Thawing
A.C. Nielsen

some
ADULT CONTENT

by Paul Carey

This book is a work of fiction. Names, characters, places, and incidents are the product of the author's imagination or are used fictitiously. Any resemblance to actual events, locales, businesses, companies, or persons living, dead, or frozen is coincidental.

ISBN-13: 978-1537127200
ISBN-10: 1537127209

Brilliant young microbiologist and self-professed lab rat Kate Pearson has just landed her dream job, although she worries it might turn into a frozen nightmare. She's been hired to discover a way to successfully revive people who have been in cryonic deep-freeze stasis for years at the Chicago firm ExitStrategy, a company founded by scientist Mike "Cold Smokey" Burgess, holder of dozens of major patents.

Kate is succeeding Dr. Enzo Saltieri, Mike's partner for years, who has died suddenly under strange circumstances. As Kate sifts through mountains of Saltieri's scribbled-upon legal pads she finds paths that lead nowhere. Was Saltieri on the verge of great discoveries or just sinking into the illogical world of dementia?

Along the way, Kate has to deal with Miles Coleman, a sarcastic idiot savant assistant at the lab who's hiding his true identity; Gloria Dunham, a famous former Hollywood actress, now ninety years old and bent on taking over control of the company; plus reality show egomaniacs Dimi Konstantos and Khail Santana, megastars who've been polluting television's airwaves.

After Kate has some success reviving lab animals frozen in the 1980s such as Mr. T, the guinea pig, and John Cougar, the housecat, her attention turns to the first human subject, famous TV ratings guru A.C. Nielsen, who has been frozen at ExitStrategy for twenty-five years.

Between Mike Burgess's lofty expectations, hidden research files, secret medical procedures, switched identities, drugged drinks, randy Irish folk musicians, beefy bodyguards, plus Miles, Gloria, Dimi and Khail—Kate begins to realize that reviving A.C. Nielsen and accidentally discovering a cure for cancer may actually be a stroll in the park.

"More twists than a bag of my gourmet Bavarian pretzels!"
  - Hans Sachs, München Pretzel Werks

"A guinea pig named Mr. T, a cat named John Cougar? The 80s rock again!"
  - some person who lived in the 80s

"The characters are poorly developed, the plot unbelievable; but you'll love the punctuation!"
  - Sarah Gooseflesh, Schenectady Public Library

"A total waste of your time! Enjoy!"
  - Ziggy Zneuzel, President, Procrastinators' International

"As a top literary agent, I usually love cross-genre books. That is, until I read 'Thawing A.C. Nielsen'. Sci-fi/Comedy/Satire/ Medical/Mystery plus guinea pigs? I think not!"
  - Natasha Fatale

"Please read my son's book. I think it's pretty creative. I'm just sorry he wrote those racy parts."
  - Paul's mom

ACKNOWLEDGMENTS

This book actually began as an idea for a screenplay. But after consulting with an experienced documentary and feature film cameraman I know, I decided instead to make it into a novel. Little did I know how much work that would be for a newbie writer!

Many thanks to Jennifer Mattison of Mattison Editing for her patience over the last year. She has been instrumental in fixing so many issues and polishing the manuscript. Also, thanks to Katherine Otte for her insight upon reading the full manuscript. Tara Pegasus, the wonderful author of Alameda's Awakening, was another very helpful reader. Many thanks for the encouragement from my older brother Jim Carey, CRNA, who acted as the medical technical consultant.

CHAPTER ONE

February 2013

"Here! Here, grab this stick. Come on, man. Grab it! Hurry!"

Why grab it? Why struggle? I'm fine.

"Come on, man—you're gonna die in there. I can't get any closer. If I fall in I can't save you. Then we both die. You gotta grab it now. Please!"

I'm fine. The water is cold. It feels good. Don't be afraid. None of us ever really die.

"Damn! Stupid stick broke on the ice. Okay, listen now… I'm gonna slide out closer to you, slowly. When I get close you gotta grab my arm above the wrist and I'll grab yours. Drop that book or whatever you've got there. I can't save you if you're still holding on to stuff. We may have only one chance at this. Do you hear the ice cracking? Come on, look at me—try to focus. I know it's dark, I know you're freezing, but just stay with me, you hear? Helen, did you call 9-1-1? Keep the flashlight out of his eyes. You're blinding him!"

I need this novel. I need my notebook, too. The solutions are there. Water is a solution: a solution is the answer.

"Come on, man, focus. Look at me. What's your name? Can you talk? You understand me? I got to get you out of there fast—really fast. Oh damn, it's freezing out here. Oh shit. Helen, he's in shock! He can't move. He can't talk. He moves his mouth a little but nothing's coming out."

"Tom, you can't go out any further. Please don't do this—I'm not losing you. Be careful. I called 9-1-1. They'll be here!"

"He's gonna die if I don't pull him out soon. Helen, I have to save him. He's not gonna make it without me."

No, Tom. I'm fine. Really, I'm fine here—in the solution. The water is the solution.

"There—I got your arm. Just relax. You're in shock. I'll pull you the rest of the way out, just don't fight me, okay? See, here you go— you're on top of the ice now. Helen, I got him. Run and get some blankets out of the trunk. I'll have him there soon."

1

Let's stay in the water. It feels good, don't you think? I have friends there. Tom? Tom?

"That's it. Just relax. We'll slide low across the ice. Keep our weight spread out, right? Get off the ice and then we can walk to the car. I'm a lot bigger than you, thank the Lord. Maybe I can even carry you. Just hang in there. Stay with me, okay?"

But I have friends in the water. You'd like them. Turtles, fish, dolphins. In the water. Aqua in Latin, acqua with a c-q in Italian, agua in Spanish. Tom, water is a medium.

"Come on now. Can you feel your feet? Your legs? Do I need to carry you? Can you talk? Please try to talk. Jesus, my heart is pounding."

Water is a medium. It surrounds you. It heals you. You can breathe water if you're not afraid.

"Helen, he's totally in shock. I gotta carry him. His legs are just all locked up. Where the hell are the police? Or an ambulance?"

"I don't know. Just get him across the road to the car."

"Okay, man, we're almost there. We've got blankets, we've got the car heater. We already called 9-1-1. They'll be here soon. You're gonna be okay. See, we did it. We did it together!"

You can breathe the water. Water surrounds you. It cradles you. Air is too thin, too harsh. It can't heal you—it burns. Are you listening?

"Jesus, you saved him, Tom. Okay, quick let's get him dry. Peel the wet clothes off him. It's so dark out here. Look, I think he's already getting better. He's putting weight on his legs. Get the clothes off and we can get him in the car—crank the heat. Look at his face, he's stoned or something. He looks like he's obsessed with those books he's holding. Is he some kind of drug addict?"

"I have no idea. Listen—you hear that? That's a siren, Helen, they're almost here. Dropped their donuts and got their act together. They'll be here soon."

I'm going back. You were very brave. Helen is so proud of you. Look at her— so proud. "Good-bye, Tom! I'm going to go talk to my friends— dolphins, fish. The turtles are under the mud, 3.9 now. They'll be out soon. Good-bye."

"Tom, he just said your name. Did you hear him? Some gibberish, but your name was in there, too. He's gonna be okay. Look at you— you're shivering like crazy. Go on, get that wet jacket and shirt off, honey. There's one more shirt in the trunk you can put on 'til the cops or an ambulance gets here. Maybe they sent both."

"Okay. Shit, I can't believe I got him out. I'm freezing. I can't even imagine what he feels like. Where's that shirt? I don't see it here."

"It's somewhere in there. Let me look. There, see it in the corner? Oh, wait—Mister! Mister, stop! What are you doing? Oh no, he's going back over. No, no, no! Mister, get out of the—"

Wham.

"Oh, my God, Tom. Oh my God!"

PAUL CAREY

CHAPTER TWO

April 2013

"Look, Aria, an e-mail from that headhunter company. They have an interview for me to go to next Wednesday. Downtown at a hotel. About time something came along. Maybe I can get this and have a way to start paying off my student loans. And start splitting the rent again with you, too, of course!"

"That's awesome, Kate," Aria said. "Does it say what kind of job, like specifically?" Aria and Kate had been dorm roomies all the way through undergrad and then had shared apartments through grad school at Northwestern University. Kate hadn't found a job in the three months since she had finished her degree. She was desperate to get a career going.

"They didn't describe the job. Just said to show up. A good match, they think. You know they did tell me earlier that my biology degrees would fit in somewhere, even though the microbiology grad degree was kind of overqualifying me for some positions. I knew that might happen, but hell, I wanted that masters." Kate took a brush to her auburn hair, trying to get rid of some tangles. She always felt she was just an average-looking girl, but she actually was attractive and very fit. She just wasn't spectacularly gorgeous like Aria with her perfect complexion, flowing blonde hair, and lanky body.

"Well, I hope you get it. Just hope it isn't sitting in a sweatshop all day poking dead cows' eyes out, or slicing out frog gizzards and packing them into high school dissection kits. I was thinking about that the other day. Somebody has to put those kits together. Probably struggling biology majors like you who don't want to settle for working at 7-Eleven."

"You were thinking about the world of dissection supplies, Aria? Really?"

"Yeah, you know I'm weird. So, you get to go *pop-pop-pop*, poke the cow eyes out with your thumb and drop 'em into a rusty old pail, then hand them off to somebody else on the assembly line."

"*Pop-pop-pop*? And so now cows have three eyes?"

"Sure—yeah. Alien cows. Oh wait, no—enlightened cows. You

know, third-eye cows."

"Oh, shut up. Wish me luck it's a good job, okay? So are we ready for some wine, now that you're home?"

"Dumb question. Pour something. You choose."

"Okay," Kate said, pushing herself up from the sofa and heading toward the kitchen. They had a stash of halfway decent wine from the Trader Joe's in Northbrook. No Charles Shaw, though; they had evolved past that. "So wait, I want to know more about the frog gizzards I'm going to be packaging. Tell me more about them, 'cause I think frogs don't have gizzards. I think I knew that from actually paying attention to Mr. Zwillig in biology class sophomore year at New Trier High. I can still remember him with his squeaky voice trying to get you to focus. 'Miss Grumman, please pay attention. I assure you that this class will be important in your future endeavors.'"

"*Endeavors?* Who says that word? And he was totally wrong, the ass. I'm doing fine these days in the violin section of the Milwaukee Symphony—and I needed to know biology for that, somehow? Anyway, I said frog gizzards? Nah—oh, thanks for the wine."

"Actually yes, you did say frog gizzards, Aria. Please teach me about them. I really want to hear this."

"All right, I will illuminate things for you like I always do. I'm sorry the dark overlords of the biology world have kept these secrets from you, oh innocent one. Frog gizzards were invented by Eddie Izzard. He invented many varieties of gizzards and also lizards. Some of those sell car insurance on TV. Others, like King Gizzard and the Lizard Wizard, play weird psychedelic music."

"Oh, shut up!" Kate laughed, throwing a pillow at Aria's head.

"Hey, watch it. I've got red wine here!"

"Stop making me laugh so much. You know it makes my cheeks hurt."

"Okay, so let's think about what kind of job it could be. They don't headhunt for dumbass jobs, right? Hey, can you grab some chips or something? I'm hungry."

"You're always hungry. Where do you put all that food?"

"Into my violin playing. Do you realize how much of a workout it is to play for four hours or more a day? Have you noticed how much my body moves when I play, and my bow arm? Here, take a look at my muscles, they're totally buff, huh?" Aria rolled up her cotton shirt to show off her well-defined biceps and triceps.

"Okay, I will bring you some empty calories as you wish," said Kate. "Well, the Milwaukee Symphony is lucky to have you. A nice gig 'til you can get in at CSO, right?"

"That will be a while. Chicago Symphony doesn't hire twenty-seven-year-old violinists too often. But I'm happy in Milwaukee. It's such an easy commute from here."

"Gotta love the North Shore, huh? And we're not far from my mom's house in Winnetka."

"Yeah, the *Home Alone* house. She's so cute when she mentions that stuff."

"Eh—to me it's more like annoying when she tells people and I have to listen to her go on and on. I was three or four then; I don't remember any of it. Besides, we weren't the actual *Home Alone* house, we were just on the same block. We were the house in the last scene when the cops arrest the doofus bad guys."

"Yeah, I know. Ha-ha, the Wet Bandits! But she's so cute when she tells people about meeting Joe Pesci and the other stuff. She told me a secret once. Guess what it was."

"Oh boy, what?" Kate said, pouring more malbec in their glasses.

"She said, 'Guess what, Aria. Mr. Pesci doesn't really have a gold tooth. The makeup people put that on him. And he's such a nice man—I love how he talks. He talks funny, I think you could say.'"

"She said that? Accidentally referencing her pal Joe in *Goodfellas* with that, right?"

"Yeah, I doubt your sweet mum has seen anything as edgy as Goodfellas. I'll bet she's a rom-com girl."

"No, actually she likes mystery and crime stuff. Like *Murder, She Wrote* and whatever that Dick van Dyke detective show was."

"*Diagnosis Murder* I think it was, not that I ever watched it. Anyway, don't pick on your mom. She's still sad and lonesome without your dad there."

"I know. I go over and help her out around the house. We have fun together pretty often. Thank God my dad had good life insurance. I'm still getting over it, too. I was only twenty-one when they diagnosed his cancer. There's always a hurt in my heart, Aria, even after six years. I thought he'd be around forever to watch me become an adult, have kids of my own, you know. He would have been the best grampa ever. Well okay, enough serious talk. I'm sorry."

"No, it's okay," Aria said. She leaned over and gave Kate a long hug. "I'm always here for you, understand?"

"Yes, thank you. And likewise. You helped me through that and I will always remember."

"So, you wanna turn the TV on?"

"I don't know. What's on?"

"I saw a promo for a *Sex and the City* episode running tonight in a few minutes, I believe," Aria said. "The one where Samantha thinks she can handle dating that rich old guy. I mean the really old guy where they show her retching when she sees his sad, droopy naked butt."

"HBO is showing *Sex and the City* episodes again? Or do you mean the reruns on WFN?"

"WFN. Can you believe it? They show his wrinkly naked tushie. They don't cut that part out!"

"Seriously? Wow, that's wild. They used to be so ridiculously conservative at that station. Remember the *Farm Report* around noon? Hog belly prices from Springfield and stuff? So, Aria, new subject—how are we going to get me downtown for this interview with only one car between the two of us? You have a long day of rehearsals next Wednesday, right?"

"Eh, we have a few days to figure that out. Why do you give me wine on an empty stomach? I'm getting too drunk to look at a calendar and think straight. Let's do it tomorrow night *before* we've started drinking. Okay, sweet little girl, my little gizzard girl?"

"Stop it with the gizzards, Aria. You're crazy!"

"I know you are, but what am I?"

Kate threw a pillow at Aria, jumped up and grabbed more to throw, and chased Aria around the apartment, crashing hard into the living-room wall at one point. They yelled and laughed like eight-year-olds.

"Can't catch me!" Aria hollered with glee.

Suddenly they heard a loud *tap-tap-tap* coming from the apartment below.

They stopped running for a moment, then realized it was Old Man Drummond banging on his ceiling. "Miss Pearson, Miss Grumman, this is not a gymnasium!" he yelled from below with his grumpy-old-man voice.

"Jesus, Mr. Drummond, this is an apartment building, not a damn library! Gizzards to you—gizzards—gizzards—*gizzaaaaards!*" Aria yelled at the top of her lungs while stomping her foot as loud as she could. She fell to the floor, grabbed her glass from the coffee table, and polished off her wine.

"Guess that'll show him not to mess with a mentally impaired violin player," Kate said.

"Ha. Next time I'll go downstairs, knock on his door, and throw a big chunk of violin rosin at his head when he answers!"

Kate laughed. "Mature, Aria, very mature!"

CHAPTER THREE

The next day Kate was putzing around, wasting time doing random stuff around the apartment. To be blunt, she was bored. It was about three in the afternoon when she saw Aria's car pull in. A minute later Aria traipsed through the door with her instrument cases.

"Hey, there you are!" Kate said. "Home early, huh?"

"I was coaching a string quartet of sophomores down at DePaul for free as a favor to someone I know down there. They were sucking so much I broke it off early, told them you can't take French music like the Debussy String Quartet and blitzkrieg the thing to death with way too much down-bowing. I mean, good Lord, we gotta treat French composers with some tenderness, oui? I told them we'll try again next week after they've rethought their approach. The poor things looked crestfallen when I criticized them. Huh—I just said *crestfallen*, that's a first!"

"Hey, it's only three thirty. We could hit the tennis court," Kate suggested. "It's nice out for April. What do you say? Run over to Mitchell Park and whack some balls?"

"There's a setup line if I ever heard one. Sure, let's go. Just take it easy on me, okay, Captain Pearson?"

"Sure, no problem. We can grab some Thai on the way back and chill the rest of the evening." They got changed and jumped in the car to drive over to the park. There were only four courts, but this time of day they weren't usually all taken. Traffic was backed up so there was time to chat in the car.

"Oh my God, Aria, you wouldn't believe the dream I had. Right after you left this morning I fell back asleep. This dream was just so weird and it went on forever."

"Yeah, so what happened? I like your dreams. You know, I hardly ever dream."

"I'm sure you have dreams, you just don't remember them. Everybody dreams. I started having lucid dreams about six months ago."

"Remind me again what lucid dreams are," Aria said.

"You know, where you sort of know you're dreaming and now and then you can just slightly change stuff—like maneuver it a bit."

"Okay, so let's hear this one." Aria grabbed a bag of pita chips and ripped it open.

"Okay, so I'm sitting at an outdoor cafe and I'm like spying on this woman. Her name is Enmity Philips and she's a model. She does some commercials, too, and just low-level modeling—she's not like a supermodel."

"That's too bad. We supermodels enjoy the high life," Aria boasted, swerving to avoid a merging car.

"I don't think supermodels stuff their face like you do, Miss Distracted Driver. How about watching the other cars more and paying less attention to your bag of chips? So… Enmity used to work in a cardboard box factory, but she was depressed and wished she could invent something to go in all the boxes."

"Sounds very Freudian, Kate. When was the last time you got laid?"

"Don't interrupt. So anyway, somehow somebody decides she doesn't have to work in the box factory anymore and she can be a model, even though in my dream she's really not so attractive. So she leaves the box factory and I'm spying on her, like I said. Then up walks this guy and tells her to get to the studio. All of a sudden the dream switches to this television studio—the dream just jumps there. And there's Enmi—"

"Wait, what does that word mean? Enmity? That's not a real name. There's already a lot of weird psychological stuff in there, Kate. You need to see a shrink."

"I think enmity means you dislike someone and maybe you have a grudge against them? Like how I feel when you keep interrupting. So there's a film crew and a director and everything, and the makeup people have given Enmity like totally disgusting yellow, cracking fungus-y toenails and they're filming her trying to cut these honkin' things, and when she actually can get the clippers to work, the shards of the gross nails go flying all over. Then the director yells 'cut,' and they stop for a bit. That's when I realize what's going on. She's been hired to be on a TV reality show about weird and wacky inventors— it's called *You Wish You Thought o' Dat*. They follow various goofball inventors around for a few days and film them pitching their new product to investors."

"*You Wish You Thought o' Dat?* Dat… not that? Weird. And this is all rolling around in your precious little subconscious, huh?"

"Yeah, strange isn't it? So they set up this next scene—"

"But you said it was a reality show, why are they setting up scenes? I don't get it."

"I'm not sure I do either. It's a dream, remember? Maybe reality shows aren't all for real, anyway. Perhaps they script some of the stuff?"

"I wouldn't know. I've hardly watched any TV for the last seven or eight years or so. That's how long I've been a practice-room rat. Plus, I mean, how many reality shows do you and I watch, right?"

"Right, Aria. So anyway, the scene setup is this nerdy guy who has invented a way to catch your toenails before they go flying in your boyfriend's face in bed at ten p.m. 'Cause that would be a real romance killer, right?"

"Yes, for sure." Aria smirked.

"So they shoot this scene where the inventor shows Enmity how to use the product. It's just like one of those cones they put on dogs so they won't chew on their stitches after surgery, right? I think it's called a 'cone of shame' or something. You sit tailor-style and this thing wraps around your ankle and then the clippings fall inside of it. So Enmity thinks it's stupid, and potential investors would agree with her because when she tries it, the gnarly toenail clippings are still flying out past the cone. And that's where the dream gets really weird."

"Ooh, weirder than it's *already been*? Go on!" Aria urged as she pulled into the parking area nearest the tennis courts.

"Yeah, so the inventor, his name is Benjamin Rutherford the Fourth, says to Enmity, 'See the button? There, down at the bottom. Push it.' So she does and the rim of the cone lights up really cool, like with pulsating purple lights and the whole thing makes this amazingly cool new-age whirring sound. '*Now* try,' says the inventor guy, so Enmity rolls her eyes and clips another of the fake disgusting toenails and it starts flying out of the cone, too, except just as it looks like it's going to escape, the cone's energy field grabs the nail and pulls it back in—*tada!*"

"Oh my God, Kate, I think you've got a brain tumor. But heck, who wouldn't want one of those light-up conie things, ha-ha."

"Yeah, and then I woke up. Most of the time I was lucid dreaming. I think I made up the guy's name and nudged some details here and there."

"Well, gurl, you better register a patent for that space-age cone—or send that reality TV idea in to somebody, right? Make some slick LA producer-type give you cash for that program idea. *Dat's* what you should do!"

* * *

Kate and Aria picked up their Thai on the way back home from their tennis workout. As usual, Kate won every set—she had been the captain of her high school tennis team and captain at Northwestern for two years as an undergrad. For Aria it was simply a chance to get exercise, she knew she could never beat Kate. They settled in with the Thai and opened a bottle of wine, intending to keep the vino consumption a little more under control than the night before.

"So, please," Kate said, "can we figure out Wednesday? I'm getting nervous about this interview and I really want to get it planned."

"Sure, what time is it again?" Aria asked, as she dug voraciously into her Pad Thai.

"Downtown, ten a.m. at the Winston House. When's your rehearsal in Milwaukee?"

"Noon. Some dreamboat French pianist Andre-something is coming in to do the Bartok Three. Good thing he's not doing One or Two, he might permanently damage his precious little French fingers, never to uncork a Beaujolais again."

"Okay, so sounds like this could work, right?"

"Yeah, I'll drop you downtown about nine, then I'll drive up to Milwaukee, rehearse, tie Andre to his hotel room bed and ravish him, and then be back to get you."

"Super, and if I have to I can kill time at the Art Institute. Sounds like a plan. Can you pass that chicken satay?"

"Sure. Hey Kate, I started thinking again about what your job could be at this company. You wanna hear?"

"Sure. Serious this time, or no?"

"Serious, for sure. I think they want you to clone Hitler's moustache. They have some of it in a vault in Berlin, I hear."

"Jesus, you're crazy."

"Well, my mom says my dad dropped me on my head a lot when I was a baby. He says I was really squirmy—that's the excuse they make."

"Wow, Aria, that explains a lot!"

"Yes indeed, I believe it does. But you'll still be my friend, woncha?" Aria said, pouting her lips and batting her eyelashes.

"If I have to, goofball!"

CHAPTER FOUR

Wednesday, the big day. Aria dropped Kate in downtown Chicago at the front door of the Winston House on Wabash Avenue, a classic old hotel with a gorgeous lobby full of enormous Oriental rugs, leather chairs, dark walnut and rosewood coffee tables, crystal chandeliers, dual curving marble staircases leading to the mezzanine level—swag, swag, and even more swag. At any moment, one might expect to see Fred Astaire and Ginger Rogers glide into the room doing the tango. Kate, dressed smartly in a black suit with a peach-colored blouse, approached the main desk. She was fifteen minutes early, which to her meant she was on time. Her father had drilled some old-fashioned good habits into her when she was a teenager. She had hated them at the time, but now, especially with him gone, she appreciated that he had done so. In a few minutes she was escorted into meeting room C.

"Good morning, Miss Pearson, please have a seat," a gentleman with a deep baritone voice said, bowing slightly and extending his hand. "My name is Franklin Burgess. I'm part of the ownership of Energy Source. We're the ones interested in your expertise." Franklin was tall, at least six one and had a deep tan but very few wrinkles for his age, which was fifty-five, she guessed.

"Good morning," Kate said, shaking hands with Franklin and then with the other gentleman present.

"And I'm Mike Burgess, Franklin's uncle. We're so happy to meet you today." Mike was a hefty man and even taller than Franklin. You could tell they were family. They both came across as very friendly and gracious. "If you don't mind, we'd like to skip talking about the weather and just cut to the chase, as they say—tell you about the position and why we're so interested in you. Is that all right?"

"Well, of course, I'm all ears and, frankly, I'm excited to be here for this interview."

"That's wonderful, Miss Pearson," Mike said. "Our company is called Energy Source and we're a privately owned enterprise. The ownership consisted until recently of me, Franklin here, our associate Dr. Enzo Saltieri, another major shareholder who lives in California like Franklin, and then a few people with quite minor stakes in the company. Dr. Saltieri recently passed away and we are interested in filling his position. We're located in Northbrook and we are a private energy-provider to North Shore corporate complexes. We also run a bioresearch project called ExitStrategy, which Dr. Saltieri headed. I'm the CEO of the whole shebang, and we have a small but dedicated staff. Shall I continue?" he asked, smiling.

Kate's jitters were already going away. The man was a charmer.

"Certainly."

"Dr. Saltieri had recently fallen ill right in the midst of some important bioresearch. He was battling cancer and, sad to say, Alzheimer's disease. We wanted him to get more-intensive therapy, but he kept putting it off. He was placing our research ahead of his health and his future. We were all saddened when he passed a few months ago. He was a great man."

"I'm so sorry, Mr. Burgess."

"Thank you. He went quickly. So now we need someone to keep the research going forward and we think you just might be the right person." Kate sat up taller. Research—just what she wanted. This sounded very promising so far.

"We're impressed with your résumé and all the research projects you've been part of," Mike said, thumbing through all the documents in hand. "First of all, the person we're seeking needs to know their biology down to the most minute cellular level. That's you for sure."

"Thank you," Kate said. "I spend a lot of time with microscopes. A whole lot of time. The opportunity to do major research has been my goal since I was eight or nine. Yes, I'm a biology nerd—totally."

"Understood," said Franklin Burgess. "My uncle Mike is also a supernerd. Engineering. You will get along famously in our Northbrook Nerdsville location, I'm sure. And honestly, Miss Pearson, we also need younger blood in our company—many of us are on the wrong side of fifty." Franklin smiled.

Kate smiled back. *Yes, Kate, remember to smile and be personable. Don't look grim—or desperate. Use your people skills.*

There was a knock on the door. Room service entered with a cart of fresh coffee and pastries.

"Oh, this looks good, doesn't it?" Mike exclaimed. "I've got a weakness for sweets; you can see it by my waistline. Please, Miss Pearson, avail yourself before my nephew and I hog the offerings. Coffee?"

"Yes, please. This is a nice surprise. And I'll just grab that little brioche there, too."

"Of course," Franklin said. "You'll find that Mike and I appreciate many of the smaller delights in life. In fact, Mike hired a chef recently to create cooked-to-order lunches for our employees. No more need for them to run out and buy fast food!"

"Very nice," Kate affirmed. "A wonderful idea."

"So, as we were discussing," Mike said between bites of a cinnamon roll, "we need someone to look at Dr. Saltieri's latest research and see if they agree that he was onto something, something big. We want to hire someone with fresh eyes and no preconceptions about the research. Your Northwestern University track record is impressive, as are all your references. We also hope you don't mind that we had a consultant read through your master's thesis."

"Oh, yes," Franklin interjected between gulps of his coffee, "I have a copy here. 'Transcriptional Activators as Antirepressors,' et cetera, et cetera, and something-or-other 'Polyphonic Pathway Genes.'"

"That's pentose phosphate, not 'polyphonic,' sir," Kate said.

"Well, of course it is—you'd know the title of your own thesis," Franklin said sheepishly. "Maybe I'll have to give in and finally get bifocals."

"The point is," Mike said, "our consultant was impressed. And then we saw something that grabbed us from your work experience—the cryogenic research you've done over the last few summers. You've stated that the project included research on new cryoablation treatment methods for breast cancer—new techniques that might revolutionize approaches to treatment. Could that be overstepping a bit? An exaggeration, Miss Pearson?"

"Well, no, not at all. And I didn't actually use the word 'revolutionize.'"

"Oh, I was paraphrasing, not a problem," Mike said.

"We've found ways," Kate explained, "to finely control not only the cryo level of the needle probe but also directly deliver real protection to the healthy cells nearby. I hope what I have summed up in a few words in the résumé doesn't appear to be a gross misre—"

"Oh no, Miss Pearson, you don't need to defend yourself." Mike waved off her concerns. "We're not here to attack you. I was trying to see how passionate you are about this topic. Cold—heat—the whole spectrum of its effect on the human body; this is *precisely* the area of research that Enzo—Dr. Saltieri—and I have been working on for years."

"Wait, I'm sorry, I don't quite understand," Kate said. "You're an energy company but *also* do bioresearch. Is that what I heard?"

"Yes. And I'm not a doctor or a biologist," Mike pointed out. "My expertise is in cryotechnology, as an engineer."

"That's right, my uncle is the master of all things cold—*very cold*," Franklin said, about to mount an attack on a French cruller.

"Actually, Franklin, I don't make things cold as if I were Jack Frost—I design cutting-edge heat-transfer systems. Everything in our world contains some amount of heat. Heat-transfer systems simply move precise amounts of heat from one place to another. It's all one big canvas that can be painted on—hopefully without Jackson Pollack results."

"Uncle, I stand corrected." Franklin bowed his head.

These two are entertaining, Kate thought. This all sounds very interesting. And they're not cookie-cutter businessmen.

"Miss Pearson," Mike continued, "we want to keep investigating the intersection of biology on the cellular level with new ideas in cryogenics. That, in the proverbial nutshell, is the job. Interested so far?"

"Very. This is what I want to do: research. Nothing makes me happier than being in a lab running a hypothesis through its paces. When people call me a lab rat, I take it as a compliment!"

"And just to clarify," Mike continued, "your job has nothing to do with the energy-provider part of the company. That's a no-brainer I run. It creates income on a monthly basis that goes toward our bio research."

"Understood. So what's next?" Kate asked. *Oh my God, this sounds like a dream job. Keep up the positive vibe—smile, be professional. I hope they are okay with me being so young.*

"Just so you know," Mike said, "I was employed at a well-known corporation for years. I know full well what people hate about job interviews. I must have interviewed hundreds of people over the years to fill positions in my department. So, what's an interview question people hate? Go ahead, speak freely—and this isn't a trick question!"

"Well, I would say when they ask you what your weaknesses are."

"Precisely! A ridiculous question," Mike said. "One we won't be asking you. And just so you know, our other large shareholder, the other one from LA, is coming in Friday to meet you personally. If Miss

Dunham asks you that question Friday, we will shush her, right, Franklin?"

"Yes, we would do that. She's elderly and sometimes speaks out of turn, just so you know. And, then, what is the other thing people hate about interviews, Miss Pearson?"

"Well, the other one is that until you jump through all the hoops you don't have any idea of the salary. You're poked and prodded, but all the while kept in the dark. Of course some salaries are posted I sup—"

"Precisely, again," Mike said. "So we will tell you now the starting salary. I see no reason to withhold that information. You'll know it now and have less anxiety when we meet again. We'll start you with a two-year contract at a salary of two hundred fifty thousand dollars per year with options for continuation, plus very generous benefits. What do you think?"

"I think I am seriously interested in this position, Mr. Burgess... and Mr. Burgess," Kate said nervously—she was having problems taming the ridiculous butterflies that had just fluttered in her stomach. "It sounds like a dream job to me."

"Excellent!" said Franklin. "And if you would agree, we have set up some standard pre-employment screening tests. In addition to doing the usual due diligence like any other company, we have to screen out possible hires who might be prone to leaking proprietary information. We have very new research areas that cannot be compromised. Understand?"

"Of course. I can do whatever you need. When would that be?"

"Can you do tomorrow at eleven a.m.? The screening firm is in Evanston."

"Eleven a.m. is fine. I'll make it work."

"All right, here's my business card, their address is on the back. After that we'd like to see you here Friday—say ten in the morning again?"

"Not a problem. I look forward to it. What is the company name again, the part you need me for?"

"It's ExitStrategy," Franklin said. "In a sense, it refers to being prepared for what's next in life—like the old saying 'when a door closes, a window opens.' And if you're going to go through that window, you better have a strategy in place, right? You'll see what it all means Friday. You know, it's rare that anyone bothers to ask about the name, but you did. Shows you're attentive and curious!"

"I like the name. It captures your imagination."

"What Mike and Dr. Saltieri have been doing is just that—imagination on an epic level," Franklin said. "I think you'll be impressed once you learn more, Miss Pearson—actually may I call you Katherine?"

"Yes, of course, but I go by Kate most of the time."

"Well, then, 'til next time, Kate. We'll see you here on Friday."

CHAPTER FIVE

"Chris, man, you writin' this all down? You gettin' all I got to say?" Khail asked.

"Yes, Khail, I got it. But you know, kale chips are supposed to be healthy. You can't make them that crazy way. Mixing them up with fried pork skins in the same bag? Ridiculous! It doesn't make any sense. It won't sell."

"Chris, everything I think up sells. All the little stuff, the big stuff. Dimi's reality show, all the other shows, all the products. You'll see, we make Khail Chips and people will eat 'em bag after bag after bag. People are conflicted, Chris. You know that word?"

"Yes, Khail, I think I know that word."

"People try a little bit to be healthy, but the devil inside 'em wants to eat that salty, greasy food. I'm just playin' to their angel and their devil inside. People like when they get played like that. It's a delicious scenario, right?"

"*Scenario?* Another fancy word, huh?"

"You bet. Glad you noticed. So we'll call 'em Khail Chips: Yo, Fatback Flavuh. So maybe they get fat from part of the bag, but the kale part keeps 'em healthy. And you know most people want to have a big ass these days anyway, Chris. Even white girls. Big ass, fat lips, too. Hell, maybe we find a crazy spice to put in there to plump up their lips, huh? Yo, Chris, you so outta touch with the people. You're like twenty-eight, but you think like an old man—it's sad. I'm telling you now, Khail Chips will sell just fine. Anything with my name on it does."

"You know how to spell kale, right? It's K-A-L-E, it's not like your name."

"Chris, don't go naggin' on me again. Okay, next idea. You writing these down? So I heard there's fires in the hills. Too dry, way too dry here in SoCal. I heard some report they puttin' stuff in clouds to make it rain. Say it's damned expensive to do. You hire me some smart dudes to make it work cheaper. I know you know smart dudes from where you went to school. Stanford, right? We make that stuff and we call it Khail Hail and we make millions. Save Smokey the Bear. Write it down, Chris."

"Okay, done. That should be an easy one." Chris rolled his eyes.

He'd been suffering for what seemed like forever through these idiotic weekly brainstorming meetings with Khail Santana, superstar male-model/reality show star. Khail had hired Chris three years earlier to be his financial adviser, then decided to make Chris his personal adviser as well. What Chris couldn't figure out—couldn't for the life of him wrap his head around—was how often Khail's moronic ideas clicked and made money, as in many *millions* of dollars. "So if I get these going you'll green-light them? We put a lot of work into developing some of these ideas and you don't always pull the trigger on them like you should."

"What's he mean, green-light, Khail?" asked Theo, one of the bodyguards employed by Khail and his wife, giant-boobied reality TV megastar Dimi Konstantos.

"Green-light means go, go, go—do the damn thing," Khail exclaimed, pacing his production studio office. "Stop stokin' yo' joint at the stoplight and accelerate your damn Escalade. *Do the damn thing*—that's what Chris and some of those other white folk do. I got no damn time to do that stuff. Sometimes I don't even got the energy to make the green-light sign. My life is exhausting. I got the modeling—got to be The Ebony Adonis everyone loves. I gotta be with Dimi and make her feel special all day long, I gotta slug paparazzi dudes, I gotta pretend to be crazy on our reality show. You fuckers know hard that is?"

Theo broke out laughing, dropping the dumbbell he'd been using to do curls. "Yeah, Khail, you're not crazy—you *perfectly normal.*"

"Damn straight," Khail declared, shooting Theo a dirty look. "Okay, here's another one."

"Whoo—you on fire today, Khail."

"That's what *she* said," Khail answered, flashing his perfect smile.

"Ooh, yeah bruthah!"

"Okay, listen now, Chris," Khail said, "I'm tired of bein' sweaty. I got some perspiration issues. It works for the modeling, 'cause they don't gotta mist me with water or oil me up to look amazing on that runway. I got my own supply of slickness. Know what I mean?"

"Yes, Khail, I have noticed that you perspire a lot. So what's your plan?"

"Something new for Khail's Kustom Klothes—shirts with built-in antiperspirant and a damn sick odor. Maybe like it smells like money—rolls o' Franklins. You smell like that, all the bitches go down on you."

"So we embed all these chemicals into the fabric? And what happens when you wash it, Khail?"

"You don't need to wash it—evah. It's fresh forevah, *man*! Don't you get it, Chris? Got 'nother scent—Cristal. You sweet like Cristal, muthah. Theo, good thing Chris here is good at minding my money—he sure got no creativity for anything else, that's for sure."

"Mmm hmm," Theo said, nodding. "Hey, all y'all, you want some protein drink? I'm mixin' some up."

"Nah, man, I'm cool. Gotta work these new ideas. Chris, you want some of Theo's drink? Boost up them flabby muscles on you? Damn, we gotta work on you. You pasty-white. You skinny. You got no bling. You got no imagina—"

"He gotta get out his comfort zone, Khail," Theo bawled, testifying. "Say, how 'bout we give him a new name to start? Maybe like Chris X-X. Like X marks the spot, but he so damn awesome he got two Xes. What all y'all think?"

"Yeah, Chris, what you think—you like Theo's idea?" said Khail. "Make you into Chris X-X? Get you some gold chains, get you a kickin' grill—find out where Lil' Wayne dumps his used ones at?"

"Sounds good, Khail," Chris X-X lied, trying not to visibly cringe at the image of putting some rapper's used dental grill in his own mouth. "Looking forward to it. So, are we done for today?"

"Yeah, Chris."

"Okay, now remember about next week. We have a staff meeting to go over all those new show ideas."

"You on top of that, right? How many submissions we got in so far? Five hunnert, six hunnert?"

"Khail, your flagship show has way more fans than that sending in their ideas for this competition. We're up to four thousand submissions. I've got every intern on staff weeding through them during their entire shift. We have e-mail, we have videos. You should see them all. The grammar in the e-mails makes me want to heave, but hey, maybe that's my problem, right? And the story lines—Jesus H. Christ, I didn't know there were that many weirdos living here in the good old US of A."

"That's good, though, Chris. That's our people, man. We got personality—they got it, too. We give them a chance to compete to be reality stars, man. And our people are special; they don't work nine to five for the man. You think anyone in boring old Iowa or Minnesota got personality like we all, Chris X-X? I rest my case."

"Case *closed*, muthah!" Theo exclaimed, back to pumping his weights.

"So you think there's some shows worth producing out of all them?" Khail asked, finished with his pacing and now stretching out on the office sofa.

"You and Dimi and the production people can decide that, Khail. You're the creative brain trust. You know, at this point, I mostly just protect your wealth. I've only been helping on the show stuff for a few months now." Chris doodled absentmindedly on his legal pad. *An MBA from Stanford and this is what I'm doing with my life? Lord, did I just call Khail and Dimi and those pathetic producers a brain trust? Shit.*

"Okay, Chris," Khail said. "Just make sure there's some baby shows for that meeting. Cute babies, screwed-up parents, right?"

"That's the recipe. And we've got those. Plenty of them. Wait 'til you see."

"And midgets, too, Chris X-X. People *loves* their midgets."

CHAPTER SIX

Kate arrived back at the Winston House on Friday morning. This time she was directed to take the elevator to the fifth-floor suites. She found room 525, took a deep breath, exhaled, then knocked on the door. In a few seconds it swung open and Franklin Burgess greeted her again. "Miss Pearson—Kate—so good to see you again!"

"Likewise, Mr. Burgess," Kate responded.

"Oh my, she's so young" came a crackly voice from across the way.

"Yes, she is, Gloria. That's a *good thing*," Mike assured her. "Kate, I'm so glad you are here. May I present Miss Gloria Dunham and her attorney, Mr. Randolph Morgan."

Miss Dunham motioned for Kate to approach, then slowly reached out, barely grasping Kate's hand. The whole process seemed odd—as if Kate were a lowly peon being presented to the Queen of England. Morgan, barely thirty-five, yet appearing world-weary, just nodded ever so slightly in Kate's general direction.

"This room is gorgeous," Kate remarked. "I've been to the lobby and ballrooms for a few meetings and events, but I've never seen the rooms here."

"Yes, this is the only hotel I stay at while in Chicago," Gloria said. "The rooms are not large, but they are of quality. This room, number 525, is my favorite—I always request it. I have many special memories of my times in this room."

"Well, let's get started," Mike said. "I've ordered the little tray of coffee and pastries like last time, Kate. I know you enjoyed that."

Kate took a moment to eyeball this Miss Dunham. *Judging by the multitude of age spots and her crepe-paper skin, she must be at least ninety, Kate surmised. But look at those eyes—so blue, so piercing. The elegant clothes, the fine jewelry—yes, she looks wealthy.*

"Kate," Mike said, "your profile from the testing Wednesday came in. You passed with flying colors—no surprise. So let's talk more about this job. We've already told you the starting salary and much of what we expect from you. Have you thought of any questions for us?"

"Well, I'd like to know what Dr. Saltieri was researching—specifically."

"Wait, you haven't told her what you do there yet, Mike? Franklin?"

27

Morgan inquired, rolling his eyes. "Oh, *this* should be interesting."

"Randolph, this is why we do things in stages," Mike countered. "I'm sure we will have no problem. Kate, the research is centered on cryotechnology. We hinted that to you. You've already worked in this area with your cancer ablation studies, right?"

"Yes, of course."

"And you know that doctors can revive people who have fallen into icy waters, even people whose hearts have stopped beating or slowed down to a faint pulse. That doctors at times will purposely place people into cryogenic comas, lowering the patient's body temperature to slow damage from a severe trauma and allow themselves time to repair the body, yes?"

"Yes, I am familiar with all this."

"And you may also be familiar with the fact that for many years it has been possible to freeze human organs—donor organs—and use them to help others, people who are desperately ill, correct?"

"Yes, I've been to labs that do that. In my senior year we visited one as part of a project."

"Kate," Mike said, making sure he had eye contact with her as he spoke, "ExitStrategy is a cryonics facility. We are the leading cryonics company in the country—the world, actually. And Dr. Saltieri was finalizing a revivification procedure for those patients under our care in our facility in Northbrook."

"Cryonics? Cryonics, not cryogenics? Wait, you mean you freeze people? Oh my God, you *freeze dead people?*" Kate blurted out. She felt nauseated. Her heart began to race. She wanted to escape or hide somehow, or go into a fetal position.

"Well, there you have it, Mike. She's obviously shocked, now what?" Morgan shook his head in disapproval.

"Kate, yes that's what we do," Mike began explaining. "But at our company we're *scientists*, not crackpots. And think about it—over the centuries, how have people defined death? It's changed drastically over time. First it was defined as lack of breathing or lack of a heartbeat. That was death. For a long time now we have been reviving people who have fallen into icy waters, like I said, or who have been electrocuted. We restart their hearts, don't we? On the other hand, we sometimes, again, as I already stated, purposely *stop people's hearts* to do surgery on them. Did we kill them, Kate? No, not by today's standard. But what are our criteria for declaring death right now—today? There isn't anything close to exact agreement on the topic today, is there? What separates life and death has never been well defined and the line between the two is more indistinct now than it has ever been, won't you agree?"

"Yes, that is true, I guess," Kate admitted faintly. Yet despite Mike's finely crafted words, she still felt awful and very panicky. Her heart was still pounding, her palms sweating.

"Kate, what if we could give hope to people stricken with terrible diseases—give them a fighting chance? Help them survive far enough into a future society where there is a cure for their disease—for cancer, for ALS, for MS, for muscular dystrophy, for all the terrible diseases that claim people far too soon. Also, what if we didn't have to let our greatest minds disappear into the void? Think of the work geniuses like an Einstein or a Hawking could do if they could live again in the future."

"I don't know, I really don't know… I'm shocked right now," Kate murmured. "I'll be okay, just let me sit here. You can keep talking, I suppose."

"You can make a dash for the door if you like, Miss Pearson," Morgan offered with a sly look on his face. "I don't think anyone here is spry enough to tackle you and hold you here against your will."

"Randolph!" Gloria yelled, shaking her cane.

"Sorry, ma'am," he muttered nonchalantly. He actually had seemed far more concerned about the pipe he was trying to light than the conversation going on in the room.

"Look, Mike," Gloria said, "look, she's a strong girl. She'll be fine. Go ahead, continue."

"So, Kate," Mike began again, "what do you *know* about cryonics? Probably you have vague knowledge of its history and its practices. What you have to understand is that when cryonics came about in the 1970s it was considered speculative at best. And that's reasonable, since yes, anyone or anything can be frozen using liquid nitrogen. I could freeze a tree stump if I wanted to, but then what? Let's say, instead, that we cryo someone who has cancer, wait twenty-five or fifty years, and doctors of the future have devised a way to revive them and fix what killed them. Most people think it simply can't be done. But what about the people who see the glass as half-full. Perhaps it can be done—and that's the thing, there has always been that *perhaps* out there, the idea floating around in the minds of dreamers, I suppose."

"Mike, you're waxing particularly poetic today, which is well and fine, I suppose," Franklin said. "But Kate needs to know the other issues that were going on in the early days, don't you think?"

"Yes, Franklin," Mike agreed, "you're right. Kate, besides a few firms with healthy agendas, there were money grubbers—hacks who started up primitive cryo labs just to cash in, asking for people's money and freezing them any which way, sometimes even just freezing their chopped-off heads if the client didn't have enough money to cryo their whole body."

"Like Ted Williams, the famous baseball player," Franklin interjected. "I met him once. Rather conceited fellow. His head is in a cryo facility in Arizona. Ghoulish to the max."

"Wait, can I just get up and use the bathroom for a moment?" Kate asked. "I need to splash some water on my face."

"Of course, Miss Pearson," Gloria answered. "It's down to the right."

Kate entered the bathroom, shut and locked the door. *Now what do I do? The dream job is more like a nightmare. A frozen, subzero nightmare—ugh. Do I stay and listen, or just get the heck out? Oh, my God, this can't be real.* Kate used the toilet and then splashed water on her face and the back of her neck. It felt very good, calming her. Finally she rejoined the others.

"Kate, glad you're back," Mike said. "The pastries have arrived. What can we get you?"

"Nothing for now. But I'm feeling a little better. I'm ready to listen to more." She took note that Mike was doing almost all the talking. *He's the one in charge, obviously.*

"Kate," he continued, "back in the early days CBC News did an exposé accusing cryonics labs of being complete scams, hauling in big money while just creating 'corpsecicles,' a term they coined for the report, and that it was all pseudoscience. Honestly, what they uncovered when they visited a few firms was appalling. There were practices that couldn't be defended. The damage from this report was so overwhelming that many companies folded in a short amount of time and no new companies started up after that point—with one notable exception—our company, founded by Franklin, Dr. Saltieri, and me."

"And so when was that, Mr. Burgess?" Kate asked, trying to respect him enough to listen and engage, instead of sitting blankly in a fog. She could tell the two Burgess men were passionate and highly intelligent and really didn't seem crazy. She felt she owed it to them to hear their story.

"We started up a while after I left General Motors and Frigidaire," Mike continued. "I had met Dr. Saltieri and we both developed an interest in this field. We had the expertise, and surprisingly to me, were able to develop the capital to go into business. My training was in engineering and he was an internationally respected medical professor. We enlisted Franklin here to find our first clients. Franklin was a well-known character actor in Hollywood for years and knows literally everyone in the business there, including our Miss Dunham. We didn't have to wait long to have interested, wealthy clients, especially the Hollywood types. In fact, thanks to Franklin's charm and connections we never had to solicit business—clients found us."

"So ExitStrategy, it's your plan for when you die? Close a window and open a door, or close a door and open a window, like whatever you said the other day?" Kate asked Franklin.

"Precisely!" he said. "Kate, we're totally under the radar. All that bad publicity hurt companies who started up way before we did. Most people, including the press, still don't know we exist. We have no website—nothing—but the right clients still find us. It's word of mouth among the elite. Signage for our power-generating facility is what people see when they visit and step through our front door. They don't get much farther than that entry and a conference room. They have no idea we're doing something else, too. That is, unless they've contacted us about being an ExitStrategy client."

"Sounds very cloak and dagger," Kate said.

"Correct," Mike said. "And over the years that we've been successfully operating a truly scientific facility, bad things happened to our remaining competitors. One cryo firm went bankrupt—fortunately another facility took over the clients. Another one had a serious power failure; all their liquid nitrogen tanks failed. Terrible. It was days before they had their tanks functional again. What do you say to the client families in that situation? 'Oops, sorry!'? That's another reason we wash our hands of those people—all the corpsecicle creators."

"So what specifically makes you different?" Kate asked. "You've piqued my interest a bit and I think I've gotten over my initial shock. Whew, I was not prepared for that, I have to say. Are you doing something different to store people? And did you hint that Dr. Saltieri

31

had an actual plan to revive these people?"

"Yes and yes would be the answers," Randolph Morgan interrupted. "Yes, they are doing something different. Radically different in the intake and storage realm. And yes, Mike firmly believes he can bring people back to life sometime." Morgan puffed on his pipe as he dragged a chair over so he could sit directly in front of Kate. "Here's where we stand right now, Miss Pearson. I must insist, as Miss Dunham's attorney, that you tell us if we should proceed with this interview process or if you may wish to exit now. We have no intention of divulging further proprietary information just to satisfy your schoolgirl curiosity. We need to know if you have possibly overcome your initial outrage and may be seriously interested in this employment opportunity. Does that sound fair to you?"

"Yes, we can proceed—and yes, I was shocked at first," Kate explained. "I'm sorry I reacted that way. Go ahead, Mr. Burgess, either Mr. Burgess."

"That sounds wonderful, Kate," Franklin said. "And let's make it easier on you, call us by our first names from now on, eh?"

"That would be nice. So, the question left hanging—what makes your company different?"

"Well, look at that!" Mike exclaimed. "Sometimes it pays to have a lawyer in the room to focus people's thoughts and motivations. Kate, Saltieri and I decided that maybe the press was right. Who's to say that someone frozen down to liquid nitrogen temperature could ever be revived? And, let's ask you now, what kinds of problems would max-freezing create? Think about it from your expertise area."

"Well, on the cellular level, any decent amount of water within or between molecules would expand and crack everything. There might be massive damage. That's what I would say on a first pass."

"Exactly," Mike agreed. "So I invented a way to avoid using liquid nitrogen and the ridiculously low temperature it would naturally dictate. I invented something new around 1985—we don't ultra-freeze our patients until their skulls fracture, we don't expect them to survive as if they were dumped into Antarctica. No one else even knows about our new processes, they've never been revealed. You can understand why Mr. Morgan stopped us for a moment. We have many proprietary inventions and procedures at ExitStrategy."

"But also at that time," Franklin continued, "Mike realized that he could build storage tanks—we call them pods—out of an acrylic instead of aluminum or steel. The acrylic has decided advantages over the metal."

"Yes," Mike said, "and there is much more that we can tell you later. We feel that our patients from 1985 and onward stand a very strong possibility of revivification. Another major development around 1989 further strengthened our chances for success."

"So, Miss Pearson, what do you think?" Miss Dunham asked. "Is Mike Burgess delusional?"

"Well, no—um, I don't totally know. It sounds like he is employing real scientific methods. It does sound like your firm is far more successful than your competition."

"Uncle Mike, tell her your background—as a young man. When you were her age," Franklin encouraged.

"Well, all right, I suppose," Mike answered. "Kate, keep in mind I don't like to talk about myself. I dislike braggarts and don't want to be one myself."

"Go ahead," Kate said, "this whole meeting has become curiouser and curiouser… I'm ready to hear more."

"Ah, look at that, she knows Lewis Carroll. Very good, my dear," said Gloria, with a little giggle. "Now go on, Mike, don't be so modest. Start at the beginning, please."

"Oh all right," Mike said hesitantly, "but it's really not that interesting. I wasn't a spy or anything or an actor like my nephew Franklin. I was smart—that's not a lie. I finished high school at age fifteen. I had a bent for math and science that came out of nowhere, I guess. My parents didn't even *finish* high school. My dad was military and was based at Chanute Air Force Base in Rantoul, a little ways from Champaign-Urbana and the University of Illinois. So when I was this little math and science *wunderkind* my parents found out that a great university was just twenty-five miles away and decided that they needed to get me there. I started at U of I at age fifteen and majored in mechanical engineering, but eventually focused more on electrical engineering. When I arrived as a freshman, people on campus looked at me funny for a couple years because I was so young, short, and scrawny—not the big hulk of an overweight old man you see today," he added with a grin. "But by my junior year I had grown up a bit and was working lab projects for John Bardeen. You may know the name."

"Oh yes, I do!" Kate said. "We studied the development of the MRI and other imaging devices my sophomore year."

33

"Well, Kate," Mike continued, "Bardeen spent over twenty-five years teaching at the engineering school. He won Nobel prizes in two different fields. He and a fellow named Shockley invented the first transistor when they were at Bell Labs. Think about that—the first transistor! It won him the first Nobel. Then at U of I he pioneered research in a fledgling field at the time—superconductivity. In fact, we have an MRI at ExitStrategy, and that MRI was made possible by Bardeen's work. And getting back to me, I was there as his number one assistant for seven years. He won a second Nobel for the superconductivity research. I went with him to Sweden for the ceremony, and, this is funny—Professor Bardeen had brought two of his kids to the first Nobel ceremony. The king of Sweden chided him for it, but Bardeen pushed back, saying 'I'll bring them all next time.' I was there for that second Nobel ceremony and sure enough, he brought all seven of his kids right up onto the podium. This time the king approved! After that, Frigidaire lured me away. I was able to use crazy side aspects of superconductivity research to invent ridiculously efficient heat-transfer systems. And that's how I made my name and a boatload of money working for Frigidaire and their parent company, General Motors. So, is that enough about me? Does that help you realize we're doing real science and we're not delusional?"

"Well, it would appear so. You seem to have had an amazing career. Yes, color me impressed. But I'd really like to see this facility—get a sense of it," Kate said.

"Sure. I know why you said that, Kate," Mike answered. "The way a lab looks tells a visiting scientist everything. Is it clean and neat, or is it sloppy and dirty? Does it house cutting-edge technology, or is it just a bunch of dirty test tubes and Bunsen burners? We'll drive up to see it in a bit if you like. We have technology there that you've never dreamed of."

"Technology, real science—that's what I'm looking for in a job. I just realized I'm hungry now. Mind if I go visit the pastry cart?"

"Not at all, Kate. Go dig in, have as much as you want!" Mike insisted.

While Kate poured herself some coffee, grabbed a croissant and smeared a bit of blackberry jam on it, the others exchanged smiles and nods. "She's perfect, isn't she? Just what we've needed," Mike whispered.

Kate returned with her plate of food and coffee. The tension in the room had disappeared. Even Randolph Morgan had become less gnarly. After Kate ate a few bites of her croissant, Gloria showed her around the suite as if they had been friends for years. After the little tour and a few more minutes of small talk, they reconvened the interview.

"Well, Kate, are you ready?" Franklin asked.

"Ready for what?"

"On Monday you called yourself a nerd—a lab rat. Want to see your lab?"

"*My lab?* Hmm, so you're the salesman, right?" Kate gave Franklin a little smile. "Sure, yes—no harm in looking, right? I'm ready when you are."

CHAPTER SEVEN

Before parting ways at the hotel on Friday, Gloria insisted on scheduling a lunch date with Kate for a month later. "Time for us girls to get to know each other better," she'd said as she kissed Kate on the cheek. Then it was time for Mike and Franklin to show Kate around Energy Source/ExitStrategy. They left the hotel and drove north on Lake Shore Drive since I-94 was a mess. It was a beautiful day—people out on the lakefront jogging trail, Lincoln Park harbor and the zoo off to the left. They zoomed on, eventually zipping onto Green Bay Road. Mike was driving, so Kate engaged Franklin in some small talk in the backseat.

"So, Franklin, you were an actor? What was that like?"

"Oh, it was great fun. I never hurt for work. And I lived in sunny LA—I still don't know why Mike insists on living here year-round, brr."

"Might I have seen you in any films?"

"Yes, and no. When I was really young I did stand-in work. I'd be Ryan O'Neill's or Warren Beatty's or someone else's backside. Did some stunts, too. Just about got killed by a crazy horse one day—threw me and started kicking me. I was in the hospital for a week. I graduated from that racket and did television work back in the 1980s through most of the 1990s. In fact, if you watch reruns I'll turn up somewhere, of course looking a lot fitter than I am now."

"So when you had speaking roles what kind of parts did you play?"

"I was typically one of the bad guys. You know, the guy who's trying to punch out Jim Garner on *Rockford P.I.*—stuff like that. I had some recurrings for a while, too—*Law & Order*, a couple other more forgettable shows. I was crap at comedy, so I was pretty much typecast as a bad guy in dramas. The directors liked my threatening scowl. Wanna see?"

"Sure." Franklin glared at her, his eyebrows arched, his mouth parted to show off some pretty wicked incisors. "Whoa—that's good."

"Yeah, I had steady work. No problemo."

"Kate, Franklin knows everyone in Hollywood," Mike piped in. "Not just actors—directors, cameramen, grips, set design, makeup people. Everyone big and small."

"Ha, maybe because I had a weakness. Well actually, I still have it," Franklin said.

"And what's that?" Kate asked.

"I pick up tabs. My dad and Mike taught me that. Always happy to treat others when there was a great get-together. You watch if we ever go out with a group sometime. Everyone will sit there and keep their mouths shut, looking around pretending to not notice that the check has come. They'll all be waiting for Mike or me to pick it up."

"We don't mind—it makes us very popular fellows!" Mike added.

The small talk continued for a while more. They drove past the corporate offices for many Fortune 500 companies. Sandwiched between were small, yet amazing tech start-ups.

"What are all these green and white circular buildings I see?" Kate asked. "Right in back of these companies?"

"Ah, good eyes, Kate," Franklin exclaimed. "Those are ice system air-conditioning units. I'm glad you noticed them! They're designed, constructed, and licensed by my uncle."

"So, Mike? Ice systems?"

"Yes, Kate. It's heat transfer—what I do. This type is simple enough that a third-grader could understand it. You know there are variable rates for electricity from the power company, right? This system makes ice at night when electric rates are low. Then in the morning, say about six a.m., we shut off the ice production and let the ice melt. Air blown over the ice is cooled and circulated throughout the building. Just repeat every day and voilà—you've got a forty-five percent saving in air-conditioning costs. It's a ridiculously simple formula and it's an easy Energy Source revenue stream to help out what we're doing at ExitStrategy. I sure as heck didn't invent the idea, but I tweaked it for efficiency. And here—we've arrived!"

There it was, the home of Energy Source/ExitStrategy and to dozens of patentable discoveries in heat-transfer research, cryonic stasis, and more. Kate was impressed—the building looked like something out of the future.

"Oh my, it's so huge and so modern," Kate gasped. "A massive solar array? That must produce crazy amounts of wattage. I wasn't expecting this. Huh, you have a tennis court off the parking lot—seriously?"

"Yes, built just for you," Franklin quipped.

"Don't listen to him," Mike said. "Gloria Dunham had it built for someone. But you can use it whenever you like."

"So, this is a big circular wall, and then that's the building rising out over the top of the wall?"

"Actually, no," Mike said, prying his girth out of the car. "What looks like a wall is the outside edge of an enormous circular hallway that goes all the way around. If you could see the building from the air you would liken the design to a wagon wheel. That tall part rising up in the middle—see it there? That's the hub. Then there are five spokes, or wings, which connect to the outer ring you're looking at now. You'll get a better idea of it once you're inside."

"This must have cost a fortune to build."

"It did, but in baby steps. We started with the central hub and two wings. The other wings and what we jokingly call the 'collider ring' were added later."

"Collider ring? Oh, yeah, I get it," Kate said.

"So let's go in the main entrance, which is the A wing," Mike said before calling security and then entering. "So, Kate, this wing holds all the offices, including mine and yours. Also, a few office staff, a few people who do the ice construction; licensing, also the sales of the solar energy electricity to our neighboring buildings. There's my office, and right here is yours. Let's pop in and take a look."

"Mike, you make it sound like I'm totally ready to sign a contract," Kate protested.

"I don't think that will happen until you see the lab," Franklin interjected.

"Oh my, this is swanky." Kate walked here and there, checking out all the highlights: multiple computers and monitors, a video system apparently running a live feed from the lab, whiteboards of various sizes, filing systems, a large steel and glass desk in the center of the room, voice-commanded direct and indirect lighting, a mini-kitchen, a private bath with shower. "It's beautiful, such a modern design. I think you could live here. This office is as big as my whole apartment."

"Check out the coat rack, Kate," Mike said.

"Ooh, look at that, upscale lab coats with my name embroidered by hand, it looks like. All different colors. You're sparing no expense."

"That's true," Franklin said. "Now walk back out and go to the end of the hallway and you'll be at the center—the energy center—of the whole building."

As they left the hall, the space opened up into the circular hub area—the ceiling extended to about forty-five feet. At the center of the hub was a giant monolithic tower.

"Oh, my God. It's huge. What is that?"

"Well, guess," Mike said.

"I'm guessing it's your main power generator. But it's almost silent. Is this where the solar energy comes in, over here? And you've got some kind of heat-transfer system, maybe this part over here, I'm guessing, to run your cryosystem?"

"That's pretty close."

"He's got about twenty-five patents just sitting there, Kate," Franklin said. "Not that we're planning on disclosing the workings of all this yet."

"Wow, oh wow. This is amazing," Kate gasped as she walked the entire circumference of the towering steel and copper monolith. There were monitors, displays, dials, and weird-looking gizmos here, there, and everywhere.

"Oh, here come Chrissy and Norm," Franklin said. "'Clipboard Norm' people call him. He's married to that thing—the clipboard, I mean, not the woman with him. Norm, Chrissy, come on over. I'd like to introduce our new head of research, Katherine Pearson. You know, the one we've been telling you about."

"Oh, it's so good to meet you, Kate," Chrissy exclaimed, shaking Kate's hand. Chrissy appeared to be about fifty, a very fit woman with wavy brown hair, green eyes, and an abundance of freckles. "When do you start?"

"Well, I haven't even agreed yet. Although I already seem to have a number of lab coats with my name on them."

"Sure, Mike is wooing you big-time. Resistance is futile—you will be assimilated," Norm quipped.

"These two have been with me for years," Mike said. "Chrissy from day one and Norm a little after. I stole him from GM. Norm is the brain behind the brawn of that beast you see in front of you."

"No, you invented it, Mike. You are the brain. I just keep it running, and happy," Norm said.

"Mike, what if you had a power outage? What's the backup?" Kate asked.

"Kate," Norm interjected, "we are so redundant on energy supply it's ridiculous. Don't worry about that!"

"All right, Kate, you ready to see your lab?" Mike asked. "It's near the start of B wing, over this way. Walk with us, Chrissy, Norm."

They entered the B wing and immediately ducked into a large room that opened up to total about two thousand square feet.

"Oh my God, look at this," Kate gushed, trotting from spot to spot. "Electron microscopes—the latest models? Eppendorf centrifuges, a speed vac concentrator, an ELISA washer—this looks like custom glassware over here, right? And computers and monitors everywhere, a sample preparation station, oh wait, three stations? Oh my! Wait, is that what I think it is? A brand new proton ion DNA sequencer? They just bought this model at Northwestern, but they wouldn't let me touch it—for full professors only. Oh my God, this is insane!"

"Like a kid in a candy shop, right, Mike?" Chrissy said, grinning over at him.

"You bet," he replied. "Can you blame her? A very expensive, well-stocked candy shop, I might add!"

Kate discovered more and more gadgets and toys to drool over. Maybe it was finally time to put up or shut up, she thought.

"So shall we talk now, Kate?" Mike asked. "Let's just you and me step into my office and see what you think."

"All right," she answered, still overwhelmed by the totally tricked-out lab.

* * *

"So first let me ask you a couple questions," Kate said. "Why me? Aren't I awfully young? All I have is a master's degree. And why am I replacing a doctor? Shouldn't you simply just get another MD?"

"Kate," Mike confided, "we talked to your advising professor at Northwestern. He said you have more potential for creativity than any grad student he's seen in years. Went on and on about you. We're looking for serious potential, new ideas. We're trying to find someone who can do cutting-edge hard science and add a hell of a lot of imagination, too. And someone who isn't afraid of a failure or two along the way. He says you're the one, and we believe him. And you're humble, too. We could just have Norm keep the cryosystem running forever, but we want to go way further. We want to revive these people, not just keep them frozen. What's the point of that?"

"And what makes you think you can do it? I know we talked about this a little bit, but then Miss Dunham's lawyer shut things down. Do you want to talk freely to me now? I might be about to commit to this, now that I've seen some of the operation. But I need to know where you are, where you are trying to go, and I really need to think about the ethics of this, too. Understand?"

"Yes, we will talk honestly now. Franklin and I believe in the importance of being earnest, Kate. Just to clarify, Randolph Morgan does not work for us. He's just Gloria's lawyer. And Gloria has a habit of poking her nose into people's business. We usually let her do what she thinks she wants because then we just circumvent her anyway. Sometimes this is just a big game for Franklin and me—the 'Outfox Gloria Game,' I suppose you could call it. That game goes all the way back to 1985 or so. Franklin has been into mind-games since he was a kid. Believe me, he played devilish tricks on me the whole time he was growing up."

"So Gloria is a bit of an oddball, I take it. Is she senile, or just weird? Both?"

"Hmm." Mike doodled on some stationery, trying to decide how to answer the question. "You saw the tennis court. She had it built for an individual who has been here in cryo for years. What does that tell you, Kate?"

"What? A tennis court for someone in cryostasis? That's crazy."

"Agreed. Watch yourself around her, okay?"

"Sure. Should be interesting when we have lunch together next month, huh?"

"You'll be fine. Ninety percent of the time she'll blather on about her show-biz career and how awful her two ex-husbands were to her. You can just sit and nod. But I have to say that when she learned you played tennis it made her even more interested in meeting you. You also went to the same high school as her tennis-playing friend here in stasis. She tells me it's fate that you're here."

"New Trier? This person went to New Trier High? Hmm, interesting."

"Yup."

"All right," Kate said. "So what truly sets you apart from the corpsecicle places, like you called them? What do I need to know?"

"Saltieri and I agreed, let's stay away from deep cryo. It's unnecessary. We go to just before the glassy state and hover there. We don't chill people to the point that their skulls crack—hey, I noticed that made you gag when I mentioned it. Sorry, but that's what those hacks do. But don't worry, they say, the doctors of the future will fix everything! We say stop being barbarians. We can do far better if we apply real science to this field."

"Keep talking," Kate said, nodding.

"Enzo and I set out to scientifically reinvent the whole cryonics field—blow past the pseudoscience our competitors were doing. We had a lot of ideas, and some of them were shots in the dark—just hunches. But we think we nailed a lot of stuff. 'Stuff,' Kate—that's a scientific term, you know," Mike said, his eyes twinkling.

"Hunches or dreams can yield results. You and I know that they've been there throughout the history of science, right?"

"Agreed, and I've been blessed to have had those moments myself now and then in my career. So we decided to perfuse the body with helium, driving out moisture. In addition, I invented the polymer pods, which are more stable and are less prone to icing and so on. A few other tweaks and changes in procedure I can tell you later. And then the final piece of the puzzle—what Enzo was working on."

"Yes? Yes? What was it?" Kate asked eagerly, moving forward on her chair.

"I don't know. I honestly don't know," Mike said, grimacing in frustration. "That's why you're here, Kate. He was up to something. But between the lung cancer and the Alzheimer's he was struggling. It seemed like he had ideas percolating. But when he would tell me about them and I didn't understand immediately what he was getting at, he would get very frustrated, and then the Alzheimer's would kick in. He would lose his train of thought and storm away—mad at me, mad at the world. You'll have all the files to look through. Vet whatever of his you can decipher, or discover solutions yourself. That's the opportunity here, understand? You're the one who can decide if we can truly revive these patients—all these wonderful people here, waiting. Let's walk down to Enzo's office."

They walked down the hall to Saltieri's old office. Mike swiped a keycard, opened the door, and motioned Kate in. "What does this look like to you, Kate?"

"Ha. It looks like Albert Einstein's office—that famous photo of his office taken on the day he died. It was a mess. Well, to us it looks like a mess, but I'm sure to him it was just how he worked, right?"

"Right. And what you see here is the desk of another genius—Dr. Enzo Saltieri. Enzo taught medicine at the University of Bologna in Italy for years. A small man with a ginormous brain. Johns Hopkins lured him to the States. He was guest lecturing at University of Chicago when we met, and we discovered that we both had a bent for this crazy idea of cryo. Anyway, Kate, all the work is here—and yes, I know it's a mess. His notes are a jumble, sorry. Some of it is on computer drives, but a lot of it is page after page of scribbles on legal pads. What Franklin and I want you to do is this—take some time, say ninety days, and evaluate absolutely everything Enzo was studying. Beyond that, your real bottom-line assignment is to formulate a procedure to revive the patients here. Make a magic potion, click your ruby slippers three times, or whatever else it might take to turn them back into normal, healthy, walking and talking people again. That's it in a nutshell. Not so hard, eh, Kate?" Mike grinned.

"Mike, you do realize that *every* internal organ has to work in order to pull this off, right? And right away we have to fix what killed these people in the first place. What was wrong with most of them when they died?"

"Cancer mostly. And just remember, no cryo company ever promised revival and the cure for any patient's disease or illness. Cryonics just presents the *opportunity* for a human body to exist into the future where cures might be discovered, right?"

"Hmm, so much to think about." Kate stood and paced Saltieri's office and pulled at her hair—a habit of hers when she was trying to blast through a tough problem. "So what do people pay to be here?"

"What do you think people pay at other facilities?"

"I have no idea, sorry," she said, stopping to finger through the pile of scribbled-upon papers heaped on Saltieri's desk.

"For a full-body cryo, the tab is anywhere from eighty thousand dollars on up to two hundred thousand. Pretty steep, huh?"

"Hey, you want immortality you better have the buckos for it, I would guess," she said, suddenly realizing this whole day was the strangest one of her life. She wondered what Aria would think of all this and how many goofy, comedically inappropriate questions she would ask Mike if given the opportunity.

"Right. So that's what others charge. Our fee is *one million dollars*," Mike declared.

"One million? Wow. Oh my gosh, all I've been saying since we got here is 'wow,' huh?"

"Yes, I noticed, but who wouldn't say 'wow'? You see, Kate, the people we've brought in, mostly from Franklin's networking—the famous actors and directors, painters and sculptors, novelists and sports stars, the old money folks and the nouveau rich lottery winners—none of them are going to try to do this Walmart style. The wealthy can be a pain in the ass and do plenty of stupid stuff, but overall most of them are damned smart with their money. They rarely bargain shop for anything, whether it's shoes, cars, homes, boats, or a cryo facility. We're number one because they've learned by word of mouth that we are the *only* ones who care enough about science and have a chance to make this work."

"And who regulates this? State health agencies? The FDA? No, wait, that makes no sense," Kate said, confused about how this could be monitored in any logical manner.

"No one. Can you imagine some state-employed drudge comprehending any of this?"

"They'd be very confuzzled," Kate said, borrowing one of Aria's favorite made-up words.

"Confuzzled indeed," Mike said, grinning. "There's a little patient paperwork involved. Some minor legal issues that I'll explain to you later. They're really not a concern. How about some food? I'm starving. Let's hop over to our lunchroom, okay?" They jaywalked through the hub and entered the cafeteria. They saw Franklin was already there, getting himself an iced tea.

"Hi, Kate," Franklin greeted, smiling. "Glad to see you again. Walk over this way. So here we've got our own chef from eleven a.m. until two. You can order anything you want as long as James has the ingredients on hand. It's a company perk. Nice, huh? James, this is Katherine Pearson, she's going to be our new head of research. Are you ready to show off your talents for her?"

"Sure, Franklin. So, Miss Pearson, what have you got a taste for? I do have some killer avocados today, maybe we can work them into something for you," James said. He was a tall, hunky young man, maybe twenty-five or so. I would definitely enjoy having this man cook for me every day, thought Kate. *Bet Aria doesn't have a chef cooking for her at the symphony in Milwaukee. The best she can usually do is pop into Usinger's for brats and a beer. Tasty food, but mostly guys with well-developed beer bellies there.*

"Well, James, first, just call me Kate. And I would absolutely die for a fajita with those avocados being one of the stars of the day."

"Not a problem. Chicken? Beef? How do you want it?"

Hmm, there's a line Aria would jump on. She always knows how to flirt with hunky guys. Wait, I'm here for a job, need to get my mind back on business. "Why don't you surprise me, okay?"

"Sure thing," James said, flashing a million-dollar smile.

"Okay, Kate, go get something to drink over there and meet us at a table," Mike said.

Kate grabbed a bottle of Italian soda. In a few minutes their food was ready and they continued their talk.

"So, Kate," Mike said, between bites of beef stroganoff, "our operation doesn't look like a scene from a Svengoolie movie, huh?"

"That's for sure. But I guess that other lab with Ted Williams's head, as you told me, would certainly qualify."

"Kate, do you like tuna?" Franklin asked.

"Sure, why not?"

"Well, don't gag, but they decided to place each head upside-down on a can of Bumble Bee Tuna to keep it, I mean the head, from sticking to the cryo unit surface. Not kidding!"

"Well, that'll make her lose her appetite, Franklin. Stop torturing the poor girl."

"Never you mind, Mike," Franklin answered. "And then, Kate, guess what happened once when they tried to transfer one of those heads. They picked it up and the can was frozen tight to the head. Now there's a Svengoolie picture for you, huh? So, they started banging at the can with a hammer, but it wouldn't pop off until they slammed it like fifty times. I kid you not. It's all in a book written by a former employee of theirs. Can you imagine?"

Kate suddenly broke out into a fit of laughter. Just the absurdity of it all had finally bowled her over. Mike and Franklin grinned at each other and finally laughed, too.

"Okay, Kate, ha-ha—that was good. We laugh a lot around here, by the way," Mike said. "Hey, we don't know how much of that book is true. But there it is. Anyway, back to reality, in your résumé you mentioned a doctor from the Caribbean somewhere, a fellow you worked with now and then on cryobiology projects. What was his name again?"

"Oh, yes, Edouard—Edouard Radelet. Brilliant man. Bet you he's head of the World Health Organization before he hits forty. An amazing mind."

"If you're on board we want to hire him to work with you," Mike offered. "Would you like that?"

"Would I? Of course. That lab and me with Edouard? That would be amazing, although I don't know if he's available." Kate finished off the last of her delicious lunch. This was a great perk, she decided.

"We'll figure that out. All right, listen, I have some things to attend to for a few hours," Mike said. "Could we drop you by your place— it's close, right? And then meet us back here maybe about seven and we'll tour the operating room and walk you down a wing or two to see the actual patients. Okay?"

"Sure. Aria—that's my roommate—can drop me back over."

"Wait, Mike, why don't we let her use one of the company cars?" Franklin said. "Enzo's is sitting there doing nothing except collecting tree sap and bird droppings. He won't be driving it anytime soon, right? Keith, the head of security will start that car up and hand you the keys, Kate. Meet back here at seven. We'll have a fancy gold pen for you to sign your contract, won't we, Mike?"

"Fancy pen? Oh yes. My lucky pen you're talking about. Right, Franklin?"

"Yessir, Uncle Mike. The lucky pen!"

PAUL CAREY

CHAPTER EIGHT

"Miss Pearson is here, Mr. Burgess."

"Very good, Keith. Thanks for staying late. You can take off now."

"Thank you, Mr. Burgess."

"Thanks for letting me use the company car, Mike. That was very nice of you," Kate said.

"Not a problem. Well, how about I show you the last remaining things you need to see? Shall we?"

"Of course."

"All right. So over here, Kate, opposite your lab, is the operating room. This is where all the patients make their transition—their 'exit strategy.' Step on in."

"It looks just like a hospital operating room, I would venture. What are some of the procedures?"

"Well, first let me tell you that all the patients have signed a Body Donor Agreement. Technically they are donating their body to ExitStrategy. But instead of the usual, you know, a body going to an educational institution as a cadaver for students to study, or to a research project, we're going to put them in stasis as quickly as possible. The donor status ensures that we are covered legally. We have other forms as well—agreements made between our patients and us, and these are not meant to be divulged to the outside world. We also, at times, videotape patients just before their procedure. They are on camera stating their wishes for cryo. It's a pretty good idea, especially since there have been a few times where we sensed that certain patients' family members might want to battle us."

"So you've had battles?"

"Nope. Knock on wood—it's never happened. We've been surprised by that. Ironically, the only battle we've had was with an actual cryo patient. She was insistent on getting what she wanted. Enzo decided she was right, so she got it. Franklin and I gave in. In the long run, she and Enzo were right. It actually changed how we do things around here."

"What happened? What did she want?"

"It's a long story, I'll tell you later. Let's just stick to the mini-tour script for now, okay?"

"Sure, that's fine, Mike. Wait—so do these people have funerals? It would seem antithetical to their beliefs. They're denying death, right?"

"They usually will have a memorial service. Some who don't want to divulge that they've gone into cryo may stage a funeral, but there's no body in the casket. In those cases, only a few people at the service may know about the choice for cryo. However it plays out, we haven't really had any problems. Don't forget, most of our clients are wealthy, powerful, and famous. They've been calling their own shots for years. Not too many people around them are going to buck them when they choose to be a part of ExitStrategy."

"I understand. So walk me through the procedure."

"I'll give you the highlights," Mike said. "The body is cooled quite a bit to minimize any chance of early decomposition. As quickly as we can, we open the femoral arteries. We drain most, but not quite all of the blood out of one, while we inject our glycol-based cryofluid on the other side. For the most part, Chrissy and a partner do this. They are very good at it."

"Wait. You have licensed medical people for this? You can't just use anybody, right?"

"Chrissy is a licensed RN. She studied to become one specifically so that she could participate. Enzo Saltieri was the supervising MD, of course. We had other doctors and nurses on call when needed."

"You said 'had,' not have. What's that mean?"

"Good catch, Kate. We haven't cryo'd anyone in three years."

"Why not? Wait, what about Enzo? Didn't he want to go into cryo?"

"We'll get to that soon, Kate. Anyway, no one alive right now under contract with us has died recently, for one thing. We've been okay with that. You mentioned you wanted to think about the ethics of all this, right? Well, actually that hit us a while back. Enzo and I began to realize that we needed time to review the ethical implications of going the next step—of reviving people. I mean, who's responsible if we bring back someone now, or years from now, and they're alive but a vegetable? Who is responsible for their quality of life? What if their family doesn't exist in the future? What will the society of the future say? Enzo and I rushed into some of this too quickly. We were too excited to start the company and get it running. But as we got older we realized that there were issues, big and small, that colored this whole thing. Understand?"

"Of course. I *totally* understand that, Mike. And I'm actually glad you're saying this. We are in an ethical gray area, right? Life, death, some kind limbo in between? It does raise millions of questions."

"Correct, Kate. So, moving on, after we have the cryo preservative in their body, the fluid that protects against icing, as well as the helium gas perfusion of the entire body to protect against ice formation in between cells, we start really dropping the temperature. As I told you before, we don't just do the knee-jerk thing the other facilities have always done—simply freezing all the way down to liquid nitrogen level. We don't even hit the glassy state I told you about, so we're nowhere near liquid nitrogen temperature. At the temperature we use, there can still even be a tiny amount of biological process going on at the molecular level, believe it or not. I mean laymen don't get that, but I'm sure you would appreciate this as a biologist. Granted, there is no measurable heartbeat, no EEG. We also cycle the temperature up and down and periodically force more helium into the environment. You'll see the readout and hear that at each pod, and it's all computer controlled."

"Why the temperature shifts?"

"Enzo believed the body needs variety, that some kind of external stimulus, or at least change in the environment is good for the body. I don't understand his research and formulas on this—maybe you will!"

"Yes, I get most of the ideas I'm hearing. Brilliant, actually. And your expertise in heat transfer is what makes all this possible and affordable over many years, right?"

"Correct, Kate. We think that our process will result in the least amount of cellular damage and the best chance for revival. Of course, that's your new job, understand? Examining all of that. My fresh set of brilliant, young eyes."

"Wait, let's go back a sec." Kate drummed her fingers on the steel table in the room, trying to keep her focus on what questions to ask. "When you begin this process, these people have just died, right? They have a death certificate from a doctor, correct?"

"Yes. But we don't actually agree with what that certificate says. A death certificate is just a piece of paper that society thinks should exist. In our case, the patient has just shown the early signs of physical death, just initial function failures—that is all. We believe that they are still alive. That is our position here. Did you know the most recent studies show that brain cells last far beyond the current definition of death? People can laugh all they want at us, but those are folks who don't know recent research. When we place someone in cryo, we are preserving their more important functions for them. You stopped breathing or your heart stopped—so what? We will preserve you, we will save you—*literally save you*. We really do believe in this, Kate. Remember what I said about the brain cells? Let me ask you, Kate— what makes you, you? What is it about Katherine Pearson that makes her the person she is—that people say, 'Oh look, there's Kate Pearson'?"

"Well, other than my appearance, I would say personality, I guess. They would know my smile, how I talk, what I think about the world."

"And where is that? Where is it stored?"

"In my brain, obviously. Memory, the collected basis for my views and my personality, right?"

"Correct. That recent research I mentioned posits strongly that brain cells, especially core memory cells, are still functional far beyond the point where a doctor would readily agree to sign a death certificate. These cells do not die quickly—they are still functional for hours, even days past so-called death. I'll show you the research from legitimate cutting-edge sources, not quacks."

"Wow, seriously? So you honestly believe that the patients here have much more than just their physical bodies in stasis, that you have preserved their memories as well, and that you can restore full brain function upon revival?"

"Absolutely. I have to, otherwise we are just freezing and thawing flesh—not real human individuals. And as you mull all of this over, it goes to show you, again, that we really don't know what divides life from death. We are still stumbling blindly, just guessing at things."

"This is pretty amazing stuff. So now what?"

"Let's walk down the B wing. Ready?"

* * *

"Okay, here we go, Kate," Mike began. "This was the first patient wing built. The cryo system control starts at the center of the hub— you know, the big tower of power, as Chrissy calls it, and runs right underneath the floor we're walking on. As you see, we have people in cryopods running down each side of the wall. These first forty or so are the steel pods, not the new design. The equipment below us feeds up to each of these pods. There's an outer pod, and then an inner one. We've got readouts on the whole system and each individual pod. Norm oversees all this with the help of a young woman named Deirdre. She also helps me run my calculations. Brilliant kid, just a little older than you. Actually, you two might hit it off—not everyone here is an old-timer."

"This is amazing. So who are all these people? It looks like there are about eighty stations along each wall—so about 160 patients in this wing alone?"

"You're a bit off—there are sixty on each side, thus 120 patients in this wing. Evens over here and odds on the opposite side. So here, let me tell you about some of them. B34 here—she's a ballerina; B36, an author; B38, a well-known scientist. Across there is B39, a politician whose name you would know. It's an impressive assemblage of people."

"So, they just lay here and wait? And what killed most of them? You mentioned cancer earlier today."

"Yes, a lot of these people have cancer, especially pancreatic or metastatic cases. ALS, MS, MD, late-stage Alzheimer's—there are many illnesses represented here."

"So, they wait, right? But really, how long?"

"Maybe not too long for some of them. As you know, almost every day around the world there are new treatment ideas and promising medical research. And frankly, it depends on you, too, Kate. After you look the research over, you tell me when we could take a try at it. Try it out on some animals we have frozen here. If it works with the animals and you've finalized a procedure, then we could hunt for a patient here whose illness is curable in today's medical world. I'd sure like to see it happen soon—most people my age have been retired for a while and are out playing golf in sunny Arizona, right? Well, here we are the end of this wing. That's Benjamin, in B120. He was a public school teacher. He met Franklin at some museum in LA. We have no idea how he saved up a million dollars to spend with us. But here he is, nonetheless."

"Interesting," Kate replied. "Do you think they dream? I mean all these people. What would they dream about?"

"You're quite the romantic, aren't you? Well, I don't think they dream of electric sheep, we'll leave that to the androids—maybe more like how to get ahold of a plush electric blanket and set it on extra-high, I bet," Mike said, chuckling. "I'm curious. When we first revealed what ExitStrategy does, you panicked. You were nauseous. How did that change so quickly?"

Kate had thought Mike might get around to asking this question. She stared at the floor for a moment, then spoke slowly, yet clearly. "My dad died from cancer. He was in so much pain. It was terrible. Yes, I freaked out for a while the other day. But then I started thinking of my dad—how I lost him and he's never coming back. Here he would have had a chance." Kate fought hard to not tear up in front of Mike.

"I'm sorry for your loss. I'm sure it must have been hard for you. But here were are now, in the present, right? And the big, big question is this—are you ready? Do you want to be the new head of research at ExitStrategy?"

"Yes, I've decided to be bold. I'm young. If I can't go out on a limb now, take a risk—maybe make a difference in the world—when will I? Sure, this is all quite unusual, but I see your commitment to hard science. The lab alone screams that. You seem to be a brilliant man. So heck yeah, I'm in!"

"That's fabulous, Kate. I'm so pleased—you have no idea. Franklin will be, too. Welcome aboard! Oh, hope you don't mind—I got ahold of your friend Edouard. We talked over Skype. Lovely young man, very gracious and ridiculously smart. Get this, he said he would be available to you for six months if you want to pursue this."

"Seriously? You talked to Edouard?"

"Yes, he says he is leaving his current position soon, and he has a new government health appointment lined up with some other Caribbean country. It starts late spring of next year, I think he said. Until that job kicks in he's available to the highest bidder, he joked."

"Wow! That's great to hear."

"Yes, just the man you hoped for, right? So when I told him what we do here he wasn't shocked like you were back at the hotel. After all, he's from Haiti, right? He took it completely in stride. When I explained it all he said Saltieri and I should be in the Vodoun Doctor Hall of Fame!"

"That's pretty funny. So what's next?"

"I have your contract here. Take your time and read it over. And you can keep that company car, too. We'll add a rider to that effect."

Kate took the document. Everything seemed straightforward. She smiled at Mike. *What a wonderful, brilliant man,* she thought. "Okay, I'm ready. Do you have that lucky pen your nephew mentioned?"

"Oh yes, somewhere here." Mike patted his pockets. "Here it is. Kate, I've kept this pen for years. Just looking at it now and then keeps me from becoming complacent. Same thing you seem to want to avoid, eh? It's the pen that General Motors handed me years ago to sign my forced resignation."

PAUL CAREY

CHAPTER NINE

Mike Burgess, Fall 1980

Do a line, then I'm outta here. A raise and a promotion, piece of cake. Stop sharing me with Frigidaire, GM all the way now, baby. Today's the day—I can feel it.

Mike Burgess trotted out of his Glencoe, Illinois, apartment and jumped in his car, a 1979 Oldsmobile 88 with the optional 260 Olds engine. He wouldn't be caught dead with the Buick six-cylinder engine they were dropping into most of the 88s now. Mike had every possible option added to the car and it drove like a dream. He especially liked the headroom, since he could slide his six-foot-four-inch frame behind the wheel with ease. Mike had not only created the coolant system and heating/air-conditioning design for this car and every other GM car since 1972, but he also had a part in redesigning the assembly line it was built on.

Okay, looking good. Not much traffic. Get through this stretch past downtown and then drive like a bat out of hell through goddamn Gary, Indiana, stinkin' armpit of the Midwest. Just zoom on past that stench from the steel mills. Then hit the Michigan state line—smooth sailing from then on.

A few hours later Mike pulled into the GM corporate headquarters parking lot with time to spare. He parked his car and strode on through the famous entrance doors, smiling and shaking hands left and right as he made his way toward the elevators. He was a big man with an equally large personality—people were naturally drawn to him. As he stepped into the elevator and pushed the button for the boardroom floor, he saw McDonald, one of the chairmen. McDonald tried to scramble in but the doors closed too fast. He tried to call out to Mike but it was too late. *Wow, he looked kind of sour. Just from missing the elevator? Oh well, he'll catch up. Good guy, doesn't take any shit from Moore. McDonald has an electrical engineering background. Gotta like him, we engineering guys stick together!*

Mike got off the elevator and shook hands with more pals in the hallway. *This is gonna be a red-letter day,* he thought. *How much more money are they offering, I wonder? Hell, all the patents and the new work in plant design—I think I'm making senior VP, easy. And they won't be sharing me with Frigidaire anymore.*

"They're ready for you, Mr. Burgess," the receptionist controlling access to the boardroom said.

Mike straightened his tie, then winked and smiled at her, "Here I go!" he announced. She looked blankly back at him. The Mike "Cold Smokey" Burgess charisma hadn't yet won her over.

Mike pulled the door open and walked in with his usual confidence. He looked around and saw all the usual exec faces, but also two others he didn't know. *Bean counters probably*, he thought. He moved around the room shaking a few hands, and then McDonald entered from the private entrance and sat down at the head of the table. There were ten or so men in attendance, plus a secretary taking notes.

"Greetings, Mike. Glad you got here safe and sound," McDonald said.

"Glad to be here. I survived driving through Gary and the mills. No matter how many times I drive through there I can't get used to that smell."

"Well, Mike, don't forget, a lot of that Gary steel winds up in our cars. Or in a lot of the stuff you've designed for Frigidaire over the years."

"Sure, I was just making a joke. Guess it wasn't that funny."

"So, Mike," McDonald announced, "I'm going to be running this meeting since we've known each other a long time. I've always respected your work. You're a multitalented hardworking man and I appreciate all you've done for Frigidaire and GM in your time here. Carl here will start things off."

"Thanks for being here, Mike. I echo Mr. McDonald's sentiments," said Carl Castle, a bald-headed fellow who always looked like he'd been sucking on lemons. "Mike, we're all here because we've become aware that you like money."

"Well, of course. That's what GM is about, Carl. Didn't you get the memo?" Mike zinged back. He looked around and to his surprise no one seemed to get his little joke—his sly putdown of Castle, the goddamn jerk.

"Yes, Mike. I understand. Clever. As I said, we've noticed you like money. And actually girls, too."

Carl Castle? Really? The guy hates my guts. Everyone knows it. What's he talking for, anyway? "Well sure, Carl, I think it's safe to say we all like money here. And girls, too, right? We're men, aren't we?" Stone-cold silence. Even the fellows in the room who'd been his best work pals looked away, avoiding eye contact.

"Mike, there's a difference between girls and women, wouldn't you say?"

"Well sure. So, really, what's this about, Carl? I thought this was a business meeting. Say, if it's about production on that new thermocouple for the Impala I've got the specs in my car. I can go get them." *Jesus, something's not right here. Damn fucking Castle, what the hell does he know? Dammit, dammit, dammit!*

"Carl, get back to the main point, please," McDonald insisted, looking pissed off.

"No, sir, I'm sorry. We need to go over this point first, do we not?" Castle said, looking over at a fellow who Mike had never seen before in his life. The man who stuck out by virtue of his ill-fitting $39.95 Montgomery Ward's suit gave a tiny nod back to Castle.

"No, Mr. Castle," McDonald said, "I said for you to move to the real point of this meeting. Ultimately I'm in charge here. Stick to the main point or you won't speak any further."

"All right, understood," Castle said, trying to hide his disdain not only for Mike but for McDonald, too. "Mike," Castle snarled, "bottom line is that I don't have to be nice to you. I can just hang you out to twist in the wind. You know why? Because right now I'm going to introduce you to someone who has become very interested in you. This is Special Agent Springer from the Internal Revenue Service here to my right. He's got a few things to say." This wasn't the poorly dressed man Castle was trying to introduce before—this was a different fellow, trying, with little success, to herd a giant pile of folders on the desk, papers spilling out every which way.

Oh shit, they got me. Damn it, fucking goddammit, and fuck Castle. I should cold-cock him right now. Mike could feel his face turning red, his blood pressure going through the roof. His urge to walk over to Castle and kill the bald-headed bastard with his bare hands was overwhelming.

"Good afternoon, Mr. Burgess, I'm agent Dirk Springer of the Internal Revenue Service out of Cincinnati. For a while now Frigidaire and GM accountants have been reviewing your expense accounts and have also been trying to resolve how you had access to and control of certain company bank accounts. They asked us to investigate and we've been doing so for about nine months now. Your personal bank has been cooperating with us for at least the last six months. I would like it on record that the IRS feels that GM and Frigidaire have done a poor job of controlling situations like this. We'll be working with you to clean up some processes, correct, Mr. Wyatt?"

"Yes, GM will oblige and we're ready to work with you," said Larry Wyatt, GM head legal counsel. "That's completely understood. Mr. Springer—please continue."

"Mr. Burgess, I am here to inform you that the IRS is prepared to file charges against you next week for felony tax fraud in regard to massive unreported income, alleged to be embezzled GM funds, for tax year 1978. We are talking about criminal tax fraud, a felony. The files here on this table represent just a fraction of the information that will prove our case. The case against you is substantial. I suggest you listen closely to Mr. McDonald and GM legal counsel Mr. Wyatt when they lay out a path for you which may resolve this matter quickly. Just to be clear, the IRS is not charging you with embezzlement. That's not part of the IRS—we are simply a taxing body. Embezzlement would be a state of Michigan matter. However, if the state did press charges we would fully cooperate. Thank you, Mr. Burgess for your attention." And with that, Springer simply sat down. There was no drama—no vendetta. He wasn't there to crucify Mike like Castle was. Mike hated the IRS, but at least he could give credit to Springer for treating him with decency and respect while speaking to him in front of his colleagues.

"So, there we have it," Castle said. "And now I am going to turn to Mr. Bendek like I first wanted to. There is more to this situation. Mr. Bendek?"

The fellow with the cheap suit stood up. "My name is Jussi Bendek, I'm a private investigator. When the IRS started investigating this situation, they confirmed that they were only investigating his financial activities. But Mr. Castle desired more information about Mr. Burgess's daily activity. He hired me, and in my investigation I found that he purchases cocaine for his private use. I also discovered that he seems to like young women, often taking them out to either what you might call dive bars but just as often to nice restaurants. Over the last year we identified these young women and determined their ages. Mr. Burgess, you met a Hazel Morganthaler in Flint, Michigan, on December 31, 1978. Do you recall that?"

"I refuse to answer your questions," Mike said, recovering a little bit of his cool. "You're obviously a tool of Castle's. This is a hatchet job. I have nothing to say." McDonald's sour expression finally turned into a smile. He nodded his approval to Mike, as did several other men.

"You drove Miss Morganthaler from Michigan," Bendek continued, unfazed, "through Indiana to Illinois while she was, at that point, seventeen years old, in order to engage her in an act of prostitution, a violation of the Mann Act of 1910."

"Oh, really?" Mike bellowed, pounding the table with his fist. "Castle, you asshole, you hired this two-bit sleaze ball PI to follow me around? Yes, okay now I will choose to respond, dammit. I met Hazel at a New Year's party at the Flint plant. She had come to the party along with her uncle Bill, who works for us. Did you even know that, Castle? She needed to get to Chicago for a job interview. She had dropped out of high school the year before, but now she was starting to get her act together and wanted to get a job like everyone else in the world does. I offered to give her a ride back to Illinois with me. I knew exactly how old Hazel was—seventeen—and Bill shook my hand and thanked me for helping her out. You tailed me and just assumed the worst of me, is that it, you idiot? She slept on my couch for two nights until she found a place to stay with another young woman she knew. And I bet you never asked her the details, did you? What else did you discover, Bendek, you sleazebag?"

"I'm prepared to turn this over to the FBI right now, Mike," Castle interrupted, waving Bendek off.

"Carl, shut the hell up," Wyatt snapped, glowering at Castle, then turning to Mike. "Look, Mike, you do seem to have a weakness for young women, the Morganthaler girl aside. It's fairly apparent. For now, though, let's calm down and put things in perspective. If the board were to allow Mr. Castle to go to the FBI they can probably fabricate a case to make against you somehow, even though I personally think you never slept with anyone underage."

"Damn straight, Larry," Mike said. "I'm not a pervert."

"I understand, Mike," Wyatt agreed, "but right now the FBI isn't a friend of GM. I simply don't want to deal with them. The IRS, however, is our friend. They work with us, not against us. The Mann Act is the FBI's baby, but they know nothing about any of this yet. We'd like to keep it that way and I don't believe Mr. Castle's character assassination of you will prevail. Carl, I'm head legal counsel here. I'm telling you right now to stay out of my territory, and I highly advise you to stop drumming up support with various board members about what your PI was up to. You brought the IRS in on this before we had even finished our internal investigation. That doesn't sit well with me or anyone else in this room." Wyatt turned back to Mike, softening his tone. "Anyway, Mike, the real situation is this—you embezzled the money. You know it, I know it. It's a fact. You have a coke problem as well. And right now we don't want the media to have any juicy stories to print about us. Fighting off the Japanese for market share is our big job right now, understand? We don't want shareholders to worry about this kind of stuff, too. Therefore, we have no choice but to keep this quiet and let you go."

"Mike," McDonald jumped in, "does this have anything to do with situations where you were expecting bonuses from us? You know, when we licensed out patents you worked on? I'm pretty sure you were angry about that."

"You bet I was angry," Mike answered. "You made ten million selling off my new coolant recycle design and didn't give me a penny. All I asked for was some part of that pie. I thought I was working for GM—not those other companies."

"Mike, it wasn't *your design*. You know how this works. Anything you did while an employee was the property of GM to do with as the company pleased."

"And the board couldn't give me anything? I've made this company millions of dollars. Many fucking millions. So yeah, that's why I did it. I was damn angry. I did it to mess with GM—to prove I was smarter than GM. And it wasn't hard, by the way. You've got a lot of leaks in your system. Come to think of it, fellas, if GM's fiscal security was a radiator, you'd be on the side of the road with steam blasting out the hood."

"Duly noted, Mike," McDonald said with a slight grin.

Mike let out a deep sigh as he pushed himself away from the big table, trying to figure out what to do or say for the moment. It wasn't their fault. He had been in the coke haze weeks, months on end, plotting revenge like a maniac. How could he have had such a serious lapse in judgment, in character? And now it was over. A relief, actually. Thank God for friends. Sure, Castle was a total asshole, but there were other men in the room who, he knew, loved him as a friend and as a colleague. He had let them all down. And even just McDonald being there, sort of on his side, meant the world to Mike now.

"So, Mike," Wyatt continued, "GM knows that we have a number of people in the company with cocaine problems, it's a problem all over the country, I hear. You'll have to sort that issue out for yourself.

Frankly, it's neither here nor there to us right now. GM leadership believes along with me about you and the women. None were underage, just good-looking twentysomethings, correct? Don't listen to Castle. Don't let him rattle you. When Cunningham and Farrell leave the board in about six months, he'll be fired. He pretty much hung himself when he spilled all this to the IRS without coming to me." Wyatt shot a withering look at Castle, who shriveled under the glare. "The amount you embezzled would seem very large to John Q. Public, but to GM it's a tiny piss in the ocean. So here's where we stand with Agent Springer—GM will not ask you to turn the money back in—it will still be viewed as income. We've worked out a deal wherein GM will pay your taxes, late fees, penalties, the whole nine yards. We're settling with the IRS and after today they don't know you from Adam. All you have to do is resign and walk away. Plus one more thing. We want you to write down how you got the money—how you did it. We want that so we can tighten things up, understand? We've got papers here for you to sign. Everyone else is going to walk out now except for Agent Springer, McDonald, and myself. You look over the papers and I'll answer any questions you have, but you need to sign these today, understand?"

"Yes, Larry, thank you. I apologize to you all. It should never have happened. Thank you, and I hope you can forgive me," Mike said sadly, looking from face to face. The other men shuffled out of the room, most of them giving him a firm handshake or a bear hug as they went. Wyatt brought the resignation papers over to Mike.

"Okay, Mike, go ahead and read all this. Please note that you can't take any of our intellectual property to your next employer. That's very important." McDonald, Wyatt, and Springer sat patiently while Mike read everything. It was all straightforward. There was zero mention of the cocaine or of the Mann Act crap.

"Okay," Mike said. "Now what?"

"Here's a pen. You've got to sign here and there, and initial over here on this page a couple times, see? Press hard for the carbons, okay?"

"Okay," Mike said, "what else?"

"Now you need to sign this amended tax return the IRS has prepared for you," said Wyatt. "Look it over and sign that and you're off the hook with the IRS. No charges, no prison, nothing. The state of Michigan and the FBI will not be brought in. And for your own sake, Mike, clean up your drug problem. You don't want to risk going to jail for that, do you? Anyway, look at this way out as GM's thank-you for your many years of inspired service, and we're sorry this happened just as much as you are." Wyatt gave Mike some time to read over the IRS amended return. "Okay, now take this piece of paper and write down how you got into those accounts. You can just sketch it out for us. Listen, Mike, there's nobody on this planet who can replace you at GM. It'll probably take three guys to do what you did for us. Best of luck as you move forward with your life." Mike finished up the quick narrative on how he easily funneled GM money into accounts he controlled and then handed it to Wyatt.

"Mind if I keep this pen, Wyatt?"

"Sure, of course."

"You can have this, too, Mike." McDonald slid an envelope over to Mike.

"What's this?" Mike asked.

"It's our thank-you," McDonald explained. "The board decided, who amongst us is without fault? The chairman says we made a mistake by not rewarding you enough. We should have done more all along to make you happy. You made a mistake, a big one, and maybe there should have been a public punishment—that's what pricks like Castle would like to see happen. But having to resign from GM is a gigantic punishment just in itself. We hope you'll reinvent yourself. I mean hell, that's what you do, man. *You invent!*"

"Thank you all," Mike said humbly as he rubbed his tired eyes. "Mr. Springer, I'm sorry—and I didn't think I would ever say I'm sorry to the IRS for anything, but here I am doing it now. Thank you all," he muttered again as he stuffed the envelope in his suit. "Wait, Larry, do I have someplace to sleep tonight if I drive back to Glencoe?"

"Yes. The company lease for your apartment is good for another seven weeks. Drive carefully going back, okay? Can you handle that?"

"Yeah, I can. Hope to see you sometime." Mike shook hands with all three men, walked out of the room, and got on the elevator. Half an hour earlier, in this very same elevator car, he had been dreaming about nabbing a senior VP job and a fat raise. That sure as hell didn't pan out. The elevator brought him down to the lobby. He sat down on a bench, took a deep breath, then slowly tore open the envelope McDonald had given him. Inside was his final Frigidaire/GM check—all his company retirement account money and other accrued benefits added together, then rounded up, way up to the figure of exactly $750,000—GM's way of somewhat turning a blind eye and thanking him for his years of genius and dedication.

CHAPTER TEN

Speeding west across Michigan at ninety miles per hour, Mike realized a strange feeling was overtaking him. What was this new thing? Perhaps absolute, newfound fricking freedom? He had thought the next ten or fifteen years of his life had already been mapped out, but now look. Funny how his mind had put certain things in boxes, like the embezzling. He had compartmentalized it, shut it away, didn't think about it. That money, that gross error in judgment—it was as if someone else, some other Mike Burgess had done it. And maybe it was some other Mike Burgess. That version got caught by the IRS, forced out of his job—the Mike driving the shiny Olds 88 heading back toward Chicago was a free man—with a brand new canvas for the future and a helluva lot of dollars' worth of fresh paint to play with.

By early evening he was about to say good-bye to Michigan and roll back through Indiana—good ol' Indiana. Maybe it wasn't such a bad place. A flood of feelings—happiness, melancholy, confusion, nostalgia—swept over Mike. What would he do now? What was out there for him?

A few minutes before the Chesterton exit he noticed a big billboard: "Johnston Brothers Dy-no-MITE Fireworks Superstore, Buy One, Get Five Free!" *Well there's a deal if I ever saw one,* he thought. His lucky day just kept on getting better and better. Mike turned off 94 and rolled up to the front of the big sheet-metal building. It was almost six p.m., the posted closing time. Mike hopped out of the car and walked in. There was only one person there, the owner it looked like, lazily tallying up a poor day's worth of sales. He was an older fellow, sporting a completely illogical comb-over and some snazzy red suspenders, which almost distracted your eyes from the greasy food stains on his shirt. *He might afford a nice toupee and some new clothes if he didn't give so many fireworks away.* It had always amused Mike how these Indiana fireworks joints always tried to one-up each other with their hokey old bait-and-switch advertising tactics.

"You still open?"

"Sure, fella. Slow day, maybe you can make it better. Name's Tucker J. Johnston. I'm the owner."

"Pleased to meet you. I'll just wander. You got a bag I can put stuff in?"

"There's carts over there. Fill it on up. I'll stay open for as long as you like. Got some great new aerial cakes in aisle three."

"Thanks." Mike grabbed a cart and started down aisle one in no hurry. Heck, no place to go but home and no work for tomorrow. He picked a few things out from aisle one and two, then got to three. There they were, the item the owner had suggested, with a special banner proclaiming their awesomeness:

NEW! Junk Dawg Thumpers $19.95
10 shot 500 gram aerial cake
Double breaks of glittering mines
Strobe willows/timed mines w/3-shot finale

Well, look at that! Mike had no idea what any of that meant but it sounded pretty spectacular. *I better get at least two of those. And these and these over here. Heck, fill up the cart, make the old man at the register happy.*

"Well, look at you, sir! You got yourself a full cart, don't ya? You just made my day, big fella. Just watch your fingers with all those. Take a lookey here," Johnston said, holding up his right hand, which was missing two fingers. "So you got a celebration comin' up?"

"Oh yeah, I just got fired. Time to celebrate."

"Oh, I'm sorry, that's a shame. Wait, you're celebratin' you got laid off?"

"More like celebrating the money they gave me to get out. Seven hundred fifty grand."

"Cash or check?"

"It's a check. You wanna see it?"

"No, sir, I meant cash or check for the fireworks? We don't take no plastic here, that's not real money."

"Oh sorry, I thought you were asking about my big payday."

"Well actually, it would be interesting to see a check like that. How much did you say it was for?"

"Seven hundred fifty thousand real US dollars. Here, take a look." Mike pulled out his wallet and showed the certified bank draft to the old codger.

"GM, huh? You build cars of the future for them or somethin'? Flying cars, mebbe?"

"Nope, just kept all the GM cars nice and cool in the summer and toasty in the winter. I'm Mike Burgess, but I got stuck with a nickname back a few years, Cold Smokey," Mike said with a smile, reaching out to shake the old man's hand. "Kind of a mix of what I do, the cold part—you know, air-conditioning, and then a mix of my name, Mike Burgess, with that White Sox pinch hitter from a few years ago, Smokey Burgess. Remember him? Put it all together and it's Mike 'Cold Smokey' Burgess. A guy on the line at the GM plant in Flint made it up. I thought it was dumb at first, but now I kinda like it."

"I ain't never had a nickname myself. Always wished I could have one," the owner sighed.

"Well, you know since you showed me your hand," Mike said, "there was a baseball player called Mordecai 'Three Finger' Brown. Born here in Indiana, I think maybe Nyesville, or maybe it was Terre Haute. He pitched for the Cubs. When he was a kid his hand was injured in a farming accident, but he still learned how to pitch. I'm a baseball nut, in case you hadn't figured that out yet. So there's a nickname for you, I suppose."

"Well, I can't take another Indiana fella's nickname. That don't seem right, Mr. Cold Smokey. Gotta be a fresh one picked out for me, don't ya think?"

"Sure. Well wait, let me think. Hey, I got an idea, ready to hear it?" The old man shook his head up and down. "What sound does your best firework make? Make that sound right now."

"It goes *ka—booooom!*"

"There you go! Nice to meet you, Kaboom Johnston!"

"Hey, I like that. Thanks, Mr. Smokey. You got a new friend. Come back anytime." He gave Mike a big fat smile, exposing gaps here and there where teeth had jumped ship.

"So, I buy one and get five free, right? This won't be too expensive, then, huh?"

"Oh, well them are over there, in that old blue garbage can in the corner. Now you pick one of them deluxe sparkler packs there, and you sure do get five more, no charge. We been running that special for twenty-five years, I bet," Kaboom bragged.

"Ah, that's great. Yeah, well then add that to my order. Thanks!" Mike grinned, happy to experience the scam in all its hokey glory. The old man rang Mike up, absentmindedly whistling the first eight bars of "*On the Banks of the Wabash*" over and over. "Well, sir, nice to do business with you today," said Mike, shaking Kaboom's hand.

"The pleasure was all mine, sir. G'night. Drive safe now, big fella."

* * *

Mike loaded the fireworks into his trunk and got back onto 94. A beautiful peach-colored sunset was lingering in the sky, taking its sweet time painting some scattered clouds. Mike drove about ten miles and then saw some open space along the road, a field with no crops. He stopped the car and got out, took the boxes of fireworks out of the trunk and walked them over into the field. He went back to the car and got a couple boxes of matches he had grabbed when he stopped for a late lunch at La Cantina restaurant in Paw Paw. Next he rigged up a few of the smaller fireworks and lit them—*pow, pow, pow* they went, lighting up the sky with green, red, and silver streaks. He shot off a few more, building to the larger purchases he had made. A few passing cars slowed down to watch the display, a couple of them honking in appreciation. Mike now bundled a few together and set them off. At one point, one of the fireworks had fallen loose just as it exploded and whizzed past Mike, just missing his left ear. The burnt black powder hung in the air, stinging his nose. As night crept closer the sunset's colors intensified to a dark orange, and the fireworks showcase grew even more exhilarating. One rocket swept high in the air, exploded into an anemone shape, made little whistling sounds, and then the cinders fell toward the ground, glittery gold all the way down. *Good stuff*, Mike thought. *Now time for the finale.* Mike set up the big investment of the day, the two Junk Dawg Thumpers. He aimed them up high and toward the field, away from his car and the road, not knowing how wild these bad boys might be. He paused for a moment, then said out loud, "Good-bye Frigidaire, good-bye GM. It was fun while it lasted. But now I'm moving on. Wish me luck!" He lit the bundled fuses and stepped back. The fuses hissed and then *whoosh*, the Thumpers blasted into the sky, higher and higher. Multiple explosions and a wild array of colors and patterns took over the sky. Then more glittering lights and pinwheels spun out into the darkening sky, and finally the payoff, the advertised three-shot volley (times two)—*kaboom, kaboom, kaboom, kaboom, kaboom, kaboooommmm*. Mike felt the heavy concussion of the volleys slamming into his chest and then heard the waves of sound bounce off the barns of surrounding farms—a series of smaller kabooms echoed on for at least ten more seconds. Thoroughly satisfied, Mike stood and watched the waning sunset for a few minutes. *It's so beautiful, this show the sun puts on for us every night and then the sunrise in the morning—every morning. Why don't we watch these more, make the time to see them?* He tried his hardest to etch this moment into his mind forever. Not just the beauty of this big evening sky across the flatness of an Indiana field, but also the feeling of new freedom, the exhilarating opportunity to reinvent himself however he chose.

CHAPTER ELEVEN

May, 2013

"Kate, do you have a few minutes? I'd like to introduce you to a few people this morning," Mike said over the intercom.

"Sure, give me a sec. I'll come on over." Kate closed her laptop, stood up, and strolled over to the mirror in her office. *Yeah, looking good in this fancy monogrammed lab coat. Wonder how you get a job as a healthcare clothing model. Yeah, I'm totes the girl for that. Unless I spill food on it, then I'm a dead ringer for Tina Fey in 30 Rock. And who doesn't want Liz Lemon to be head of research for their frozen zillionaire Grandpa?*

"Okay, I'm here," Kate announced as she arrived at Mike's office.

"Good. We're going to stroll down to the end of the C wing. That's where the more modern pods are, where the patients who have the best chance of revival are in storage. There's one more room down there that you haven't entered yet, I believe."

"Yes, I've noticed it. Sometimes there are people hanging around there, so I haven't gotten too close. Some kind of special room? Or are those security people? Though they sure don't look like security."

"I'll explain when we get there. It will be an unusual experience for you. I think I can say that with confidence." They headed to where the C wing spun off the hub onto its own path and walked down the long passageway where the more modern pods aligned along the walls to their left and right.

"Here it is. Notice the name on the brass plaque?" Mike asked.

"'The A.C. Nielsen Apartment'—huh? An apartment? Like somebody lives in there all the way down this wing? Isn't A.C. Nielsen that TV ratings company from back in the day?"

"Yes. And actually, the company still exists right here in northern Illinois. It's based in Schaumburg, near Woodfield Mall and the Legoland. Mr. Nielsen is in the apartment. Let's go ahead and knock." Mike rapped on the door three times, paused, then knocked two more times. The door swung open a few seconds later.

"Hello, Mr. Burgess. How you doin' today?" a friendly African-American gentleman of about forty or so inquired. He had closely cropped gray hair and was dressed quite nattily, sporting a bright green bow tie and brown tailored suit, with a green vest that matched the tie. He looked like a young version of Morgan Freeman.

"Very well, DePaun. Doing very well," Mike answered. "And you? I see we have a crowd in here today."

"That we do. We're about to watch *Leave It to Beaver*. Bennie thinks he's got the dialog down for this whole episode, but Miles the naysayer, of course, says otherwise. There's fifty dollars riding on whether Bennie can nail it. So come in, Mr. Burgess. Come on in, miss."

"Thank you, DePaun," Mike said. "Fellas, you're going to have to turn the TV down. I brought someone important in to meet you. DePaun, you know you don't have to hang here all the time. When your shift is over you can go home, or go feed the birds in the park, or whatever else you want to do. Anyway, I have someone here I want you to meet. DePaun, this is Miss Katherine Pearson, our new head of research. She's a smart one—graduated from Northwestern *summa cum laude*. Bachelor's and master's degrees in microbiology."

"Glad to make your acquaintance, Miss Pearson," DePaun said as he reached out to shake Kate's hand.

"A pleasure, I am sure," Kate responded.

"And here, coming your way is Bennie," Mike said. "Never missed a day of work—not a single day."

Bennie smiled and shook Kate's hand. He looked to be Filipino. A big man with an even bigger smile. She guessed he was about six feet tall and three hundred pounds or so.

"And this," Mike added, "is Miles. He's our resident brainiac. Knows more about anything and everything than you would ever care or dare to stuff into your own brain. Also quite the dresser, eh, Miles?" Miles looked to be in his early to mid-thirties, Caucasian, dressed very slacker in a faded Hanson *MMMBop* T-shirt, severely wrinkled khaki shorts, and dirty orange Crocs. Greasy hair and an underachieving goatee completed the look. He was the sartorial opposite of DePaun. *Please, Lord,* Kate thought, *let the T-shirt be a satirical comment on the state of the pop music business.*

Miles stepped forward and shook Kate's hand. "Glad to meet you, Miss Pearson," he said, barely making eye contact.

"Oh, please, you can call me Kate. Katherine or Miss Pearson I can do without."

"Katherine, huh?" Miles said. "But you should call yourself Kat, not Kate. Kat like in *The Hunger Games*, you know. Kat—Katniss Everdeen.

That would be epically cool."

"Hmm, well I don't know about that. Why would I want to be like some pop figure in a big-budget movie or in a book read by sixteen-year-olds? I'd rather just be myself," Kate said. Mike nodded in approval.

"Well, suit yourself," Miles said with disdain. "You've got a chance at an awesome nickname and you don't take it? Weird."

Kate tried to hide a smirk. "And your name? Miles? Got a last name to go with it?"

"He won't tell us his last name. Must be pretty bad. Maybe it's Miles Mussolini," Benny teased.

"My full name is none of your business!"

"Yeah, tell us your whole name, man. We've been waiting," DePaun said, "come on."

"I'll bet payroll knows his full name," Kate ventured, grinning slyly.

"Nope, Kate," answered Mike Burgess. "He's a volunteer—working for free here."

"Well, now I am even more impressed with Miles, the man with, apparently, just one name—like Bono or Madonna, huh?" Kate let a hint of sarcasm slip out just to see if anyone might notice.

Miles cracked his knuckles over and over, then said, "You know, I have a better idea for you if you don't want to be Kat from *The Hunger Games*. How about Kat, the main character from *Gravity Rush*? You play it?"

"Um, no." Kate wondered if this Miles fellow expected her to revert back to life in high school, or, shudder, junior high. Didn't he realize that most girls-slash-women just weren't into video games?

"Seriously? It's an awesome video game for PS3. You get to control gravity, battle the Nevi monsters, and you also have a rockin' black cat, too. If I were a girl I would definitely dig having the name Kat."

"I'm just happy she doesn't have red eyes like Kat in *Gravity Rush*," Bennie exclaimed. "Those red eyes are really creepy, you know."

"Yeah, whatever," Miles looked away, shuffling his feet.

"Well, gentlemen, I'm quite happy to make your acquaintance, but I think I will pass on the name Kat for now. I'm happy with Kate or Katherine. And besides, I have no time for movies and video games. There's this thing called work I do." Once again, Mike nodded his approval and grinned. Kate was taking down the nerds in the room, especially Miles.

"What about you, DePaun?" Kate asked, sensing he, at least, wasn't a tool like Miles. "What's your nickname?"

"I don't have a nickname, but I guess sometimes it could be 'Hey you,'" he said with a laugh.

"So, Kate," Mike said, "now that you've met this motley crew, what do you think of this 'apartment' as we call it? Look around for yourself."

Kate wandered about while the men turned their attention back to the TV. First, she noticed some photos on the wall—a shot of a middle-aged man with wire-rimmed glasses wearing a classic black suit shaking hands with John F. Kennedy while a beautiful blonde woman looked on. There were beautifully framed photos of the man with other presidents as well: Eisenhower, Richard Nixon, Gerald Ford, and several more photos of the same man posing with old-school entertainment people—Bob Hope, Dean Martin, Lucille Ball, Red Skelton, Dan Rowan and Dick Martin of *Laugh-In* fame, and a young Alan Alda in his *M*A*S*H** getup. It looked like this fellow knew everyone. Kate circled back to the old Magnavox console TV the men were watching. Who knew how old that thing was, but the picture was great. *Somebody must have access to a big-ass supply of vacuum tubes*, she thought. Miles, Bennie, and DePaun seemed obsessed with old sitcom reruns. They had given up on their bet for the day since Mike's interruption to introduce Kate had spilled past the beginning of *Leave It to Beaver*. By now, Eddie Haskell had already invaded the Cleaver's kitchen and was fully engaged in small talk with Mrs. Cleaver, munching away all the cookies she had made, much to the Beaver's chagrin. The caffeinated laugh track urged viewers to chuckle or guffaw about every three seconds. Kate noticed that now and then Miles would feed the other two some trivia about the show. Obviously this guy was totally OCD. They were watching WFN Platinum, according to a little promo icon in the corner of the screen that Kate noticed. She had never heard of this so-called platinum version of good old WFN, the iconic, locally owned Chicago station. In the 90s they had followed the lead of Ted Turner's WTBS, shedding some of their conservative, local ways and becoming a superstation.

"What's WFN Platinum, DePaun?" Kate asked.

"It's all the great old vintage TV shows 24/7, mostly sitcoms. Platinum means no commercials, no news. Just show after show. You know, like *Three's Company, The Dick van Dyke Show, I Love Lucy, F Troop,* that kinda stuff. For dramas they got *The FBI, Mannix, Wild West, Cannon, Mission: Impossible, Bonanza*, that there Western with Barbara Stanwyck—I forget what it's called."

"*The Big Valley*," Bennie yelled out.

"Right, good show," said Miles. "It's basically the epic stuff from about 1965 through about 1985. It was designed to fit our purposes perfectly. And they air the original—none of the episodes are shortened or sped up like how a lot of stations today butcher a show to cram in tons of commercials."

"Fit your purposes? What's that mean?" said Kate.

"Excuse me, Kate, but have you not noticed there's a cryopod along the wall? Honestly, I thought you'd ask about that first," Mike asked, looking perplexed.

"Well, of course I noticed it. It's the 800-pound gorilla here. And let me deduce that the gorilla's name must be Mr. A.C. Nielsen. He's a favored client obviously, and that's him in all the photos and inside the pod as well, correct, Dr. Watson? And are these three babysitters or something?"

"See, I told you she was smart, DePaun!" Mike boasted. "You nailed it, Kate."

"But why?" Kate asked. "Why the TV and the babysitters and all the memorabilia? The photos and plaques, the old fake-walnut paneling on the walls, the Barcalounger like my grandparents used to have? Oh, wait, what's that on top of the TV?" Kate walked back to the TV and examined a small black box on top of the Magnavox.

"You like it?" Miles asked. "It's an original Nielsen Company black box from the 1950s. The machine that made the company famous… and richer than God. Look close and check it out. Pretty cool, huh?"

"I feel like I'm stuck in maybe 1975 or 1980," Kate ventured. "Oh wait, I get it, this is some kind of weird shrine to Nielsen. Right? Is that the deal?"

"Yes, that's pretty much it," Mike answered.

"But why? He's there in that cryopod, right? He doesn't know you've got all this vintage furniture and cheap paneling and TV stuff going on. And why does he need babysitters? Hello, he's not exactly conscious. Why the heck are you doing this?" Kate pleaded.

"It's all about Gloria Dunham, the part-owner of ExitStrategy, who you met when we hired you," Mike explained. "She's the one who finances this apartment, and honestly, she bankrolls a lot of our recent research that you're in charge of now. In case you didn't figure it out, she was vetting you just as much as Franklin and I were. Anyway, she was a dear friend of Mr. Nielsen and credited, whether it was true or not, his company with the success of her acting career. She loved him dearly. And, just so you know, it was a purely platonic relationship. There were times in her life when Gloria was a very troubled person, and often her behavior frustrated people to the point that they would write her off, whether it was professionally or personally. Being able to talk to Nielsen in person or over the phone helped her out, kept her closer to being psychologically whole. He was a bit of a father figure to her, even though he was only a few years older. I think you could venture a guess that she had father issues—maybe she was abused as a child. I don't think anyone really knows but her. But if that was true it would explain a lot of her erratic behavior over the years."

"'Erratic'? Yeah, that and a few other choice adjectives," Miles interjected, elbowing Bennie in the ribs.

"Anyway, Kate," Mike continued, "Gloria's career kind of sputtered about 1960. Radio shows were disappearing and she was getting older. Like a lot of film actresses of her generation, she did some TV series and guest spots on various TV shows. Older audiences still loved her, but she wasn't gaining any young, new fans. About 1963 she got married to Frank McMurtry, her costar on what you could call a family values sitcom, *The Front Porch Swing*. You know him?"

"Maybe. I think I've seen him in a few movies, maybe *The Caine Mutiny?*"

"Yeah, he was in that, you're right," Mike agreed. "He went from being a Hollywood film noir bad guy to playing boilerplate likable dad parts on TV—kind of an odd transformation, but he made it work. He constantly pinched his pennies and invested his income in California properties. Plots of land scattered all over around LA and Orange County, large tracts of land in San Diego North County, also some beautiful properties up in Santa Barbara. He was worth three or four hundred million when he passed away. When Gloria went totally schizophrenic and he couldn't handle any of it, McMurtry divorced her pronto. He just threw oodles of money at her to hasten the divorce. So now we're around 1967, she's in her forties and has gobs of money. More money than you will make in your entire lifetime."

Kate shook her head. "Wow. So, really, what's with this room?"

"It's simple," Mike explained as he straightened one of the photos on the wall. "Gloria was a partner with Franklin and me from the beginning. We have a lot of entertainment types here as patients and a few others who have small investments in the company. Gloria loved Mr. Nielsen so much that she paid the tab for him to be here. After he passed away she insisted that we create this apartment and make it like a comfy home, so that when he comes back he'll feel welcomed. He'll see all the photos, the memorabilia, the Magnavox or an RCA 1970s television, and so on. That's how it started. It wasn't until about five years ago that she got all obsessed about him waking up and nobody being here to greet him."

"Whoa, wait!" Kate said. "Nobody here to greet him?"

"She actually thinks he could wake up, unfreeze himself, open the cryopod from the inside, step out, and ask one of us for a Swanson Salisbury Steak TV dinner," Miles said. "We have explained a billion times that he can't revive himself from inside the pod, but she's convinced we're lying."

"Wow! Just wow!"

"She became so obsessed about this issue that she decided to foot the bill to hire caretakers here 24/7," Mike said. "Find some pleasant folks to welcome A.C. back to life. You said that the room makes you feel like everything here gives you the vibe of 1975 or 1980, right? That means we've been successful. Not only does she want caretakers to greet Mr. Nielsen, but she also wants the apartment to be a sanctuary or a cushion from the shock of waking up in 2013, like if it happened now, or 2050, or whenever. We would ease him psychologically from a time he knows, like the 1970s or 1980s, to the world of the actual year he comes back."

"But you and Dr. Saltieri already have that in your process," Kate ventured. "I liked when I read that in the company handbook. It shows you care about these people here. 'Psychological mentoring' I think Dr. Saltieri called it. Easing patients into the present, right? Doesn't Miss Dunham know about that?"

"She just wants things her way, as you can see. She has the money and Franklin and I don't really have a problem with it. It's all a bit amusing to Franklin and me in its audacity or idiocy, or whatever you want to call it!"

"And seriously, she really does think he will just wake himself up and crawl out of the pod," Miles interjected.

"Check out the TV, Kate," Mike continued. "At first there was simply a set in the room that Nielsen would notice when he 'woke up,' with the old Nielsen box on top. But when she decided that she absolutely had to have caretakers she wanted them all watching the TV 24/7 and ready for Mr. Nielsen to wake up, sit down, and join them watching Sonny and Cher or whatever. That's what these guys are doing here. And they're forbidden to watch anything but WFN Platinum. You'll find that there is nothing in the apartment that will tip off that it's the year 2013. Everything in here is vintage. The caretakers can't bring an iPod or a laptop or cell phone in here, per Gloria's rules."

Kate still couldn't believe her ears. This was crazy.

"Oh, there's more," said Miles, the only attendant interested in helping Kate understand the whole bizarre situation, since DePaun and Bennie were arguing about some trivia regarding *Petticoat Junction*, which had just started. "Ever hear of Howard Hughes?"

"Of course. Everyone knows who Howard Hughes was," Kate answered.

"Yeah, but how much do you yourself know about him?"

"Most of the stuff, I guess. Are we on Jeopardy or something?"

"Miles, settle an argument," DePaun yelled, "who was sleeping with Nat King Cole right before he died? Which sister from Petticoat Junction was it?"

"Easy. It was Billie Jo, the second Billie Jo, who was played by Gunilla Hutton. She was on *Hee Haw*, too."

"See, I told you so." DePaun punched Bennie's arm. "You owe me ten bucks."

"Damn, I thought it was Meredith Baxter," Bennie said. "Listen, I gotta pay you tomorrow. I got no money on me today." They both laughed and launched into the *Petticoat Junction* theme song, battling to see who could do the best steam locomotive engine imitation at the end.

"Guys, hold it down," Mike yelled. "We're trying to explain to Miss Pearson why the apartment is here."

"Ha, you gotta call her Miss Pearson, but she says we can call her Kate. Guess you don't rate so much, Mr. Burgess," DePaun said with glee as he walked over to the fridge to grab a Dr Pepper.

Miles rolled his eyes at his coworkers' shenanigans, then cleared his throat. "All right, so Howard Hughes decided to move to Las Vegas. He buys a hotel and lives in the penthouse, and by the way, this is before his schizophrenia and drug abuse kick in hard. So Hughes is becoming more and more reclusive up in his penthouse and gets pissed that there are no all-night TV stations in Las Vegas. All he wants to do is watch movies and TV shows day and night; he's got insomnia issues. So what does he do? He frigging buys a crap little Las Vegas TV station, KLAS-TV, in 1968 and then instructs them to go 24/7 playing mostly old movies that he loves, or rebroadcasts of his favorite TV shows like Ben Gazzara in *Run for Your Life*, or *Hawaiian Eye* with Robert Conrad."

"Okay, keep going. This is actually getting fascinating in an epically weird kind of way," Kate admitted.

"So, the station programmer proposes three or four days' worth of programming at a time to Hughes for his approval. But Hughes sometimes even calls the station up at like four a.m. and tells them he fell asleep and woke back up. 'Rewind the show back a half hour and start it back up so I can catch up,' he tells them. And they do. Why? 'Cause he's their boss. Crazy, right?'"

"And somehow this connects back to us how?" Kate asked, confused but also amazed at Miles' steel-trap mind for minutia.

"Here's how it connects. Money, Kate, money. Hughes had gobs of it and so does Gloria. So it's like Six Degrees of Kevin Bacon, man, except now it's Six Degrees of Gloria Dunham. Or whatever. Gloria did two pictures for Hughes when he owned RKO. The films both sucked, but who cares now? The point is that she knew Howard pretty well and they stayed in touch. After A.C. Nielsen, Howard Hughes was her second lifeline, not that it did her much good, since he was a hundred times crazier than her. Anyway, Gloria knew all the details about Howard and his Vegas TV station. When she decided to drop a ridiculous amount of money and sponsor Mr. Nielsen's little hotel stay here at ExitStrategy she was just borrowing from Howard's playbook. Wait—Mike, is it okay if she knows all this inside stuff?"

"Absolutely, Miles. You're on a roll, obviously. No reason to stop now!"

Miles cracked his knuckles loudly. Kate realized he did it all the time. She was right about his OCD tendencies. "Okay," he continued, now that he'd reduced his stress load, "so Gloria is messed up, not bizarro-world like Hughes but still pretty weird, narcissistic, a bit schizoid, that kind of stuff. Her whole history in Hollywood spells it out, as much as she tried to hide it. She treated her first husband like crap. I've read he was a nice guy, a great trumpet player, very talented

81

and handsome. They had a messy divorce. All along she was obsessed with Nielsen even though he was just a nice guy businessman. He never asked for any of this. Even with his company's success he never had a ton of money himself, he'd just roll his money back into the company's future. But she had the dough to support his cryo, bankroll the creation of this goofy apartment, and then later hire us to attend it 24/7 and… wait for it, as they say…"

"What, what!" Kate pleaded, totally sucked into the story.

"She went to WFN here in Chicago and tried to convince them, a la Howard Hughes, to sell their station to her, which of course, as a major corporation they would never do. But they did take oodles of her money and agreed to create WFN Platinum. Kate, think about it, in reality WFN Platinum exists for one viewer, a person who still hasn't even seen a single show. It wasn't meant for the regular *schlub* out there, flipping absentmindedly through crap station after crap station with his remote." Crack went the knuckles again. "It was created by crazy Gloria solely for A.C., so that when he wakes up he can stumble out of the pod, scratch his ass, see one of us in the room and say hi, watch *M*A*S*H** on whatever vintage Magnavox or RCA or whatever old set Brown's TV in LaGrange can supply us with and he'll be a happy camper in the epic Barcalounger. He'll ask us for a Hamm's beer and some Jay's Potato Chips and he'll think it's still like 1985 or so, and he won't freak out that it's really the twenty-first century. That's what Gloria created here. It's like a freakazoid episode of *The Twilight Zone*, huh? And, by the way, did you see the tennis court outside? Nobody here plays tennis. But Nielsen did, so that's why it's there. Insane, huh?"

"Yes, seemingly insane," Mike interjected. "But she's in total control of her senses even now in her nineties. Sure, she's stubborn, wily, conniving, evil, and a whole lot more. But be warned—she's still a consummate actress. She can pull off anything she wants in any situation. Franklin and I continue pleasing her, and of course continue accepting all her many dollars. We let her get her way, at least on the surface, even if we know we can circumvent her. We let her think she's in charge. Remember I told you about this, Kate? It's complicated but manageable, that's how Franklin and I look at it. And look at this— you can play tennis here now, how's that for a perk?"

"Ah yes, the tennis court. Now it makes sense that it's here." Kate laughed.

"Yup. So, Kate, that's the backstory on Gloria, A.C., WFN Platinum, DePaun, Bennie, and me—all the crazy shit," Miles bragged, running his fingers through his greasy hair, trying to fluff it up, but failing. "Things are pretty strange around here. Like Mike said, he and Franklin play this weird game with her. They actually enjoy it, I think. I guess they like the challenge of seeing how much money they can pry from her bony fingers even when she's plotting against them and the rest of the world. Am I right, Mike?"

"Well, that would be a 'no comment,' Miles, especially in front of a new employee. But unofficially, yes, you might be onto something there. Why do you have to be so damn smart all the time?"

"So if Gloria's The Brain, who's Pinky?" Kate asked.

Miles smiled at Kate's reference. "Probably that lawyer of hers. He's not buck-toothed, but he's weird. He's maybe thirty-five, but he acts like he's sixty. Of course, that's why she likes him. Anyway, sorry for the 'Kat' thing earlier. I'm not always that nerdy or difficult."

"Hmm, after hearing all this strange stuff are you still going to stick around and work here, Kate?" Mike asked, feigning concern.

"Yup, no doubt," Kate bubbled. "You might have thought I'm a regular girl, but... wait for it—I actually like weird!"

CHAPTER TWELVE

"Kate, hi, can I join you?" Kate looked up from her boring little chicken Caesar salad to see Chrissy holding a tray crammed full of food. Apparently she believed lunch should be a rip-roaring power meal. It was still only eleven thirty and no one else had arrived in the cafeteria yet.

"Sure," Kate said. "'Set a spell, take your shoes off. Have a heapin' helpin' of some hospitality.'"

"Huh?" Chrissy cocked her head. Kate noticed how gorgeous her deep brown eyes were. Even at roughly fifty Chrissy was still an amazingly attractive woman.

"Sorry, I'm still weirded out from my morning meeting in retro-TV land down in the C wing. My mind has been invaded by old sitcoms."

"Ha, oh that. A little odd, huh? So what do you think?"

"I don't know. The whole thing is bewildering. Especially all the demented stuff that Gloria Dunham is up to. I left there and started to think—what's the one thing that a businessman like A.C. Nielsen would be livid about in regard to this WFN Platinum station that Gloria concocted? The one thing he would be outraged by?"

"Hmm, I don't know. I haven't thought about it much." Chrissy didn't care to tax her mind for she was far more focused on the epic mac and cheese Chef James had created for her. She swirled the golden sauce with a flourish, encouraging it to thicken and weld itself to the pasta. Meanwhile, the tendrils of steam rising from her minestrone soup were making Kate realize her stomach might rebel and insist on more satisfaction than the puny salad in front of her could ever offer.

"Chrissy, if Mr. Nielsen came back and saw WFN Platinum *without any commercials* he'd go totally bonkers. His company's ratings and research determined not only the price of TV ads but also which shows survived and which went to the graveyard. The Nielsen ratings were pretty much the sole arbiter for years, right? For him to see TV with no commercials would tell him that his company had become a total failure. Instead of being consoled by seeing old TV shows on WFN Platinum, he would be bewildered by it all. Gloria is crazy, right?"

"Well, I suppose. Kate, Gloria Dunham and logic don't pal around too often. Anyway, why should you worry about any of that?"

"I worry about everything, Chrissy. I was born a worrier. Can't get over it. Anyway, enough about me and my day so far. We should get to know each other. What are you up to these days?"

"Well, I don't know. Norm and I are just holding down the fort. With Dr. Saltieri gone, we've been staring at the walls. We're waiting for you to give us something to do, frankly."

"I understand. Say, answer me this. Why do Saltieri's records swing so much from meticulous to shabby? I mean, I find files that are impeccably detailed and others that look like a fifth grader was writing them up."

"Saltieri was a genius. Record keeping was probably a bore to him. Hey, you want to try the soup? It's really good."

"Sure. Mm, that is delicious. The food in this cafeteria is going to spoil me rotten!"

"Hey, it's all healthy food," Chrissy countered. "That's what Mike wants Chef James to make for us. So, Kate, guess where Mike found James."

"I don't know. A cooking school or something? He's great, but really young, obviously. He can't have cooked that many places. You think he's dreamy, Chrissy? James I mean, not Mike."

Chrissy laughed. "Yes, he is a bit of eye candy but I'm too old for him. Mike found James from the backseat of a cab. James was driving and was taking just about the worst possible route to where Mike needed to go. At first Mike thought the kid was trying to run up the meter on him, so he finally started telling James how to get to the destination. Then James kind of lost it and kept saying, 'I'm sorry, I'm sorry' and admitted he didn't know his way around. He's broke and took the cab job out of desperation. His only family is down near Little Rock, Arkansas, and besides, they can't help since they're all poor as dirt."

"So then what happened?"

"Mike asks him what he's good at doing. He tells Mike he loves to cook and watched cooking shows on TV all the time when he lived in Arkansas. Mike finally gets to his destination, and as he gets out of the cab, he gives James his ExitStrategy business card. Tells him to come here the next Saturday—come and show what he can cook."

"Seriously? That is so cool. How long ago was this?"

"Like six months ago. Oh sorry, I slurped my soup while you were talking."

"Doesn't bother me," Kate replied. "So he shows up and cooks for Mike?"

"Mike and Franklin, and get this—Dieter Schantz is here, too, you know, the famous chef. He's a friend of Franklin's from way back. So Mike has some banged-up pots and pans here and Schantz stops at Treasure Island and grabs some groceries on his way over. Of course, the kid doesn't know who Schantz is and that this world-class chef is here—right here in this cafeteria. But James just goes and whips up this great dinner—oh wait, there's Norm. Come join us, Norm."

"Hi, Kate!" Norm said, sans clipboard for once.

"I was just telling her how Mike found James. What was the food he cooked up? You know, when Dieter Schantz brought the groceries."

"Um, let me think. Oh yeah, he made a salad with goat cheese and pomegranate seeds, a deep-dish cheese and pesto pizza totally from scratch, and a fresh blackberry cobbler. Not bad for a twentysomething with no formal training, huh?"

"Yeah," Chrissy added, still slurping the soup, "so Mike hired him part-time to cook lunch for us and at night he's over at Schantz's kitchen learning the art. See, this is what Mike does, he's a Finder."

"Meaning what?" Kate asked. "'A Finder'? What's that?"

"He finds struggling souls and helps them find their true path, you could say. There was a whole show about it on Oprah."

"Oh, here we go. Chrissy and her hero Oprah," Norm poked.

"Oh, shut up," countered Chrissy, sticking her tongue out at Norm. "It was a good show most of the time. Anyway, I don't think Mike ever watched an Oprah in his life, but this guest author on the show happened to describe what Mike does to a T. She was touring and publicizing her new book about all this. Kate, I'll bet you've noticed he can strike up a conversation with anybody."

"Yeah, he's got the gift of gab," Kate answered.

"That's right," Norm said, "and when we were both at GM he could talk corporate strategy with a top executive one minute and then go out in the factory and talk transmissions with any guy on the line. Heckfire, he's so garrulous it's crazy. Chrissy, what's that crazy theory of yours? Something about toes? Talking toes or something?"

"It's the talkative toe, Norm," Chrissy answered, grabbing a thick slice of seven-grain bread. "Jesus, I'm hungry!"

"You've got a tapeworm, Chrissy," Norm offered.

"Shut up, dork!"

"No, you have one," Norm insisted slyly. "I'm convinced of it. I think you should give it a name. Then the two of you could politely discuss and negotiate your meal plans."

"Wait, you two. Back up a sec. A 'talkative toe'?" Kate was getting more interested in the conversation but also noticed her stomach was now grumbling. *Feed me*, it kept saying.

"You're gonna think I'm crazy, but there are theories about people's toes." Chrissy shot Norm a dirty look to keep him quiet. "One of them is about that second toe. If it's longer than the big toe, it means you talk a lot. People like to listen to you, please you, do what you say. You've got the gift of gab, like you called it, Kate—you're the master of small talk, maybe the class clown in high school, in a good way. Or maybe you're more serious and you're the class president. You can easily woo the opposite sex. So let me tell you, Mike's got a really long, talkative toe. I saw it once when he was in the hospital."

"Okay, my day just keeps getting weirder and weirder." Kate smiled.

"Why? What was weird before I sat down here?" Norm grinned.

"She met the renegades down yonder at the Nielsen homestead," Chrissy offered, now launching into a supposedly low-cal white chocolate brownie.

"Mm, can I have a tiny bite of that?" Kate asked.

"Sure, honey, here you go!"

"So what was on TV this morning?" Norm asked.

"*Leave It to Beaver, Petticoat Junction,* then *Perry Mason* I think," Kate said. "They were making bets on whether Bennie could recite all of today's *Leave It to Beaver* dialog. I guess I screwed that up by showing up with Mike."

"Oh yeah, they do that." Norm nodded. "Miles has over a hundred TV shows totally memorized. Sitcoms and even full one-hour dramas. The others have some, too, but he's the one who can parrot back tons of entire shows. That young man is amazing."

"I thought he was rude, actually," Kate replied. "Well, at least he was rude to me. You know, it sounds like they're a dumbed-down version of *Fahrenheit 451*—you know, the Ray Bradbury novel."

"Oh, yeah!" Chrissy said, her eyes brightening. "Where books are banned and there's a whole underground of people who've each memorized an entire great novel to keep it alive, right?"

"Kate, you can't always look down on people like Miles and the others," Norm asserted. "Maybe they're just memorizing moronic TV shows, but they're still using their minds. And besides, look where they each came from. Hang on, I'm going to finally go get some food—I'm really hungry now. Kate, can I grab you something?"

"Yes, please. The minestrone—a big bowl! And it's okay for you to call me out if you think I'm ever being snooty. Most people view me as a rich little North Shore girl, and maybe sometimes I'm guilty as charged."

"I get it. And I'll go get the food," Norm said.

"So, Chrissy, what does he mean, 'look where they each came from'?"

"Mike again. The Finder and the Fixer of people. I can see his aura—it's deep purple—quite beautiful. Anyway, the name of the book the lady was talking about was *Finders, Fixers, and Rocks*. All three of those guys Mike found on the streets. Bennie was morbidly obese and had suffered a stroke, lost his job as a school bus driver because of it. His insurance didn't cover everything, so he went broke and wound up on the street. Mike met him living in some haphazard assembly of cardboard boxes down near DePaul University. They started talking and Mike offered to buy him food at the Burger King nearby. Bennie said no, he couldn't eat that kind of food, he was scared of having another stroke. So Mike walked with him somewhere else and bought him a salad. Next time he saw Bennie he did the same thing, but then he asked him all sorts of questions about whether he was an alcoholic or used drugs. When Bennie swore he had nothing like that going on, Mike hired him to come here and do maintenance. When Gloria came up with her loony round-the-clock attendant scheme, Bennie was promoted to that instantly. And oh yeah, he's lost over a hundred pounds. You should have seen how big he used to be."

"So Mike's a guardian angel, according to that book?"

"Well, maybe," Norm said, arriving back with the vittles, "but he's not perfect."

"Yeah, okay, of course. What about DePaun?" Kate asked.

"DePaun has early-onset Parkinson's disease," Norm explained. "Mild enough you don't always see the symptoms. Mike struck up a conversation with him when he was living on the street selling *Street Savvy* papers near the Art Institute. You know, Street Savvy, the homeless people's newspaper? Mike brought him up here and put him to work in the A.C. Nielsen apartment, too. Our company insurance and the docs have his Parkinson's under control now. You can hardly tell he's got it."

"Wow! And Miles?" Kate asked.

"Nobody knows the whole story," Norm explained between bites of James's low-cal Reuben sandwich. "He and Mike don't talk about it. Maybe they will at some point. Obviously something happened for Mike to want to bring him in here, and Miles is as smart as anyone under this roof. That kid's IQ has to be one fifty or higher. He won fifty grand a few months ago at a national tournament playing that card game Yu-Gi-Oh. But there's something going on there—some kind of hurt, some kind of damage. I think I've figured that out. He's got the potential to do far more than just sit in that room, but right now he's not ready. I think Mike's giving him time to sort it out. If Miles acts like an ass to you, just keep in mind that it's a defense mechanism. Give him some space and grant him a little basic respect, and I bet he won't always be obnoxious when he sees you coming his way."

"This is just a lot to process. Between all the personalities and all the odd files from Dr. Saltieri and not knowing exactly what Mike wants from me, I'm kind of in free fall. Maybe this isn't the job for me," Kate said, feeling a bit numb.

"Oh no, Kate, we need you," Chrissy insisted. "Mike is a Finder and a Fixer. But you're the Rock. Like in the book—that's you, I can sense it. You anchor the whole thing, everything around you, everywhere you go. Didn't you say you were the captain of the tennis team in high school, or was it college?"

"Both actually, but so what? That's just a sports thing I did growing up. How important is that now that I'm an adult?"

"It was important then, and even now it proves you are a natural-born leader. A true leader. That's what Mike and Franklin see in you. It doesn't matter that you're young; in fact, maybe that makes it even better."

"So how about you, Chrissy. How did Mike find you?" Kate felt a little better about herself. Chrissy was so supportive, so friendly.

"Well, it was over the top, I can tell you that." Chrissy winked at Norm. "I was in the restaurant where Mike had his heart attack. Did you know he had a massive heart attack?"

"No, I didn't. Really?"

"Well, he did, a while back—quite a while. Like I said, I was there. I was on a second date with Enzo Saltieri. Seems like a million years ago."

"Dr. Saltieri? *Our* Dr. Salieri?" Kate asked, surprised.

"Yes, but the dating didn't last long. We realized we would be better off as friends. I was a lot younger than he. I was working as a veterinary assistant and didn't like my job much—it just wasn't challenging enough. Plus my boss was hitting on me. What a prick. Anyway, Enzo and I were nibbling on an appetizer one evening and just talking and I was thinking this guy is so nice, I wonder where this is headed and all that. Oh my God, I was a silly young thing, can you ima—"

"You're getting off the story, Chrissy!" Norm interrupted.

"Oh yeah, right. Sorry, Kate. Anyway, Enzo and I were talking, and for a while I had noticed this big brawny man at the bar pounding down shot after shot, and then he goes over to the payphone in the corner and he's talking to someone for a while, the receiver in one hand and a drink in the other. I remember pointing him out to Enzo and telling him, 'Hey, that man doesn't look like such a happy camper.' Well, he looked terrible, in fact. Suddenly the guy, which was Mike, got the strangest look on his face, like total panic. His face turned the weirdest color, he dropped the phone, staggered for a bit, and then went straight down, straight down like *bam*! Everyone in the whole restaurant jumped. He had landed square on his face and there was blood everywhere. People were screaming at the sight of that big man lying unconscious with a broken nose and gashes all over his forehead. Enzo and I ran over, pushing our way through people to get to him. Mike was in full cardiac arrest so Enzo and I dove in and did CPR. It took forever to get a pulse back and for the damn ambulance to arrive. And that, Kate Pearson, was the very day Mike had lost his job at GM."

"Wow, that is amazing. He would have died if you two hadn't been there. Sounds like you and Enzo saved his life." Kate shook her head as she felt tingles run up and down her spine.

"Well, yes, we did. It didn't hurt that I had just taken CPR at the community college. Enzo needed my help to get that big man's heart and lungs going again. Anyway, Mike had been driving all that day, from here to General Motors in Detroit, where they canned him, then back here again. He wound up at that bar, downing shot after shot of Maker's Mark. He says now that it was a great day, all the freedom and the future opening up, but I guess his heart disagreed with that assessment. Mike's world imploded on him that day, but think about it, Kate—without that heart attack none of us would be together here today. ExitStrategy was born out of Mike meeting Enzo that day and then them getting to know each other and building their crazy cryo ideas together. I came along for the ride and then Mike stole Norm away from GM, and it was just us four for a while. Some people would say that Mike was lucky that Enzo and I happened to be there. But that wasn't just dumb luck, no ma'am. Somebody or something put all three of us together in that building that day, that hour. And pardon my new-agey Oprah-speak, but I believe that some great power—God or Allah or the positive energy of the universe, whatever name you want to use—was at work that day. And no matter what name you choose, that's the ultimate, the original True Finder and the True Fixer of all our souls."

CHAPTER THIRTEEN

"Khail, honey, you know we have a production meeting in half an hour. Stop working out and get yourself ready," said Dimi Konstantos, star of the number one reality show on TV, *Dimi & Khail: U Wish It Wuz U*. Dimi's ascent to stardom began when she appeared as a dancer on some hit music videos in 2005. But her dance moves weren't what caught the imagination of viewers—what fascinated them were her mammoth breasts, weighing in at size 34DDDD. And these weren't implants—they were the real deal. By 2007, she was a YouTube sensation after a series of nipslips, which were certainly not accidental. By 2009, the reality show launched and went straight to number one. A year later Dimi's line of lascivious lingerie, Saturday Night Sexsations, exploded across the malls of America.

"Sweetie, I gotta stay in shape," Khail grunted, about to hit sit-up number two hundred. "You think The Ebony Adonis can take days off? You know what I gotta do to stay on top? Plus I like to be the entrepreneur. All the stuff I invent, the ideas and shit. I got more goin' on now than just our show."

"Put the show first, Khail. You can stay on top by being a bigger part of it," Dimi insisted. "You've been away modeling too much. We're going to be at show one hundred soon—we need something great for that and you haven't had a single idea for that show, have you? On top of that, now we have all those submissions from the fans who want to be our next hit series. Do you even know where we're at on that?"

"Not too much. Chris told me a little. So okay, I'll be at the meeting. Where's it at?"

"Jak's office. Be a man now and show those people you have real ideas for TV—some innovation. You can't just be a pretty black man parading your abs around. Remember when you told me I should be more than just my titties? When you broke up with me because you said I wasn't respecting myself? Don't forget, we got back together because I saw you were right. I listened to you then. So now, listen to me, Khail. You can be more than a stupid fantasy for all those suburban white women out there, getting their perfect little JC Penney white cotton panties all damp, starin' forever at you in a shiny magazine. Besides, on our show being pretty is supposed to be my thing. I'm supposed to be the pretty one—not you. You don't wear the leopard thongs. I do. You're the man. So act like one."

"Hell, Dim, you don't got to go shootin' me down so. I got a big launch coming up. There's crazy money goin' on in the fashion world—you just don't understand. I gotta be in Toronto, then Paris, then Hong Kong. I can't be the king of the runway unless I work out. Plus I'm more of an entrepreneur. This acting is buggy."

* * *

"All right, people," said Jak Hammer, executive producer of *Dimi & Khail*. "Who out there in Middle America wants half a million dollars' reward? And who wants that and more—their own reality show produced by us, the best in the business? I'll tell you who. Four thousand rabid fans of Dimi & Khail across the country."

"Ha, rabid is right!" Chris Bronsteyn muttered.

"Four thousand? Damn!" Khail said. He was wearing torn jeans and a two-thousand-dollar designer linen shirt.

"Jak," Dimi whined, "can we please turn off the cameras? My nails look terrible. I can't be darling Dimi 24/7, okay?"

"Yes, Demetria," Jak sighed. "Lennie, have your guys take the rest of the day off. We've got plenty of random office footage already." Dimi blew Jak an exaggerated kiss. She loved the cameras only as long as she looked fantastic at all times.

"All right, so let's get this meeting started," Jak said, rolling up his sleeves and popping open a Red Bull, which was now, sadly, his only vice since his doctor forced him to give up hard liquor. "Trish, start taking notes. For the record, today we've got Dimi, Khail, and Chris Bronsteyn, Khail's baby-faced adviser; plus Julio Campana, Shontae Bridgewater, and myself from the production staff. So, people, today all I want to cover are the e-mail and video submissions from the public for the competition. FYI, the social media on this thing has gone wild. Great idea, Julio, as usual. Chris, Khail insisted we put you on point for this. Where are we on this thing?"

"Yes, Jak, we're actually now at five thousand submissions. We've hired extra interns to weed through them. We should give them hazard pay, I think, considering the possibility that their eyes, ears, or brains, or all the above might start to bleed or even explode from what they've been subjected to. Some of the submissions have been mailed from prisons and mental institutions. And there have been plenty more from just plain folk that were scary as hell. By the way, spelling and grammar? Not a part of the equation."

"Okay, Chris, we get it, not everyone is Stanford material like you." Jak had already drained his first Red Bull and was popping another open. "This will just make you feel even more superior, right? So drop the 'I'm better than you' crap and give us the stories."

"Jesus, Jak. Take a chill pill along with your caffeine, will you?" Chris shot back, determined not to be cut down by Jak the sleaze. "Anyway, OMG FYI OMG, here are the promising ones so far—"

"Chris, you little fuck, OMG FYI OMG is my fucking catchphrase, understand? You know how many times TNZ has shown me saying that? Cut the crap!"

Chris rolled his eyes and sighed, making sure everyone noticed, then spoke. "First off, there's a show these down-home folks have tentatively named Bike Path Lovers. It's about this divorced man and divorced woman in Nebraska who met on a bike path. They're both about forty-five or so. He's got dental hygiene issues, but they're not too gross. They keep meeting secretly on the bike trail because the teenage kids on both sides totally disapprove of them being in love. The guy calls himself 'No-Tush' because he says riding his bike all the time has smashed down his ass. Weird. The woman's name is Kiki. She runs a delivery service and she's got tattoos everywhere. I mean— *everywhere*. We could really play with that. Jak, I know that's a thing for you, the tats in private areas, right? Kiki's a big girl, but she gets her exercise on her old pink Schwinn, streamers and all, that she had as a girl, pedaling every day to go hookup with No-Tush."

"You said *hookup*?" Jak said. "So they actually do it out in the woods? On the trail or whatever?"

"Jak's getting a woody from this one," Shontae whispered to Julio.

"Not sure, Jak," Chris responded. "They sent a bunch of photos of themselves on the trail, standing there by their bikes. Such sad faces. You can see there's a lot of passion and pain going on at the same time. The kids on both sides are totally obnoxious, all except one. She's the sweet nerdy twelve-year-old with braces who just wants her daddy to be happy. Apparently the others beat her down and make fun of her flat chest. We're talking big-time, up-and-coming young effing white-trash talent here. Pass this photo around, Trish. These are the kids."

"Ooh, damn. I don't wanna meet up with them out back the Walmart," Khail yelped. "Check out that white boy's mullet, whoo-ee!"

"There, see what I mean? And here are a few photos of No-Tush and Kiki. They found a photographer in Omaha to make it up in sepia-tone. Gotta love it."

"Aww," Shontae purred. "They're in love. You can see it. They're sweeties!"

"I like it. Yeah, this has real potential." Jak tousled his one-thousand-dollar frosted 'do.' "Kind of a Romeo and Juliet upside-down. Instead of Daddy Montague and Old Man Fucking Capulet, we got the kids hassling the adult star-crossed lovers."

"What's a *Schwinn*, Jack?" Dimi asked.

"It's an old bicycle, Dim. Used to be the top brand back in the day. But by today's standards they're kind of heavy and clunky."

"Like Kiki, then, huh?" Dimi asked. "Yeah, I dig it. She looks so sad. Too bad she's fat. Look at this other pic—her ass is like two big wobbly dumplings."

"Oh yeah, I forgot," Chris said. "She has a tattoo that's misspelled. Priceless. It says 'Love Fourever'—F-O-U-R-E-V-E-R.'"

"Well, that's an OMG—FYI," Julio said, winking over at Chris.

"Yup." Jak ignored Julio's swipe. "Okay, moving on. Chris, what's ne—"

Suddenly, Khail's 2 Live Crew ringtone blasted away at full volume. He grabbed his cell and began talking. Jak, used to this kind of interruption from Khail or Dimi, sat and waited, drumming his fingers on the table.

"Hey, all y'all, sorry, I gotta take this. It's the modeling gig in Toronto. I gotta get the details. I'll go in the hall and talk."

"Okay, Khail," Jak said. "Chris—go!"

"All right, number two—*Baby Got MBA*. Three couples in Palo Alto who are constantly one-upping each other to make sure their precious tiny toddler makes it into Harvard or Yale, MIT, my alma mater, et cetera. They're the ultimate helicopter parents and they're proud of it. Their little superbabies are learning Chinese in multiple dialects; they have chess tutors, math tutors, Suzuki violin classes, subliminal motivational tapes that loop all night while the kids are sleeping.

They've got them set to enter exclusive private kindergartens and even have the kids' names on internship waiting lists here and there. It's pretty messed up."

"Oh wait, aren't these *your parents*, Chris?" Jak asked with a smirk.

"Sounds interesting," Shontae said. "More upscale than the usual stuff. Tell us more."

"Here are photos." Chris ignored Jak. "Check out the diversity. A white couple, an Asian couple, a gay couple with an adopted black kid. And they all hate each other. I mean *really* hate each other. They've only banded together with the submission because each couple is desperate to get their kid on television. One of the gay guys used to be a porn star—hetero porn—totally not kidding you."

"Damn. Winner, I think," Julio declared. "But can't we get some Hispanic people on there, too? We got to represent my people more. Make sure there's a kid named Miguel who isn't just going to grow up to excel at yard maintenance—that's all I'm saying. We could cast that, you know."

"I'm sure Jak could do that if he wants," Shontae said.

"Like I said," Chris pointed out, "these people are desperate to get on TV. And they're weird. I can tell you they'll battle the directors on everything."

"Good, that's what we want, Chris. Don't you know what drives production of reality TV? Haven't you been paying attention to the behind the scenes?" Jak railed.

"Yeah, okay, Jak. They battle each other, they battle your directors, they kidnap each other's kids and do secret lobotomies on 'em. Great stuff, right?" Chris said. *Oh my God, did I just say all that shit? Lobotomize toddlers? Where did that come from?*

"Good!" Jak pulled another Red Bull from the mini-fridge. "Okay, what's next, Chris, my little man? We're on a roll, right?"

Khail came back in, still scrolling through messages on his cell. "Yo, people, I gotta be in Toronto for sure next Thursday. They finally figured out when I gotta be there to try on the threads for the new Xania Latrois trunk show. You won't see me for about five days, 'zat cool with all y'all?"

"Baby, I'll go with you. I haven't been to England in forever. We can go to Piccalilli Circus, honey," Dimi said, smiling all pretty for her man Khail.

"England, Dim? Whatchoo mean, England?"

"Well, Toronto's part of Canada. It's somewhere in England, right? They got the damn Queen on their money, I know that. I had some of those bills when I was in Vancouver opening one of our lingerie stores, Khail." Dimi looked over at Chris, batting her eyes. "Toronto's in Canada, right, Chris?"

"Well yes, definitely," Chris concurred with a smile.

"Dim, we got to get you a map to look at or a globe or sumpin'." Khail shook his head. "Canada ain't in England. It's north o' here. Like on the way to the North Pole."

"That's Alaska, honey," Dimi responded. "Alaska is what you're thinking of, sweetie. Anyway, now you're fighting with me and I don't appreciate you fighting with me when the cameras aren't rolling."

"Oh shee-it! Yeah—okay, I'll shut up now. No sense. Go ahead, Chris. What's next?"

"You'll like this one, Khail. Proposed title: *Little Men/Big Gas.*"

"You say little men, Chris? Is that what I think it is?" Khail flashed his perfect male-model smile.

"You got it, Khail. *Little people*—your favorite, I know."

"Khail, you're sick," Dimi protested. "What, were you a little people in a goddamn past life? You've got a strange obsession with them. Jak, when is this meeting over? I got things to do. I got to shop for dresses, I don't have time for this stuff. You decide—you and Chris and Julio. And Shontae. Just don't let Khail have his little people. He's done enough of that." Dimi reached into her handbag and pulled out a bottle of antacid, chugging down at least eight ounces. When she was done, there was a little pale-green antacid moustache on her face. Chris and Julio noticed it and grinned at each other.

"Dim, this is just a meeting to look through the entries so far," Jak explained, weary of being the peacekeeper when things boiled over between Dimi and Khail. "We're not deciding anything final today."

"Fine then, I'm so outta here." She gave Khail a withering look and sashayed out of the office.

Jak sighed. Now only one cray-cray person remained in the room. "All right, Chris, tell us about the little people," he said, wishing that a sultry, scantily clad young barmaid would bring him a perfectly prepared 7 and 7 right about now.

"Two brothers, about twenty-five. Yes, they're little people and they live in Reno. They've had chronic, very noisy flatulence issues for ten years. The doctors can't figure out why. They have both had a hard time holding a job, especially if it's someplace where quiet is important. They were dealers in a casino for a while. The casino was pretty noisy, which benefited them, but the fetid reek of some of their constant gassiness was too much for the tourists to handle. Result? Another lost job for the lads. I feel for these two. They're actually pretty sweet and quite funny fellows."

"We could have them trying to get a job in a library," Shontae suggested. "Set up hidden cameras to get all the people's reactions when they let a big one fly. Put that in the pilot."

"Another winner, Chris," Jak said. "You tell the interns they've done a great job. How many more?"

"One more," said Chris. "Now this one is out there. Ready? Okay, there is this bunch of inbred pig farmers. Somehow all the men are Jesus H. Christ damned butt-ugly but every wife and daughter is totally, bodaciously drop-dead freaking gorgeous."

"Wait," Julio said, "the pigs are inbred? Or the farmers?"

"Ha, good one, Hooley." Chris chuckled. "So these guys say that there are aliens trying to capture their teenage girls and impregnate them. An epically evil outer-space plan to create a whole new race of beautiful blonde three-legged mutants. They say they have footage of a spaceship, supposedly, and all sorts of crazy stuff."

"Weird. Where are they from?" Jak asked.

"Take a guess."

"Texas."

"Alabama."

"Um, Oklahoma?"

"Nope, you're all wrong," Chris said. "Khail, you've been quiet so far. You got a guess?"

"I don't gotta guess, Chris. I know these things. Gotta be Loosiana, where I grew up. Swamp gas state. Aliens use the swamp gas as a cover. Everyone down there knows that."

"Heck, you're right, Khail. Good for you."

"Of course I'm right. Why you so surprised? Why you think I'm stupid, Chris? I mean really, tell me why. Just 'cause I'm pretty? 'Cause I'm a male model? 'Cause I'm black and I'm proud, but I didn't go to college—some hotshot college like you? But that don't make me stupid. Besides, I got me a tutor now. Teachin' me words, man. New words. Here, I got a list o' power words I'm studying for my teacher." Khail pulled a ninety-nine-cent spiral notebook out of his five-thousand-dollar Bottega Vaneta alligator-leather handbag and flung it at Chris.

"Hmm, these are tough words," Chris said, in all earnestness. "Let's see: reciprocate, pummel, generosity, gorgonzola, emancipate, twerk. Wait, huh? *Twerk?* Khail, who is this tutor?"

"It's Theo, one of my bodyguards. He's done some junior college and he's damn smart. Listen, man, I can use those words already. Like listen. 'Hey, muthah, better *reciprocate* my *generosity* when I done gave you that *emancipated gorgonzola* or I might have to *pummel* your *twerkin'* ass.' See, Chris X-X—not bad for three weeks, huh?"

"That is very impressive, Khail," Jak said emphatically as he stood up, straightened his tie, and threw on his gold blazer. "Without a doubt, we're all going to have to stay a safe distance from you and your cheese. Meeting adjourned."

CHAPTER FOURTEEN

June 2013

"Deirdre, what do you make of these?"

"Those are all the five-by-eight cards Enzo made on each patient, Kate. Remember, I showed you how they were placed into a database?"

"Yes, I remember, you showed me that a couple weeks ago when we started plowing through this stuff in Enzo's office. But you're missing patients—many of the most recent ones, of all things. How can that be?"

"It's the best I could do, Kate. When Enzo was getting sicker and sicker he knew this was all a mess. That's why Mike glued me to Enzo virtually 24/7 to try to make sense of it. And besides, we have a sort of master file on each patient, they just don't all include the same forms. It's not like we don't know who everybody is, right?"

"Well, yes, I get it. But it's so helter-skelter. Do you think there might be some forms or files in storage somewhere?"

"I don't think so. Enzo would have told me, right?"

"I guess. Well, thanks for helping on all this." Kate stood up and stretched. She had been going through Enzo's messes for three hours straight before Deirdre had walked in. "Just you and me sorting all the piles of papers into zones has really helped—internal research papers over there, outside stuff on that back table, patient files here by me— you know."

"Yay for us, huh, Kate? So what do you think of the research?"

"Oh, I keep working on summarizing that every night at home until about two a.m. My social life came to an end when I took this job. My fun-loving roommate hates me now."

"I doubt that. But anyway, who said you had to work sixteen hour days?"

"That would be me, Deirdre. Give me a problem and I bulldog it to death."

"Bulldog? You sound more like a Gila monster. Bite hard and don't let go. Or maybe a Komodo dragon. Bite hard and spread nasty bacteria from H-E-L-L."

"I doubt you mean that as a compliment." Kate laughed. "Am I that obvious a Type-A?"

"Duh! Mind if I sit down?"

"Sure, please do. Anyway, it seems to me that reviving some of these people might be doable. If you piece together bits and pieces of various university research, it points in that direction. And keep in mind, none of them are trying to bring back frozen folks like we are. They're making impressive advances in cryogenic medical methods, not cryonics. We can easily restore function of frozen organs. You know, I look at various things in the field and I see a bunch of ideas which we might apply here. But as far as how to do it, step by step—I absolutely don't know. And Enzo didn't have it figured out. Some interesting ideas in his last days but also a lot of weird doodling. Whatever he may have said to Mike, I think he was just stringing him along or exaggerating things."

"He was really weird toward the end—the Alzheimer's. Hey, Kate, come over here—see this empty fish tank?"

"Yeah. So what?"

"He killed all the fish that were in there with the chemical in this bottle. I don't think he was coherent and aware how much stuff he was putting in there, like round the clock. The fish all died, but he said it was the solution."

"The solution? Not in the amounts you're talking about. Wait, the solution or a solution? It is, literally, a solution—malachite green, a phosphate in solution. It's a salt—three forms. I think it's used to kill parasites."

"Well, he was overdosing them. This stuff, too," said Deirdre.

"Methylene blue, which is a misnomer—it also turns things green. You said he was putting this in there more than once a day? Weird."

"Like once an hour. He would stare at the drops swirling in the water. Of course, the fish died, but he hardly noticed. Look at all the stains from this stuff on the tank stand. See what I mean? Oh yeah, even his fingers were stained from these chemicals."

"Jesus, that is odd," Kate muttered, absentmindedly running her fingers along the crusted, stained edge of the tank.

"He played with other chemicals, too. Put them in water inside clear glass bottles, then lined them up and stared at them. All different colors. They were kind of pretty, but eventually we poured out the water and tossed the bottles."

"Hmm, very strange, Deirdre."

"Well, yeah. So, back to the present. Everyone knows you're a biology genius. I bet you've got something."

"Nope. Pretty much nothing. Nothing that I can be proud of—that makes total sense. Just thaw these people out and zap their heart? An eighth grader could try that. It can't be that easy."

"I'm sorry to hear that. But keep plugging, right?"

"Mike has me on a deadline. Ninety days. Then submit a report."

"That sounds like him. Hey, I'm going to make some tea. Enzo was a big tea drinker. Look at all these. Obviously you're stressed. Want some?"

"Yuppers to that. Something herbal, okay? But no malachite green tea."

"Funny. Okay, I'll get it started. Anyway, you're blasting away at cryonics and cryogenics scientifically. You'll figure it out."

"I hope so. I need more time, or we're not going to succeed." Kate's frown disappeared. She began to chuckle.

"What's so funny, Kate?"

"I just remembered something that my gramma told me from when she was a little girl."

"What was that?"

"She was trying to learn how to tie her shoes and got more and more frustrated that she couldn't do it. Her dad—my great-grampa R.B., who was a character, by the way, told her, 'If at first you don't suck a seed, fry, fry a hen'!"

"What? Why did he say that? Some kind of nonsense verse?" Deirdre asked, confused.

"'If at first you don't suck a seed—fry, fry a hen.' She was mishearing the old phrase—you know, 'If at first you don't succeed—try, try again.' Get it?"

"Oh God, that's funny. How old was she at the time?"

"I don't know. Five, maybe? But she remembered that bit of childhood silliness the rest of her life. Pretty cool, huh? Anyway, sorry to sound like a broken record, Deirdre, but what do you think of the five-by-eight cards?"

"Well, they're pretty straightforward. Name and patient number, which of course is their cryopod number as well. Last address. Next of kin. We make sure to keep updating that for changes. Attending physician and their illness diagnosis. A few other things."

"Right. And what about this: 'VT'? What does that mean?" Kate shuffled through a dozen or so cards, hoping something would leap out and grab her attention. Meanwhile Deirdre laid teabags in their mugs and poured the hot water over them. "I don't know, Kate. But VT isn't just marked on the C wing cards. It goes back to halfway through the B wing. As far as what it means, I really don't know. It's like Enzo was notating only for himself. He probably never thought that someone else might be stuck looking at all these cards and his random abbreviations and such."

"Right, makes sense," Kate agreed. "Now look here at this little scribbled entry, 'E.S. signed.' The few cards I have from C wing all say that. So that's obviously Enzo's initials, but what did he sign? I don't get it. If you look in various C wing patient folders, there's nothing with his signature on it. It's baffling me."

"Hmm, yeah, you're right. I never noticed that—you have an eye for detail, don't you?"

"Those patients also don't have any death certificates on file, Deirdre. You think their doctors or attorneys held on to those?"

"Could be. Anything was possible in The World According to Enzo." Deirdre handed Kate the cup of lemon zinger tea, then stirred some honey into her own cup of Earl Grey. "You know, Kate, I was trying to help transcribe things, clean things up, get them from old paper records onto the computer as much as possible in the time I had. I wasn't trying to interpret anything. You know I'm a mathematician, right? That's why Mike put me on all this. I'm the data chick, the data go-fer. My real job is being Mike's number cruncher when he's running theories or producing prototypes of his inventions. So, just remember that I have no medical background. I'm happy to help, but you'd have to tell me specifically what you're looking for."

"So, Enzo never shared any inside info on any of this with you?"

"Nope, sorry."

"Okay, but work with me for a second, because trying to figure this out isn't actually medicine. You see some of these cards with little gold stars? Like these here. See 'em, Deirdre?"

"Sure. I thought that was weird and kind of funny."

"Why funny?"

"Oh, I remember when my piano teacher used to put a gold star on pages of my method book when I'd done a good job."

"Yeah, sounds about right. 'Yay, I got a star, Mommy!' Right?"

"Yeah, a little kid thing. Not very scientific. I get it, Kate. Enzo was weird—weird and super smart. He always had his own odd ways of doing things, that's for sure."

"And here, A.C. Nielsen has a gold star and a red star. He's the only one I can find with the red star."

"Well, he's obviously a special guy, huh? His own apartment and the coveted red star of cryo awesomeness."

"I've been staring at this all morning. It's driving me crazy."

"Yikes. Let it go. And drink your tea, girl. You haven't touched it yet. Relax and try a different angle, maybe? Have you thought of that?"

"Yes of course, but what? I'm stuck. And this weird paperwork—I hate being mystified by dumb details. My Type-A personality again, I guess. So why can't Enzo's ghost flutter in here and answer all my questions? Is that too much for a girl to ask?"

"He's dead and buried, Kate. Want to go visit the cemetery? Oh, I forgot something. Mike wants you to have this list of veterinarians we could hire to start the animal-based research you told him you want to tackle. Take the list and explore it. These are cutting-edge dudes who are available to us for some highly paid freelancing. They're all on LinkedIn, by the way. And let me know what else I can do. You'll figure this out. After all, if you get too frustrated you can always 'fry, fry a hen'!"

Kate shrugged. "Very funny. Yeah, I guess so."

CHAPTER FIFTEEN

"How's Jerry today, Miss Kate?"

Kate pulled herself out of her foggy reverie to see Clipboard Norm standing next to her with his usual lopsided grin and truly unfortunate Moe Howard haircut. "Huh, what?" she muttered.

"Touchdown Jerry. You two are having a chat? Is he bragging about that bootleg touchdown he scored in the Super Bowl a zillion years ago? He never shuts up about it."

Kate suddenly realized who Norm and his monotone delivery reminded her of—Droopy, the ultra-droll Warner Brothers cartoon dog. "Oh yes, patient C1. Jerry Hastings. I'm trying to memorize all the patient numbers."

"Seems like an odd way to memorize. Make him come to life, think of him as Touchdown Jerry, a man who made the Pro Bowl five times. A bit conceited, but he had a hearty handshake and a million-dollar smile. Forget the C1 label."

"The C1 label is science, Norm. We're supposed to be scientists."

"Ugh. Just numbers, Kate? Just data? Are you telling me you want to be one of those dreadful scientists without a sense of humanity? You don't want to be that person, do you?"

"Yeah, whatever. You can claim touché there, I guess," Kate answered tiredly. "Mike talked like you do about these folks when he first showed me the pods. But you guys knew these people. I never met a single one of them when they were alive. It's hard for me to visualize them as real people, especially in this sci-fi cryopod environment."

"Well, just learn their nicknames. Touchdown Jerry—not C1. That'll put you more on track. Hey, over here, C9, 'The Darling Diva,' Michaela Gretry. Famous opera singer and really sweet woman—so much talent and a whacked out sense of humor. Matter of fact, Mike asked all these people their nicknames, and if they didn't have one, he'd ask them to make one up that they liked before they entered cryo. Mike is a nickname guy—surprised he hasn't slapped one on you yet."

"I'm afraid of what some of you might call me—like Overachieving Girl, or Nose-to-the-Grindstone Girl, or something far worse. Oh well, that Mike is different, that's for sure."

"Yeah, Kate. He's out there sometimes. But I enjoy it."

"I'm frustrated, Norm. There's a lot of crazy in Mike. Also, a lot of 'you figure it out yourself, Kate' in him, too. He won't help me with anything other than giving me Enzo's mess to trudge through. He doesn't want to talk at all about Enzo's personal life and why he's not in cryo. There's all sorts of stuff where he's closed the door on me. He gave me ninety days, plus clerical help from Deirdre, to come up with a report. Here I am closing in on ten weeks, totally exhausted, and I'm still struggling for some kind of direction. I'm afraid I'm totally failing this."

"I'm sure you can do it. We all believe in you. You don't have any quit in you, that's for sure. Besides, Mike's intent is to keep you unbiased. Didn't he tell you from day one that's what he wanted? And he's told the rest of us to leave you alone, not to compromise your take on all this. He keeps talking to me and Chrissy about your fresh set of eyes."

Kate sighed, wishing Norm hadn't happened upon her. "Well, they're very tired eyes right now. Anyway, thanks for the pep talk. Say, so what if you hate nicknames?"

"You don't have to have one. And we also have some anons in here. Only the Burgess boys know who they are. Heck, for all we know Elvis may be here anonymously."

"That's funny, Norm." Kate giggled, finally letting go of some tension.

"Kate, have you met Rainbow Jenny? Or Jenny's Mom? They're here together—C3 and C5." Norm tapped on the two pods gently. "Starting here and all the way down are all your patients most likely to become President of the USA in 2060 or so. These people benefit from our most recent advances in procedures, hardware, software. Rainbow Jenny and Jenny's Mom—or C3 and C5, if you must—have you researched them yet?"

"No, I haven't. What's their story?"

"Jenny has Hutchinson-Gilford syndrome; it's quite rare—accelerated aging. She was only ten years old when she went into cryo, but she looked like a tiny old lady."

"Oh, that's sad. I've read about that. Genetic, right?" Kate seemed to remember reading an article in *Scientific American* about the syndrome. And now here, in the strange world of ExitStrategy, she was encountering it.

"Right, and absolutely no clue how to solve it presently. But that's the beauty of cryo. Maybe in ten or twenty years there will be an easy cure. Stem cell research, genetic manipulation. There's going to be a cure for this. She just has to wait it out."

"And her mother—Jenny's Mom? That's a sweet name. How is she here?"

"Cancer, metastasized. She's a feisty one. Gave Mike and Franklin a lot of grief. She was darned if death was going to defeat her daughter and herself all at once. You'll run into her husband sometime. He comes by about once a month to visit his girls. Andrea, Jenny's Mom, that is, wrote a lot of passionate and sometimes even angry letters to her MD and to Mike and Enzo, looking for a cure, or some kind of hope. You should read them sometime. She really stirred the pot."

"Norm, that's an amazing story—the two of them here side by side, waiting for cures, for a miracle. Really sad, but amazing. I'm beginning to get it now. We have to know each person's story. We have to be passionate about them being under our care, right? I think you just taught me a lesson. Thank you." Kate gave Norm a long hug, then sighed deeply.

"That's what old-timers like me are supposed to do, Kate. Pass on our supposed wisdom. Too bad you have to listen to all our complaining to hear the occasional nugget of truth! So, stroll with me down the row." As Norm passed each pod, he gave it a little pat, a little touch. Kate copied him, trying to force herself to truly connect with the people inside. "Kate, I'm sorry Mike has been so reticent to talk about Enzo with you. I didn't know that. So here's the last occupied pod, C53, one of the anons, and then here we are, C54; this was supposed to be Enzo's pod. We were actually getting ready for his journey into cryo. The lung cancer and the Alzheimer's were getting quite bad. He kept working even when he was so sick. And we'd have to watch him closely. He would wander off from the building when the Alzheimer's was extreme."

"Someone keeps putting flowers here. I see them all the time."

"It's Mike. Sometimes Chrissy. They really loved him."

"So, Norm, can you, for my edification, tell me why he's not here? He had lung cancer, the Alzheimer's. Why couldn't they put him in cryo when he died?"

"You have no clue, do you? Seriously?"

"No. No one has told me, Norm. Please, what happened?"

109

"Remember I said he would wander at times? One night he took off. We didn't know where he was. He'd been muttering stuff all day that we couldn't understand. Reciting numbers—Celsius temperatures that would not have anything to do with what we do here, his usual gibberish about the ocean or water or something, healing this or that. Anyway, he disappeared that night."

"Then what?"

"He must have been wandering aimlessly in the cold for hours—we don't know. But at some point he wandered onto a frozen lake not far from here. A small lake, but the water is pretty deep. This couple drove by, saw that he had broken through the ice and was in big trouble, and rescued him. Pulled him out and got him to their car. Heroes, really. They started to get his wet clothes off of him, but they looked away for a few seconds and he started to cross the road again—said he had to go back, he had friends under the ice, in the water—crazy stuff. Just then a semi drove by. The poor driver didn't have a chance to avoid hitting him. Enzo walked straight in front of the truck. He was killed instantly. The truck jackknifed severely, but the driver was okay. The whole scene was such a bloody mess that they had to close the road down for hours. We didn't find out what happened until the next afternoon since Enzo wasn't carrying any ID. We had filed a missing person report that morning, but you know how those usually go. Mike was devastated—utterly devastated. We all were, but especially him. I'm not surprised he doesn't want to talk about it. He's hiding his grief from us all, and mostly from you. I'm guessing he doesn't want you to have to grieve for someone you didn't know, to bear any of Mike's own guilt. That's the story, Kate, the whole story."

"Oh, my God," Kate murmured, shaking her head slowly. "Now I understand." Tears welled up, even though she had never met the man so beloved by everyone at the company. "He was sick, but he never got to go to cryo like he and Mike assumed would happen. The redemption was ripped away. I get it. In an instant Mike lost his best friend, his business partner, his colleague. Instead of being alive and working, or in a cryopod here at ExitStrategy with a possible future, he's six feet under. That wasn't how it was supposed to go."

"Yes, you're right. And you see these—all the flowers? They don't heal the pain, Kate. They're here, mute. They don't change anything, but I think we'll be placing flowers here anyway for a long time, maybe forever. And we'll never use C54, this pod—Enzo's."

CHAPTER SIXTEEN

Liebesleid

"Why the sour face, Kate? I know you're working hard, but right now you really look like shit."

"Thanks for the encouragement," Kate grumbled. "Oh wait, Aria, sorry. I'm being an ass. Keep playing. The music is wonderful. I'm sitting here hitting a total dead end at this work. I've only got three days until I'm supposed to tell my boss I've solved everything."

"Including world peace?"

"Yes, including world peace, and whirled peas. And I'm supposed to teach Americans when and when not to use apostrophes," Kate said, finally smiling a little.

"Have some more wine, Kate. Wine solves everything, right?" Aria put down her violin, grabbed the bottle of malbec they'd been sampling, and poured a little more in Kate's glass.

"Wine just makes you sleepy. You pass out and you forget your problems."

"And what's wrong with that?" Aria asked. She picked her instrument back up and absentmindedly began to pluck random notes, then tuned up her E string. "Oh yeah, I've been meaning to ask you— what's that book there and what the hell happened to it? It looks like it got run over by a truck."

"Well, literally it was. This weird sci-fi book and this notebook full of doodles were the two things Enzo Saltieri had with him the night he was run over and killed. The police brought it over to the lab a week ago. Apparently my boss wasn't in the mood to go in and claim Enzo's possessions. Mike doesn't want to face Enzo's death at all."

"Oh, I'm sorry. I didn't know."

"Not a problem. I never knew the guy. I'm just trying to sort things out. The police released these two items to me and I've been plowing through both of them looking for clues."

"So what's the book about?"

"It's called *Startide Rising* by David Brin. I guess he was a hotshot sci-fi author in the 1980s. The cover's half-torn off from the accident and it was covered with mud. I've cleaned it up as best I could. Here, take a look." *If Aria can figure this out,* Kate thought, *I'll give her a month or two of my salary.*

"Hmm, dudes and dolphins? What are they up to? Battling Klingons?"

"No. There's an original overlord species in space that comes and gives humans advanced brains and then dolphins and chimps get to be smart, too."

"Hallelujah for the chimps!" Aria yelled.

"Yeah, right. Weird. Anyway, when someone gives you this gift, they say you've been 'uplifted.' Of course there's the usual sci-fi techno-babble and battles and stuff. I don't get what Saltieri saw in this book. He apparently liked diving headfirst into its watery weirdness. He seemed to obsess about water toward the end."

"So what's in those chapters with all the yellow Hi-Liter?" Aria asked, sizing up the book. "Geez, this thing is falling apart. Hang on... let me skim this for a sec."

"Sure, no problem, I'm not going anywhere." Kate laid her weary head on the table, defeated.

"Wait, so the dudes are underwater with the dolphins?"

"Yeah. The humans learn how to breathe water. It's actually a pretty cool description about how scared you would be to do it for the first time. They don't quite breathe it directly, though. And anyway, what the hell would that have to do with our research? I don't get it." Kate sighed.

"Did you see this page toward the end? Something about a psi-attack? It's a torturous thing or sound that gets inside your brain. And then look at his scribble, 'like my Alzheimer's—terrifying voices won't go away. Pain.'"

"Sad, huh? Yes, Aria, I read that. When he was lucid he was aware how much the Alzheimer's was taking its toll. Can you imagine how frightening it would be to know that your mind is literally being taken away from you, piece by piece, day after day?"

"It's terrible, Kate. And the notebook? Hand it to me."

"Sure, let's see you figure this out."

"Hmm yeah, Doodletown, USA, that's for sure. And numbers— 3.9 Celsius. Then 4.2. Then 3.9 again, but he goes and crosses that out? Epic amounts of indecision, right? And what are these in Fahrenheit? I've forgotten how to convert that."

"About forty degrees Fahrenheit, Aria. We don't do anything at that kind of temperature. Nothing. But he looks like he's obsessed by these numbers."

"And here," Aria pointed, "more obsession, but temporary I guess. Two whole pages with O2 and O4 written all over, and then he crosses that all out violently."

"Those are types of oxygen molecules, Aria. Common oxygen is O2. O4 doesn't exist like he would have been thinking. And anyway, I don't know why he'd be all worked up about it."

"And here's another page with those first numbers—the 3.9 C and 4.2 stuff. Wait, this guy has like zero art skills, Kate. Is this supposed to be an armadillo next to those numbers? Or maybe a turtle—what the hell?" Aria handed the book back to Kate, apparently giving up on making any real sense of it. She grabbed her little hunk of black rosin and began tending to her violin bow.

"I don't know. Probably a turtle. From what I'm told by a few coworkers, he seemed to be obsessing the last two weeks he was alive about all things water. He was dumping chemicals into fish tanks, talking about turtles, and then the damn dolphins from the book. Also, a few days before he was killed he had a run-in with the same cop who wound up being the first responder to the crash scene. Saltieri was at the YMCA pool telling little kids that he could breathe underwater."

"What? That's messed up."

"Yeah, and he told them they could do it too if they weren't afraid. A parent heard him, freaked out, and called the police. That cop kicked him out of the building."

"Kate, have you ever been around someone with advanced Alzheimer's? I have—my great-aunt had it. I helped take care of her for a while. It was tough. They can get far beyond the early-stage forgetfulness that most people associate with the term Alzheimer's. The late-stage is really bad—hallucinations, severe paranoia—nasty stuff."

"Yeah, maybe that's it. I keep wishing that something will click in my brain, that the seemingly random crazy shit here in front of me means something, and somehow it can go from his addled brain into my supposedly healthy one, and I can proceed to use it."

"Well, Kate, you should take a breather. You're pretty blocked, right? Here, have some more wine and I'll play for you. I'm taking requests and not even putting out the tip jar, okay? What will cheer you up? Maybe a Bach gigue? Some Telemann? Prokofiev? Some hoedown fiddle music? You name it."

"I don't know. I don't know anything right now. Meh. You're right, I can't even think straight. I'm screwed. I should resign."

"Jesus, just relax, okay? Take a deep breath and think of a song you like," Aria said, yanking some loose hairs off of her bow.

"Okay, let me think. Oh hey, sure, I've got one. How about that Fritz Kreisler piece—what's it called?"

"Oh, this one?" Aria put her violin to her chin, and her agile bowstrokes began spilling out the bold leaping double-stopped notes of the opening phrase, exaggerating the craggy descending hemiolas. "The *Liebesfreud*—that's what you want? The one that sounds like horny mountain goats prancing proudly about with their enormous erections?"

"No, no, no! Jesus, Aria, goat erections? Are you ever truly serious? The other one—the companion piece. You know, the sad one. I love that tune."

"You sure you want sad tonight, Kate? I could play you a polka and cheer you up. Or a pirate song?"

"No, play the *Liebesleid*. Love's Sorrow, right? It's so beautiful. I don't care if it's sad."

"Okay, but this is the last tune for the night—I gotta put my baby back in its womb with the case humidifier. You run the AC so much my instruments are all drying out."

"Sorry. I sure as heck couldn't live in Florida."

"Oh, I could. Florida or Costa Rica, somewhere warm like that. Anyway, here's your little tune, sweetie." Aria's smile waned as she closed her eyes; she was entering the zone of silence out of which the great mystery of music emerges. She gently laid her bow on the D string and began simply, slowly—coaxing each note along so it joined with the next to make a phrase, then a little sentence. Limpid notes slid into each other here and there. The sentences grew by sequence into a story, a wordless story of love lost, the violin's wistful soul echoing the secrets of the heart. Subtle shifts from major to minor were like tiny daggers, gently piercing the heart, yet for some reason there was no pain. Scars had been built to protect the one no longer loved, the abandoned one. A quicker tempo, a moment of hope in the middle section. Aria's body swayed as she played louder, more vehemently. The violin was alive, singing sweetly, encouraging, pleading for love to return. But Kate already knew how the song ended; sadness returned, love indeed was lost, and yet somehow through this grief Aria's sage two-hundred-year-old instrument arrived at the central vibration of truth—the pearl inside the shell, despair crystallized into strange beauty: the scarred heart was, miraculously, still beating. Aria released the last tiny note into the air and finally opened her eyes. She saw Kate hunched over the table, sobbing silently. Tears rolled down her cheeks, their saltiness touching her lips, spilling onto her paperwork, onto the torn and tortured copy of Startide Rising. Kate tried to wipe her tears away, but they kept coming in waves. Aria gently laid her magical violin in its case, walked back over behind Kate, and leaned over her, enfolding her. She held Kate for what seemed like an eternity.

* * *

Kate finally picked up her head and tried to swipe her matted hair away from her face, still very damp from all the tears. Aria moved back to the other side of the table, facing Kate.

"You okay now?" Aria asked.

A smile gradually blossomed across Kate's face. She wiped the final tears away. She sighed, closed her eyes for a moment, then opened them, still smiling, looking deeply into Aria's eyes. "Aria, I think I've got it. It just came to me. It was all there waiting for me to stop trying so hard."

"What? You solved it? What Dr. Saltieri was trying to do? The crazy scribbles and walking out on a lake and then getting hit by a truck?"

"Yes, I think so. Ever put two and two together?"

"Of course. I think we did that in kindygarten, Kate. I'm going to get you a washcloth for your face. Keep talking. You're sure you're all right now?"

"Yes, completely. I owe you, girlfriend. You knocked down the wall. Anyway, Aria, I just put it together."

"See? Two plus two, right? Who needs algebra and trig?"

"Exactly."

"So come on, spill the beans. What's it all about?"

"I still have to dig in, check stuff out. I'm pulling an all-nighter, wanna help?"

"Sure. But tell me something at least. You're killing me here."

"Okay. Dr. Saltieri was trying to cure his cancer himself. Nothing else was working. He was trying to find some kind of water-based cure."

"What do you mean?"

"Eh, gotta research it more. But you helped, too."

"Yeah? But I made you cry with that damn piece."

"Yes, you did. And I tasted my tears, like it was the first time ever. That was the beginning of the epiphany. I tasted them and they were so salty and so wet. It was like I was inside my tears there for a moment, like I was inside a primordial sea. I was overwhelmed. And look at the book cover, some of my tears fell on it and I looked down and saw them—my tears on the people and the dolphins—and I thought of the people breathing under water in that weird chapter. It's all about water, saline water. Stuff you can dissolve into water, too. Like Saltieri's 'solutions.' Also, there's a molecule he diagrammed in his scribbles that looked crazy to me. Never seen anything like it. I'm thinking now that it's some weird water-soluble cancer drug. Something not approved in the US, perhaps? He had been to Mexico, but no one knows why he went. Anyway, then you added another clue."

"What else did I do beside make you cry?"

"You said you wanted to put your violin, your baby, back in its womb. Keep it safe—keep it moist. The womb, the water, safety, all that and more. When you hugged me I could feel your heartbeat like I was in that womb and you were my mother. Aria, I think I can make Mike's deadline. I've got three days. Do you really want to help me pull an all-nighter like I said?"

"For sure."

"Okay, ready?"

"Yup. Kate, sweetie, do you remember when you were about to interview for this job and I was joking about third-eye cows?"

"Pretty hard to forget. Of course I do, Aria."

"I think you just used your third-eye to get inside of all this. Cool, huh?"

"Sure."

"Okay, let me bring my laptop out here. We're gonna go 'Gangnam Style' on this, right, sistuh? What do you want me to Wikipedia first, Oh Enlightened One?"

CHAPTER SEVENTEEN

"Skinny girl? We got *you* covered, too. We *all* mothers."

"*Cut!* Dimi, the line is 'we all *sisters*.' That's what I'm reading here," Bryce McClanahan shouted, suffering through a commercial shoot for Dimi Konstantos's lingerie company, Saturday Night Sexsations.

"*Sisters, mothers*—whatever, Bryce honey," Dimi said. "Damn, I got a chipped nail, we can't shoot this now."

"Dim, you've always got a chipped nail. And I'm sorry I was late to the set. Traffic was ridiculous all the way here from Santa Monica. But that's why we have assistants, right? We have it under control. So let's get that nail fixed. Everybody take five. Makeup, touch-up that pinkie for Dim. And somebody needs to tell me what the hell is going on with this ridiculous new script. This is totally not the script Jonni e-mailed me. So fess up. You don't just hand me a new script without any warning when I walk in the door. That's not professional."

"Excuse me, Bryce. Khail pumped up Jonni's script," Dimi explained, sloppily popping an enormous wad of blue raspberry bubblegum while grabbing and shifting her two-or-more-sizes-too-small bra in a doomed attempt to get her giant breasts to fit. She finally gave up on the bra issue when the nail artist came over to fix her chipped nail.

"What? He did what?" Bryce said, grimacing.

"Pumped it up. He said Jonni's script was flat. How can we be talking about curves and have a flat script? That's what he said. It's logical." *Pop* went the gum.

"Jesus, Dimi, we're aiming at a new demographic here. Women with actual money to spend on high-end merchandise, not the trailer park high school dropout gurlies who are using their kids' lunch money to buy the cheap stuff. There's a whole new set of classier customers your marketing team has decided to tap. Khail scripting for that? Are you kidding?"

"Well, Khail did what he wanted. And now you see how good it is, right?" Dimi said, all bright-eyed. Pop.

"Well yes, of course, *I see it now*. It all makes sense." Bryce skimmed all the way through the script, rolling his eyes. "Yeah, this crap sounds like Khail talking—his own very special take on the English language. And obviously that's why this script says you're supposed to say 'cleavage is a man's best friend' at the end. That's a Khail thing, too, right? Jesus." Bryce tossed the renegade script on the floor. "This crap will not get shot today!"

"It's not crap, Bryce. It's from a real man's perspective," Dimi said. "I love it. And people like the word 'cleavage.' It's sexy. It makes people get all hot."

"If these are Khail's words have *him* say them. He should be on camera with his finely crafted script. I mean it's a masterpiece, isn't it? And I'm not sure making skinny girls, as you and he call them, feel like you're sorry for them is going to help your business. But hell, I'm just the director. What else do you want to change? The lighting? The set design? What?" Bryce bellowed, getting even hotter under the collar.

"What we're saying—" Dimi was playing with her extensions and blithely ignoring Bryce's brusqueness, "—is that Sexsations bras and panties can even make a skinny, tired old non-MILF look great. Even when her husband is sober he'll think she looks smokin' hot in our lingerie. They both'll get some. That's how Khail explained it. He's pretty damn smart now, don't you think? See the logic? You know, coming from a real man like my Khail?"

"*Non-MILF?* Yeah, okay, that totally sounds like something Khail would say."

"I think everyone here would agree with Khail," Dimi insisted. "And I can't imagine what it must feel like not to be hot. Think about it, if you're all worn out and got five kids to watch and no time for your looks, you better be praying that some of the men out there will still look you over and call you a MILF. Pad up those tiny titties with our amazing bras and you're a hit on the street."

"Jesus, Dimi, you set women's rights back thirty years saying that stuff," said Shontae Bridgewater, assistant producer of the Dimi & Khail show. "Not to mention you saying, 'we all sisters' instead of 'we're all sisters.' Not every black person talks like Khail. I sure as hell don't."

"Shontae, don't you go all Black History Month on me." Dimi pushed the nail artist away, then walked over to Shontae and got in her face. "Some women got curves. We're the real deal. Skinny women like you are losers, but I'm gonna help you all if I can. Sexsations will rescue you."

"Seriously, Dimi? Or should I say *Dim*? That's right—your precious little nickname fits you perfectly—*dim*." Shontae sneered. "And you're going to help them how, exactly? By telling them to be sluts like you? Fancy lingerie is all that matters? Really? You know, Dim, people with a brain haven't forgotten how you got your start."

Everyone gasped. Talking about Dimi's early music-video days of cleavage eruptions and nipslips was taboo. Something had been brewing between Dimi and Shontae for a while now and it looked like they would finally have it out.

"Go to hell, Shontae! You can't talk to me that way. I can fire your ass, like that," Dimi barked, snapping her fingers.

"Give it a try, you stupid whore," Shontae hissed. "I've got a multiyear contract. You've finally pissed me off so much I can't keep my mouth shut. I've been holding this inside for months, but no more. You've been treating me like shit lately. Actually, treating everybody like we don't matter. All the ridiculous stuff we do to make your life easy and that's the thanks we get? You and your fancy nails, your ugly bras, your insufferable skanky fake leopard-skin thongs, your obsession with your stupid megabreasts like they're all that fucking matters in the whole world. You're a goddamn total embarrassment to women. And you're a racist, too!"

"All right, ladies," Bryce yelled, trying to regain control of his studio. "As much as the men in the room would love to see you launch into a full-scale catfight, I'm going to ask you both to back away. Just back away, you hear me, you two? Dimi, you need to put a leash on Khail. Honestly, he can't be getting in the way of professionals, understand?" Dimi shot Bryce a look, a "don't you join in and start messing with me" look. *Pop-pop-pop* went the bubblegum.

"You're getting all this, right, guys?" asked Moses Smythe, unit director of the *Dimi & Khail: You Wish it Wuz U* reality show, speaking softly through his mike to the camera crew.

"Oh yeah, Moses. We got it all," camera one operator Bill Sampson whispered sotto voce. "Isn't it amazing how easily they forget we have the show cameras on them virtually 24/7? And Shontae? I don't blame her for blowing up, but I'm pretty sure her contract is standard. It most likely says that any footage she appears in can be aired without any recourse. *Booyah!* Not a good idea to get caught on camera crossing *The Dim*—not with how her fans support her."

"Ratings rule, Bill," Moses whispered. "Dimi's stirring things up on purpose. She sure as hell knows we've got the cameras rolling! Look, she heard me; she's winking over this way. See, Bill?"

"Yup. Poor Shontae. Twice the IQ of Dimi, but half the street smarts. Being played for a fool!"

CHAPTER EIGHTEEN

"Hello? Miss Pearson? Is that you there? The sun is so bright."

"Yes, it is. I've been standing here watching for you." Kate was dressed to impress in her swankiest outfit. After all, it wasn't every day you had lunch with a famous gazillionaire movie legend.

"Help me out of this cab, dear Katherine," Gloria Dunham said, "and then help me into the lobby. And why ever did they change the name of this place? It's absolutely sinful."

"You mean the hotel name, Miss Dunham?" Kate helped Gloria through the doors and into the lobby of The Public Chicago Hotel, formerly the historic Ambassador East. "I don't know. And honestly, I didn't realize The Pump Room was still in business inside here."

"Of course it is, Katherine. You can't kill The Pump Room. It's an institution. Kings and queens have dined here—and all the film greats. Have you ever been here?"

"No, but I've heard about it. The hopping place to be back in the day, huh? If you were really on fire you got Booth One, correct?"

"That is correct. I see you are not as ignorant as most people your age."

"I'll take that as a compliment, I guess." Kate tried not to respond with anything too snarky.

The suave maître d' recognized Gloria as she approached. "Oh, Miss Dunham, so happy to see you return to The Pump Room. What has it been? Six months… a year?"

"Hello, Roberto. I'm not sure how long it's been. Too long, I'm sure. But you know I'll always come visit you when I'm in Chicago. Can you give us a table over by that window there? I sat there with Bogart and Bacall maybe about 1955. I see Booth One is already occupied."

"Next time call ahead and Booth One is yours. We're always happy to serve you," Roberto said graciously.

"Come, Katherine, let's sit." Gloria dropped her tired old bones into her chair with a grimace. "It's not easy being this old, Katherine. I've got some advice for you: live hard and die young. Not that I've done that. I've outlived almost all my enemies, and my friends. It's strange and exhilarating, I must say."

Exhilarating to outlive friends? That's odd. Well, Mike and Franklin warned me to watch my step. Hell, I'm not scared of her. And anyway, what does she want from me?

"Hello, Miss Dunham. Greetings to you on this fine day," Tony deAngelo crooned. "I'm very happy to serve you today. Shall we begin with a beverage?"

"Yes, Tony. I'll have a Bloody Mary, the usual way. What will you have, Katherine?"

"I see you've got a pomegranate martini featured. That sounds good."

"Very well, then," Tony said, with a slight bow.

Kate looked around at the photos of generations of celebrities and politicians plastered on virtually every square foot of wall space— Frank Sinatra, Bette Davis, Ronald Reagan, John Belushi, Jimmy Carter, Doris Day, Johnny Cash, Harry Truman, Lucille Ball, Victor Borge, Jack Benny, Charles DeGaulle, and hundreds more. The celebrity photos fascinated Kate. But there were also many faces she didn't recognize, maybe singers and actors who had enjoyed their fifteen minutes of fame but now were largely forgotten. Yet their youthful, smiling faces still held court at The Pump Room.

The drinks arrived and Gloria stirred her Bloody Mary over and over before she took a sip. She sized up Kate, as if she were trying to figure out if she was an easy mark or a true adversary.

Kate took a sip of her pomegranate martini and started the conversation. "So, Miss Dunham, what was it like to be in the movies, especially back in the Hollywood glory days?"

"It was exciting, of course. But it was hard work."

"I'm sure. But it was glamorous, right?"

"Do you see the man with the cigar in that photo over there? He was a big-time producer. I did three films for him. He told me over and over that I was a failure as an actress, and I believed him."

"That's a shame," Kate said. *Ah, here comes the part where I just listen and nod. I can do that. Besides, this drink is tasty.*

"I was working in radio and Hollywood during those years. Constantly flying back and forth between New York and Los Angeles. The public loved me, especially the people who listened to radio shows in the 40s and 50s. I was always the sweet girl next door. Maybe hard for you to picture when you see me today, right, Katherine?"

"I'm sure you were a great beauty in your youth. And I have to say, your eyes are still totally amazing. They must have been something you were famous for, right?"

"Oh, yes. I'm Norwegian. Blonde hair, the bright blue eyes. My real name is Gloria Swenson. Of course, that wouldn't fly in Hollywood. Gloria Swanson was already an enormous star. So I became Gloria Dunham. I grew up in Minnesota. That's what we all look like up there. Hollywood loves blondes, Katherine." Gloria had already reached the bottom of her drink. The waiter noticed and brought another. "You know, if your eyesight is better than mine, which I'm sure it is, you might be able to spot me here and there on these walls."

"Really? Shall I look and see?"

"If you like. I'll give you a little help. I'm with men in each of the photos."

"All right," Kate said, standing up. "I'll prowl around." Kate walked slowly through the room. A few other people were doing the same thing—examining all the photos of the rich and famous lining the walls of the restaurant. Kate finally latched on to a photo that seemed like it might be Gloria. She called out from across the room. "This one? It looks like you, with, I think, Alan, um, Alan somebody, right?"

"Alan Ladd, nice fellow. Decent actor. But no, that's not me. That's Veronica Lake. That's from when she and Alan were publicizing The Blue Dahlia, her only decent movie. Notice the chin? Not mine. Plus I hated her."

Kate kept wandering. *Oops, guess I flubbed that. Aha, how about this one. Blonde, blue eyes, the right chin.* "I've found you, Miss Dunham. Right here, correct?"

"Very good, Kate. And who is the fellow, do you know?"

"I have no idea. But you look like you're in love," Kate speculated, returning to her seat.

"That's me with my first husband, the first time I was ever here. I was so young and innocent; can you see it? He was a trumpet player. Started out playing with the Jimmy Dorsey big band before going out on his own. He was fairly famous in the day. Over the years, we drifted apart. We were both traveling too much, and then later he had health difficulties. I was having my own problems holding on to my sanity what with all the pressure of Hollywood. I started taking a lot of pills. There were pills all over our house, I'm sorry to say. I don't blame him for our breakup and all my problems. I was nasty to be around. Of course, the public didn't know any of that. That's how Hollywood worked. Your personal life could be going down the crapper, as they say, but no one would know."

"You're quite candid about your past, Miss Dunham. I admire that."

"There's no sense in pretending when you're my age. Whatever happened, happened. I had problems with men my whole life. And pills. Oh my God, the pills. Katherine, you need another drink, don't you?" Gloria snapped her gnarly old fingers and the waiter appeared. "Please get Katherine another martini, Tony."

"And would you like to order now, Miss Dunham?"

"No, I'm not really hungry. I don't eat very much these days, Tony. Shall we just keep chatting and sipping, Katherine?"

"Whatever you wish." Kate smiled.

"All right. Can you find another?" Gloria asked, reaching into her purse and pulling out some ruby red lipstick.

"Well, let's look again." Kate stood up and walked over toward a little alcove. More famous folks—Bing Crosby hamming it up at Booth One with Bob Hope and Dorothy Lamour. The Monkees, Harrison Ford, Twiggy, Steve Martin, Mel Gibson. And there—the amazing blue eyes, the delicate lips and nose, the halo of wavy golden-blonde hair. "Here you are, and that's Frank McMurtry. I saw him in a Hitchcock movie. Am I right?"

"Yes, Katherine. You're quite good at this!" Gloria smiled.

"I spend hours looking through microscopes. My eyes better be good. And my dad forced me to watch a lot of old movies on videotape with him when I was a kid. We'd sit there with popcorn and watch together."

"That's nice. Maybe I can meet him some day."

"No, he passed away a few years ago from cancer. My mom is all alone now except for me."

"I'm very sorry. That's sad to hear. Well, you are right, that is Frank McMurtry—husband number two. When our movie careers were fading we did a TV situation comedy. It wasn't so bad. I think it lasted four seasons."

"And then what?"

"Well, then I was a little bonkers again, dear Katherine. I couldn't keep a grip on much of anything. I was angry that the studios were passing me over for actresses who were much younger and less difficult to deal with, I suppose I should add. I took it out on Frank a lot. Boy, did I ever take it out on him. He wasn't as forgiving as my first husband. Would you like to hear the story? You'll learn where virtually all my loot came from."

Kate's second drink arrived. She took a sip. It was delicious but strong. *I guess it's a liquid lunch today,* she thought. *Better watch myself.* "Sure, go ahead, Miss Dunham."

"Frank had become one of the richest men in all of Southern California. He had built up oodles of dollars from real estate investments. When he got tired of dealing with me and my problems he finally gave a big chunk of his money to me, just to convince me to go away, to disappear quickly and quietly."

"Wow, that's amazing," Kate said.

"Uh-huh. So would you like to hear a funny story about this place we're in?"

"Of course."

"In 1957 or 1958 Queen Elizabeth came here. Some big event was going on in Chicago. She stayed at the hotel and ate here. After she left, some smart alecks unscrewed the toilet seat from her hotel suite upstairs, mounted it in a frame, and had a brass plaque engraved for it. Guess what it said."

"I don't know. What?"

"*Her Majesty, Queen Elizabeth the Second sat here!*"

"Ha, that's funny. They put it on the wall here?"

"No, they didn't dare do that, but they gave it to the hotel owner to take home. It's a true story." Gloria coughed, shrunk down in her seat, and hacked up a little phlegm, which she hid in a napkin. She sighed, touched up her makeup, and then sat up straighter, ready for more fun. "Okay, back to work, Katherine, chop-chop. You've got one more to find. Do you like this game?"

"Well, yes I do," Kate said, even though two strong martinis on an empty stomach were making her feel a little weird. And martini number three had just arrived, thanks to the ever-attentive Tony. "All right, let me look some more. Do you suppose people watching me think I'm some pathetic tourist from Kansas or something?"

"Oh, I am sure of that. You have a Kansas look to you, Katherine. Has anyone ever told you that? Fresh from the farm. But who cares? We're having fun, we have refreshments, and we have time on our hands." Gloria's blazing blues eyes twinkled.

"Okay. Let me wander over by that door to the kitchen. I haven't looked there yet." Kate searched but couldn't find Gloria. But Elvis was there along with Colonel Parker, plus photos of Sophia Loren, Warren Beatty and Faye Dunaway from the *Bonnie and Clyde* days, as well as Tom and Dick Smothers. And holy cow, The Rolling Stones, appearing quite baby-faced, were there, too!

"I believe you're very cold, Katherine. Go over near the sommelier station." Gloria motioned.

"All right," Kate said, not exactly walking a straight line due to the Belvedere vodka in her drinks. "Where are you? Hmm—no, no. Wait, here you are. You're with James Arness, right? From *Gunsmoke*? And the other fellow with the glasses is…?"

"That's Mr. A.C. Nielsen, of the A.C. Nielsen marketing company. Our friend at ExitStrategy, yes? He was always such a gentleman. Even when I was having problems keeping my life together, I could always call him up and he would steer me gently. He was from Minnesota, too, but he was Danish, not Swedish like me. Lovely men—those two," Gloria added wistfully.

"Well, this is all quite amazing, Miss Dunham."

"Oh, let's drop the formality. Please call me Gloria from now on."

"And please call me Kate."

"Well, actually you can't be a Kate. A Kate has to be feisty, like Hepburn. You're too nice, too polite for that. But you're a pretty Katherine, I would say. Pretty, I suppose, but not beautiful. You have that Kansas look of yours, but maybe you should try using more makeup. Try to make more of some of your average features. Anyway, Katherine is the name I shall use for you. Do you mind?" Gloria flashed her sweetest smile. She snapped her fingers again and within two minutes, two more drinks appeared. She had The Pump Room waitstaff well trained.

"So, Gloria, tell me more about your first husband—a musician, you said?"

"Yes, conservatory trained, but he decided jazz was more for him. We were so young and he was so handsome. Of Spanish heritage, with lovely thick hair and mysterious eyes. All the women threw themselves at him."

"But you got him."

"Well yes, I did." Gloria smiled proudly. "I was doing a lot of radio at the time and I was at a charity ball that all the actors from my show were attending. The Jimmy Dorsey band was playing for the event and

I saw this gorgeous god of a young man with his shiny silver trumpet. Dorsey raved on and on to the audience about his new find, this trumpet player who had just left some fancy East Coast music conservatory to join the band. And then Dorsey featured him on the next tune. He picked up that shiny horn and dazzled us all, and I fell in love right then and there. I was dizzy in love, Katherine. I'm not kidding you. We were married within six months."

"Wow, like right out of a fairy tale."

"Yes, for a while. We decided to live in California and I would go back and forth—New York for radio and the movies out west. Unfortunately, Raimondo was pretty much living out of a suitcase with the band. It caused a lot of stress on the relationship. I begged him to settle in LA and return to classical, maybe play in the Philharmonic or do the Hollywood Bowl or something. We fought about all his traveling, but he loved jazz too much, and I guilted him about it. Sometimes things would get better, sometimes worse. And then I had my problem with the pills. At times the pills made me a monster. But sometimes not taking the pills was even worse."

"Well, you just wanted to have a little love nest and be happy, right?" Kate asked as she swirled her drink, trying to prop up Gloria's spirits.

"Yes, I did. And that's why I agreed to finally stop nagging him and go see what the jazz life was really like. Go with him on a tour and enjoy the road life together. A little getaway to rekindle the romance. Of course, this was a small group. Ray had become a be-bopper and I wasn't always happy with some of the types he was hanging out with. Lots of alcohol, drugs, you know. So we went on this tour and—"

"I'm sorry to barge in, Miss Dunham," Tony said with his trademark bow. "You've got fans across the way. They've engaged me to ask if you'd sign an autograph for them."

"Katherine, my eyes aren't very good today. Do they look like nice folks?"

Kate smiled and nodded.

"Go over and invite them to our table here."

Kate, again doing her best to walk in a straight line with all the alcohol she had downed, brought the three grinning fans over, all of them over seventy-five. Gloria chatted graciously with her devoted fans and then signed three Pump Room napkins for them. The three left after a while, smiling as they clutched their bounty.

"Now, Katherine, where were we?" Gloria asked.

"Your first husband—a trip with him and his jazz group."

"Oh, yes." Gloria's lovely smile, so evident during the moments with her fans, gave way to a painful frown. "Actually, I'm tired of talking about the past. Let's rejoin the present and talk about you and ExitStrategy. I'm sure you're excited to be there, yes? It will take a while to figure things out—all that science, all of Mike's gizmos. But you'll be fine. I am, however, concerned about a few things at the company."

"What sort of things?" Kate felt more and more woozy from the four martinis. She had always made a point of not drinking on an empty stomach, yet somehow here she was, doing it to keep pace with an old lady.

"Oh, just things in general. I am wondering if you could let me know, since I am a major shareholder, if you think there is anything I should be concerned about. Just look at me as the guardian angel of the company and please make sure Mike isn't doing anything unwise. I actually have knowledge of an incident in the past where he was in dangerous waters. Illegal matters, believe it or not."

"Really? That surprises me. Well, I'll think about it. I don't really know what else to say." *Except this, Old Lady—now I know for sure why you wanted to do lunch. You want me to be a mole, a spy for you? No way, no how.*

"Consider it," Gloria cooed, unaware of Kate's disdain for the little trap she had tried to set. "I, for one, think that Mike makes plenty of mistakes and there is no one to point them out. After all of these years, he won't listen to me." Gloria frowned and shook her head for effect.

Wait... four strong Bloody Marys in fifty or sixty minutes on an empty stomach? She's a little old lady and she still looks perfectly alert? Still doing her best to play me? How does she do that? She must weigh all of ninety pounds— what the heck? "Well, I'm new on the job," Kate said, remaining cool and not tipping her hand. "It would be difficult for me to tell him what to do, other than from a purely scientific viewpoint."

"I understand, dear." Gloria shrugged as she searched for something in her purse. "If you do see something at ExitStrategy that doesn't seem right, just know that I'm available to you. You can talk to me discreetly whenever needed. Absolutely whenever. Oh, look at the time. I must be going now. There should be a timed cab out front waiting for me right now, I believe. Roberto will make sure the bill goes to my account. Stay and finish your creative drink. Pomegranate, was it? I've never tried such an unusual drink. You young people are quite into the exotic, I must say. I'll have the staff help me down the stairs and out to the cab. Katherine, my dear, it was so good to talk to you today and get to know you better. Call me whenever you wish." And with that little farewell speech, Gloria squeezed Kate's hand ever so slightly, stood up, ambled slowly out of the restaurant toward the hotel lobby, and was gone.

"So good to get to know me?" Kate mumbled. *She didn't ask me anything about myself. It was all about her getting my guard down and trying to plant me as a spy at ExitStrategy.* Suddenly an odd hunch came over Kate. She eyeballed Gloria's fourth Bloody Mary, still sitting on the table half-full with gross lipstick stains on it. Kate picked up the glass and brought it to her nose, sniffing, then took a taste. *Well damn, I've been played by a crazed old woman. There isn't a trace of alcohol in this drink!*

CHAPTER NINETEEN

Gloria and Ray, October 1961

The members of the Raimondo (Ray) Machado Quintet, accompanied by their wives, rolled into San Francisco for a Tuesday through Saturday engagement at the Black Hawk, at the corner of Turk and Hyde in the Tenderloin district, down near the bottom of Nob Hill. The district was famous for its jazz clubs, bars, billiard halls, and wild goings-on. Dashiell Hammett lived there for a while and he portrayed his famous character, Sam Spade, as living in the district at 891 Post Street. The club suffered from stained carpeting, lousy plumbing, and other problems, but the musicians didn't care about the peeling paint and the backed up toilets. They just wanted to jam. Billie Holiday and Ella had sung there, but the club was best known for showcasing the best of the bop world, both hard and cool—Miles, Monk, Dizzy, Coltrane, Chet Baker, Ahmad Jamal, Stan Getz, plus Gerry Mulligan and other wet behind the ears West Coast Cool players all played there. On a Tuesday or a Wednesday it might be blues in the night—a local piano trio, with dirty needles and used condoms littering the alley out back. But Friday or Saturday it could be heaven on earth—beautiful young women in slinky red dresses sipping fancy drinks at the bar, and name touring acts with intense young men wailing on their shiny horns.

"You ready to get over to the club, Ray?" Gloria asked.

"Yeah, sure. Jesus, who'll show up on a Tuesday night at nine? If no one shows we're just playing for ourselves."

"You can play for me, Ray. Which dress?" Gloria held up a couple choices.

"Neither. You look mighty fine in that sexy satin slip," he said, arching his eyebrows and walking around behind her, wrapping his arms around her and caressing her warm, soft belly. They could see themselves in the full-length mirror in the hotel room. It was a turn-on for them both.

"Mm," Gloria moaned softly. Ray could hear her breath quicken. She placed her hands on top of his, then pushed her ass back slowly into his groin, sending a not-so-subtle message to the bulge in his crotch. *Oh, she wants it now, right now*, Ray thought. He could feel his cock growing harder and harder, his balls tingling. His hands slid up to her breasts, the sweet mounds of tantalizing flesh. He teased her nipples through the sheer fabric until they were hard. Her breathing grew even faster.

"Ray, what are you doing?"

"Feeling you up. You like?"

"Mm, yeah. You like my tits? You wanna cum all over them, baby?"

"No, I wanna fill you up, fuck you hard."

"Yeah, Ray, talk dirty to me. Real dirty."

"I'm gonna bend you over and fuck you hard. Fast and hard. Like an animal," he said as he started grinding his cock at her sweet ass. They kept watching themselves in the mirror. He started pulling his pants down.

"Yeah, fuck me, Ray. Throw me on the bed and fuck me, baby. Come on!"

"Yeah, here we go." He pushed her roughly onto the bed, her face buried in the pillows. He pulled her ass up in the air and yanked down her damp panties. Her heat and scent drove him crazy when it hit him. His cock got harder and harder, ready for action.

"Come on, Ray. Come on, give it to me."

He pushed hard, one damned hard penetrating thrust. She gasped loudly, then started panting. He thrust in and out. Hard thrusts, which she met with a variation of her own. They were a doggy-style fucking machine. On and on. Faster and harder.

"Ray, you like Veronique's titties?" Gloria said out of nowhere.

"What?"

"You like her tits? I saw you staring at them."

Ray slowed down his thrusting, then stopped, even though he stayed inside her. *What the hell is this all about?* "No, I like you, I like *your* titties. Come on, let's do it," he said, thrusting harder again.

"Okay," she said, picking up his rhythm.

Geez, he thought, *she just ruined this. Killed the moment.* He slowed down again.

"Ray, what's the matter?"

"I'm trying to make love to you and you ask me if I like *someone else's breasts?* That's weird." He felt his erection going down.

"I saw you staring at 'em. It's a fact."

Ray stopped thrusting. "Geez, you're crazy, Gloria."

"Yeah, I am!" She quickly reached down between her legs and put a vise grip on his balls with both hands.

"Shit, stop it. That hurts. It's not sexy at all."

"Keep fucking, Ray. Come on, get it back up and be a man."

Ray couldn't help himself, Gloria's power play made his cock harder, his full balls aching from the pressure she kept on them. He thrust like a madman. In and out, harder and deeper.

"That's it, Ray. Harder, harder. Harder. Cum now, cum, goddammit," she yelled. "Now, now, now!"

Ray's head felt like it was exploding from the quick rush of dopamine. His cock spasmed over and over, way longer than usual as it pumped his hot cum inside her. She kept hold of his balls, squeezing everything out of him. He couldn't tell for sure if she came or not. *She wanted to mindfuck me—grab my balls and make me cum or rip 'em off. Be the boss, intimidate me. She's getting crazier. I bet she stopped taking the pills Dr. Gordon prescribed.*

Gloria finally released her death grip on his testicles. He plopped down next to her on the bed. He didn't know what to say. What the hell was all that about Veronique's breasts? It wasn't talking dirty, it was an accusation. That's Rollo's wife—out of bounds. Band members didn't do that to each other. Yeah, Gloria's definitely weirded out. Won't even talk to me now. Look at her, lighting up her Pall Mall and now the silent treatment. Still trying to mess with me. Fucking castrate me. That wasn't making love.

After a while Gloria stood up and padded off to the shower. Ray heard her turn on the water. All he could do was shake his head. "Hell, where is this gonna wind up?" he muttered out loud.

* * *

The Tuesday night crowd was decent. A mix of locals and more-dressed-up traveling business types. Some had beautiful young escorts on their arm. After all, the Tenderloin was an easy place to procure whatever a man with some dough wanted. The band members' wives sat together in a dark corner so Gloria wouldn't be spotted by some stumbling drunk fan. The girls dressed low-key, saving the fancy dresses for the weekend. After a few tunes, Ray noticed the wives giggling a lot when Gloria was talking. *Shit, is she giving them all the juicy details of that strange quickie two hours ago? Oh well, what can I do about it?* Jojo, the piano player, was going chorus after chorus on "Cherokee," giving Ray time to observe Gloria. After a while it looked like the other women were shunning her. *What was she telling them? About grabbing my balls like a crazy woman? I don't think they're that kinky. If that's what she told them, no wonder they're ignoring her now.* Ray grinned. "Serves you right, Gloria," he muttered. He was so deep in thought that Calvin had to elbow him hard back to reality. He almost missed coming back in on the repeat of the melody.

"Man, where yo' head at?" Calvin whispered hoarsely once the tune ended.

"It was pounding Gloria a little while ago. Sorry, man. It was intense. I think she's over there telling the girls all about it." He didn't care to tell Calvin how weird the sex had become.

"*Hell, no,*" Calvin said. "All they talk about is makeup and clothes. And money, man. Money, money, money. They shoulda married advertising executives or sumpin'. Listen, stop thinking about sex and play your horn. Do what I say."

"Yeah, Calvin. I got it. Won't be no problems, boss," Ray said with a grin.

"Yeah, yeah. Shut up, asshole! Blow some spit outta that horn and play the damn thing."

* * *

Wednesday night. A smaller crowd than Tuesday. Go figure. Weekday gigs, hardly worth doing. The boys began their second set with "Round Midnight" in a new, avant-garde arrangement by Ray. After an intro and the full head, Calvin took up the first solo on his tenor sax. As he finished, the small crowd lazily applauded. Ray was next. He started with the tiniest germ of an idea, a single note on the dominant tone of the mournful, yet harmonically complex tune written in 1944 by Thelonious Monk. Ray's single spark traveled in strange syncopations above the half notes in the bass part. Then suddenly, a flurry of eighth notes appeared, outlining ascending and descending ninth and eleventh chords through the changes of the head, then back to the single tone, but now up an octave. The sidemen exchanged glances. Where was Ray going with this? Then a new rush of eighths and sixteenths, but this time the storm of notes outlined modern quartal harmonies borrowed from contemporary classical composers like Bartok and Hindemith. The true jazz aficionados in the room stopped slumping over their drinks and sat up straight, trying to follow Ray's leaps of improvisational genius as he spun out ever-longer phrases. They tried to hold on while Ray led them through the storm to the Promised Land. Jojo kept feeding Ray even more complex harmonic underpinnings for the free-play, nodding his head at Ray. *You want that? Yeah? Okay, I gotchoo. Go here now? Yeah, I'll catch you—sharp 11, man. Yeah, that's it, I got you! Yeah, minor with a major seven, Ray? Yeah, sure!*

Ray's quicksilver notes hung in the air with a strange, yet beautiful logic—a musical vision of Utopia all right there and then in a dark, smelly club in the Tenderloin. When the solo ended, the room erupted in applause, drowning out the rhythm section as they headed into the coda. Ray and Calvin joined in for the last few measures, the string of secondary dominants everyone knows if they've ever heard the tune. Then a fadeout with bowed bass and mallet-rolled cymbals dying away into the distance. The crowd went crazy again. Everyone in the band stared at Ray.

"Man, I wish Monk coulda heard that," Calvin declared. The other men nodded.

"I'll tell you this, Miles Davis wouldn't want to hear it—he plays that tune. You just done run circles around Miles, Ray!" said Rollo, the bass player.

"Well then don't tell him!" Ray said, still sweating profusely from his gymnastic efforts.

"Jesus, Ray, you're like from a different planet. I wish someone was recording that," Jojo said. "Catch it for posterity."

"I can do it again. Go get a recorder somewhere. Tomorrow night. I know every note I played. If you wanna hear it again."

"You mean you wrote it out? All that crazy stuff? You memorized it?"

"No, I improvised it all," Ray said. "But I can tell you every note I played… unless you don't believe me."

"No, man, I believe you. I ain't disagreeing with anything you got to say!"

"That really is a fuckin' great tune, isn't it?" Ray smiled and winked at Calvin.

"Yeah, Ray, damn fuckin' great tune," Calvin agreed. "Hey, you ever met Monk?"

"No, but I'd like to."

"We gotta go out east, New York, sometime. Play that for Monk. See what he thinks," Calvin said.

"Yeah, see what he thinks," Ray echoed absentmindedly. The magic moment was suddenly over. Gloria's crazy shit was already back on his mind.

CHAPTER TWENTY

Thursday morning Ray slept in. He wasn't up until past noon. When he tried to walk to the hotel bathroom he weaved left and right, feeling like he was hungover, but he only had two drinks the night before. He sat on the toilet forever, dizzy and miserable. Instead of getting in the shower and looking for resurrection through hot, steaming water, he stumbled back to the bed. "Shit, I'm sick," he whispered out loud to no one, since Gloria didn't seem to be there. He fell back asleep immediately.

"Ray, where are you?" Gloria called out later as she entered the room followed by an eager-to-please bellboy. The young lad plopped down six boxes of swanky new shoes Gloria had purchased and held out his hand for his reward. Gloria handed him a ten-dollar bill, gave him a peck on the cheek, and shooed him out the door, his face blushing crimson.

"In here, in the bedroom," Ray croaked.

"Why are you still in bed?"

Ray rolled over toward where her voice was coming from and squinted. He was still groggy and disoriented from a strange dream he had.

"I'm sick. Terrible. Dizzy—I can't stand up or the room spins. Ugh."

"But you've got a gig in a few hours. You have to play tonight. That band's nothing without you."

"No, I can't. I really can't."

"You have to. You've got no choice. Sit up, let me see you." Ray complied with the taskmaster. He hated when she bossed him around like he was some slack-jawed assistant to the assistant director on one of her sets.

"Yeah, you look bad. How much did you drink last night?"

"Nothing. Almost nothing. Two drinks."

"Be honest. Don't lie to me. What were you boys doing in back between sets?"

"I wasn't doing nothin', Gloria. Geez, listen to me," Ray protested.

"But they were. They were, right?"

"Who cares? You're not their mommy, and you're not mine," Ray pushed back.

"Don't you talk to me like that! It's bad enough you gave up being a legit musician, but now you hang out with these addicts? I don't mind slumming a bit for fun now and then, but you turn into an addict and the press finds out? I can see it in Variety—'America's sweetheart married to lowlife needle-marked devil.'"

"Oh, so this is about you now?" Ray said, getting testy. "I'm sick. I got a bug. But you've got a bug up your ass."

"Fuck you, Ray!" she said and slapped him hard on the face. She backed away from the bed and glared at him.

"Don't fucking hit me. I'm sick. Dammit, keep your hands off me!" Ray yelled, rubbing his face. "Jesus, Gloria, go to hell!"

"No, you got to hell, you loser," she countered.

"Okay, I will go—playing jazz. You try to stop me. That's me up there on the stand, the real me. When I'm there I'm not just any old *schmuck* reading the notes someone else threw onto a page. I just got a record offer from a big label. You don't know 'cause you don't even care about what's going on with me. I like classical, but I love jazz. Do you even get the difference?"

"Ray, if you weren't so stupid and artsy you could be leading pop concerts at the Hollywood Bowl. You got the dark Spanish looks and the talent. You could be bigger than Carmen Dragon, making a ton of dough, but you think it's beneath you."

"Who cares about looks, shallow shit like that? Lame Hollywood stuff. Is that really all you care about?" Ray could feel his heart pounding, his temples throbbing. *Why can't she leave me alone, let me sleep?*

Gloria just stood there, glaring at him, her arms crossed over her chest. The almighty Gloria, all five foot three and one hundred and five pounds, ready to do mortal battle with a sick man. A minute of silence ensued—it seemed like forever.

Ray finally spoke. "So, Gloria, which are you choosing?"

"What do you mean?"

"You're not married to me, you're married to your career—to Hollywood."

"I'm sure as hell not going to be married to a drug addict, dammit!"

"Why are you talking like this? I've never done any drugs. You're acting crazy!"

"You're doing drugs with your band."

"Hell no, I am not!" Ray yelled incredulously, stumbling to his feet to walk toward her.

"Yeah, get up, walk over here, show me your arms. You got tracks I bet, just like goddamn Calvin and Jojo."

"Okay, you are totally crazy. You must be off your meds. Don't you realize you sleep with me every night? Any damn day or night you can see my arms. You'd know if I have needle marks on my arms. Have you seen any?"

"Then you're snorting something, liar."

"Let it go. Seriously."

"Look in the mirror. You look like an addict."

"I'm sick, I got the flu. If you loved me you'd be taking care of me now, not yelling at me like a madwoman. Enough with the crazy shit!"

"Crazy shit? Yeah, okay, come here and I'll show you crazy shit. You wanna see it?" Ray couldn't figure out why she was going so totally ballistic and paranoid. Had to be from not taking her pills. She was certifiable right now.

"Come here, Ray, I'll show you crazy shit," she taunted, gesturing for him to come closer.

Maybe I can get my arms around her and try to calm her down. Slowly come up to her and see if I can get a grip on her, a bear hug, he thought. He moved closer and just as he was about to reach out to her, she grabbed a small metal sculpture with a marble base off the breakfront by the couch. She raised it quickly and slammed it as hard as she could on the side of Ray's head. Pow. His head jerked sideways, and he tripped over the edge of an Oriental rug and toppled over hard, like a decrepit old building being razed by dynamite.

Gloria stood victorious, peering down at him—her face like a devil. "There's crazy shit, Ray," she yelled. "You wanted it, you got it. You don't ever backtalk me again, mister. Don't ever mess with me again, Ray. No way, no how. You try, and I'll destroy you."

He was out. Luckily for Gloria he wasn't dead. Not that she really cared much in her present mental state.

* * *

Ray regained consciousness about twenty minutes later. He pulled himself up off the floor and staggered back to the bed. *Jesus, the whole day in bed. First sick, now a bashed-in head. A great Hallelujah day.* He lay there trying to get his mind to work, to figure out what had happened with Gloria. *Jesus, she could have killed me.* He looked around, trying to focus. No sign of her and no sign of her stuff. *She's cleared out—she's gone. Left me to die on the floor. That's the end of that. Damn, it's gonna be ugly, though.*

There was a knock on the door. *Rat-a-tat, rat-a-tat.* It made his head hurt more. *Rat-a-tat, rat-a-tat.*

"Go away," Ray groaned.

"Ray, what's going on? Why aren't you at the club? Let me in." It was Dorothy Love, Jojo's wife. She was a sweetheart, the daughter of a respected Baton Rouge Baptist minister.

"I'm sick, Dorothy."

"Ray, come on. The gig starts in ten minutes. Hurry up and we can still get there during the first set. Calvin sent me to get you."

"I can't play tonight."

"Ray, what's wrong? You never miss a night as long as I've known you. Where's Gloria? Is she in there? Gloria?" Dorothy yelled.

"She left."

"To get medicine?"

Ray wondered what to say next. He couldn't decide. What the fuck did it matter?

"Ray? Ray? Dammit, let me in. What's going on? You're getting me worried. You sound like shit."

"Just a minute," he said, grabbing for a robe as he stood up. Still dizzy, he reached out and braced himself against a desk and then a leather chair as he wobbled over to unlock the door.

Dorothy entered and took a long look at his haggard face, the blood matted in his hair. She let out a whistle. "Whoa, what happened to you?"

"I've got the flu or something, really dizzy. Gloria came in and we got into a fight. She thought I was lazy, or on drugs, or something. She got totally paranoid. I think she stopped taking her pills. She got crazier and crazier and then she hit me with that thing over there on the floor, whatever it is. By the time I saw her swinging it at me I couldn't get my hands up fast enough."

"We got to get you to a doctor. You look bad, Ray."

"No. What's he gonna do, anyway? Give me aspirin? It's not bleeding anymore. I just need to lay down."

"Well, you need ice on that head. I'll call for some. Go lay back down. Maybe we can get a doctor come over here."

"Okay," Ray sighed, once again traipsing back to the bed.

"Room service? Yes, can you send up some ice right away—like quickly? Okay, thanks. And then can you send up some aspirin, a pot of strong coffee, and a BLT? Okay, thanks!"

"I don't want a sandwich, Dorothy. Cancel the BLT."

"Fool, the coffee is for both of us, the BLT is for me. I'm starving!"

Ray smiled weakly. Dorothy was a good woman. The ice arrived before long and Dorothy wrapped some in a hand towel and placed it on Ray's aching head. She used a wet towel to clean up the blood encrusted in his hair.

"You got nice hair, Ray. Soft and pretty."

"Thanks, I guess," said Ray.

"Man, she got you real good. I'm sorry, Ray. I'm real sorry. She's pretty and she's a movie star or whatever, but there's somethin' wrong with her."

"Tell me about it." Ray moaned.

"Ray, you said somethin' about pills, right? We were in the ladies' room at the club Tuesday night. She took a whole bottle of pills and flushed 'em down the toilet. Laughed and said they were pills from men who wanted to control her. She went on and on complaining about every man in her life, even you."

"That sounds about right. The pills are to keep her steady. Not too manic, not too depressed. Like in between. She's got problems. And I guess I'm one of them."

"It's not your fault. I think she just don't like men!"

"You think?" he said with a weak smile, pointing to his head. Dorothy smiled back. She got a fresh towel, moistened it, and kept cleaning Ray's wound. This is what a good woman does, he thought. *Jojo's got a good woman.*

"Well, she's gone now, right, Ray? Maybe you don't go chase after her—that's my advice."

"I think you're right, Dorothy. Hey, at least she didn't hit me in the lips. I can still play my horn!"

There was a knock at the door—room service again. Dorothy took the aspirin bottle and tapped out three pills into Ray's hand. He gulped them down with some water while Dorothy took a bite of her BLT.

"You want some?"

"No, I'd probably throw it back up. I'm still dizzy. But I'll take a cup of coffee. Give it to me black."

"Oh, black's the best. You know it."

"Don't make jokes. My head hurts too much if I laugh, Dorothy!"

"Okay, sorry! Hey, I'm gonna call the club. I'll tell Calvin you really can't make it."

"He'll get lots of solos tonight. Tell him I ain't dead. No little hotel statue gonna kill me off, goddammit!"

"Well look at you, gettin' your sense of humor back. See, everything gon' be all right." Dorothy dialed the club, taking bites of her BLT as the phone rang and rang. Someone finally answered and she got her message through to Calvin. "He's real upset, Ray. He says he'll get a doctor over here. He'll get him here soon."

"Okay," Ray said. "Hey, at least it's not Friday or Saturday and the big crowds. Maybe I am hungry now. I haven't eaten all day."

"Okay, I'll get you somethin'. What do you want?"

"Soup and crackers, something like that."

"Okay. Say, why don't you close your eyes and try to relax."

Ray took the advice, but with his eyes closed he felt like he was spinning, spinning fast. He opened his eyes and the spinning stopped. Dorothy ordered for Ray and then hummed a little tune while they waited for the soup and the doctor to arrive. After a while, there was another knock on the door. It was the doctor. Dorothy ushered him in.

"Hello, folks, I'm Dr. Julius Sands. You're Mr. Machado, I presume?"

"Yes, thanks for coming," Ray said. Dr. Sands wore a fine wool suit and crisply starched Van Heusen shirt with a beautiful silver and turquoise bolo tie to set himself apart from the crowd. He was a small man, but somehow had a great booming voice, the kind of deep voice that might scare a child, but command respect from adults in his care.

"So what seems to be the problem, Mr. Machado?"

"Well, I suppose the biggest problem is that my wife tried to kill me by bashing my head in. That's for starters."

"And this is our wife here?" Dr. Sands eyed Dorothy.

"No, a friend. I'm sorry. This is Dorothy Love, a good friend and a pretty good nurse."

"Oh, I see. So there's the 'for starters,' as you put it. A wife with a flair for the dramatic. There's more?"

"Yes, I think I have the flu. I've been dizzy and feeling bad all day. The cracked skull was the icing on top of the cake."

"Ray, do you realize you're on the thirteenth floor of this hotel?" Dorothy interrupted.

"What? No, I'm on the fourteenth floor. I'm in 1403, Dorothy. Besides, who cares?" Ray said, giving her a disapproving look. "The doc is here. He's trying to talk to me."

"There's no thirteenth floor here, Ray. Well what I mean is they don't say there is one, so the fourteenth floor is really the thirteenth floor. You shoulda stayed on the seventh floor like me and Jojo. I plan these things."

Dr. Sands fiddled with his bag, pulling out a stethoscope and the like, and sat patiently while this odd conversation ran its course.

"No Louisiana *juju* or *mojo* talk, Dorothy, please. I've heard it all before. Not tonight, okay?"

"All right, Mr. Machado," Dr. Sands said, "let's see that noggin." He moved Ray's head around at different angles, got a good look, and let out a whistle. "Well, it's a doozy, that's for sure, but you'll survive it. The bleeding is superficial. Did you lose consciousness when it happened?"

"Yes, Doc, I did. But you think it'll be okay?"

"Yes, I do. Ice it, aspirin, the usual stuff. Looks like you've already been doing that, right? Rest, too. I still need to look you over in general. Let's take your temperature, blood pressure, and so on—the usual drill." He stuck a thermometer into Ray's mouth and then pulled it out after a while. "98.8—no fever. Pulse next." He reached out for Ray's arm, then eyed his watch. "One sixteen, a bit high, but you've been under stress, eh? Now let's get this cuff on your arm. Hold still." The doctor pumped up the cuff, then released the pressure, watching the little gauge. A look of concern crossed his face.

"What is it, Doc?" said Ray.

"I'm not done yet. Let's listen to the ticker." He placed the stethoscope on Ray's chest, moving it here and there. Ray sat there trying to remember the last time he'd been to a doctor. He hadn't been sick in ages. Sands checked Ray's eyes with the light from an ophthalmoscope, making a little tsk sound now and then as he peered in.

"Mr. Machado, do you smoke?"

"No, I'm a trumpet player—professional. I can't afford that vice."

"Drink?"

"Not that much, I try to be a good Boy Scout. Stay healthy."

"Very good. And this trumpet playing, do you enjoy it?"

"Yes, I do."

"Good to hear. A man should enjoy his profession. This trumpet playing, tell me about it. Do you have to blow hard—like really hard?"

"Not so much. I'm classically trained. I know how to play without doing anything crazy."

"Like what would be crazy?"

"I've seen big band guys get dizzy or even pass out from blowing high notes."

"Interesting," Dr. Sands said, rubbing his chin.

"But I've never played much first trumpet, and now I mostly play bebop. You won't hear me playing too many high Cs."

"You say you were dizzy earlier, heart pounding and so on?" Dr. Sands asked.

"Yes," Ray answered.

"Mr. Machado, your blood pressure is dangerously high—160 over 115. Has anyone told you that you may have serious high blood pressure problems?"

"No. Well, I've hardly been to a doctor. I've been healthy," Ray said.

"I don't think that's true anymore. This trumpet playing is dangerous. You need to have a full battery of tests as soon as possible. Your resting pulse is very high—the blood pressure, the dizziness. You may even have heart damage. You may have to quit playing your instrument, Mr. Machado. Any vision problems lately?"

"Yeah, maybe." Ray started to become truly perturbed by this know-it-all.

"Like what?"

"Sometimes I see like stars or flashes. I thought it was in my head."

"Well, it is in your head. Your eyes are in your head and all this blowing pressure is causing eye problems. I believe you have a retinal tear in your left eye. We'd need to look at it with better instruments than what I have with me. Listen, I'm most concerned about the blood pressure and your heart. You need to see a cardiologist as soon as possible, hopefully tomorrow."

"We still have three more days at the Black Hawk, Doc. I have to play those or we lose a lot of money. It's a serious gig."

"Mr. Machado, have you been listening to me?" Dr. Sands insisted, staring intently at Ray and then swiveling for a few seconds toward Dorothy, hoping to enlist her support. "You look like you are healthy; you're a handsome, successful man and all that, but you're a ticking time bomb, to be blunt about it. If I were in charge of your welfare, I would forbid the trumpet for now. Take it away, lock it up. There's a name for what you've been doing to yourself, it's called the Valsalva maneuver. An Italian fellow in the 1600s named Antonio Valsalva discovered it."

"Yeah, so what is it?" Ray asked defiantly. "What's it got to do with playing the trumpet?"

"Oh, it doesn't have to be trumpet playing. It could be, pardon me, about straining one's body to try to force a bowel movement. You know, holding your breath and forcing down. That's the potty version of Valsalva. Your version is eminently more artistic. You professional trumpet players probably stoke up on air, hold it, then blast away. Am I right?"

"No, I don't do that!" Ray protested.

"You don't realize, even a split second of doing so strains the heart. The pressure from the left to the right chamber becomes dangerously unequal. Some people's hearts can take it, some can't. Do you know who King George the Second was?"

"I'm not sure, Doc," Ray answered.

"Well, George the Third was the King of Britain when we fought for our independence. George the Second was crazy George the Third's pappy, of course. I'm a history buff, medical and otherwise."

The phone rang, and Dorothy went to answer it. While the band was on break, Calvin was calling to find out how Ray was doing.

"By the time George the Second was sixty he was blind in one eye, hard of hearing, severely constipated, as well as gout-stricken due to his awful English diet," Sands continued. "One day he popped into the loo to do a poo. Well look, I made a rhyme!" He chuckled. "Anyway, he sat down on the porcelain throne, not his golden one, held his breath, grunted, pushed really hard, probably over and over, doing his royal version of the Valsalva maneuver, and right then and there burst his heart—aortic aneurysm. Totally blew it out. A quick death on the potty. Very dignified for a king, wouldn't you agree? Sorry, I am often in the habit of speaking in facetious tones. Interesting, eh?"

"I guess. So I should try not to poop, Doc?" Ray asked sarcastically. "Is that what I should do?"

"Well, just don't strain, lad, don't strain at it!" The doctor smiled.

"Duly noted. I'm sorry, I guess I was raised by savages."

"That's okay, I give all my patients little lessons like this. Ray, you've got symptoms like what killed George the Second. What are you going to do about it?"

"Okay, Doc, I get it. I'll get some tests. I promise."

"And you have to put the trumpet down. Now. Get the tests and then maybe pick it back up if the specialists clear you."

"I don't know… this is my life. Music is my life."

"It won't be your life if it winds up killing you. You may think you are indestructible, but I can assure you that you're not," Dr. Sands warned. "Ray, there's a book I love called *The Medieval Reader*. Big book, maybe five hundred pages with tiny type. It's all contemporary accounts about a smorgasbord of old stuff from the Dark Ages. A recipe for stuffed eels, how to burn a witch or draw and quarter a man, some folk remedies, firsthand accounts of famous battles—you get the idea. One chapter contains obituary notices from newspapers in merry old London. They're sad to read, especially the ones about children, but some are also funny in an Edmund Gorey sort of way. You know Gorey?"

"Yeah, sure. Spooky funny guy. He's in the papers, I think," Ray said.

"Yes, he's a master of what's called black humor. So here's one from the book. I've memorized a few to use as small talk at parties.

"'Julia Dovesmore, age thirteen, dared by her drunken Uncle Onslow to balance upon the top of a wall with her eyes closed, said wall being part of an enclosure within which were several recently captured wild boars, did lose her balance, fell into the filthy enclosure, and was devoured by the warty animals. Requiescat in Pacem, June 18th, 1599.'

"There's an interesting side note," Dr. Sands continued with a chuckle. "'The bishop of Warwickshire ordered the boars destroyed since placing their meat on the dining table would constitute what was then considered by the church to be a secondary level of cannibalism. The mischievous drunkard uncle was ordered to compensate the owner of the boars ten gold pieces!'"

"Okay, I get it. You got a knack for telling a story, but what's that got to do with me? Besides, it's getting late."

"Wait, there's one more—a short one, more modern, humbly composed just now by myself, based on Dickens.

"'*A Tale of Two Trumpeters* by Doctor Julius Sands. It was the best of times. It was the worst of times. Joshua fit the battle of Jericho. He blew his trumpet and the walls came a-tumblin' down. Ray Machado blew his trumpet. The people cheered at his art, but the high notes burst his poor heart. Requiescat in Pacem, 1961.' Get the drift?"

"Yeah, it wasn't so subtle. So go home now, you're up way too late. I'll get those tests when I get back to LA. That's where I live. I'm married to a movie star. It's a charmed life for me, Doc." Ray glanced over at Dorothy, whose expression indicated that she had been taking the doctor's words far more seriously than Ray had been.

Dr. Sands stood up, reached over and placed his right hand on Ray's shoulder for a moment, then touched and patted Ray's cheek as if he were blessing a small child. "Be safe, Mr. Machado. Be well and be safe." He then turned for the door.

CHAPTER TWENTY-ONE

October 2013

"What do you think, Amman? How does he look?"

"What you see is what you get, Kate. At least for now," replied Dr. Amman Vishwanathan, the expert veterinarian Mike and Kate had hired to oversee the animal revivification project. "This Mr. T of yours isn't quite ready for his next scene on *The A-Team*. But hey, nice of somebody to have shaved this guinea pig's head, chest, and abdomen in advance for us, huh?"

"The shaving? That was me—last century!" Chrissy announced as she entered the exam room to join everyone else, put on a hair net, and washed her hands. "I wanted to give him a little Mohawk like his namesake, but Enzo said no."

"Brownie points for you, Madame!" Amman said, giving a little salute. "Anyway, Kate, not much to tell right now. He's damn cold and stiff, obviously. I'm used to guinea pigs squirming like crazy when I try to treat them."

"Okay, Chrissy, document everything, all the usual parameters," Kate said. "And remember to X-ray him, too. Listen, people, we want to continue to catch everything we do here on tape, so try to not block the cameras with your body as you proceed. Everyone besides Chrissy come back in thirty minutes."

"So I'm curious." Amman was eager to chat more with Kate, since they had hardly had any one-on-one time since he had arrived, "I'm sure you had other qualified candidates for this job. I didn't ask you yet why you picked me."

"They gave me five names. While I was being a responsible professional and checking you all out the usual way, my goofy roommate just looked for your names on YouTube."

"Oh, I know where you're going with this."

"Yup. Over a million hits of you doing an emergency C-section on an elephant. I said right then and there—I want that guy! Besides, that Bollywood dance you and your assistant did as the credits rolled was awesome."

"I didn't post that thing, the Berlin Zoo community relations people did. It still seems weird that it went viral," Amman said.

"Well, they made it into a heartwarming feel-good story. The mom okay and the baby delivered healthy—a total success. They didn't show much blood and stuff, but I'm sure you must have been covered in it!"

"Yes, I was. By the way, I stayed a few extra days after the surgery and the mother elephant began recognizing me as a friend. When I went back six months later to see her and her baby, she came up to me and draped her trunk around me, hugging me. It was amazing."

"Wow. Well, I'm glad you're here—really glad."

"Well, Kate, speaking of amazing, your protocol is epic."

"We can call it epic when it's proven itself. It won't be long from now that you're going to be here bringing our furry friend back to life. The protocol is the prep work to get you and Mr. T. into that final scenario."

"Yup. I get to bat cleanup—bottom of the ninth."

"That's right, Amman. And I'm hoping we'll have a happy little critter eating, pooping, sleeping, and happily wiggling his nose as he runs around with glee. Chrissy has already spent her own money on a cage, food, some toys. She loves animals."

"Listen, I have to ask—I've been hearing conflicting stories. One guy I met said that your Dr. Saltieri killed himself, that he stepped in front of that truck on purpose. But that's not right, is it?"

"Where did you hear that, Amman?"

"When I first got here last week I parked in the wrong lot and there was a guy from your neighboring business who pointed me over this way. He's the one who said it. So he didn't have the correct story, right? I heard your doc had Alzheimer's and lung cancer. That's tough."

"Yes, he had both. He had been to Mexico looking at alternative cancer treatments. He started getting these ideas—pretty much obsessions—about putting himself in a tank of super-oxygenated water and slowing his heart rate and breathing rate to something like hibernation levels. Then, while he was floating in this tank there would be cancer-curing chemicals in the water solution, also vitamins and other things."

"That's wild."

"You bet. He studied the hibernation of turtles, under the mud at about four degrees Celsius. Well, three point nine to be exact. He was probably going to propose doing all this, but he never got the chance. One night Dr. Saltieri wandered off in the cold, broke through some ice on a lake. These people saw him out there and rescued him. They were getting all his wet clothes off of him, but they turned their back for a second. Right then he started going back over the road, said he was going back to the lake to see his friends he called them, dolphins and turtles apparently. According to the police report I read, he must have been in shock the whole time. He hadn't spoken a word to his rescuers until just then. A truck doing about sixty miles per hour hit him. He died instantly."

"The truck driver—was he okay?"

"Yes, thankfully. Poor guy. He had no chance to swerve and avoid hitting Dr. Saltieri, it happened so fast."

"So you combined some of these crazy ideas Saltieri had with your own, huh? That's a pretty fantastic mashup, Kate!"

"Well, all along I had been thinking that just thawing someone out and then zapping their heart wasn't going to work. I mean, it's too simple. No way could it be as easy as grabbing a pizza out of the freezer and slapping it into the microwave, right? Enzo and Mike, or any cryo lab out there drove so much moisture out of these bodies just to keep ice from expanding and causing damage—how could anyone expect essentially freeze-dried folks to come back to life when the time came? I was stumped. I had literally nothing. Then I had a moment of discovery, an epiphany while my roommate was playing a piece on her violin. I realized that I could adapt one of Enzo's alternative anticancer ideas—float the patient in a vitamin-enriched liquid environment, gradually hydrating and warming them. Plus a liquid environment can be controlled with more subtlety than what we could do in air, right? And they're kind of like in their mother's womb, sort of cradled in amniotic fluid all over again, get it? I started sketching out ideas and it all seemed to make sense. And by aiming initially at four point two degrees Celsius, which is just a little higher than Dr. Saltieri's hibernating turtles' body temperature, there's no chance of any early decomposition. We aim for that temperature and then continue on, quicker at the end."

"This sounds amazing, Kate. New ideas. Bravo!" Amman declared, scribbling down some notes for himself.

"There's more. My most radical idea, which I admit may mean nothing—all through the process we pulse sound waves at the rate a maternal heart would be beating. Of course for a guinea pig that will be faster than a human. I have this hunch that cells and organs know they're alive in a sense. I believe that they are at least partially sentient and can recognize the mother organism, and the most obvious stimulation we can give the cells is sound waves mimicking maternal heartbeats. As we try to revive the patient, that maternal heartbeat will be there constantly, and as we reach the last stages the stimulus will be especially important, uplifting the unconscious brain toward consciousness, awareness, and hopefully, full function. I got that uplift idea from the sci-fi book I showed you that Saltieri was obsessed by. Yes, I know it sounds new-agey crazy, but I'm doing it anyway. And then you enter the stage."

"It's brilliant, Kate. You're quite the free-thinker."

"Amman, do you know the book *Lives of a Cell* by Lewis Thomas? It's a book I read over and over as a teenager. That book inspired me to become a biologist. Living cells, whether you're exploring their reality or thinking metaphysically, are smarter, more connected to each other, and more aware than we give them credit for."

"Extremely interesting. I can see why you were hired for this job. And yes, I know the book. If this works you'll have page one headline news."

"Thank you, Amman. Of course we won't be telling anyone just yet. Our real goal is to revive humans, of course. There are some other interesting details. I believe Dr. Saltieri thought he could learn to breathe underwater, that or breathe ultraoxygenated water somehow. There were some scribbles that by doing this, more of the cancer medicine could get into his lungs and effect a cure. Weird."

"May I join the conversation," Norm asked, reentering the operating room.

"Sure," Kate said. "So, Norm, when you opened the pod, the inner one, what the heck was that?"

"That was pressurized helium. Did you like the little *whoosh* sound, or did it freak you out?"

"Yes, it totally freaked me out," Kate admitted, "and then the little vapor cloud hanging over Mr. T? For a second I thought it was his soul escaping from us. I'm like 'Mr. T don't go, we're here to save you!' Yeah, it was weird. Then I said to myself, stop thinking negative thoughts, you dummy."

Amman laughed. "You remind me of my grandmother back in New Delhi, Kate. She's so superstitious. When I laugh at her for it, she hits me. She's a tiny woman, but she packs a wallop!"

"Okay, Chrissy's done, folks are back. Here we go." Kate checked her watch, then turned toward the main camera and spoke slowly and clearly, reading from a script she had prepared:

"This is Katherine Pearson at ExitStrategy. The time is 10:43 a.m. October 21, 2013. We shall now proceed with our next step. Dr. Amman Vishwanathan is now placing a flotation device on the subject to keep his head above the water line so that fluid does not enter his lungs. In a moment, he will place the subject into the solution tank. The tank holds one hundred gallons of a special vitamin-enriched solution. The exact chemical composition of this saline solution is recorded in our files. The temperature is four point two degrees Celsius."

Kate paused while Amman lowered Mr. T. into the tank, adjusting the flotation device. Then she continued reading her script:

"The subject will remain in the tank for roughly seventy-two hours. The body temperature will rise slowly toward the temperature of the tank. Data leads are already attached to the subject's skin. At the forty-eight-hour mark, assuming we have sufficient warming of the body, special catheter devices will be installed through the urethra. These dual-purpose devices will provide temperature readings as well as deliver small amounts of extra warmth to the kidneys. We expect that proper kidney function may be a challenge, according to Dr. Amman Vishwanathan. We will also make small incisions in the abdomen to place heating devices there. Thus over the final twenty-four hours the conduction warming through the skin will be accompanied by internal warming of the core abdominal organs. Sound waves mimicking the sound in utero of a mother guinea pig's heartbeat will pulse constantly throughout the revivification process. In addition to the data collected electronically, the subject will be monitored around the clock by a staff member. This is the end of this portion of the procedure."

Kate folded up her script and everyone came over to shake her hand. There were no hugs yet. That would happen later, assuming success.

"And now we wait," Chrissy said.

"Yes. And now we wait," Kate echoed.

CHAPTER TWENTY-TWO

"Okay, everyone, it's almost time to proceed. I'm excited about how things are going so far," Kate said. "Right now, I'd like to introduce you to two new people in the room. First we have Dr. Ritika Pandey, Amman's surgical assistant from his practice in Boston. If you've seen the famous elephant C-section video, that's Ritika as his chief assistant." Ritika smiled shyly and waved her hand at Kate, Mike, Norm, Chrissy, Deirdre, and two lab assistants present, Nick Costas and Jeremy Palvar.

"Let me tell you that Ritika did as much or more than I did that day. It was a team effort," Amman said, smiling proudly at Ritika.

"Also," Kate continued, "I am thrilled to introduce my friend and research associate Dr. Edouard Radelet, with whom I have worked in designing new cancer cryoprocedures. As you know, Edouard will be our MD, working with me to develop a protocol for human revivification. Edouard is from Haiti and he's been leading a multinational initiative to close the enormous gap in health care between the have and have-not nations in the Caribbean. His passion for medicine and that winning smile of his has generated millions of dollars of donations for the cause from Fortune 500 corporations with Caribbean interests. He's finishing up that work and soon will be the health minister of Trinidad and Tobago. All this and he's still under forty! We'll have him for a few months while he is between those two jobs. Please welcome Edouard."

Everyone applauded. Mike walked over to give him an ultrafirm Cold Smokey Burgess handshake. Edouard was handsome and athletic, with a warm chestnut complexion and dark, piercing eyes.

"While most of you were sleeping," Kate said, "Amman, Ritika, and Chrissy were here getting Mr. T ready for the final step. I was here to observe and record. The internal data and warming leads are in place and the computer has been raising the heat of the solution in the tank. We are ready to go, right now."

Mike stood up and cleared his throat. "I want to thank everyone in this room and wish you good fortune, not good luck. I'm not a medical guy, but if there's anything I can do, let me know. I don't mind being a go-fer today for any of you!" Everyone smiled, then exited Kate's office and reconvened in the operating room, donning surgical gowns and masks before they entered.

"Okay, have we got our cameras on, Norm?" Kate asked.

"Yup, ready to go."

"Okay, Amman you are in charge. Everyone take your cue from Amman and Ritika, okay? Amman, we've got Dr. Radelet here plus lots of extra hands here if you need anything."

Amman took over. He spoke in a firm voice, narrating as he went through the procedure, cameras rolling. "All right, people. Mr. T is now up to thirty-five degrees Celsius. We've matched up his outer and core temps over the last few hours. I'm removing him now from the tank. Here we go. And now we'll place him on these towels to dry him. There we go—thank you, Dr. Pandey. Now fresh towels and the heating pads, please. Dr. Pandey, please remove the internal heating devices and sensors and let's recheck all the traditional leads: EEG, EKG, blood pressure, everything."

Ritika sprang into action. Kate had never seen anyone move so quickly. "Chrissy, are you getting standby readings on your equipment?" Ritika asked after a few moments.

"Yes, Ritika. Everything's good," Chrissy answered.

"Okay," Amman continued. "All we need is about two more degrees of warmth. He looks good, I see no visible problems or damage. First we will insert a breathing tube to ventilate the lungs, supplying oxygen when the time comes. Once we've got the centrifugal pump going we'll be removing cryosolution, and then we'll be creating normal flow of oxygenated blood. Later, once we've established a pulse, the pump will assist removal of carbon dioxide until we're certain he can breathe on his own. We will now make incisions to access his femoral arteries. The pumping cycle will begin on the left side and force the cryosolution out of the right artery. Dr. Saltieri's glycol-mix cryosolution has hopefully minimized damage to Mr. T during his years in cryo. By the time we've got that exchange completed, Mr. T will be at thirty-eight degrees and ready for chest compressions followed by defib. Got it?" Amman made sure that everyone was with him. He looked up at the camera and smiled, appearing cool and confident.

Kate was trying her best to emulate Amman's calm demeanor as he and Ritika started the procedure, but in truth her heart was pounding. She tried to breathe more deeply to see if that would help. Her tendency to let negative thoughts creep in got the better of her. What if the effort to revive Mr. T was an utter failure? Would a negative outcome that day be proof that the universe quite often loved to thumb its nose at human imagination and daring? Kate feared with all her soul the possibility that absolutely nothing would happen during the revival process, that Mr. T would just lie there like a blob or roadkill, or even worse, like some fuzzy stuffed toy mocking them. But, she thought, what if they at least got a spark? A heartbeat, some EEG activity, anything that would give them hope.

"Okay, we are ready to go to our final stage," Amman announced about twenty minutes later. "All leads attached, body temperature is thirty-eight degrees, cryosolution out and blood already circulating via the centrifugal pump. His lungs and all passageways are clear. Dr. Radelet, would you free Dr. Pandey and me up a little and call out vitals for us when you get them. Do you mind? And now, Mr. Burgess and Miss Pearson, I am now going to bring your Mr. T back to you. I hope you like pets!"

"You bet!" Mike said, smiling broadly.

Amman began with chest compressions, about two per second, using his fingertips on the tiny animal. After about two minutes, he traded off with Ritika, in order to avoid fatigue in his hands.

"What's going on, Amman?" Mike asked, concerned that nothing seemed to be happening.

"Standard procedure, Mike. Don't worry. This is just our starting point."

Ritika kept pumping away, her compressions intended to simulate the natural coughing mechanism and its effect on the heart. "That's two minutes," she announced.

"Okay, I'm taking back over, get the small dose epinephrine ready," Amman said.

Kate couldn't help herself, her whole body was becoming more and more tense. She found herself trying to breathe for Mr. T as Amman and Ritika did their work.

"All right, dose number one epinephrine administered," Ritika announced. Amman continued his compressions. "Recheck the breathing tube, Amman."

Amman stopped for a moment to double-check everything. "We're good. No problem there. Moving on. Okay, Mike, now we bring out the artillery." Amman tweaked the knobs of his favorite veterinary defibrillator, a bright yellow state-of-the-art machine he knew inside and out. He had brought it with him all the way from Boston. He picked up the small defib paddles, then turned and locked eyes with each person in the room, one by one, gaining their full attention. Kate's maternal heartbeat sound waves continued to fill the air.

"All right, here we go. Three joules to start." After Ritika applied gel to Mr. T's chest, Amman picked up the paddles and positioned them, then simultaneously pressed the start buttons on each paddle with his thumbs. *Zap.* And... nothing... nothing. Everyone studied Amman. He was breathing deeply, almost as if he was willing his patient to copy him. To have a heartbeat, to fill his lungs, to live again. Amman didn't look up, his focus was only on Mr. T. "Moving up to five joules. Here we go." He repeated the process and everyone in the room held their breath. Zap. And... nothing... nothing... nothing again.

"Dr. Pandey, inject the second dose of epinephrine," Amman instructed. "He's a stubborn little guy, but I know he can do it. He's coming back, people. Lord Dhanvantari and I can feel it."

Ritika injected the stimulant, an amount so small a person would hardly even notice it, but for the little guinea pig this was a healthy dose, much bigger than the dose they had first administered.

"Here we go. Seven joules." Amman once again centered his breathing. He placed the paddles and applied the shock again. Zap.

Beep... beep... beep....

Then nothing.

"You had it!" Radelet yelled. "Those were heartbeats. They were. I know it."

"You're right," Ritika said. "Amman, you almost got him back. Ten joules?"

"Too high, Ritika, we'll fry him. Maybe eight? And we can't give him any more epinephrine. So now the joules are the only chance we have. Ready, everyone?" They all nodded, some staring intently at Amman, the others at the motionless Mr. T.

"Okay, double-check that cart. Is everything there? Lidocaine, yes? Okay, we're going to get him this time. Here goes." While Ritika applied more gel to Mr. T, Amman reached for a different set of paddles, then moved the dial on the machine one more notch to eight joules. He brought the paddles to Mr. T's chest. Then zap. Still nothing. Kate's heart was sinking.

"Again, Amman, again, Come on, do it!" Mike yelled.

"This is it, people. One more try. Here we go!" Amman declared.

Zap! The blast of eight joules of hair-raising electricity jolted the body into the air. Everyone gasped. Then they heard it—the magic sound.

Beep... beep... ...beep... beep... beep-beep... ...beep... ...beep... beep... beep-beep... beep... beep... beep... beep... beep... beep... beep...

"We've got him! He's alive! Listen, he's trying to breathe," Kate yelled, noticing the little snuffles and gasps the pig was emitting. Amman and Ritika swung into warp speed, while Edouard yelled out blood pressure and heart rate numbers. Mr. T's heart and lungs were struggling to coordinate—to establish a rhythm, to live again. Amman, not satisfied with the halting breaths, administered chest compressions, far more gentle this time, while Ritika double-checked the blood gas monitors. Oxygen was going in and carbon dioxide out, everything as it should be. Soon Mr. T's breathing became fairly regular.

"Dr. Pandey, be ready with that lidocaine. I don't want him to lose this rhythm. Sure it's fluttering a lot but for now it's damn good, huh?" Amman said to Edouard, a huge grin on his face.

"Damn straight," Edouard answered. "So, eight joules on that little body? That's interesting. I'm glad you didn't go wild and give him eighty!"

"Blood pressure now?" Amman asked Ritika, who had taken over reading the data.

"It's up and down, but nothing too crazy. Maybe it will stabilize soon. Not sure. Do we need the lidocaine?"

"No, he's fine for now, at least. The flutter is going away, see? We'll just keep watching. And we've definitely got ROSC."

"All that epinephrine and he's still just lying there? What do you think of that?" Kate asked. "Oh I'm sorry, I should shut up, right?"

"He's okay. Look at those vitals," Amman said, nodding his head toward the monitors. "ROSC is *return of spontaneous circulation*, Kate. It's a very good thing. His heart and lungs are ready to do all the work now. There are some crazy swings in the readings but there's nothing there that says we're going to lose him in the next few minutes. He may be close to normal soon. The epinephrine dosage was normal, Kate. The joules were a different story, but, hey, sometimes you do what you gotta do, right? Anyway, Mr. T will wake up when he's ready, my dear

Miss Pearson. Guinea pigs sleep a lot. Trust your friendly veterinarian, okay?"

"For sure, Amman," Kate said. "I wasn't doubting you. I study cells of creatures, you operate on them. What do I know?"

"Look at that EEG, people. Pretty damn nice. He's got brain function. Oh my! Look, his heartbeat is synching with Kate's synthesized mommy guinea pig beat, what do you know?" Amman grinned at Kate as he removed the breathing tube. Everyone stood and watched the EEG and all the other screens, readouts, blips and bleeps. This little piggy was alive and looking good—no big bad wolf was lurking close by. "Put a little blanket on him. I want to keep him nice and warm. Twenty-some years—that's a long time to be chillaxing, right?" Everyone laughed, then realized that they could relax now, shake hands and congratulate each other. Mike pulled out his cell phone to call Franklin with the good news.

Amman put on his stethoscope and listened to Mr. T's heart. Finding nothing wrong, he entertained his audience with guinea pig trivia. "Some of you don't know much about these little fuzzballs, but I am here to tell you that they are wondrous creatures. They share a lot of design with humans, and that's why they're such a valuable lab animal. And of course, nowadays, lab animals don't have the awful life they used to have. We vets were instrumental in pushing for reforms, but hardly anyone knows. Vitamin C was discovered through research on guinea pigs. Working on them helped further the development of a whole bunch of vaccines. Even such amazing things like replacement heart valves, and our modern anticoagulants and asthma medicine were brought to you by these guys. So anyway, I'm really pleased with everything I'm seeing here. He looks great. And you all are a great team. Thank you so much. But Kate is scared of how sleepy he is. How about we check for some reflexes to prove he's really got the brain function the EEG equipment says he has. And maybe he'll wake up and play with you, right, Kate?"

"Yes, right, Amman," Kate said, feeling a bit picked on.

"Okay, let's see… how about you, Mike? You can do an easy reflex test that will probably even work on a sleeping guinea pig. Wanna try it, big guy?"

Mike stepped forward. "Sure. What do I do?"

"Well, guinea pigs have awesome ears, inside and out. Great hearing and very sensitive to the touch. And they are really similar to human ear design and function. The first success in regrowing stereocilia, that's inner-ear hair cells, was in guinea pigs a few years ago, meaning we might have a way to reverse hearing damage if we can develop it for humans. Just pinch the edge of his outer ear for a second. Give it a good pinch." Mike did. Mr. T jerked a little, then went back to snoozing.

"There you go. Classic pig response. He's awesome." Amman beamed at Ritika as he removed all the leads attached to Mr. T.

"But still asleep," Deirdre said mock-glumly, giving Kate a funny look as she said it.

"Okay, then, Kate, your turn. Next is the Preyer reflex, a test for deafness. Give a little whistle right by his ear and you'll probably see his outer ear move, like maybe even wiggle. It's a fun reflex to watch." Kate stepped forward and bent down. She gave a soft whistle and sure enough, even though Mr. T sure looked totally asleep, the ears wiggled.

"That's cool!" she said and stepped back.

"No, Kate, I don't think we got the full response. Whistle louder," said Amman. She whistled louder and got the same response.

"Hmm, that doesn't seem right." Amman appeared concerned. He hovered over the animal, checking him over again. Kate began to worry. Was there something wrong with Mr. T?

A few minutes went by as Amman continued to check the animal. Now everyone was looking worried. "Let's try the whistle with something added and see what happens," Amman said.

Clap! went Amman, slapping his palms together loudly while giving a shrieking whistle. Simultaneously the whole team jumped in surprise as Mr. T leaped into the air, opened his eyes, and started running wildly around the table. Everyone yelled and laughed.

"Catch him, catch him!" Nick yelled.

"He's gonna run off the table. Quick, keep him from going over!" Norm said.

All Kate could do was laugh at this little circus act. The whole team jabbered away as they tried to catch Mr. T. Finally Chrissy got hold of him and petted him, calming him. The Amman and Mr. T show was a huge hit. Things settled down and then all eyes were on Amman.

"Amman, you could have scared him to death," Kate accused.

"No, I think you might have that totally backward, Katherine." Amman winked. "I scared him to *life*, you might say."

"How did you know he was okay enough that you could pull off that crazy trick?" Chrissy asked, continuing to stroke a now very relaxed and happy Mr. T.

"Ten minutes ago," Amman said, "when I first examined him really closely after the defib, I could see he was in REM sleep. His little eyes were moving about under his eyelids. Also, his little nose was twitching a tiny bit. I think he was having a nightmare about how bad your lab smells with some of the chemicals you have in here. He'd rather have sweet dreams about the scents of carrots and lettuce."

"So all that reflex testing stuff was a big gag at our expense?" Mike asked.

"Yes, sorry. I couldn't resist it. Didn't you call any of the personal references I listed? The first thing they, or Ritika for that matter, would have warned you about me is that I am the world's biggest practical joker!"

CHAPTER TWENTY-THREE

The next morning Kate, Amman, Ritika, and Edouard began their day with a visit to their furry little patient. Chrissy was fussing over him as he sat in his cage chewing on some shredded carrots, wiggling his little nose and whiskers. She was assigned to chart his health and behavior and had been with Mr. T almost nonstop.

"Look, y'all, he's such a sweet little guy." Chrissy smiled, obviously very happy with her new pet.

"You might not know this," Edouard said, "but in much of South America, guinea pigs are served up grilled or roasted on a spit, Chrissy. A low carbon footprint source of protein. You're not hungry right now, are you?"

"You're barking up the wrong tree, Edouard," Amman advised. "You can't tease Chrissy. You'll never get a rise out of her. Believe me, I've tried since the day I got here."

"That's right. And if you try to roast Mr. T, I might roast all of *you*," Chrissy said, sticking her tongue out.

"Okay, everyone—relax," Amman said. "We just want to look him over. Do we have your permission?"

"Yes, of course." Chrissy stepped back from the cage.

Amman stepped forward to watch Mr. T for a while. He took him out of the cage and checked him over. He seemed satisfied. "As soon as he poops we'll be looking at that. He's been eating a lot, right?"

"For sure," Chrissy answered. "Don't worry, he's gonna have some little pellets for you sometime soon."

"And we'll draw blood now. I also want to hook him up and see that EEG again. We'll do a few more tests, too. Say about one p.m., okay?"

"So what do you think of him, Amman, now that he's been with us for a day?" Kate asked.

"Well, I definitely think he's a guinea pig, just not as cold as before. That I'm pretty confident of. So he was on that TV show in the 1980s, right? *The A-Team*? I've never seen it, though. What other animals were on that show?"

"Very funny, Amman, very funny!"

* * *

"Kate, do you have a minute?" Amman asked, stopping by her office later that afternoon.

"Sure, what is it?"

"We're running a full battery of bloodwork tests. Also, our guy pooped. We'll be able to look at his blood chemistry, enzyme levels, and lots more. Now it's our turn to digest things, sift through the info he's giving us. Lots of good stuff going on. So, you've got the old charts and info on this animal, right? Cause of death back in 1987? Can you pull all those files back out for me? Also, bring me all the documentation Chrissy made—especially the X-rays she took right before we revived him. I think maybe what your charts say about this guinea pig and what I just noticed when I examined him don't match up." Edouard was passing by and popped into the room to join them.

"Here, Amman, here's everything. It's been on my desk all week." Kate waved the binder that held everything they had on Mr. T.

"That's everything? Right there? And you're sure it's this animal, correct?"

"Yes, it's him. Here's a photo. His markings are pretty unique and it's his gosh darn file, I'm sure. It's all right here. What on earth are you up to?"

"There's film here, right?" Amman asked. "X-rays of tumors? Let's look at them again."

Kate dug into the file and pulled out six X-rays taken a day before Mr. T's cryo procedure in 1987. They walked into the lab and threw the first one up on the illuminator.

"Okay, look, tumors, a bunch of them as described in the file in that horrible scrawly handwriting," Amman said. "Look at them—big, little—scattered all over the abdomen."

"Yes, so what?" Edouard asked.

"Throw the next one up, Kate," Amman said impatiently. "Okay, now here is the best view of the tumors on the spine, see? Also described in the file. Look—one, two, three in a row. Then a gap and then that large one there, see?" he asked, pointing them out for Kate.

"And the other X-rays?" Edouard asked.

"They're just slightly different views of the two you just saw," Kate said. "These are the two best views of the tumors. I'm not a doctor, but believe me, I've looked at these a lot. Don't forget, I've been here months longer than you guys."

"Kate, hand me the X-rays that Chrissy just did. Let's look at them."

Kate gave Amman the X-rays and he threw them up on the illuminator. "See here? Nothing! He looks totally normal. All the tumors are gone. Every single one of them. Do you see?"

"That can't be," Kate protested. "I know this is Mr. T and these are his files. Can either of you detect anything that would tell you that we're looking at the wrong X-rays from the past? That the old film is a different animal?"

"Actually, comparing them I would say without a doubt that it is the same animal," Edouard said. "Look here, Amman. He had a broken tibia at some point. Agreed?" Amman nodded. "It's the same on both sets of film. It healed kind of weird, notice? It's clearly the same animal."

Amman scurried toward the lab with Kate and Edouard following. "Good timing. He's asleep. All right, Dr. Radelet, gently palpate this patient and please update the status of the tumors we just looked at. These tumors right here," he said, shaking the film from 1987 and jabbing at it with his index finger.

Kate unhooked the top of the cage and lifted it off, which allowed Edouard access with both hands to the drowsy guinea pig. He methodically felt Mr. T's abdomen, attempting to find the tumors they had seen on the X-ray.

"They're gone, I think, Amman," Edouard declared, shaking his head in disbelief. "I can't find a single one of them, and from the film it looks like they should be easy to find. Some of them near the skin surface should even be easy to see."

"Right!" Amman said. "They've vanished. They're all gone!"

Kate whistled, and Amman shot her a look. "Don't whistle near the patient, Kate. Remember the Preyer reflex?"

"Sorry, couldn't help it."

"What's going on, you guys?" Chrissy asked, approaching the group. "Is there something wrong?"

"Chrissy, something is right, but it makes no sense. Watch," Amman said. "Now, Edouard, the spinal tumors. Those you should easily be able to feel since there's no fat there to get in the way of locating them, right? That big one we saw on the film—if that's not there I'm going to faint."

"Right." Edouard began probing along Mr. T's spine. Mr. T kept slumbering through all the pushing and prodding. "Lord in heaven, Amman, there's nothing there, absolutely nothing," he said, dumbfounded. "All the tumors are gone. Amazing! But *how?*"

CHAPTER TWENTY-FOUR

November 2013

Word spread quickly throughout the building, even to the people watching over A.C. Nielsen—somehow cryo had cured Mr. T's cancer tumors from 1987. But how in the world was that possible? No one knew the answer. Amman and Ritika, with Kate's help, kept studying Mr. T day and night, combing their data for anything that might tell them more. Meanwhile, Mr. T kept on wiggling and piggling away. Ritika eventually had to return to Boston, and Edouard would leave soon for a week or two in the Caribbean, so most of the continuing work fell on Amman. Chrissy had already taught Mr. T a few tricks to the amazement of everyone. He was the number one attraction at ExitStrategy—so much so that Mike had to occasionally shoo people away and yell at them to get back to their actual work.

Despite these happy times, Amman had found some issues that weren't to his liking. He kept these to himself for a while, waiting to gather evidence to confirm or deny them before he told anyone else his concerns. Norm happened upon him once, as Amman stared almost cross-eyed at some EEG readouts, drumming his fingers for minutes on end. When Norm asked if he was okay, Amman snapped out of his trance but looked troubled. Norm decided to not press the issue, figuring that perhaps Amman was simply sleep-deprived. However, this all came to a head three weeks after Mr. T had rejoined the living.

One morning, Amman entered ExitStrategy with a newly arrived guest from San Francisco, a veterinarian named Dr. John Shipley, who had attended grad school at Cornell's revered veterinary program with Amman. Amman had asked Mike and Kate to let him bring in Shipley as a consultant. Amman and Shipley disappeared into Amman's temporary office and were holed up in there for hours. Kate wondered what was going on, but left them alone. Amman finally emerged, looking exhausted. He walked into the lab and sat down beside Mr. T's cage. Mr. T was hard at work rearranging his wood chips for the seventh time that day. Amman stared at Mr. T for what seemed like forever. Kate noticed him there but held back—she could see that something was bothering him. Shipley entered the room and stood quietly by Kate. She finally broke Amman out of his trance.

"So what do we know, Amman?"

"What I've always told you, Kate. He's a guinea pig."

"Right. And you brought him back to life," she said gently.

"Yes, the whole team did. It wasn't just me."

"True, but you were the one with all the training, all the knowledge."

"Yes, and Ritika, too." Amman kept staring at Mr. T, not even looking up at Kate. Finally, he stood up and walked back to his temporary office. Kate looked to Shipley, who just stared back at her without expression. Amman returned to the lab with his laptop and brought up the report he and Shipley had created for Kate and Mike to read.

"Kate, come over here, look at this—page one, page two, page three, and so on. This could be any guinea pig in the world."

Kate squinted at the data and charts. "That's good, Amman. We want him to be like all the other guinea pigs, right?"

"Here—" He stood. "—take my seat. Go ahead and keep scrolling." Amman started pacing the room slowly. Meanwhile, Shipley remained like a statue, expressionless. Kate kept reading and scrolling. As she went through more and more pages her face lost its luster, and her usual cheerful smile turned into a frown. At page forty, Shipley's observations as an expert in mammalian behavior appeared. Over the past week Amman had sent him hours and hours of video footage of Mr. T, and Shipley had summarized his observations for inclusion in the report. Kate read on about ten more pages. "That's far enough, Katherine. Just technical-shmechnical stuff there now. Go ahead and skip to page seventy-five. There's a fairly succinct summary there," Amman said softly.

Kate found page seventy-five and read more slowly, mouthing each word. When she finished she took a moment to steel herself before she spoke.

"Amman, thank you. Dr. Shipley, thank you for reviewing this case and sharing your expertise with us. We really appreciate it."

"You're welcome, Miss Pearson. I'm sorry," he said.

"Shall I call Mike in, Amman?" Kate said.

"Yes, I think so," he replied. "But better yet, why don't you get everyone in here? We'll tell them all together."

"We could do that. Almost everyone is here now. I can get the rest of them here by one this afternoon."

"Let's do that, then," Amman said, placing his hand gently on Kate's shoulder. "I'm sorry, too, Kate. I never expected this."

CHAPTER TWENTY-FIVE

At one p.m. on the dot, Mike entered the lab, looking very anxious. The rest of the employees had arrived, sensing something important was about to be revealed. Kate noticed that Miles, the odd dude from A.C. Nielsen's apartment, was there as well. *Guess he's curious about what's going on*, she thought. She had become so focused on her lab work over the last number of months that she hardly remembered what his face looked like. She did, however, remember his brash attitude.

Amman and Shipley entered the room and Kate got right to business. "Thank you all for being here. Today we have a guest from San Francisco, Dr. John Shipley. Amman and he earned their advanced veterinary degrees together at Cornell, the best vet school in the country, I'm told. Amman and Dr. Shipley have been reviewing Mr. T's case for the last week via e-mail and Skype. Dr. Shipley has been helping interpret Mr. T's well-being since his expertise is in animal behavior. Amman, please go ahead."

"Hello, everyone. First I want to tell you what incredible things you've done here lately. I've never been on a team of people with so many amazing and quite diverse backgrounds."

"They are a heck of a Venn diagram, that's for sure!" Kate said, attempting to lessen the tension building in the room.

"Think about it, folks—we're pioneering in areas where most would fear to tread," Amman continued. "We've brought an animal back to life. He's right here in this room with us and he's been here for three weeks already. We've proven that Mike and Dr. Saltieri were right, that it can be done. We also seemed to have stumbled upon a possible cure for cancer. That alone is beyond incredible, and there are probably years of research that could come out of that. You have an amazing young leader in Katherine Pearson and an inspirational, visionary founder in Mike Burgess, but now a very large challenge has presented itself here. We know that Mr. T stabilized quickly. By the second day he seemed pretty normal. But on that day I thought his EEG looked a bit unusual. I gave it some time, checking twice a day to see what would happen. Well, every few days it looked more and more odd, but I still just thought it might have had something to do with the fact that he had been frozen so long, that his system still had some kinks. However, as time has passed the EEG has become much worse, I'm sorry to say. Mr. T's brain is damaged. The damage is progressive. He has two to six weeks to live. There is no known cure for his condition." Everyone in the room gasped and looked around at each other, stunned.

"He looks fine. How sick can he be?" Chrissy said, trying to fight back tears.

"Amman and I are sorry to bring you this news, but you have to be scientists here," Shipley said, jumping in. "If any of you have fallen into this trap, you really have to stop thinking of him as your pet."

"So what's wrong with him?" Mike asked grimly.

"Like I said, his brain is not functioning properly," Amman began. "It's in rapid deterioration. He will start sliding more and more and you'll see the progression plainly every few days. Here, take a look at this EEG printout Dr. Shipley brought in of a normal guinea pig, and then look at Mr. T's." They watched intently as Shipley showed the comparison. "Do you see the little rapid zigs and zags in Mr. T's EEG? This is from week one. And here's a sample from week two. More zigs and zags and far more frequently. And here's today—quite pronounced, you see?"

"Now take a look at this video I prepared," said Shipley as he opened his laptop. Everyone gathered around. "Guinea pigs wiggle a lot, right? Here is a healthy guinea pig wiggling around, eating and drinking, moving about in his cage." After two minutes Shipley closed the video. "Now next, this is Mr. T from this morning." Shipley started the second video. "Notice anything?"

"No, not really." Chrissy said. "They look the same to me."

"I can't see anything either." Deirdre shrugged. "Maybe I'm stupid."

"No, you're not," Shipley said patiently. "Pretend you aren't expecting a guinea pig to be such a wiggler and watch it now in slow motion." Shipley ran back to the beginning of Mr. T's behavioral video and set it to play in slow motion. Suddenly it was obvious—Mr. T wasn't wiggling, he was convulsing. It didn't appear normal at all when viewed in slo-mo. Now that Amman and Shipley had sharpened their eyes, everyone in the room could see the pronounced difference between the healthy pig and Mr. T. They all nodded to Shipley—now they saw it.

"What do you think, Dr. Radelet? Diagnosis?" Amman asked.

"Wait, I'm thinking, I'm thinking," Edouard said, cradling his head in his hands and concentrating. A few seconds later, "It's something neurological, obviously. I can't pin it down. Give me a minute."

"Take your time. We know you're not a veterinarian. Anyone else—ideas?"

Edouard was still deep in thought, his eyes rolling up toward the ceiling now and then, in concentration. "I've got it. It's progressive myoclonus epilepsy."

"No, Edouard, but yes, the EEG would look similar," Amman conceded. "Anyone else?"

An unexpected voice in the back of the room leaped out. "It's sporadic prion disease, similar to mad cow disease!" All heads whipped around to see who had spoken. It was, to their great collective surprise, Miles, the geek from the A.C. Nielsen apartment. "Prion disease—proteins folding over on themselves and destroying their own function, deforming and encouraging other proteins to fold over in the brain, too. The brain goes haywire and destroys itself. The rapid EEG zigs and zags are the signal of chronic myoclonic jerks caused by the progressive brain damage."

"Please, somebody slow down and tell me what the hell is going on," Norm pleaded.

"Norm, have you ever had a massive spasm or jerk in your body just as you almost drifted off to sleep?" Miles asked. "I think we all have them. That's called a hypnic jerk, which is a type of myoclonic jerk. Some people say the hypnic jerk, the one, like I say, where you jolt as you fall asleep, is a survival tool from our past. Like 'Hey, don't fall asleep too fast, Mr. Caveman. Take another look outside your cave and make sure some saber tooth tiger isn't about to eat you,' that kind of thing. In modern humans, myoclonic jerks happening quite frequently can be a sign of Parkinson's, Alzheimer's, and some forms of epilepsy. You're correct there, of course, Dr. Radelet. It's generally a sign of a damaged brain. A jerk just now and then is fine, as you all probably think I'm one and you only see me now and then." Miles paused as people chuckled. "But you can see Mr. T has them all the time. It's a symptom of the prion-created brain damage. And just so you know, myoclonic jerks are part of the puzzle on the second episode of the first season of *House*, the TV show. There they are a sign of subacute sclerosing panencephalitis, which is a persistent measles infection in children, usually fatal. But I don't think Mr. T has the measles." Everyone stared at Miles as if he were from some other planet where somehow everyone is a master medical diagnostician. "Hey, when I'm at home I don't watch *Happy Days* or *Mork and Mindy* all the time." He shrugged. Everyone chuckled. Now it made sense. The supergeek was also, apparently, an *idiot savant* riffing at them from an old episode of *House, M.D.*

"Very interesting, Miles," Amman said, "and also quite accurate. Remarkable employee, Mike! Miles has conjectured correctly. This particular prion disease we're looking at is not the mad cow variety or the chronic wasting disease you see in large animals like elk. Not that there's that much difference. Either way the brain loses function quickly. All those proteins folding over cause cellular damage and holes all over the brain. We call it spongiform encephalopathy because the normally compact brain looks, under a microscope, spongy where the holes start appearing. The abnormal EEG and the associated myoclonic jerks I first noticed are early signs of the disease. I'm sorry I took so long to put it together. It wasn't something I would have expected to pop up. It's amazing that your Miles recognized it so easily. Kudos to you, sir. Anyway, look at this photograph—I'll pass it around for each of you to get a good look. This is severely damaged brain tissue in the later stages of the disease so that you can see what we mean by spongiform. See all the holes, the dark spots?"

"Wow, look at that," Norm gasped, examined the photo closely, then handed it to Mike. "That looks bad."

"So what causes these diseases?" Mike asked.

"The mad cow form is transmitted through contaminated animal feed, or in a lab due to poor attention to cleanliness," Amman explained. "It can be transmitted via contaminated surgical equipment and so on. But Shipley and I are pretty sure that this is the other form, the sporadic version that Miles mentioned, where the source of the prion problems is completely unknown. In this form, the prion attack is similar to how viruses attack the body. In fact, for years researchers thought a virus was at work. But prions aren't viruses, they're proteins. We all have proteins in our bodies and some of us may have a few of these mutant proteins, the prions, inside us, too. They're out in the natural world as well, even just laying around in the earth's soil. They're proteins with a demented, super-nasty streak."

"Without quibbling too much right now about these details, people," Kate said earnestly, "the main point is that we have a patient with some form of prion disease leading soon to death. That much is certain."

"Hang on. I'm still catching up, Kate." Mike fiddled with a pencil and a spiral notebook. "I'm not a biologist or a doc, remember? Prion, how do you spell that?"

"P-R-I-O-N, Mike, rhymes with *neon*," Kate said. "We'll take a day or two and get everyone up to speed on prion diseases, mad cow, the whole nine yards. We'll compile a *Prion Diseases for Dummies*."

"Here's a factoid for you all," Miles chimed in again from the back of the room. "In humans it's called Creutzfeldt-Jakob disease. People go from normal, to messed up, to dead very quickly. In diagnosis, CJD can be confirmed by biopsy of the tonsils, since they harbor a significant amount of the PrPSc prions, thus distinguishing the CJD from other suspects such as Alzheimer's. Oh, and cannibals can get it, too. From eating damaged brains—yum. Hannibal Lecter be warned!"

"And all that was on *House*, too?" Shipley asked.

"No, it's just stuff I know. Mr. Burgess knows where I get all this," Miles said cryptically.

"So, what I want to know is, are we in danger?" Norm asked. "Is this contagious? That's not something I want to deal with."

"No, Norm," Amman assured, "it's not easily transmissible in humans or from animals to humans. Most forms happen out of nowhere. The sporadic version most likely is genetic. But we're not totally sure of that. It's a strange disease presenting in multiple forms and we really know very little about it."

"And a cure? Did you say we can't save Mr. T?" Chrissy asked.

"There's no cure, Chrissy," Shipley said. "It's a degenerative disease. Once you have it, it's all downhill. No cure for animals, nor for humans. Some people are hunting for one, but so far, little progress has been made. Some people think there may be an environmental issue involved. Anyway, Mr. T will soon convulse more than ever. It will progress to where he will look like he's having severe grand mal epileptic seizures. After that subsides he'll become listless, lose his appetite, lose his sense of direction and balance, become zombie-like, and die as his brain commits suicide in front of your eyes. I know some of you have become attached to your patient, but you must let go of that. He won't be in any pain during any of this. Now is when we put on our lab coats and study him and learn. And, remember, who knows where this came from. Maybe he already had this disease before he was frozen. It's likely this has nothing to do at all with the cryo process. But you must research all that. By the way, I like Miles' tonsil idea. We should biopsy them and also run him through the MRI in the other room. What do you say, Amman?"

"Right—great idea. Prions are everywhere, keep in mind. We don't think about them until they malfunction within the brain and we become aware of them. We don't know much about why they do this folding over of their material and how or why they encourage other proteins to do the same. But I am going to assume that all of you will be prion disease experts very soon."

"It sounds like Miles already is," Mike said. "Thanks for joining us, Miles. I thought you might be interested in this."

"Thanks for inviting me, Mr. Burgess."

"'Thanks for inviting me,' he says?" Kate mumbled to herself. *Yu-Gi-Oh tournament dude Miles standing there in the torn Whitesnake T-shirt? Mike invited him to show up? Really? Wow, I never—totally never saw that coming.*

CHAPTER TWENTY-SIX

May 1990

"Hello?"

"It's me—geez, this cell signal is crap. Anyway, I'm here. I found him. You'll never believe it, that shit old hippy Volkswagen bus of his is sitting in the side yard. It's rusting away like it always was. He must have hauled it two thousand miles just to watch it rust some more. Crazy."

"That's funny. This whole idea of yours is pretty epic karma. You're a genius."

"Ha, that's what they always call *you*. Anyway, I'm gonna ring the bell in a sec. Let's hope he likes the plan. I can't see how he wouldn't, right?"

"Right. He'd by crazy not to. You're not going to mention you-know-who right away, are you?"

"No, of course not. But it will be interesting to see his reaction when I get to that, don't you think?"

"For sure. Say hi for me and call back when you're done, okay?"

"Okay, bye!"

* * *

"Oh my God! Look who the cat dragged in! How did you find me?"

"It wasn't too hard. I just asked around. You know, people in the biz."

"Come in, come in. Here, sit down."

"Thanks, so... Iowa? Why exactly Iowa—Mason City? And isn't this where *The Music Man* was filmed or something?"

"My parents left New York City and settled here, not really sure why. I went to high school here, but I didn't fit in very well. Anyway, Music Man was based on Meredith Willson's childhood here in Iowa, but it was filmed in LA. Of course, you should know that, right? My sister is out back with her two granddaughters. We'll let them keep playing, okay?"

"Sure. No problem."

"So what in Sam Hill are you doing here?"

"Well, I heard you were sick. I can tell—you don't look too good. Hope you don't mind me saying it. We were always straight with each other, right?"

"Yes, true. So you're still in La-La Land? Working?"

"No, those days are over. But it was fun, wasn't it?"

"You bet. So what brings you here? Why are you looking up old friends? Got something to sell me? A vacuum cleaner? Hey, I know. Maybe you're the new Fuller Brush man!"

"Ha, no. Well, come to think of it, maybe I do have something to sell you. That would be one way to put it."

"Okay, pretend you're Willy Loman and give me the pitch."

"Sure. Well, like I said, I heard you're pretty sick. Word travels in LA."

"Yes, real sick. Lung cancer. Should never have started smoking, I guess. And you see how skinny and yellow I am? Got stomach and liver problems. Cirrhosis—too much drinking. And to think I was such a model of moderation when I was younger. Anyway, I've got about a month now, something like that. There's nothing anyone can do about my condition."

"And you're okay with that? You don't act too worried."

"Sure, I'm worried. All those two orphan girls out back have are me and my sister. Her daughter Grace and her husband were killed in a car crash last year. Damn drunk driver. Of course, he lived. The drunk drivers always walk away from the crash, dammit. When I die I don't know what's going to happen. We don't have much money at all."

"Yeah, that's what I figured and it's why I'm here. Say, can I get a glass of something to drink?"

"I've got some lemonade. No hard stuff anymore. I do miss that at times. All the carousing and drinking you and I used to do. Remember?"

"Sure, I remember those days. They were pretty friggin' epic, right? So listen close now. What if I told you that you don't have to die?"

"I'd say you're fucking nuts, pretty much fucking cuckoo, but go on, keep talking. I can hear you from here in the kitchen."

"And what if I said that I have some money laying around that I could put in your sister's name for those girls out back. And there'd be some for you, too. But you'd have to wait awhile to get yours."

"Here's your lemonade. It's from a mix, nothing fancy. Wait a second, so what did you just say? I have to wait for this miracle money? Wait how long? I'm dying, man."

"No, you aren't going to die. *Not going to*. Understand? The girls can have their money as needed for school and whatever. But you yourself might have to wait fifteen or twenty years to get your money. It'll be worth the wait. Still interested? Intrigued?"

"Yeah, but what do I have to do? Who do I have to kill? I'm not exactly the assassin type, you know. Especially now—look at me. And you think I can live another fifteen years, maybe twenty? Me? Look up terminal lung cancer in the encyclopedia and they got my picture there. This sounds nuts."

"Maybe. But you're interested, right? You trust me?"

"Of course I do. You've always been an honest man. But you do sound pretty crazy right now."

"Right now I may be crazy—crazy like some kick-ass fox in a storybook. Go ahead and call me looney tunes if you want, I don't care. I've got all the angles figured out. This is a thing of beauty. You wanna hear why I say that?"

"Duh, yeah, man. I'm ready. What else have I got to do today besides cough up my lungs laying here watching crap TV?"

"Then strap yourself in, old buddy. Here we go…."

PAUL CAREY

CHAPTER TWENTY-SEVEN

January 2014

"Okay, everyone, break time is over. Let's get back to business."

Norm groaned. "Geez, Amman, you're such a taskmaster."

"True. You can hate me if you want," Amman answered. "Okay, it's been three weeks now since Mr. T passed away. A week since Laverne, the other guinea pig we revived, died from the prion disease as well. I know this has been painful to watch, but we've collected a ton of data. So let's review. Where are we now? Let's slap it all up on this whiteboard, okay?"

"We've got the EEG readings, the gradual decline in behavior," Kate said.

"The brain autopsies you did, Amman," Chrissy added.

"Right," Amman answered. "We've established the prion disease in Mr. T. and Laverne. But where did it come from? What have we got on that? And don't forget, on the positive side, all the tumors these animals had somehow disappeared miraculously. As strange as that seems, it's true." The door opened and Mike and Miles entered quietly.

"Edouard is out of town for a week, but we've been talking via e-mail about the cancer," Kate said. "He's a bit stumped. He doesn't think the prion disease has any relationship to the disappearance of the tumors. He'll be back here in a couple days."

"All right, so there's some input from our oncologist—that's good." Amman scribbled all the observations on the whiteboard. "So, the prion origin—we think it's not lab contamination, right?"

"Correct," said Ritika, who had returned from Boston to help out. "When we revived Laverne we got the same results. She had the prion disease and died, too, but she came from a different source. The odds are that lab contamination here is not the issue."

"All right, people, look at the board," Amman challenged. "What connects? Where is the prion disease coming from? Two animals in a row have sporadic prion disease? I find that an unlikely coincidence."

"I dig the whiteboard approach, just like on *House*, huh, Amman?" Miles ventured. "*House* was a good show. But I wish season six hadn't been such a downer."

Kate couldn't help but roll her eyes. "Well hello, Mr. Miles, hello, Mr. Burgess," she said. "Miles, we're already aware of your fondness for television and *House, M.D.* in particular. Right now, we're trying to figure out where the prion disease is originating."

"Well, I've been doing some research," Miles announced "And, by the way, props to whoever named all those lab animals back in the 1980s—Mr. T, Laverne & Shirley, Urkel the white rat—pretty funny."

"That would be Keith, our chief security guard. He made those all up. We have his cat in cryo, too," Chrissy said.

"Okay, Miles. We're trying to work here," Kate said impatiently.

"Let him talk, Kate—seriously," Mike said.

"So, research, Miles?" Amman interrupted. "What do you have for us?"

"I may have changed my mind from back when I said the prion disease we found was the sporadic form. Who here has seen *The Walking Dead?*" A few hands went up. Kate's blood was boiling—all this Miles TV show nonsense.

"Well, here's the deal," Miles explained. "We're all *Walkers.*"

Silence. Dead silence. Finally, Chrissy squinted her face and asked, "What the hell do you mean?"

"If one of you volunteered here right now and let me crack open your head, I'll find prions. You're a *Walker*-in-waiting."

"C'mon, man, you're nuts," Norm said, derisively.

"No, I'm ninety-nine percent certain," Miles insisted. "It's there. Remember when Shane died in season two of *Walking Dead?* He hadn't been attacked by a Walker, but he reanimated when he died. Then they start figuring it out. The Walker pathogen was in everybody. Pretty spooky, huh?"

"So you're saying we all have prion disease?" Amman asked.

"Yes, in varying degrees. And this theory easily explains why you had two guinea pigs in a row with prion disease, understand? In modern times it's no longer an anomaly, an outlier."

"Okay, Miles, I think you're crazy, but hell, I'll go down the rabbit hole with you," Amman said. "Norm, roll that other whiteboard over here. Let's give this one a clean slate."

"Dang, this isn't an episode of *House*—it's a fucking full season," Chrissy whispered to Ritika.

"Okay," Miles explained, "here's what I've got. I've dug around and found out that we've got an explosion of incidences of CJD—that's the form people get, remember? It's being hushed up, by the way. And we're now easily detecting the presence of more and more prions in our soil, especially in the Midwest corporate farming zone, like Illinois, Indiana, Wisconsin, Iowa, Nebraska, et cetera. Also, the numbers are highest where the heaviest pesticide usage is. Prions love pesticides. Over the last three decades they've become more and more present in the produce food chain—tomatoes, carrots, watermelon—and really big-time in corn. And that's a big uh-oh, I am sure you can imagine why. From the ground, through the corn plants, then into all the thousands of crappy corn-based foods and beverages being produced—it's all contaminated. All the people eating the shit that the mega food companies churn out are in danger. And I haven't even started talking about what corn-shit we're feeding our cattle and other livestock."

"Quite a conspiracy theory, Miles," Norm said. "And your sources for this—more TV shows?"

"No. Emphatically no. University research, independent labs, private foundations that actually care about our health. All the folks that the FDA doesn't want to listen to since everybody there is controlled by the corporate farming PACs. There's so much dirty money going on. Hell, I think they all know what's happening, but the greed still stops them from admitting we have a catastrophe lurking here."

"So we're all going to die from this? A big epidemic? Like *Walking Dead*?" Ritika asked. "It sounds pretty far-fetched."

"Anything's possible," Miles said. "It could go really bad, hard to say. Things could go better if people actually wanted to stop being so damn lazy—if the whole country decided to stop stuffing their faces with corn chips and stop drinking high fructose soda. Say no to crap food and get off their fat asses and exercise."

"And what else?" Kate asked.

"Like start eating true organic food. No pesticides. Maybe your apple isn't so pretty, but it won't kill you. Stop eating corn products completely. Some trace metals, like manganese, make the prion condition worse. Some others may actually help fight the effects. Pot makes it better—cannabinoids, especially the Cannabichromene form—CBC. There's also a cure in development."

"Wait, Miles—you said a cure? For animals? For humans? Who's developing it?" Ritika asked.

"A research agency in Iceland of all places. They're even willing to ship dosages for use in experimentation. They have partners signing up in a bunch of countries. Right now it's being tested in Malaysia on animals with mild symptoms. Nothing as extreme as what Mr. T had when we brought him back. US big pharma doesn't care about this—at least not yet. Not enough money in it for them, obviously. But if this thing goes *Walking Dead* wacko, we're going to need serious kick-ass drugs to fight it. Then the big Fortune 500 pharma boys will be all over this like a hobo on a ham sandwich."

"Hobo on a ham sandwich, Miles? I haven't heard that one in years," Mike chuckled. "So there you have it, folks, some of Miles' ideas. I thought they would interest you."

"And tell me again where you got all this information, including the stuff about some Iceland research place." Kate was still not convinced Miles wasn't totally cuckoo.

"Here and there, but the really meaty stuff came from Bonesaw."

"And that's another TV show, right?" Kate asked. "Yup, that's what I expected."

"No, Kate, I know what Bonesaw is," Ritika volunteered. "Some young Russian-American doctors based in LA. It's a weird history. A tight-knit bunch of Russian Mafia dads grouped together and put all their kids through US law school or med school, making the next generation legit. The medical kids have created this amazing medical info subscription service. You pay them to research things for you—global reach. It can even be the most obscure item you're curious about, but they'll find it. They'll also personally translate anything you want into English or whatever language you want. And it's not like wonky BabelFish translations. They each speak like ten languages. There are five or six guys and three or four women, I think. It's a big deal. I'll show you their website. Oh yeah, they've also gone on record publicly condemning all the illegal stuff their dads do."

"Yeah, Kate, Ritika's got it pegged," Miles said. "I've got a subscription and I'll bet Edouard Radelet has one, too. I'd be surprised if he didn't. These guys' custom-built search engine makes Google look like an ugly baby with a fully loaded diaper."

"All right, I have some good news to share," Mike said. "I've located a brilliant MD, a gifted surgeon who thinks outside the box when necessary. He's available immediately and that could really help, since Radelet can't do everything. We could add this doctor to our team. What do you think?"

"I'm for it." Amman nodded. "A surgeon plus Edouard Radelet? Sounds great. And let's not forget—you want to bring back people. I'm a vet. I'm not going to be participating in that."

"Everyone agree with Amman?" Mike asked. They all nodded. "Kate, Amman, Miles, can I see you in the hallway for a moment?"

* * *

"What is it, Mike?" Kate asked. "Why are we out here in the hall?"

"Out of respect to you. I wouldn't do anything to upset you in front of your team."

"What would upset me?"

"Kate, I want to bring this doctor in. He's a bit unorthodox, but I think he'll grow on you. He's not only a gifted diagnostician but he's also a cardiologist. He could be the one to reboot all these people, understand? Add this fellow's skill set to Edouard Radelet's oncology and cryogenics background and we've got one heck of a medical team."

"Okay, I'm game, Mike. When can I meet him?"

"Kate Pearson," Mike said, then nodded toward Miles, "I'd like to introduce you to Dr. Milstein Coleman the Third. Dr. Coleman, Miss Pearson." Miles tentatively extended his hand toward Kate, smiling sheepishly. Kate hesitated out of shock, then slowly reached out and shook Miles' hand. Amman likewise shook his hand, then grabbed him and gave him a giant bear hug.

"You're a doctor?" Kate gasped. "What? Really? I don't get it. Mike?"

"Yes, he's a doctor. A fine doctor, even if he might be a little rusty. But his license to practice is current. Got any warts you want removed?"

Miles grinned, speechless.

"Wait, are you Milstein or Miles?" Amman asked. "Which is it?"

"I prefer Miles for now. But it isn't my real name. I'm supposed to be Dr. Milstein Coleman the Third but that didn't work out too well for me. My grandfather was a GP. A nice man. My father is way higher in the food chain. He's a well-known plastic surgeon in San Diego. Pretty damn rich. He's also known for being a complete asshole."

"But why do you spend your time at the Nielsen apartment," Kate implored. "A.C. doesn't currently need a doctor, right?"

"Well, long story short, I kind of got hit by a double or triple whammy about eighteen months ago. First off, I never had a choice of careers. My father told me I would be a doctor when I was six. That was his expectation and I didn't dare say no to him, ever. And all along I had what's called Imposter syndrome. You've heard of it, perhaps?"

"Sure," Kate said, "I have problems with that myself from time to time. It's damned annoying."

"So you're getting a feeling for what my life was like. As a kid I hung out with the goths, the skaters, the potheads, any group that I thought might get my dad's disapproval. And I was into television, movies, gaming, useless trivia, all the stuff he hated about pop culture and all the stuff you know me for, right? I was trying to get my dad's attention, let him know that maybe I didn't want to grow up to be him. But that didn't really change anything. I still wound up at med school. It sort of worked out. I was a very good doctor and I was still young and doing well. Many people envied my success, I'm sure of that. But one day I made a terrible mistake. We had some blood pressure problems with a surgical patient, but I kept going." Miles fought to make the words come out. His voice grew quieter, now just a harsh, desperate whisper. "I ignored the anesthetist, ignored the nurses, ignored the machines beeping angrily at me. I wanted to have my way, like my dad drilled into me, and kept going when I should have stopped, sewn the patient back up, try the procedure sometime later. But no, hotshot Dr. Milstein Coleman the Third kept going... and I lost the patient. I killed her. It was all my fault. If I hadn't grown to be a conceited jerk carbon copy of my father, she would have lived. I couldn't believe what had happened. There in front of me was this young woman, flatlined, dead on the table. I was stunned, speechless. The nurses had to help me walk out of the operating room. I had been sitting there forever in disbelief." Miles looked off into space. He couldn't bear to look Kate or Amman in the eye.

"I'm so sorry, Miles. That's tough," Amman said softly. "But we all lose patients. It's part of the bigger picture. They're supposed to tell you in med school that sometimes patients die, right?"

"Tell that to my father, Amman. He was so ashamed of me, told me I was a pathetic failure. Called me garbage. Here I was thirty-two and killed someone in an OR and he told me it had never happened to him in his entire career. So I believed him—believed that I was garbage. I quit, just quit cold turkey. People tried to get me back, but I refused. Everyone thought I was crazy. They probably started thinking that I really was a loser, a crazy loser." Miles perked back up a little, he had told them the worst of it. "Eventually everyone gave up on me— all except Mike here and his nephew Franklin. I had met Franklin at a hospital fundraiser in San Diego. When word got around and Franklin heard what had happened, he and Mike asked if I'd like to come to Chicago and take some time off from the pressure, all the expectations from my father. So I agreed. And I've been getting my act together, little by little."

Mike, the Finder and Fixer, nodded, smiling proudly at Miles.

"So now," Miles continued, "here's the thing. I've been watching all of you. Kate, your dedication, your drive—you just won't quit. There's not a thing that can stand in your way. I've really admired that. Amman, you are one smooth operator. Amazing. So I've been seeing all this and that's why I told Mike I was ready to come back. I'm ready to be a doctor again. I want to help if you think I can be of some value at all."

"Well hell yeah, Miles," Amman said as he slapped him on the back. "You seem to have a photographic memory of anything you hear or see. Your IQ must be sky-high. You could probably diagnose what's wrong with a rock or a sea urchin, I bet. Why wouldn't ExitStrategy want you?"

"It all makes sense now, Miles," Kate said, smiling. "That day you rattled off all that medical knowledge about prions and the Creutzfeldt-Jakob's and the other stuff—I thought somehow you were like Dustin Hoffman in Rainman. Now I get it, and I'm sorry for treating you like crap now and then."

"Ditto. Kate, not Kat."

"And," Amman added, chuckling, "you should tell your father to go to hell, I think."

"Ha, yes. I should get to that—soon!"

"So one big happy ExitStrategy family now, eh?" Cold Smokey said, wrapping his big meaty arms around both Kate and Miles. "Let's go back in the room and make the official announcement!"

CHAPTER TWENTY-EIGHT

"Okay, losers, here we all are again. Nobody could find a real job?" asked smartass Jak Hammer, executive producer of *Dimi & Khail: U Wish it Wuz U*. "Trish, it's the usual crowd minus Khail. You ready with your brand new Bic Rollerball?"

"Hey, I happen to have a new job," Chris said. "And it's in reality TV, therefore it's a real job, huh?"

"Oh yeah, that's right," Jak answered. "Somehow Khail convinced me to put Chris here in total charge of the one hundredth show. And we're giving Chris an associate producer tag in the credits. Listen, Chris, just make sure this thing is celebratory, okay?"

"What?" Dimi whined. "I'm not going celibatory. I have needs. How the hell am I supposed to keep my hands off that gorgeous man of mine? That's messed up, Jak."

"Oh Lord, Dim, *celebratory*—like happy. You either need your ears cleaned out or buy a purse-sized dictionary, thesaurus, something."

Chris waited patiently while Jak and Dimi sorted through their crap. He had decided to go all in, for a while, on the reality TV meal ticket. Stop being so sarcastic and snide, make some fucking money for a year or two and then get the hell out. "Okay, can I talk now, people? Here's what I've got for the one hundredth episode. First of all, Khail's in Hong Kong modeling, okay? Dimi's moping, she misses him so much. And I guess maybe she can talk about being horny with him gone. There, Dimi, we'll add that in, okay? You can show off your vibrator collection to your sister. Anyway, speaking of Konstantina, she and the other female entourage members come get you and take you out to get your nails done and—"

"Nails *did*, Chris," Dimi interjected.

"Huh?"

"You get your nails *did*—you don't get 'em done. Don't you have a girlfriend?"

"Chris, she's right. All us women of color get our nails *did*," Shontae added. "Even if most of us speak perfect English the rest of the day."

"Wait, I'm a woman of color now, Shontae?" Dimi asked.

"Well, you're Greek. That's enough color for me."

"Well, thank you, then… I guess. I'm glad we had our little fight,

Shontae. Now we can be friends again."

"Okay, wow!" Chris said. "Going on—you get your nails *did* and then Konstantina sees those little fish that some salons have that eat away the dead skin on your feet. You know about them?"

"Hell, yes. But I'm not putting my feet in there. They're not eating my toes, Chris," Dimi said, squirming in her chair.

"Lord, I need a vacation," Jak moaned, popping open a Red Bull.

"Well, that will be the fun part," Chris said. "The girls will dare you to do it. It will be hilarious. We'll make sure the background music is funny, like cartoon music. Plus we'll get plenty of cleavage shots when you're bending over to see the fish."

"Hey, that's good, Chris," Julio said. "Then what?"

"Then they all hit a mall and drop in unexpectedly on one of Dimi's Saturday Night Sexsations stores. Of course the store manager will know we're coming."

"Of course," Jak said.

"Well, by now Dimi's having so much fun that she's forgotten about how much she misses Khail. The girls will start doing free bra fittings on women who happen to be in the store. It'll gradually attract a crowd. We'll make sure to fit some skinny girls, too—tie it in to the new line for women with impoverished chests, right?"

"Okay, then what, Chris?" Jak asked. "You've got funny, you've got sexy, you've got cleavage, you've got product placement. Where's the celebratory, man?"

"Yeah, Chris, he's right," Julio said, turning to Chris. "We need a big ending."

"I got it, don't worry. So the girls are now sucking down cocktails at some mall restaurant—like a chain joint everyone knows, we'll line up product placement. They're sitting around yakking and laughing, getting a little tipsy when all of a sudden Khail shows up in an amazing tuxedo. But not just him by himself. All the bodyguards are in tuxes, too. We'll get shots of the girls swooning when they see what Theo looks like in a tux, right? The guys walk up and give a dozen roses to each girl. Then Khail presents Dimi with a bouquet of one hundred roses and then delivers the sexiest kiss ever on TV. Then we drop balloons and massive amounts of confetti down from the upper floors of the mall. Dimi will act surprised, like she had no idea Khail was going to show up. We get plenty of happy, excited crowd shots, this that and everything."

THAWING A. C. NIELSEN

Jak sat in thought for a moment, tapping his pen on his notepad. Everyone waited for his opinion. "Hell yes! That is an OMG FYI OMG winner. Bronsteyn, you little weasel, you hit it out of the park. I never knew you had it in you!"

CHAPTER TWENTY-NINE

February 2014

"Mike, I need to run something past you," Kate said. "We really need to pick the brains of those people in Iceland. We're set to revive the cryo'd cat soon, hopefully with success. But if we're going to have animal after animal come back with prion disease we can't even consider reviving your human patients. This is critical. I've had some e-mail contact with them and they seem amenable to helping us. I'd like to do one or two teleconferences with them, okay?"

"No, actually."

"Just like that—no?" Kate said, a little ticked off.

"Pack your bags and go there. And stop standing in the doorway. Come in and sit down."

"You said go?"

"Fly. Go. Yes, go to Iceland. You could use a vacation."

"It's not a vacation, it's work. Vacation would be Florence or Barcelona. Or a beach somewhere." Kate noticed for the first time that Mike had nothing on the walls of his office. *He sure could use a decorator, she mused.*

"Iceland would have beaches galore. It's an island, Kate."

"Yeah, right. You know it's February, right?"

"I can't fix the calendar for you. Anyway, book it and go. They'll share their research? Do they speak English?"

"Yes, and yes. I'll bet their English is better than half of our population. They say they're happy to work with us, help us in any way."

"Who are you taking?"

"Huh?"

"Who are you taking? I don't want you going alone. Take somebody with you."

"Anybody?"

"Yes, anybody," Mike said as he fidgeted with a fresh deck of playing cards Franklin had given him as a gift. A new copy of *Poker for Dummies* sat on the desk.

Hm, a new hobby, apparently, Kate surmised. *About time he gave up on his string of half-read biographies.* "Does it have to be an ExitStrategy employee?" Kate asked, the wheels turning in her head.

"Why? Is Channing Tatum available for you?"

"You know who Channing Tatum is?" Kate asked, her eyebrows furrowing.

"Hey, I go to the movies. I'm not as senile and out of touch as you assume, young lady."

"Ha, funny. Well, then, um, could I take my roommate Aria?"

"Of course. Go. Have some fun. Recharge your batteries. Spend some time with the brain trust at the institute between soaking up the sun on Iceland's white sand beaches. Just don't fall into a volcano, okay? They have active volcanoes there, I believe."

"Wow, thanks, Mike!" Kate said. She bopped happily back down the hallway to her office. *Some travel, R and R, and some research. Just what I need!*

* * *

"Road trip? Really? All expenses paid?"

"Yes, Aria. Can you swing it? What's going on with the symphony?"

"Not much. About ten more days of ho-hum and then there's a two-week break." Aria got up and wandered into the kitchen to pop open a bag of BBQ potato chips, then leaned against the fridge and stuffed her face.

"I need to leave soon," Kate said, "can you get a sub on short notice?"

"Yeah, after the next three or four days, we hop on into an All-Sibelius program. Anybody decent knows it all with their eyes closed."

"And they won't fire you for putting a sub in on short notice?"

"Nah, I'm too good-looking to get fired. Not that many hot blonde symphony girls for the horny old rich male benefactors in the audience to stare at. Haven't you noticed I'm in a hell of a lot of the promo shots? I'm whatchoo call it? *Photogenic!*" Aria said in her best hillbilly drawl, crossing her eyes and sticking her butt out as far as she could while stuffing an entire handful of chips into her mouth all at once.

Kate did a belly laugh. "Aria, if you ever get sick of playing the violin seriously, I bet you could get a job in a Branson, Missouri, show. Put on your Daisy Dukes, braid your hair into pigtails. Draw on some big-ass freckles. Hell, you'd make a fortune there on some dumb country fiddle show for the senior citizen crowd. Course they really go there for the buffets. Get on a senior bus, go to Branson and feed yer pie-hole. I think the shows are just intermissions between the buffet hogging-out."

"True. I think Branson's got it all: buffets, Elvis impersonators, and Bass Pro. But I'll never go over to the dark country music side." Aria sighed dramatically. "I can't stop lovin' classical and mah sweet violin. We're BFFs."

"I thought you and I were BFFs," Kate protested.

"No, we're um, um, BCSCFFs."

"Huh?" Kate cocked her head sideways, trying to figure out the ridiculously long acronym.

"B-C-S-C-F-Fs. Best Crazy Sarcastic Chick Friends Forever."

"Oh, I get it. Natch. Totes fer sure. Yeah, that's us!" Kate laughed.

"Wait, so where are we going? I better clean out my car, right? So road trip where?"

"'Where we're going we don't need roads!'"

"Right, Doc Brown. Ha, nice reference. Come on, seriously. Where?"

"Iceland."

"Excuse, me. What?"

"Iceland. Exotic, enchanting Iceland. I have to go there to talk to some research people about issues going on at my company. Mike says I can mix work and play. He thinks I'm stressed."

"Iceland?" Aria whined, slumping her shoulders.

"No, it's really interesting. I read a little about it. I can actually spell Reykjavik—I've practiced. They have active volcanoes. It's pretty awesome in a sparse, cold kinda way."

"We already have sparse and cold in the Midwest, Kate. Wait, so do they have men in Iceland?"

"There's a rumor."

"Okay, I'm in. I'll bet they're tall and blond like me. I'll find me an Olaf or a Sven and pop out tall, blond babies."

"Hmm, how tall would those babies be, Aria?"

"You know what I mean. They'll grow to be tall—duh. I'll feed them lots of whale blubber and narwhals. Can you eat them, do you think?"

"Jesus, Aria, you're so weird. Okay, so tell me when for sure you can leave."

"I have a great sub who can take over for the Sibelius. She grabs everything she can get. She lives in Downers Grove, out in the western suburbs. Ever been there?"

"No. Sounds like a bunch of barbiturate dealers hanging out in the woods, 'Downers Grove'?"

"It's a nice town. It's where famous New York Met Opera baritone Sherrill Milnes grew up. Also, some choral music composer was born there—I forget his name. Anyway, I'm sure I can be free in five days, okay?"

"Okay, I'll book the flight. And guess what, Mike's sending us first class."

"Sweeeet! Maybe I'll give him a kiss when you finally introduce us."

* * *

"Are you up? Hello? Are you alive?" Kate said softly while tapping on Aria's bedroom door.

"No, no. Not alive," Aria said drowsily.

"Limo is here in ninety minutes to take us to O'Hare."

"Umph," Aria grunted, trying to shift her kinked-up body around and shake off the cobwebs. "Why did you make me drink those damn gimlets of yours last night? I'm wasted, Kate."

"I didn't make you do anything. Free will. Heard of it? Anyway, you actually made the last round. You had me show you how to make 'em. You spilled the Rose's Lime Juice all over the counter, remember?"

"I did? Shit, no I don't even remember. Okay, I'm getting up. Sort of."

"Good, I'm making coffee."

"All right. Hey, I'm jumping in the shower first, okay?"

"Yeah. Just don't creative in there with the shower wand. I need time in there, too!"

"Shut up," Aria shot back.

"Love you, too!" Kate yelled.

* * *

The limo driver did his best to negotiate the midmorning traffic and dropped Kate and Aria at ORD, terminal five for international flights. After a quick, uneventful trip through the TSA line, they sank into some almost-comfortable seats in the waiting area. Two whole hours to kill now until boarding.

"How long is this flight?" asked Aria.

"I think about ten hours. Bless my boss man for the first-class seats, right?"

"Totally. And what's the weather again? I forgot what you told me."

"You forget everything. Not bad, considering it's February, like twenty degrees. Not much different than here."

"Do you think they have any ice bars? You know, carved out of solid ice. Serving drinks that freeze your tongue off?"

"How would I know? Is that a thing for you now, a special fantasy?"

"Shut up, Kate. I know there are some in Sweden or Norway. I've seen pictures of them. All the deep-freeze and ice-bar ice should remind you of ExitStrategy. You'll feel so at home," Aria teased.

"Hey, why don't you nap instead of irritating me?"

"I think I will. Yes, indeed I will. Good night." And just like that, Aria stretched her lanky legs across to another set of seats, crossed her arms, and closed her eyes.

Geez, she can sleep anywhere, just pass out and enter sleep mode, thought Kate. *Lucky!* But now without Aria's distractions, Kate could open the tour book she had found in the little bookshop in Winnetka. The cover had a dramatic photo of tundra-fringed sea cliffs and inside was info on both Iceland and Greenland. She looked through and dog-eared some pages of places they might want to visit in her downtime. Active volcanoes—that would be wild to see. And Reykjavik sure seemed like a bustling, busy city. Still, only 350,000 people on the whole darn island? A small, isolated world. So go do some work, some play. Talk to the research people a couple times plus have some fun. Time passed quickly as she flipped through the pages.

"Time to board," Kate said as she nudged Aria out of her slumbers. "Hey, wake up, we're boarding, Disney Princess!"

"Hey, Kate, while I was asleep I had a dream you were in Iceland and some bad guy knocked you into an exploding volcano and you were doing that slo-mo movie 'noooo' thing, windmilling your arms around as you fell away from me."

"Like a typical scene from any Michael Bay film?"

"Hey, I like Michael Bay movies. There's good Michael Bay movies."

"Seriously? I hope you're not referring to *Armageddon* or *The Unborn* or something."

"Shut up. You know what I mean. Anyway, the falling away slo-mo thing is awesome. It works every time, don't fucking deny it!"

"Yeah, um, whatever, Aria. So I died in your Michael Bay movie?"

"No, I woke up just in time. I saved you by waking up."

"Well, God bless us all, each and every one. Excellent. Okay, let's board."

They settled into their comfy first-class seats and relaxed while all the pathetic peons squeezed into the back. The flight attendant gave the usual safety drill, oxygen bag speech and so on. No one paid attention, except Aria, of course.

"Ya know, Miss Kate, if you gon' go down in the ocean, that seat cushion ain't a-gonna save yo' sweet li'l soul," Aria drawled.

"Shh," Kate admonished, "don't go all doomsday on me. Or the others."

"They pretend like you could even survive the impact. Ha!" Aria ranted. Overhearing the conversation, a female passenger off to their right looked over and shot Aria a grin.

"Aria, please don't make me sorry I brought you!" Kate grumbled.

The plane taxied for takeoff and was soon on its way east. *Wow, we're finally on our way*, Kate realized. The 'fasten seatbelt' light winked off and it was time to relax, browse some magazines, and have a nice first-class section drink.

"Here, Aria, look through this tour book I bought. I dog-eared a few pages for you to check out."

Aria thumbed through, squinting now and then. "Oh, this is cool! Oh wait, so is that. Lots of unusual stuff to do."

The fellow passenger who had grinned at Aria earlier got up from her seat and walked over, kneeling down gracefully in the aisle next to them, trying not to disturb others. She was about forty and stunningly beautiful. Tall, blonde, with piercing blue eyes and striking cheekbones. Kate thought she looked like a Norse goddess.

"Hi. Are you girls on vacation to Iceland? Do you want some tourism advice?" the woman said in perfectly fluent English.

"Hi. Well, I'm flying there for business and pleasure. I'm a biologist. My name is Katherine Pearson, but you can call me Kate. My oddball friend here is Aria Grumman. She's a great violin player when she isn't frightening people to death on planes." Aria nodded guiltily at their new friend.

"Oh, you've got interesting occupations! Glad to meet you. My name is Greta Jónsdóttir. Native Icelander, but I like the US, too. So you are here to study our wildlife?"

"Oh, actually not at all, although I'm sure it is fascinating," Kate said. "I'm a microbiologist—not macro. I'm here to talk to your amazing research institute about certain types of rogue protein cells they have been studying. Actually, I've discovered that they're leading the way on a lot of the research that I need to learn about for my job."

"Oh, that's what we do. Lead the way. We're a small country, but with big brains and a big drive for success. We have to keep moving so we don't freeze in place, you see. I was just in Chicago for a conference. Loved the 'Bean,' as you call it. Also, the amazing French Impressionist collection at your Art Institute."

"We aims to please in The Windy City, not that we really call it that. That's kind of a touristy name," Aria said.

"Oh, I understand. Tourists, yes. Sometimes they come to Iceland looking for penguins. Here, let me see that tour book you've been staring at." Aria handed it over to Greta, who leafed through for a moment. "Well, first you surely won't be going to Greenland, correct? So we can ignore that part of your book. You know, Greenland is not green and never was. The old Vikings said it was lush and green to try to lure foolish people to that hunk of ice. You've heard the story, I assume?"

"Yes, I have," Kate answered. "I even Snoped it. You see, I have a coworker who Snopes everything because he can't stand it if any of his precious store of trivia isn't one hundred percent true."

"Who are you talking about?" Aria asked, peering sideways at Kate. "Miles."

"Oh, that makes sense. OCD nerdy kinda dude," Aria told Greta.

"What is 'Snoped'? I don't know what that is."

"Snopes-dot-com, it's a website that tries to figure out if other sites have their stories right. Or it checks out urban legend stuff," Aria explained.

"Hmm, I'll have to look at that." Greta went back to digging through Aria's tour book. "Aha," she exclaimed, "it's here. Page seventy-five. A must-see and sure to amuse. Go ahead and read it out loud." Greta grinned from ear to ear at Kate, tapping at the page and handing the book over to her.

Kate read, "'To experience Icelanders unique sense of humor, visit The Icelandic Phallological Museum, boasting an impressive collection of animal penises from around the world. And actually, dear travelers, this is the only penis museum in the world.'" Once Kate had come across and read the word "penises" out loud, she lowered her voice the rest of the way and began to giggle. Giggles that would not stop. Aria giggled, too, and then finally she burst into a shrieking laugh, tears streaming down her face. Fellow first-class passengers stared disapprovingly at the three strange women—interlopers into the rarefied world of first class. Kate finally settled down and hoped that no one had really heard what she had read aloud. Greta had set her up.

"Go on, continue now." Greta tapped at the page in the book and gave Kate an encouraging nudge with her elbow.

"Argh, okay." Kate continued softly, "'Along with giant dried whale penises and tiny phalluses of mice and such stored in formaldehyde, you'll also see a gift shop filled with whimsical gifts, including lampshades made of scrotum skin. All guaranteed to amuse adult visitors. Laugavegur 116, 105 Reykjavik. Open daily 10 a.m. to 6 p.m. Gift store, cash only.'"

"Weird. Why cash only, Greta?" Kate asked.

"Oh, I think as a customer you'd want it that way. Do you think you'd want a family member coming across a charge card summary listing 'The Penis Museum'?"

"Wait, did you just say 'member' and then 'cumming'?" Aria asked. They all burst into howls of laughter. Once again, the heads of other, more conservative passengers in first class swiveled over to glare at the trouble-making troika of women. After a bit Kate, Aria, and Greta were able to stifle their laughter and continue their conversation.

"So where are you staying, Kate?" Greta asked.

"At the Hotel Vendavik. Is it okay?"

"Oh, it's wonderful. You'll like it. And you're doing a volcano tour? You have to. It's really what makes us so unique for the tourists."

"Yeah, we are," Aria said.

"That's wonderful. Here's my card with my phone. Call me soon and we can get together. Anyway, here's something more you might like to know about things in Iceland. We women run the country, and the bedroom. We're the most feminist country in the world."

"Oh, I like that. I like that a lot," Aria said, grinning back and forth from Greta to Kate.

"We often take extra partners," Greta explained. "Partners we choose. Understand—we choose who, the men don't. Female paradise. The men acquiesce. It's part of our history."

"So who knew? That's not in the tour book!" Kate said.

"It just turned out that way. And our men are not wimps. We love them. The rest of the world is catching up, but just barely. Pray we can take the Middle East away from the men there. They're brutal savages, almost every one, no matter which so-called religion they claim to be. Listen to me, espousing my beliefs so much. Sorry!" Greta slowed down to catch her breath. "In Iceland we don't hate men. We love them dearly. But when it truly matters, we women insist on 'wearing the pants,' as the English saying goes. So, I'm going to go back to my seat now. You've already made my flight time quite memorable for this trip. Thanks!"

"Of course, Greta, you're a dear," Kate cooed.

After Greta left, Aria leaned over and deadpanned to Kate, "Hey, do you think they have any scrotum coin pouches at the museum? Might make a great birthday gift for your mom!"

"Ew, shut up, gross person!" Kate groaned. "Ew, ew, ewwww!"

PAUL CAREY

CHAPTER THIRTY

Tap-tap… tap-tap-tap.

"Who could that be, Aria?" Kate whispered. "Who do you think that is knocking? It's like barely dawn or something."

"Ugh, go answer it. I'm too wasted."

"All right. But you have to cover the next annoying thing that pops up."

"Whatever," Aria grunted, then rolled over.

Kate dragged herself out of bed, threw on one of the plush hotel robes, and answered the door.

"Miss Pearson, I'm sorry to bother you so early in the day," said Anika Berglund, the a.m. shift hotel manager. "The people at your company in Chicago want to talk to you. They keep calling the desk, but when we try to reach you, your room phone is busy. That's why I finally came up."

"Oh, maybe the phone got knocked off, or my friend may have taken it off on purpose. Sorry about that."

"Well, they asked me to set up a video conference for you. If you can come down in fifteen minutes to talk to them, I can have it ready to go. I'm sorry. They've been very insistent."

"Oh, that's fine. I'm sorry they've been troubling you. Americans, you know? What time do you think it is in Chicago right now?"

"Maybe one in the morning. It must be quite important for them to be up that late at your office, don't you think?"

"That's for sure. Thanks, I'll be there soon." Ms. Berglund nodded, then scurried down the hallway to get the phone conference ready. *Hell, something is wrong. Why else would they be up in the middle of the night? Pod meltdown? Ha—A.C. woke up? Better get dressed and try not to look hungover. Not gonna be easy. Who'da thunk Iceland would have such rockin' clubs?*

* * *

"We're ready to go, Miss Pearson. Here's some coffee, pastries, and a nice selection of soft Danish cheeses."

"Thanks. Okay, ready when you are."

Ms. Berglund fiddled with her laptop and within a minute had a connection to ExitStrategy up on the hotel's conference room screen.

"Hi, everyone!" Kate said, waving, as the folks at ExitStrategy squeezed together so Kate could hopefully see them all. "What's going on there? Isn't it like the middle of the night? Is something wrong?"

"Oh, we're fine, Kate. Couldn't be better," Norm said.

"So what are you guys doing? I have no clue what you are up to."

"You can see we're all here in the cafeteria, right?" said Miles, who was executing the connection on the Chicago end. "Here, I'll pan around the room so you can see everyone."

"Okay, I get it—a whole bunch of you are there, but why are you—wait, Miles, what the hell? Pan back to Chrissy, okay?"

"We thought you might ask for that," Miles said with a ginormous grin.

"What is that on your lap, Chrissy?" Kate asked. "Who is that?"

"Oh, just a cat. He likes me. Of course, most animals do. They dig my aura. He's very happy on my lap right now."

"Chrissy, don't mess with me. Aria and I were up really late. We had a bunch of crazy Iceland party drinks. That cat looks sort of like John Cougar. I don't need any practical jokes right now. Where did you get that cat?" The whole ExitStrategy crew laughed—hearty belly laughs at Kate's expense. "Very funny, guys, but actually, no, not funny at all. I'm sorry, Ms. Berglund, they're making a long-distance joke on me. This has all been a waste of your time."

"Wait, Kate. Don't be such a crab," Miles pleaded, still grinning from ear to ear. "It is John Cougar, Keith the security guard's cat. It really is. We revived him and he's fine. Totally normal. And he says he wants to be called John Mellencamp now—drop the frigging Cougar thing, he insists."

"Seriously? It sure as heck looks like him—the markings and so on. Oh my God, for real?"

"Yup, Kate, he's for real," Amman answered.

"But why so soon? I knew you pulled him from the pod and put him in the womb tank, but he wouldn't be ready yet. We planned this so the final phase would happen when I got back."

"You won't believe what happened," Amman said. "The monitors beeped like crazy about four in the afternoon. Nick Costas, the lab assistant, saw it—EEG activity. Just now and then."

"Wait—but he had no heartbeat, right? EEG without a heartbeat?" Kate was confused.

"John Cougar was exhibiting what are called burst suppressions," Amman explained. "Bursts of heavy EEG activity followed by periods of almost total inactivity. It's common when entering or exiting comas, also quite common when the brain is trying to wake itself back up from hypothermia, exactly the circumstance here. When Nick started yelling and running through the building like a maniac, we all came to see. I decided that little ol' Mr. Cougar was sending us a message—'Hey, dummies, I'm a cat. I don't like water. Get me the hell out of here, I've got mice to catch.' Or something along those lines, right? So we sped everything up. It went so smoothly it was ridiculous. His heart started on the first try, and so on. Amazing, huh?"

"Geez, Amman. Wow, guys. This is so incredible. Now I know why you were trying to get ahold of me. Sorry, I think Aria knocked our phone off the hook. Hey, can you give me a close-up of the fuzz-face little guy?"

"Sure, here you go," Miles said, complying with Kate's request. Mr. Cougar was looking and acting perfectly feline, glued to Chrissy's lap as if he intended to take up residence there forever.

"He's purring really loud, Kate," Chrissy said. "Very happy, though he hasn't eaten anything. We offered him some salmon, but he wasn't interested. Keith is thrilled we brought his cat back. He said he'll be in an hour early with treats for the cat and for us, too!"

"It's no big deal he hasn't eaten," Amman said. "He may not look stressed, but I'm sure he is. He'll eat when he's ready. So what's going on in Iceland?"

"I've been to the institute twice now, including most of yesterday, before we went out to party the night. The people are nice and very supportive. But here's the bad news—they've concluded that prion manifestations can grow exponentially during environmental temperature changes. When temperatures flux the prions go crazy— totally *not* what I wanted to hear. They're saying our cryo procedure is probably a perfect storm for prions as we freeze or as we thaw, not to mention Enzo's ongoing temperature flux thing going on in the pods. The institute director thinks we're screwed. Well, he wouldn't say that. They're too polite here. Kinda like Canadians." Kate glanced up at

Anika and mouthed, "Sorry," afraid she may have insulted her. Anika smiled back. No harm, no foul, apparently. "So listen, I was going to talk to you all later today about this issue. We totally have to stop the temp shifts that Enzo loved so much. I never understood his ideas on that, anyway."

"Okay, Kate, but what temperature do you want to go with?" Norm asked. "We've been cycling through three different temperatures all this time. Now we have to pick one? Is that what you're saying?"

"Yes. Let's go to the highest of the three," Kate said as she nibbled on some pastry. "I really think the higher we are, the better. Amman, were you able to run John Cougar through the MRI—look for prions?"

"Yes, Kate. Nothing there, actually. Great, huh? We can do it again but for now I just want to let him be a cat for a few days, okay?"

"Sure. Keep me posted on any developments, okay? Great job, everyone. Does Mike know yet?"

"We texted him around eleven p.m. Haven't heard back," Deirdre said. "So you've been working and partying?"

"Oh yes, Deirdre. You and Chrissy would like it here. After I got done at the institute, Aria and I went to a museum. Lots of culture here—this was the phallological museum right downtown. Then we went and danced and partied in club after club."

"'Phallological' you said? What is that? Something about logic, or maybe a math thing, or some kind of philosophy?" Chrissy asked.

"No, Chrissy, *philology* is the study of written languages within historic contexts," Professor Miles lectured. "Iceland has an amazing, yet underappreciated place in European intellectual history over many centuries."

"No, Miles—this was the *phallological* museum," Kate said, winking at Anika. "Look it up. You're the Internet expert, right? Okay, I'm going to sign off now. Exciting news, guys. Give that pretty kitty a big hug for me, okay? But no catnip for the little dude, hear? Let's keep him calm. Love you all and see you very soon." Kate was very tired yet quite happy.

CHAPTER THIRTY-ONE

March 2014

"Okay, everyone," Mike announced, clapping to get everyone's attention. The whole group was gathered at the conference room table, chatting as they waited for the meeting to begin. "Here's why we are meeting today. Gloria Dunham wants us to revive our good friend A.C. Nielsen. I'm not a doctor, so you tell me why this makes sense to tackle or no. Who's first?"

"Oh, I'll go first," Kate said, instantaneously agitated. "We're not ready. Totally not ready. We have one cat padding around the building for a couple months and all of a sudden we're ready to revive a human?"

"That's our goal, isn't it?" Edouard looked over at Mike. "And don't forget, I'm due at my new job before long. But aside from that issue, what's stopping us from trying?"

"Seriously, Edouard? You of all people willing to be reckless?" Kate pleaded, then began to nervously yank at her hair. "I've never seen that side of you in the lab. And, Mike, why do we have to do whatever Gloria Dunham says? What's that all about?"

"We don't do whatever she wants, Kate. I'm in charge here. I'm simply here asking all of you for your scientific or medical stance on this. And, Kate, please, no drama, just professional opinions. In regard to Gloria, she is a large shareholder and as such has a right to ask what we're doing short term or long term. No matter how silly you think the A.C. Nielsen apartment and its staffing is, all of that is money Gloria has laid out." Mike crossed his arms, signaling his authority. "We may not like her, but she is part of the company and from time to time, we have to tap her assets. In fact, that may have to come up soon. We don't have the money to run all the intensive research and experiments you'd like, and this place costs a fortune to run on a daily basis, even with the energy side-income helping out—you have no idea."

"Listen, Amman has brought back animals," Edouard remarked, spinning in his chair, making eye contact with each person as he spoke. "Humans are just large, talkative animals, right? And Mike has built a tank the right size for a human. It's sitting there waiting for us to use. Kate, if you want to tweak or reformulate a few things, fine. Take time for that, no problem—we can do that."

"Kate, I assure you that Nielsen's medical issues are curable by today's standards." Miles tapped on the table to hammer his point. "It's 2014 now—Ronald Reagan and Nancy aren't in the White House. We've got new drugs and new procedures that will attack that advanced lung cancer of his, no problem. Same thing for his cirrhosis. Wasn't that the point of cryo—to stop time in its tracks until a cure was there for the people here? Who said we had to wait a hundred years?"

"We haven't thought through the ethics."

"And how long do you want to debate any of that, Kate?" Edouard asked. "Six months? A year? Five? There are no clear answers to any of the ethics questions ExitStrategy raises. What are we waiting for?"

Miles nodded. "I agree. Screw ethics. Just do it. Be bold and do whatever you think is right. We tiptoe around ethics too much. Let university professors diddle with that."

"Okay, let me jump back in here," Mike said. "When you revived the cat you added a layer to the procedure, correct?"

"Yes, once he wasn't frozen stiff we imaged his brain," Amman said. "Before he started having those EEG pulse suppressions we looked closely, layer by layer. There were no prions present, so we continued reviving him. We could spare the time since we weren't yet in the critical temperature zone for resuscitation. We didn't know why he had no prion disease, but that wasn't our concern right then. We had agreed that there wasn't any point in bringing back another animal afflicted with prion disease."

"And, Kate, remember," Chrissy said, attempting to soothe Kate's raw nerves, "once again, the cryo apparently is fixing major health problems in some strange, magical way. We've got a perfectly healthy, very frisky cat prowling around here. He doesn't even come close to acting his age. In 1991 he had advanced feline leukemia and renal failure. He was coughing up ginormous hairballs as well, all according to Keith. But look at him now—he's perfect. And for all we know, Mr. Nielsen's preexisting medical problems may be gone, just like with the animals."

"Kate, I think you're stuck in the way-back machine. Nineteenth-century moral concerns don't fit in the twenty-first century," Edouard said, exasperated. "Stop holding this thing back. We're ready to move forward. We'll scan Mr. Nielsen's brain for prions once he's not frozen solid. If there aren't any, like in John Cougar's case, we bring him back."

"And a reminder," Miles added, "you don't have that many cryo'd animals left to keep practicing on."

"So, I'm the only one here who thinks it's too early?!" Kate exclaimed, losing her control as she slammed the table with both fists. "Really? No one agrees that we need more time to think this through?"

"Kate," Mike said calmly, not taking the bait, "let me remind you that we never promised cures to these people. They signed a Universal Body Donor Agreement and left themselves in our hands. They trusted us. And think about it—out of all these patients, who has the most support from the living? It's Nielsen, Kate. Gloria is there for him. Franklin and I also developed a fondness for the man. Whatever help he needs will be there for him. I promise you."

"And if he's alive but a vegetable?"

"Kate, I just addressed that," Mike said firmly, his blood pressure finally rising as he lectured her. Kate wanted to snap off the pointy old finger he was jabbing the air with.

"Were Mr. T or Laverne vegetables when we revived them?" Chrissy asked. "Is John Cougar? We've had a hell of a lot of success here."

"So I'm the only one opposed? No one else has qualms?"

"Of course we do," Edouard said, "but I, for one, will never let that paralyze what I do professionally. Don't forget, I'm from Haiti, Kate—every day there is a crapshoot. You're too damned privileged and cautious. But it's not even really that. I'm saying it's a go because Miles is right—this guy's preexistings are curable today. This is the scenario Mike and your Dr. Saltieri were building toward. How long does Mike have to wait? Speaking as your friend and colleague, you need to honor what they created here and keep this moving forward."

"Jesus," Kate said, sighing heavily. "Miles, you'd be in charge. You're the surgeon. What do you need? I can't believe I'm saying this." Kate frowned as she tugged at her hair again.

Miles smiled, seemingly pleased at Kate's change of heart, even if it was forced upon her. "The same setup Amman had, just no guinea pig or kitten-sized equipment. I need the big-boy stuff. Also, Kate, let me assure you—if Nielsen fails the prion screening, we put him back into stasis. If I can't restart his heart, same thing. I know you think that is a big challenge, but you're not a doctor. Give a stopped heart some flow of normal temperature oxygenated blood and they're happy to reboot and take over the work. We don't have to crank open the roof and harness lightning like in a Frankenstein movie. It's not his heart I'm concerned about, it's his brain function that matters. That's the biggie."

Kate peered around the room, looking from face to face, trying to think it through. These were all very smart people—highly talented, gifted professionals. Maybe it was time to put the namby-pamby ethical worries aside.

"Kate, you've heard the medical opinions here," Mike said. "Your colleagues are ready. But it's a no-go unless you approve. You're still my number one. What do you say?" His tone continued to aggravate her, but she had to admit that the science had merit. *Why is he even asking me when it's obvious that he has already made up his mind? Thanks for the big ole plate of condescension, Cold Smokey.*

"One question, Mike. Level with me for real. Are we tackling this now just to please Gloria Dunham or because we as a team think we can succeed?"

"You heard everyone talk, Kate," Mike said, impatiently. "They don't give a damn what Gloria wants. Hell, Edouard has never even met her. They're all ready. Am I right, people?"

"Absolutely," Edouard shouted. "It's time!"

"All right, I'll agree," Kate said. *Is this a compromise or capitulation?* she wondered.

"Very good, Kate," Mike said. "I'll let Randolph Morgan know that we've decided to go for the gusto. I'm sure Gloria will be very happy."

"Fine, Mike," Kate said begrudgingly, "but we aren't doing this tomorrow."

"Day after, maybe? You know, Kate, for something this historical we really ought to have a code name," Miles said.

"You watch too many movies, Miles," Kate said.

"You know, this is one giant, epic code blue. Think about it, Nielsen's been code for how many years? I think we should call this Operation Code Ultra-Blue."

"You're really not as funny as you think you are, Milstein," Kate grumbled, her shoulders slumping.

CHAPTER THIRTY-TWO

"Kate, you finally picked up. Where are you?"

"At the lab, Aria—working. We've got a make it or break it event coming up. I'm going over everything for like the zillionth time."

"How can you spend so many hours straight, looking through microscopes? You're taking supernerdiness to new heights."

"What? Talk louder. I can't hear you. Are you in a bar or something?"

"Yes I am, and I said you're a nerd for working so many damn hours. Listen, I'm at The Skanky Barmaid, the Irish pub. Next to the sex shop where you get your flavored condoms, right? That is where you get them, I assume. I'm playing fiddle for the Arse Bros—you know, Patrick and Colm. They've got buck-a-can PBR tonight."

"Oh yeah, Patrick—my favorite male chauvinist sleazeball."

"Stop it. He likes you. He just doesn't know how to say it without insulting you. Give a poor Irish lad a break. Besides, is that such a big fault?"

"Oh no, that's nothing. And neither is it a fault that he accidentally rubs up against my boobs whenever we're in a crowded room and he thinks he can get away with it. So other than your desire to invoke the unholy trinity of Patrick, flavored condoms, and PBR in a can, why are you calling, Aria?"

"Patrick has something to show you… and it's not his freckly unit. This is really interesting. Can you come?"

"Why aren't you playing? Why are you on the phone with me? And besides, I'm in the middle of running a computer model here."

"We're on break, Kate. It's something people do. They work for a while and then rest or play for a bit. You should try it sometime. Oh damn, some guy spilled beer on me. Fuck."

"Sounds like a great time, Aria, but I think I'll pass."

"No, really. You have to come see us and hear Patrick's guitars tonight. Something weird is going on. Come on. PBR in a can! One lousy buck. You know you want it."

"I'm rolling my eyes now. Can you see me?"

"Seriously, Kate, come down here. I mean it."

"Oh, all right. I guess I can call it a night here. How busy is it?"

"For a Wednesday it's a good crowd. Wait 'til you hear the music."

"Yeah, yeah, yeah. Okay, I'll be there in about thirty minutes. Where can I park?"

"Off the alley out back. I think you can squeeze in right behind my car. You'll just barely be on the bar's property so the city can't ticket you there. Squeeze in tight—pretend it's Patrick and you."

"Shut up!" Kate yelled and hung up.

* * *

Kate parked her car and walked around to the street to enter The Skanky Barmaid. The Arse Bros, Patrick and Colm, with Aria on fiddle, were in the middle of a set covering Chieftains tunes. The place was dark and weary, but no one cared as long as the Guinness was flowing. A countdown clock, reading six days, two hours, thirty-two minutes, and fourteen seconds to St. Patrick's Day teetered on the edge of the splintery old stage. Kate grabbed a seat at the bar and smiled up at Aria, who winked back and then bounced her bow hard on double-stopped strings, propelling the beat forward on a rollicking new version of "The Foxhunt." Patrick strummed his guitar like a madman while Colm was twittering away on a pennywhistle that looked like it had been through all "the troubles" of Ireland starting in 1968. "Oh crap—in five-four-three-two-one," Kate muttered.

"Hey there, can I buy you a drink?" said a voice. It presently had no face or body attached to it as Kate had no intention of looking where it came from. *Why can't a girl ever go in a bar and just be left alone for once, and not be pestered by men?* she wondered.

"No, that's okay," she said, initiating evasive tactics by fumbling inside her purse.

"Oh, come on, I won't bite. Hey, you like this band?"

"Maybe. They're okay. Listen, I'm getting a PBR for a buck. I'm sure I've got four quarters rolling around in here."

"That's funny. You're a funny girl. I like that in a woman."

"Um-hmm." She yawned.

"You sure I can't buy you a drink?"

"Nah, I'm okay."

"Well suit yourself. I'm here all the time. Name's Sean—a relative of the owner. Seriously, I'd like to buy you a drink. Something nice, not a Pabst. How about a Guinness or a half and half?"

Kate finally looked up at the fellow. *Oh geez, he looks just like what's-his-name—Travis Bickle in* Taxi Driver. *Watch out Mr. Creepy Eyes, my friend Aria might spear you with her violin bow if you get out of hand.*

"No really, I'm fine," Kate said pointedly, putting 'Travis' in his place, and officially, from this point onward, on ignore. She turned to watch Aria take a solo, her blonde hair glowing and bouncing as she fiddled madly and tapped her right foot hard on the stage.

"Okay, suit yourself. What, I'm not good enough for you? I'm not your type, eh? Is that it? Hope you have a nice evening, bitch!" Sean snarled, sliding down the bar toward another unsuspecting young maiden.

Ah, well there would be the manners I knew would come out eventually. Yeah, very Travis-y, very Bickle-y of you, Sean of the Dead. Eh, forget about it. "Hey, can you get me a PBR?" Kate shouted at the bartender. "The epic one-dollar special. I'm thirsty here!" In a little bit she was rewarded with a can of the sickly sweet, corn-based bubble-water hipster delight.

* * *

Kate had nursed her one can of PBR as the band reeled through five or six more tunes. Patrick finished the set with an acoustic version of the old folk song "The Lark in the Clear Air" on his twelve-string guitar. Patrick had a remarkable gift for shaping a melodic phrase. The guy might be a wise-ass jerk, but he sure could play. Kate finally got another PBR and headed backstage to meet her friends in the green room.

"Kate, do you realize you still have your lab coat on under your jacket?" Aria asked.

"Oh, oops. I wasn't thinking. Hey, guys, great set." She looked around at the green room—a total dump with graffiti everywhere. It was clear that the many signs posted by the management were being ignored on a daily basis, the most obvious being a NO SMOKING sign, since the room reeked of cigarettes and pot.

"So you liked us, huh, Kate? Does Kitty-Kat want to rub up against my leg now?" Patrick quipped, making a kissy face at her.

"Of course, Patrick. But first you should go defend my honor. There was a guy hitting on me. I want to you to smack him over the head with your guitar—your most expensive guitar, to prove your love for me."

"That won't be happening, Kate," Colm said. "Did you hear his twelve-string there tonight? 'Twas absolutely steel—no wait, platinum bollocks, now, eh?"

"Yes, platinum bollocks, of course," Kate replied. These two were a hoot. Weird but funny. Colm was the older brother, about thirty. Tall with a ratty orange beard attempting to eke out a semblance of existence on his pale face. Patrick was two years younger and even taller, about six four. He was the more handsome brother. Their popularity with both old and young Irish music aficionados took them across the Midwest to venues much more highbrow than this dank little joint. Occasionally they would tour Ireland and Scotland as well as Germany, where for some reason, Irish folk music was quite popular. Aria played her neon-green electric violin with them whenever the Arse Bros schedule didn't conflict with her Milwaukee Symphony job. Her blonde good looks made the band even more popular with the male demographic between the ages of eighteen to forty-nine, according to Aria herself.

"Okay, Kate, here look at this package," Aria said.

"She'd rather look at mine, I bet," Patrick countered.

"Shut up, dummy. Kate, here's the package for the new strings Patrick put on the twelve-string. And he restrung his mandolin and the Dobro with this same brand and series of special strings. They all sound amazing tonight, right? Here, read the label."

CRYO-WHOMPERS
PH-PH-PHROZEN FOR A
PHAT-ASS PHUNKY SOUND
HSK STRING CO.
LAGUNA BEACH, CA

"Cryo guitar strings, really?" Kate asked, looking dumbfounded.

"Ha, you're not the only lab rat freezing the hell out of stuff. Heck, now I gotta try freezing my violin strings."

"Guys, what do you make of this? Where did you find them?" Kate asked.

One of the waitresses stopped by with four free pints of Guinness. Colm tipped her ten bucks. "Here, Kate," he said, passing her a glass, "now you can stop drinkin' that American piss-water. *Sláinte!*"

"We saw them at Krazy Larry's guitar shop and thought we'd give 'em a try," Patrick said, rubbing carnauba wax on his twelve-string. "Only problem is my fingers are icy-cold now. I can hardly wiggle the wee lads, damn froze strings."

"Stop clowning, Patrick. So, you like these strings?"

"Sound great, feel great. They sound like bells or somethin', like crystal bells, maybe."

"Kate, we haven't seen you in ages," Colm said. "Where have you been hiding? Aria says you're doing cryo-something. That you'd be really interested in these strings. So what do you freeze? That's what cryo is, right? Freezing stuff?"

"Yes, Colm. We chop off people's heads, freeze-dry them, then put them on spikes."

"The heads o' the English, I hope, right, Kate?" Colm said.

"Of course. To be sure, laddy. The bloody English. Their ugly mugs make righteous Halloween decorations, don't you know. And, Patrick, you'd be pretty scary if we could get our hands on your head, I must say."

"Katey KitKat. You can put your hands on my head anytime you want," Patrick said, still in lewd with Kate. "Like maybe now? In the hallway?"

"I'm not sure I could find it in the dark. Aria says she saw it once and that it's a wee tiny pecker. It might take me all night to find it."

"All night is fine, Katey. Mm hmm," he moaned.

"All right, enough clowning, you two. Kate, honestly you just make him worse," Aria pleaded.

"He's probably got blue balls now from talking about sex. He'll play better if he's frustrated. Just watch," Kate announced triumphantly.

"Well, time to go back out," Aria said. "You're staying, right?"

"Sure. And maybe I can look up this company's website while I'm sitting there fending off drunken lads."

"You do that, Kate. Save yourself for me. Don't let the English drag you away from your valiant Irish lover," Patrick wailed, in a mock drunken voice.

"Bye now. Play good!" She blew Patrick a kiss.

* * *

The band was a few tunes into the next set when Kate saw a table open up right near the front. She could leave the crowded bar and have some room to relax. She ordered another Guinness and headed on over—no more stinking PBR for the evening. Patrick set his guitar down and grabbed his bodhrán and began to bang out a raucous, driving rhythm. The crowd clapped frenetically to the beat, and eventually Aria and Colm joined in on the electric fiddle and an amplified hurdy-gurdy. The crowd cheered as Patrick leaned in to his mike and began singing the up-tempo classic "The Rocky Road to Dublin."

> "In the merry month of June, from my home I started,
> Left the girls of Tuam, nearly broken hearted,
> Saluted me father dear, kissed me darling mother
> Drank a pint of beer, my grief and tears to smother,
> Then off to reap the corn, and leave where I was born,
> Cut a stout blackthorn, to banish ghost and goblin,
> In a brand new pair of brogues, go rattling o'er the bogs,
> Frightening all the dogs, on the rocky road to Dublin.
> One, two, three, four, five!
> Hunt the hare and turn her down the rocky road
> and all the way to Dublin, whack-fol-la-de-da!"

"Ah, Geez, I gotta pee. There's the darned PBR catching up," Kate mumbled. *Why now? I wanna stay and listen, they're really jamming now. And where are the bathrooms in this joint? In back on the left, right? Head on down— oh yeah, here they are. Listen to that crowd clapping, they're actually staying with the beat. God, this bathroom is filthy. What does the men's room look like if this is the condition of the lady's room?*

> "In Dublin next arrived, I thought it such a pity,
> To be so soon deprived, a view of that fine city.

Decided to take a stroll, all among the quality,
My bundle it was stole, in a neat locality,
Something crossed my mind, when I looked behind,
No bundle could I find, upon me stick a wobbling,
Enquiring for a rogue, they said me Connacht brogue,
Wasn't much in vogue, on the rocky road to Dublin.
One, two, three, four, five!
Hunt the hare and turn her down the rocky road
and all the way to Dublin, whack-fol-la-de-da!"

Kate suddenly realized that she was yawning over and over.
*I gotta get home and get some sleep. This is fun but it's getting late. Get off the
toilet, girl, and wash your hands. And make sure you don't look wasted, right?*

"The boys of Liverpool, when we safely landed,
Called meself a fool; I could no longer stand it,
Blood began to boil, temper I was losing,
Poor old Erin's isle they began abusing,
'Hurrah my soul,' sez I, let the shillelagh fly,
Some Galway boys were nigh, saw I was a hobbling,
With a loud hurray, they joined me in the fray.
Soon we cleared the way, o'er the rocky road to Dublin.
One, two, three, four, five!
Hunt the hare and turn her down the rocky road
and all the way to Dublin, whack-fol-la-de-da!
One, two, three, four, five!
Hunt the hare and turn her down the rocky road
and all the way to Dublin, whack-fol-la-de-da!"

The crowd was belting out the one, two, three, four, five and the
whack-fol-la-de-da with the band as the tune ended. *Damn, they're a hit
with this crowd tonight. Listen to that applause. So how do I look? Hmm, no—
not drunk, just a little sleep-deprived? I'm pretty good-looking, even when I'm tired,
even if I do say so myself. "You should wear more makeup." Wasn't that what
Gloria Dunham said? "You're not beautiful, but you're pretty—like Kansas
pretty." Yeah, she said that to my face, damn old witchy bitch! Okay, stop staring
in the mirror and wrap it up, Kate. Get back to the music. Oh, Aria's singing
now!*

"I'll tell me ma when I get home

The boys won't leave the girls alone
They pulled my hair they stole my comb
But that's all right till I get home.
She is handsome, she is pretty
She is the bell of Belfast City
She is counting one, two, three
Please won't—"

Crash! Crash! Crash! The music abruptly stopped and people were screaming. Kate raced out of the bathroom as fast as she could. She fought her way through the commotion, pushing through screaming people trying to get free of the ruckus, while others moved closer, yanking out their cell phones to capture whatever mayhem was going on. Kate finally squeezed past an overturned table and saw the source of the noise. Patrick was pounding some guy to a pulp. She looked closer and realized it was Sean, the scrawny creep who had hit on her.

"What did ya put in her drink, then, eh?" Patrick screamed. "You thought no one was lookin'? I saw you. Come on, what were ya doing?" Patrick stopped punching and held Sean by the collar. A circle of men surrounded Patrick and Sean now, waiting to see what Patrick would do to him next. Kate joined Aria about fifteen feet from the altercation. Aria grabbed her hand and squeezed it.

"Jesus, Kate, he just dropped his guitar and leaped off the stage at that guy. Look—he broke two tables and there's glass everywhere. Say, did you happen to walk away and leave your drink sitting there?"

"Oh darn, I did, Aria. I knew that guy was a creep."

"I'll bet he was putting date rape drugs in your drink. What else could it be?"

"I wasn't doin' nothin'. You're all crazy," Sean yelled at Patrick.

Pow. Patrick head-butted Sean, breaking his nose. Blood sprayed everywhere. The men cheered while the women groaned. Some people decided it was time to split. An older man came huffing and puffing out from the back of the pub.

"Patrick, what are ya doin'?" said Brendan Flaherty, the owner of the pub. "You're here to play music, not bust up my tables."

"Flaherty, this guy was puttin' somethin' in my girl's drink. He's a criminal. I saw 'im do it. Ya thought no one was watchin'?" Patrick screamed in Sean's face.

"What—what the hell, that's my nephew, Patrick. Sean, what are you doin' here? You're supposed to be home with yer ma tonight."

"He's here makin' trouble, Flaherty," Patrick barked. "At your damn dive bar."

"Show me what you put in her drink, ya bastard," Colm chimed in, rather calmly. He knew someone had to play good cop when Patrick was this upset. "Show us yer pockets, little Sean."

"I got nothin' there."

"Then turn 'em out. Let us see, eh?" Patrick demanded.

"Yeah, feck off."

"Sean, you don't really want to get Patrick any angrier now," Flaherty said. "I'm telling ya now. You better turn out the pockets, Sean."

Patrick let go of Sean, then shoved him into the circle of men, who laughed and pushed him right back like a human pinball to Patrick. Finally realizing he was totally trapped, Sean slowly went from pocket to pocket, emptying their contents. He hesitantly pulled a baggy of white powder from his back pocket and handed it to his uncle. Patrick grabbed the bag away and held it up for all to see.

"Aye—there it is! Nothin', you said?" Patrick bellowed to the agitated crowd as he grabbed Sean roughly by the collar again.

"It's just health stuff," Sean protested. "Protein powder. She looked tired. I was doin' her a favor. You got this all wrong."

"I tell you what," Colm said, "how 'bout you swallow your protein powder. You don't look so good yerself right now."

"I ain't doin' that," Sean sputtered, still trying, now and then, to squirm out of Patrick's grasp.

"Don't make 'im," Flaherty said. "He's my nephew, Patrick. Please."

"Yeah, you already told us that. You must be righteous proud," Colm said. "Tell you what… Brendan, go get your phone and call the police. And make sure they send an ambulance. Yer darlin' nephew's gonna need attention, I bet."

Patrick poured some of the powder into his left hand, closed the Ziploc bag and handed it to Colm. "Now here's what's gonna happen now, little Sean Flaherty," Patrick explained, finally calming down. "You're gonna swallow this big heapin' lump o' special protein powder of yours I got here in my left hand, or I'm gonna break yer jaw with my right. Understand? You already got a broken nose—do you want the jaw t' match?"

"Or, Patrick," Kate interrupted, "just tell him he has to say what the powder really is, okay? You've hurt him enough, okay? Please. Enough's enough."

"Brendan, are you callin' the police or not? Do it right now and I'll do what Kate wants," Patrick said. The whole circle of men laughed again at the squirming Sean, dwarfed by Patrick, who was still holding him like a rag doll.

"Yes, Patrick, I'm calling them right now," Flaherty said. "Sean, dammit, just tell the Arse Bros what the feckin' powder is. And do it now."

"Sorry, Uncle Brendan. Okay, I'll say it—it's a drug that messes you up. She wouldn't let me buy her a drink. I was mad. She wouldn't even look me in the face. Like she's better than me."

"What I thought." Aria squeezed Kate's hand. "A date rape drug, eh, you little weasel? You're a pathetic excuse for a man!" Aria yelled.

"Yeah, it's GHB. So what? You're just a worthless fiddle player. I'll be out in three months or less. You'll see. And you can all go feck yerselves."

Patrick reared his fist back—everyone anticipated the blow to the jaw so much they were already wincing before the fact. However, he then slowly opened his left hand, flattened it out, and then blew all the GHB powder right into Sean's eyes and nose, causing him to wheeze and choke furiously, then pass out. The crowd broke into a cheer. Aria and Kate let out an enormous collective sigh of relief, giving each other a huge hug.

"You know, Kate, that crazy redheaded Irishman there was looking out for you," Aria said. "Ever have a man fight for you? To protect you? 'Cause I sure as hell haven't."

"No. It's a first. I guess I'll have to be nicer to him from now on, huh?"

"Yup. Guess so."

"Wow, what a night."

"So, maybe you learned a lesson tonight about keeping your drink safe in a bar, Katey-Baby?"

"Maybe. Hmm, yeah, I suppose. But there's a bigger lesson."

"What's that?"

"Don't ever step foot in a dive bar so scummy that they serve beer for a buck, Aria-Mommy—Dearest."

CHAPTER THIRTY-THREE

May 2014

"All right, everyone," Kate said. "You all know that Edouard and I have been getting a plan ready to revive Mr. Nielsen. We have made major revisions to the mix of chemicals and vitamins in the womb therapy bath. On the side, I have been trying to figure out why cryo is turning sick patients into healthy ones. Something happened a couple months ago that helped confirm some of my own observations."

"What have you got, Kate? I'm excited to see," Norm asked.

"Well, I've brought in my guitar-playing friend Patrick Flynn to provide some music to go along with my fancy slide show." Patrick nodded to the little ExitStrategy audience. "Patrick, can you entertain us with a bit of music on your guitar?" Patrick smiled and launched into some improv on the Rodrigo Guitar Concerto. It was quite beautiful and everyone clapped when he finished.

"Gorgeous," Edouard shouted. "I love that piece."

"And now," Kate said, "Patrick will play the same thing on the other guitar he has with him today." Once again, Patrick brought out the gorgeous, melancholy themes of Rodrigo's masterpiece. Another round of applause.

"That was even more amazing. Is that like a zillion-dollar guitar or something?" Miles asked.

"Nope," Patrick said. "Same brand, just a slightly different model. No real difference. Of course, you'd normally play this on a classical, but Kate wanted to use these guitars with the metal strings."

"It sounded so much richer. Were you playing with a different technique or something?" Mike asked.

"Not really, a few different notes here and there, that's all."

"So next I'm going to show you images from my favorite microscope now," Kate continued. "Take a look—these are magnifications of the strings from guitar number one. And here are images from the strings of guitar number two. I can even show them to you side by side. Here."

"Whoa. So one guitar has crap strings and the other one has more expensive strings on it?" Chrissy asked, noticing the irregular surfaces and nasty crags on the first sample, and the virtually perfect crystalline alignment of the metal alloys in the strings from guitar number two.

"Nope. Same strings—same manufacturer. Both are new sets of strings. Patrick's put in an hour of playing on each of them, tops."

"Wild. So what's going on?" Edouard sat up straighter in his chair, his enthusiasm gaining.

"The first set of strings are straight from the package," said Kate. "The second set was identical until I got my hands on them. I cryo'd them for sixteen hours."

"What the hell—cryo did that? In sixteen hours? It blew away all the crap we could see at this magnification?" asked Miles. "And the sound difference was totally noticeable. Right, everyone?"

"And, get this," said Kate. "I learned this from Patrick after he had bought a set of commercially cryo'd guitar strings. Musicians know about this. Who'da thunk, right? I talked to the string company in California and they told me all about it. All right, next group of images. Hey, Patrick, maybe some awesome background music, please?"

"Sure, no problem. How about some Django Reinhardt-style jazz?"

"Sure," said Kate. "Now here, folks, are plain old photos of Mr. T's abdomen after he was revived. No tumors, right? We all know that. I went further, however. The next images are on the cellular level from that same abdominal area, plus DNA images. What do you see?"

"We're not microbiologists, Kate. Help us out," said Chrissy.

"Miles?" Kate asked.

"This can't be Mr. T, Kate," he answered.

"I assure you it is."

"These are all perfect cells, totally clean," said Miles. "There are zero defects, zero signs of free radical damage, and so on. Your DNA images show perfect genomic stability. This looks like a guinea pig that's, I don't know, a couple months old?"

"Yet I assure you," said Kate, "these are images I took of Mr. T before he died. Apparently the cryo returns systems to their correct form, like a Platonic universal. Cryo acts on problems—if it detects matter that isn't, shall we say, natural and expected—true to design, you might say—it fixes things. Anything less than optimal gets realigned perfectly or it's eliminated, vaporized. It's like cryo knows what's right and what's wrong whether we're talking about metal alloys in guitar strings or cells in a living animal. And you can look for leukemia cells in John Cougar all day if you like, but there won't be any."

"You'd have to catch him first. That cat is so fast and frisky!" Norm said.

"So, we've discovered a cure for cancer, and other diseases, like we thought might be true?" Mike asked.

"I think we happened upon a cure, Mike, in all honesty," said Kate. "But I think they still award Nobel prizes to lucky fools like us." Everyone laughed.

"Of course, we still have puzzles," Kate said. "How is it that John Cougar has no prion disease like the guinea pigs had? He's perfectly healthy. He's got the Amman Vishwanathan seal of approval. I'm still trying to figure out that part."

"This is amazing, truly amazing, Kate. I am happy beyond belief." Mike walked up to Kate and gave her an epic hug. "So what's next? Where does this put us?"

"I think it means that when we start to revive Mr. Nielsen tomorrow, that we can pretty much, fingers crossed, expect to find that his lung cancer is gone, and that his cirrhosis is gone, too. The only other odd factor here is that, like I mentioned, the cryo doesn't seem to effect a cure for prion disease. Not sure why. Maybe we'll be lucky and Mr. Nielsen will be just like the cat, prion-free. But anyway, there's a cure being developed, right?"

"I'm guessing prion disease is just too weird and too nasty an hombre, Kate," Edouard said. "Plus, your friends in Iceland told you the prions love to do their destruction in shifting temperatures. They're thriving in this arena."

"That sounds reasonable. We wouldn't really know without a year or two of research, anyway. Speaking of which, we need to start thinking about when and to who we are going to take our bizarre discoveries to. We need partners for all this. Major universities or institutions? Edouard, Miles, start brainstorming, okay? Anyway, we're good to go for tomorrow. I thought you all would love to see this as we get ready. Mike, have you polished up your MRI? It's going to get plenty of use soon."

"It's good to go, Kate. I'll bet Professor Bardeen is probably smiling down on us from heaven right now."

CHAPTER THIRTY-FOUR

"Light reading, Kate? How's he doing?"

Kate looked up from her shiny new issue of the *International Journal of Medical Microbiology*. Miles was standing just inside the door in workout clothes and sucking on a cherry Popsicle. "Well, don't you look all spiffy in your sweats," she said facetiously.

"I was at the gym and decided to check on A.C.'s progress before I grabbed some dinner. Looks like you beat me to it. How is he?"

"Fine. Everything's the way it's supposed to be. I've been sitting here talking to him. Talking to A.C., Miles. I know he's alive. I can feel it in my gut."

"Like how we can feel the crazy vibrations in our bodies from your recorded loop of maternal heartbeats? Mike sure tuned up the resonances on that thing. Almost feels like a car subwoofer, doesn't it?"

"Yeah, it does. Do you think it helps? I know it's pretty *woo-woo* out there."

"I have no idea. But we did see Mr. T's heart sync with it when we brought him back, remember? Not the same results with John Cougar, though. I don't think it can hurt."

"Right. Well, anyway, I've been taking shifts off and on. I mostly sit here with my mind wandering, zoning in and out. I enjoy keeping A.C. company. It's like I already know him somehow. Look at him, Miles. Floating there in the tank, so peaceful. He's like a baby—a big, beautiful baby, right? Anyway, we're right on schedule with the vitamin therapy and the warmup. Not that many hours away before you get to do your thing, right?"

"Yup. Listen, Kate, you're a pretty amazing scientist, but right now you look pretty zonked. Being sleep-deprived and trying to do medicine or science isn't a good match. How about you go home and get some sleep and I'll keep watch over A.C. for a while? After all, I have plenty of experience at that, remember?"

"Yes, I do. Yu-Gi-Oh Miles and the TV shows. Seems like so long ago."

"Yes, like a different lifetime. But I needed that, as weird as it might have seemed to you."

"I understand. Okay, I'll go home. You're right, I need some sleep. Miles?"

"What?"

"Recite an *F Troop* for him, okay?"

"Sure thing, Kate. Sure thing."

* * *

"All right, everyone," Miles said sixteen hours later. "Operation Code Ultra-Blue is now in session. We're ready to run Mr. Nielsen through the MRI. Everything has gone fine so far. As soon as we get him in the machine Dr. Goldman and I will start slicing and dicing A.C.'s brain. Alex is one of the best in the business at running an MRI machine, that's why I brought him in from San Diego to help."

"That's great," Kate said. "And most of you know Miriam and Scott. They assisted Dr. Saltieri often in the past. Add in Chrissy and we've got three RNs in the room. This is groundbreaking today. I think we realize that, right? And remember, we're going to stop every ten minutes or so, do a quick EEG check for any burst suppression activity like we had with the cat. If we see that, we'll try to run him through the procedure more quickly. If he presents brain activity, we want to take advantage of it ASAP. All right, let's get him to the machine. We've got forty-five minutes to an hour before his temperature is at our final target zone."

Miriam, Scott, and Chrissy rolled Nielsen to the open MRI and placed him into position.

"Hey, at least we don't have to lecture him to be still, right everybody?" Chrissy joked, trying to lessen the tension in the room. In a few minutes Goldman was at the controls and ready to initiate the exam. The machine came to life, sounding like an angry robot from outer space. Everyone in the room had, of course, been around MRI machines except for Kate. She couldn't believe how raucous and disturbing the noises were. Five minutes went by as the trio of Miles, Edouard, and Alex peeked inside A.C. Nielsen's brain, layer by layer. No one uttered a word until Miles finally spoke.

"Wait, go back, Alex. Back it up a little." Kate held her breath, fearing that they had found prion damage.

"Here? Is that what you wanted to see again?" Alex asked.

"Yes. Oh wait, it's okay. It's a small cyst or something."

"Yeah, an arachnoid cyst, maybe there for years," Alex explained. "No biggie. Nothing to worry about. I'm going on."

"He probably has headaches from time to time. Okay, let's go," Edouard said.

Alex kept moving through the brain tissue, slowing down now and then, finding nothing worrisome, then moving forward again. Every ten minutes or so Miriam went into the MRI chamber while it was on standby and checked for brain activity. Nothing was going on. For now, that was fine with the team.

"Okay, Miles, I haven't seen a hint of prion damage, have you?" Alex asked. "It would have pretty much jumped out at us. Shall we run a little quicker?"

"Yes, I think we can wrap this part up in ten minutes. Then let's take a quick look at his heart, lungs, and liver, okay?"

"Yup, sounds like a plan." Alex ran through the rest of the brain images looking for prion damage, but there was none.

"Okay, we're done with the brain," Edouard reported. "No drama. Almost nothing to see there. A couple cysts, that's it. Certainly no spongiform issues. Are you happy, Kate?"

"Deliriously happy."

"Miriam, please tilt the table so we can image his chest and abdomen," Alex instructed. "And check him with the EEG real quick while we're resetting here." In five minutes, they were ready to continue.

"Okay, heart, lungs, here we go," Miles said. "Alex, let's do this part quicker. We're already at thirty minutes here." The machine started up again with its outrageous repertoire of clinks, clanks, clunks, and buzzes. Kate still couldn't get used to the noise.

"Edouard, you're the oncologist. What do you see?" Alex asked.

"Looks good. I need some time right here, though. Hang on."

Kate tried to stay calm, crossing and uncrossing her fingers. *Dear Universe, God, whoever is out there*, she thought, *give me good news.*

A few more minutes went by. Finally Edouard said, "Kate, you said this guy was a two pack a day Camel smoker?"

"Yup, that's right, Edouard."

"Here's his film from 1990. See the masses here and here, Edouard?" Miles asked.

"It's all gone. No cancer. This is fantastic!" Edouard exclaimed. "Alex, the liver, please."

Alex zeroed in on Nielsen's liver, allowing Edouard to look through section after section.

"What do you think, Edouard?" Miles asked.

"It's clean. No scarring. He may have had cirrhosis last century, but he sure as heck doesn't have it now. Jesus, Kate, you've found a cure for just about everything. Maybe cryo will cure erectile dysfunction, too!"

"Thank you, guys. Thank you, Dr. Goldman, for coming in," Kate said. "Success, people. Back to the operating room, please. Let's go!"

* * *

"Okay, everyone," Miles said. "We've equalized temperatures in the whole body. We're ready. Any questions? Are we clear on responsi—"

"Oh, there they are, Dr. Coleman. You've got EEG bursts," Miriam interrupted.

"Just like with the cat, Miles," Chrissy exclaimed. "What do you want to do?"

"Like I said before, if he's going to present bursts I want to encourage him, in a sense, to reboot. With our help of course. And there—now they're gone. Suppression mode. But it sort of proves he's, in a sense, actually alive right now, understand? On some level he's got electrical activity even without a heartbeat. Amazing, huh? Okay, everyone, if you will notice I have already told Dr. Radelet to start up. Edouard, are you in the left femoral artery yet? Can we start getting the cryo mix out the other side?"

"We're having problems, Miles. Nothing's flowing and the pump keeps going to standby. We've got a problem."

"Damn. I want to start him up, but not without blood, obviously. We've got to drain the cryofluid and then flush with saline until we're sure every last bit of glycol is out of his body. What's the solution? Anybody?"

"EEG bursts again, Doctor," Miriam interjected. "He's trying to wake up. Amazing!"

"I can't make him walk and talk if we can't get blood in him," Miles said. "Turn the pump off. Reboot the damn thing. Here, let me see those incisions." Miles was now in master surgeon overdrive—he would let nothing hinder success. "You're not fully in the left artery, Edouard—see? I'm making a new incision. I know it was hard to even locate with zero pulse, the fatty tissue there, and the body still a bit cool. There, got it. Turn the pump on again. We've got to get the cryo solution out, *stat*." But the machine went to standby again. It just wouldn't cooperate. They couldn't do anything further until all the preservative was out of Nielsen's body.

"Miles, maybe the artery is collapsed somewhere," Edouard ventured.

"If so, it should have popped back when we turned the machine off and back on," Miles answered, a puzzled look on his face. He stared over at the Superflow 3000X centrifugal pump ECMO system. Was the problem there or was it the patient? "Miriam, check all the clamps and stopcocks, make sure we're not defeating ourselves like idiots."

Miriam checked every detail, eyeing each connection, each possible error in setup. "Miles, it's all fine. It checks out, we should be getting flow. I've had a lot of experience with this system in intensive care units. It's kept a lot of people alive while their heart and lung problems were being solved. This is the best-designed ECMO machine in the world."

"What's ECMO stand for? I read about it but I've forgotten," Kate whispered to Norm and Alex Goldman as they sat behind the observation glass.

"Extracorporeal membrane oxygenation," said Goldman. "It's basically the modern version of what laymen might think of when they've heard the term *heart-lung machine*."

"Okay, old-school stopgap for a bit," Miles said. "Tip the patient on his right side and let gravity help for a bit. Use your hands and massage near the left and the right artery. Get things moving—whatever caveman technique it takes to try to get at least some of the cryo out while we get the machine working. Where's Norm?"

"I'm out here observing along with Mike and Franklin. And Alex and Kate, too," Norm said, waving at Miles through the glass. "What do you need, Miles?"

"Take a look at this machine. You're the mechanic, right? Find out why the hell it keeps going on vacation. The damn thing going to standby is unacceptable."

"I wasn't expecting to do anything in there. I don't have a mask and gown on, Miles. That's why I'm out here. We've never had a problem with that machine. Miriam and I ran it through its functions yesterday."

"I don't care about yesterday, Norm. Miriam, get Norm a gown and a mask and get him in here to help figure it out. Look, more EEG bursts. Damn!"

A couple minutes later Norm stepped up to the machine and checked over the controls with Miriam. "Miles, the machine is fine," Norm said. "It's supposed to go to standby if the pressure is too extreme. There's a warning code flashing, see? E44—you have a blockage somewhere. Is there any cryofluid at all coming through the exit tube there, Edouard?"

"Barely. The tube's chattering, and feebly at that," Edouard answered, gritting his teeth.

"And that code wasn't flashing before, Norm," Miles added. "What the hell? Maybe we should just kick the thing!"

"I saw it," Kate interjected, raising her voice.

Miles shot her a ferociously dirty look. "You saw a code on the machine and said nothing?"

"Miles, she's not a doctor or a nurse," pleaded Norm. "How was she supposed to know what that was?"

"It said E44, Kate? You saw it?" Miles asked.

"Yes, for a split second, and then a few times again. It would just flash for a moment."

"Jesus, *damn thing*. We had alarms set and nothing sounded? When we're done here, that thing gets dumped. I don't care how great the pump and oxygenator is if the electronics are fried somehow. Kate, see the pump, the oxygenator, the blood gas system, the priming box, and all the series of infusion bags, the new blood, all the hoses, clamps and everything attached? All of that has to get us through three steps without a hitch. We've got to drain the cryo, flush the circulatory system with saline, and then introduce the fresh blood, recirculate it to keep it oxygenated at the proper temperature, no air bubbles, and so on."

"Yes, I see it all," Kate answered meekly.

"I'm giving you a job. You're not just an audience member now. I want you to watch the display like a hawk for any codes that come on-screen. The rest of us can't watch it every second while we're working.

Can you see the display clearly from there?"

"Yes. I can do that. And I'm sorry," Kate murmured.

"And can we shut off your damn maternal heartbeat thing? It's giving me a headache." Miles had frustration written all over his face. "I can't concentrate. Sorry. I'm an ass, but seriously, I can't handle it right now."

"Yes," Kate answered. "I'm sorry again. I'll take care of it. I have no idea whether it helps or not."

"Norm and Miriam," said Miles, "we're starting all over from step one. Strip the machine down and prime the whole system again, and make sure the alarms are on—not that I trust the machine anymore."

"Okay, Miles," added Norm. "We can have it primed again in ten minutes. We'll double-check everything as we go, obviously."

Miles did a series of neck rolls, stretched out his spine, then cracked his knuckles. He sighed deeply, then took a series of deep breaths to calm himself. His eyes rolled up, and he stared at the ceiling in thought, running through solutions. "All right, I can fix this," he announced. "I'm going to try a new exit for the cryofluid at the carotid. A little slit there, no biggie. And, Scott, from now on I want you calling out all the numbers."

"Miles, you're the more experienced surgeon," Edouard interrupted, "but what about this? Run a double lumen catheter in the right internal jugular vein. It's minimally invasive and far less likely to be problematic now and later than cutting into the carotid. It also shortens the distance from our entry and exit, right?"

Miles mulled the idea over, running it through an improvised checklist in his mind. "Edouard, you're right. Brilliant! Why didn't I think of it? Come on people, let's do it." Miles began the procedure, which also gave Norm a few more minutes to try taming the Superflow 3000X.

"Are we good now, everyone?" Miles asked as he finished connecting the external section of the catheter. "Okay, Chrissy and Scott, elevate Mr. Nielsen's legs above his head, please. Like that, yes. Norm, zero-calibrate that thing and then set it on low, 1500 RPM, then press start."

Norm fiddled with the knobs for about thirty seconds. The flow of cryopreservative coming out the jugular was a bit better but still fairly minimal. At least the machine wasn't insulting them by shutting down like before or flashing phantom codes. Kate tried not to blink as she watched the machine's display intently.

"Okay, everyone ready?" Miles chirped. "We may have Mt. Vesuvius in a second. Norm, turn the knob up slowly. That's it. Take it slow. Keep going. Get us up to 3,000 RPM." Finally, they heard a muffled pop from somewhere within Nielsen's body, and a burst of cryofluid started streaming freely out the new site.

"There. Got it. Whew, that was annoying." Miles again took a few deep breaths to center himself. "Okay, where are we?"

"Everything's good now," Scott said as he and Miriam set Nielsen back into a normal position.

"Chrissy," said Miles, "you've run this particular machine before in the past, right? Tell me how many minutes it will be before I can shock him? How long until the preservative is out and he's got all real blood in there?"

"Ten minutes minimum," she answered. "Remember, everyone, Saltieri put a fluorescing agent in the cryofluid. Smart man, eh? We'll wand the rinse—the saline flow—until nothing lights up. Then and only then will we switch over and introduce the blood, force the saline out, close the whole circuit and let it run. At that point we will have established what the Superflow was actually built for—the standard ECMO procedure for maximizing optimally oxygenated blood flow, blood gas stabilization, and continuous recirculation when a patient presents poor heart and lung function."

"Okay," Miles said. "In the meantime his brain has been quiet for a while now. That's fine. I sure don't want to try to shock him during a burst. We're good here. We're bringing him back very soon."

Twelve minutes later Chrissy gave the go-ahead. All of the cryofluid was out, as well as the saline. Warm, richly oxygenated blood began circulating through Mr. Nielsen via the ECMO machine. The body temperature was now exactly where they wanted it—no longer hypothermic, yet not high enough that they needed to be concerned for now about any imminent onset of cellular decay. While Miles placed sterile patches in the abandoned right femoral incision and was sewing it up as quickly as possible, Miriam and Scott intubated Nielsen, started the ventilator, and then took turns doing chest compressions.

"All right, that's good," said Miles. "Here we go. Dr. Radelet, inject the epinephrine." As soon as Edouard withdrew the needle, Miles revved up the defib machine. "Clear!" he barked.

Zap—no response.

"Okay, Scott. Some more compressions. Sixty seconds' worth, okay?"

Kate's eyes moved nervously back and forth from Nielsen's motionless face to the ECMO machine and all the other monitors. She'd been holding her fingers crossed so tightly again that they were going numb.

"Scott, deeper please," Miles said. "Let us know if your arms tire and you need to trade off."

"I'm okay, Dr. Coleman. Sorry about that. I'm here to make this a success. You just keep telling me what you need."

"That's good, Scott. Keep going. Keep going—perfect. Okay, here we go again. Clear!" Miles yelled.

Zap. Beep-beep-beep-beep....

"We've got him!" Miles yelled. "He's back. Keep working, everyone. Keep him going. Scott, vitals?"

"BP low—not a surprise, but getting better. Hang on, I'm trying to read everything here. Okay, yeah, looking good. He's trying to breathe. Pulse irregular but improving. He's already gaining a little skin tone, Dr. Coleman. He's going to be fine!"

"Okay, Scott. Thank you, but let's not overstate things. Steady, everyone. Can we keep him stable?"

"The BP is still low. Heartbeat dropping under forty," Miriam barked before Scott even caught the readout.

"It's okay. I'm not jumping the gun here," Miles answered. "Relax. Let's keep watching."

Everyone eyed the monitors, looking for affirmation that Nielsen could, before too long, truly stabilize and start functioning without aid from the ventilator and the Superflow ECMO system. "That BP is still too low, even with the machine trying to help," Miles exclaimed. "Shit. And his lungs aren't working at all now. Oh no, we're losing him."

Nielsen's right arm quickly turned blue. Then suddenly his heart shut down. Cardiac arrest. Everyone looked to Miles for a solution. He stood totally still, focusing his thoughts. It was time to stay calm and not make any mistakes.

How does he do it? Kate wondered. *If that was me I'd be bouncing around like a crazy person trying to fix things without thinking it through.*

"All right. We start over, everyone," Miles said. "But we have to get him back fast."

"Dr. Coleman, his blood gases went way off just then, and the pH especially dropped like a rock," said Scott. "It went under seven point zero right before we lost him!"

Miles peered over at the monitors, squinting and frowning. "Chrissy, hook up that 50 mL bicarbonate and push. Let me see the bottle first."

Chrissy handed three bottles to Miles. He stared at each, making sure there was no precipitation in any of them. "Use this one," he said as he handed one of the bottles back to her.

"Still some cryosolution in the system, or helium subdermal?" Edouard asked. "You know, from the cryopod? Could it be what caused it?"

"No way. Impossible. We went through all of that when Kate, you, and I created this procedure. Damn," Miles muttered, rolling his eyes up and concentrating in his usual fashion as he mulled the whole situation over. "We had him back!"

"We'll get him, Miles," said Miriam. "You can do it. All we have to do is get his heart going again and make sure we straighten out his metabolism—the acidosis, all that."

"You're right. Okay, come on, everyone. Scott, start the compressions again. All I want is sixty seconds, then we shock him again. Kate, is that darling 3000X behaving?"

"Yes. Nothing weird on the display. It's still whirring away."

Scott set to work, performing one hundred twenty perfect compressions over the sixty seconds Miles had ordered. Miles reset to two hundred eighty joules. "Here we go. Clear!"

Zap. Beep-beep-beep-beep....

"Okay, we have him again!" Miles yelled. "Talk to me!"

"Much better, Dr. Coleman. BP in normal range. Pulse erratic, but getting better," shouted Scott.

"Look, his lungs are working. He's breathing fine now," Edouard said. "Whatever was wrong before went away."

"The carbon dioxide reading looks good," Scott proclaimed. "The acidosis issue is reversing. Yes, the lungs are functioning. Looking good."

"Whew, now maybe we can sit back and watch him continue to stabilize," Miles answered.

"Oh no, I spoke too soon," Scott yelled twenty seconds later as one of the monitors began to chime. "We've got ventilation problems. The airway pressure just shot up, the oxygen saturation is dropping."

"Damn," Miles responded. "Edouard, jump in please—six puffs of albuterol down the ET tube and bag it in."

"His heart rate is dropping—it's down to forty," Scott announced, peering at the monitors as he also double-checked the positioning of the breathing tube. Everyone in the room knew they had to bring Nielsen back right now—there probably wouldn't be another chance if he went code again. Fear was written across the Burgess brothers' faces as they watched the drama with apprehension.

"Thirty-six, still dropping, Dr. Coleman," Scott said. "Not good!"

"One milligram atropine—one milligram epinephrine," Miles ordered. "Scott, call out all the monitors."

"I think he's in bronchospasm," said Edouard. "Maybe a reaction to the donor blood, Miles?"

"Heart rate is all the way down to thirty now and erratic, Dr. Coleman," Scott reported. "BP dropping like last time. We're at six point nine on the pH and still dropping there, too."

"Okay everyone, pay attention," Miles said, eyes blazing. "I'm going to start pacing the heart through the defib pads at eighty beats per minute, then increase until we get capture. *Somewhere* in there, the patient has to follow our lead. I'm sure as hell not giving him a choice not to."

"Understood," Miriam responded. "What next?"

"One more milligram of atropine. Scott, what's the calcium level on the blood gas?"

"Three point eight," Scott answered.

"One gram of calcium. And the potassium reading?"

"Five point eight."

"That's not acceptable. We have to ventilate faster to get that down."

"The ECMO can't do any more than it's already doing, Miles," Edouard pointed out.

"I know, I know, and we're running out of time. He can't just lay on this table while we fumble away. I didn't come back to the OR to have this happen. We aren't just risking pulmonary now but kidneys and other organs, too." Miles shot a quick look out to the observation area. "Alex? Dr. Gordon! You totally sure his lungs were clean on that MRI? Healthy? Were there signs of fluid? Collapse? Did we miss something?"

"They looked excellent, Miles. Completely. Say, what if you ramp up his heartbeat more?"

"It won't be enough, his heart isn't pumping properly, and we need real metabolism unless we're happy to just keep him on the machine forever. Hell, the ECMO can't do everything. It can't revive him."

"Agreed," Edouard answered.

"Time for creativity, Miles. You're a brilliant doctor, my friend. If anyone can do it, you can," Gordon yelled out, giving Miles a smile and an energetic double thumbs-up.

Miles allowed himself thirty seconds for an idea to occur, an idea that *had to happen now, right now*. He began by emptying his mind and then inviting the answer to come to him from the universe. Yet these were thirty seconds of time they barely had to spare. "Holy shit, HOUSE SEASON FOUR!"

Kate leapt up, yet was mindful to stifle an actual cheer. *Miles and House—of course!*

"Everyone listen closely," Miles said, dropping into a hushed tone. "We abandoned the right femoral, remember? We didn't really know if it was bad or anything—we just abandoned it looking for greener pastures, right? We can go back and run an Impella through there right into the heart. Boost that heart and get its attention."

"And abandon the ECMO pump?" Edouard said incredulously. "No way!"

"No, we use them both. What's stopping us? I can get an Impella in fast, we already have the incision. Two for one!"

"Well, I'm not a cardiologist, but there are at least three contraindications and one big problem I can think of right away," Edouard said, making sure he gained complete eye contact with Miles. "There is the simple detail that you'd be on the wrong side, Miles. You can't route an Impella to its usual destination in the left ventricle from the right femoral."

"I *want* to be on the right side of the heart. I'm going to power the flow directly into the pulmonary artery and the lungs from right there. The ECMO routing in from the left side of the body is just fine. We've got all this technology and we're going to use everything we've got."

"Are you sure about this?"

"I'm sure I'm not going to lose him, Edouard. That you can count on!"

Franklin, Mike, and Kate stared over at Dr. Gordon. He could tell they had no idea what was going on. "The Impella device has a tiny, yet highly efficient motor on the end of it," he explained. "It helps spin the blood out if for some reason the heart is sluggish or partially impaired. It's an amazing invention. Even though the motor is only the size of a pencil eraser it will add another fifty percent boost to what they already have. He's absolutely frigging brilliant, your man there."

"We know that!" Mike exclaimed, gripping Gordon by the shoulder.

Miles regained access through the right femoral artery, tore the Impella packaging open, then snaked the guide catheter up toward the heart. Once in place, he slipped the Impella device inside the catheter's walls and then followed its route toward the heart. He then pulled the guide catheter back out, leaving the Impella device in positon to do its job. Nielsen's chest continued to bounce up and down with each jolt of the pacer pads as he performed the installation. The Impella and its mini-motor were ready to go. "Got it. Let's see what happens," Miles said as he started up the device, then stood back and folded his arms. "Okay, Scott, please give me good news."

"BP coming up, Dr. Coleman. The airway pressures are normalizing, and we're slowly coming back into normal range for all your blood gases. And look, he's pinking up again. Of course that's just a qualitative observation, sir." The last comment was greeted with a few chuckles, albeit somewhat of the nervous variety. "I think he really won't need the ventilator soon, too!"

"Congratulations to everyone. To the team," Mike called out. "You did it. And I think my own heart was about give out there for a while!"

"Sorry, dear Mike. There's only one operating table in here!" Chrissy shot back.

Kate couldn't believe what she'd just seen—Miles working his magical medical genius, with plenty of help from the crew. She wasn't a doctor, but to her, A.C. Nielsen seemed to be breathing just fine five minutes later when the ventilator was turned off on Miles' orders, and none of the monitors were complaining to the crew.

"Miles, what happened in the *House* episode, the one that inspired you just now," Edouard asked as everyone began to catch their breath, congratulate each other, and relax at least a little.

"Ha, he was stealing equipment from other departments to run simulations, piggy-backing a number of really expensive systems in ways no one would ever think of. Then he lied about what he was up to, of course. What I did was nothing compared to the shenanigans he was pulling off."

"So then what happened?" Scott asked.

"The usual. In the last five minutes he saved a patient with the customary ridiculously exotic disease and Dr. Cuddy threatened to fire him, which didn't happen. She had fired him in the previous episode, then gave in and rehired him. The writers knew they couldn't fire him twice in a row."

"Plus those two had push-me-pull-you hots for each other, anyway. Cuddy threatening to fire him was her own special brand of foreplay," Chrissy said.

"Exactly. A recipe for some serious steam," Miles said with a smile.

"And now what?" Edouard asked.

"Things are looking mighty fine. We'll turn off the Impella and then back off the pacing to the heart," Miles answered.

A minute or so later, as Chrissy turned down the milliamps, Nielsen's heart began to take over fully—beat by beat by beat.

"Looks like he's decided he likes ninety-two beats per minute," Scott announced.

"Very good—I'll take it. To each his own!" Miles exclaimed.

After a few more minutes, Miriam looked to Miles. He nodded back. "Miriam, pull out your penlight and check his pupils. Make sure we've got equal reactions to light stimulus."

"What does that tell us, Miles?" Kate asked as she entered the room, donning a gown and mask that Chrissy had handed to her.

"If both eyes react to the light and do so equally, we know we've more than likely got a healthy, awake, and aware brain—what we need to see. It's our first quick test," Miles explained. "I'm sorry I barked at you earlier. I really didn't mean to be so ridiculously rude."

"That's okay. You were saving a life—a really important life," Kate said, smiling.

"Look, he's fine," Miriam said. "Textbook reaction. You've got brain stem function, Doctor. Congratulations!"

Edouard let out a whistle. "Wildest code I've ever witnessed! That's one hell of a fighter lying there."

"Let's get him completely off the ECMO now. He's ready." Dr. Milstein Coleman the Third let out a long loud sigh, then took a deep breath and exclaimed loudly, "I pronounce Operation Code Ultra-Blue a success. Welcome to the twenty-first century, Mr. Nielsen!"

CHAPTER THIRTY-FIVE

"What the hell are all these papers you're dumping on my desk, Shontae? You know I hate paper. Get rid of it!"

"Shut the hell up, Jak, and please mix yourself a drink. You got any liquor hidden in here? You're so far beyond cranky. That damn caffeine drink just makes you a hyper asshole instead of a boozy one. Tell your doctors to fuck themselves. Anyway, this stuff is from Baby Boy Bronsteyn—more show proposals from the public. The deadline is almost here. These are the best, or maybe just the weirdest ones that have come in recently."

"Oh, really? I am so excited. Look at me, I'm jumping with so much joy. Oh, fuck it—what's he got?"

"Here's one, the working title is *Caboose Wars*. A bunch of female railroad enthusiasts. They fixed up some old train cars and cabooses—you can sleep in them. Kind of like a bed-and-breakfast thing. They're in South Dakota."

"And the war part of it—what's that, Shontae?"

"There's another bunch of women one town over copying the first chicks and trying to steal the customers away. You should read about the evil stuff they've been doing to each other to try to get the upper hand. Also, all the women happen to have really large—well you fill in the blank, Jak. Can you guess it?" Shontae said, winking.

"Oh fuck, seriously? They've all got big asses? What are the odds? *Caboose Wars*? Yeah, people will watch it."

"Yes, they will. And maybe we can get Amtrak for some product placement."

"Anything else?" Jak asked.

"Here's one. Hmm, let's see," said Lou Stanislav, Jak's production assistant, as he scanned another proposal. "*Blade of Truth*. It's this guy in Winnipeg who's got blades for legs, like that Olympic runner guy who killed his girlfriend. Remember that? Anyway, this blade guy is a hotshot lawyer. Takes cases no one else will. And he wins them all."

"Wait, this is for real? It sounds like a script."

"No, it's for real. I'm reading it through. Check out the pic. The dude is handsome. Chicks will dig him. His mother submitted it. She thinks it should be called *Blade of Truth: Going Out on a Limb*."

"That's so bad it's good, Lou," Jak said. "Lord. Any more? Please say no." He grabbed the tension-release gadget his secretary had given him for Christmas and started squeezing the thing. It hardly helped. *A frigging tennis ball would work just as well as this stupid, overpriced thing*, Jak thought.

"Sorry, Jak," Shontae said. "Here's one more the interns marked all up with yellow Hi-Liter exclamation marks. They call it *Who's Your Oven-Bakin' Momma?*"

"Cooking show? We don't do that. Boring!"

"No, stupid," Shontae said. "It's about a group of teen girls in Mississippi who realize there's big money in being surrogate mothers. They're not considering getting a job down at the Walmart or Hobby Lobby—that's for losers. They keep carrying cute little test tube fetuses over and over, hauling in serious dough from desperate-for-children East Coast rich couples. All these girls have funky tats, too, Jak. We all know you love the ladies with tats, right?"

"Eh, fuck you, Shontae."

"Okay, stop arguing and being such assholes," Lou demanded. "I timed Chris Bronsteyn's proposed one hundredth *Dimi and Khail Show*. It's a pretty damned good storyboard, but we're going to be eight or nine minutes short. I can't find any way to stretch these scenes out to hit our mark. What do you want to do?"

"How about we have Dimi sit on Jak's face on camera?" Shontae offered. "Watch him squirm. That could be five minutes."

"Jesus, Shontae, don't go shocking Lou's innocent mind with your filthy mouth. He's a card-carrying Lutheran, for Chrissake," Jak said, abandoning the stupid gadget and fidgeting with his tie.

"I don't get it—why doesn't this show ever just jump the goddamn shark?" Lou asked. "I mean really, who cares about Dimi and Khail? I'd rather watch Montana Mama. Now there's a woman."

"So you dig her, Lou? Isn't she kind of old for you? She's like forty-five and you're what—thirty?" Shontae said, poking hard at Lou's biceps. She loved teasing the millennials who kept coming in waves into the ranks of the biz.

"She's beautiful. I know her hair is turning gray, but it's so thick and damn gorgeous. And she's got like perfect 34C boobs."

"Oh, so you don't like Dimi's? What's wrong with them?" Jak asked as he filled a cup of coffee. He'd grown tired of the Red Bull.

"They're gargantuan," Lou explained. "She could strangle a guy with them. Lure him in, like a black widow spider or a girl praying mantis, and then suffocate him. And imagine what those titties will be like when she's fifty. Hell, we'll probably still be filming this damn show then."

"Lou, in the future we can film it in space. Her aging boobs won't sag in zero gravity," Shontae said. "We'll get NASA's approval."

"Ha, stop it. Don't make me laugh so hard."

"What, Lou?" Shontae asked. "You're getting hard? Here, just thinking about Montana Mama?"

"He likes Mama and especially all those bighorn sheep out there in Montana, Shontae," Jak said. "I think he's a real animal lover—a zoophiliac, I think they call it."

"Well, then he's got something special in common with Dimi and her ancestors. Didn't those Greek shepherd boys like to fuck their flock?"

"I believe so. Say that ten times fast: *fuck their flock, fuck their flock!*" Jak let out a long sigh—it was nice to have funny, irreverent friends. Being around them substantially reduced the daily stress of running the production company. For Jak and his staff, these wicked little office gabfests were comic relief for crass people in an admittedly despicable, yet highly lucrative business. "Oh well, seriously, guys, how are we going to pad this show? Add eight minutes? Where, how?"

"I got an idea, guys," Shontae blurted out as she stood up, grabbed two markers and started to make up a manic storyboard, scribbling wildly on the whiteboard in Jak's office. "What if we backtrack a little—make that a road trip to a spa in San Diego? There's a Saturday Night Sexsations shop in a mall there, so that works. That gives us more to work with—easy five minutes. After the mall thing, we'll tag on three minutes by following Khail and Dimi to Balboa Park. They can ride the carousel, nibble each other's ears, something sweet just the two of them. Then fade into the sunset." She added a drooling smiley-face to her presentation, plus a sketch of someone giving the finger.

"Aw, Shontae, that's precious." Jak laughed. "Okay, that will work. And if we're still short a minute or two, Dimi can look straight into the camera and flash the audience, right?"

"Yes, exactly," Lou said. "Release the twins!"

CHAPTER THIRTY-SIX

"He's stirring, Miles," Chrissy intoned over the intercom.

"Thanks. About time. What's his chart look like?"

"He's good, totally normal. We've still got the drip going on him and the muscle stimulator is still cycling."

"What's it been now, like twenty hours?"

"Yes, about that. Who else should I notify?"

"Just Kate, Mike, and Edouard. If he opens his eyes and is lucid at all I don't want to overwhelm him."

"Got it. See you in a minute or two."

Miles, Chrissy, Mike, Edouard, and Kate stood watching A.C. Nielsen stretch, moan, sigh, and everything else we all do when waking. Finally, he opened his eyes the tiniest amount, then closed them, rubbed, then reopened them—just barely.

"I'm going to turn the lights down lower," Mike whispered.

"Mr. Nielsen, good morning. How are you feeling?" Miles said gently. No answer. Nielsen stared blankly at the people hovering above him. Miles tried again. "Did you have a nice sleep, Mr. Nielsen?"

Hesitation, a look of confusion, some blinking—then finally, "What day is it?" Nielsen croaked. Everyone in the room smiled and sighed in relief. A.C. Nielsen was alive and seemingly well.

"It's Friday, Mr. Nielsen. A beautiful Friday," Chrissy answered, beaming.

"Who's Mr. Nielsen, miss?" he asked.

"Well, that's you, of course. You're A.C. Nielsen, the successful businessman."

"A.C. Nielsen?" he asked, still in the foggiest, froggiest voice imaginable.

"It's okay. You've been asleep for quite a while. Take it easy," Miles said.

"What are all these wires? Can you take them off of me?"

"A few of them, yes. Here, I can remove these. Is that better?" Miles asked. "You were in surgery, but now you're fine. Is there anything we can do to make you feel more comfortable?"

"I'm damn hungry."

"We can try to work on that. You've been on a glucose drip for quite a few hours," Edouard explained. "That won't make you feel full by any means. What can we bring you?"

"Pancakes and some Chock full o'Nuts coffee if you could. Maybe some Mrs. Butterworth's on the pancakes? You have that?" Nielsen attempted to sit up in the hospital bed.

"We can look and see. Here, let me help you sit up, sir," Chrissy said.

"We're not giving him caffeine now, Miles, right?" Edouard whispered.

"No, of course not," Miles said, "we'll find a decaf Keurig pod. But the pancakes are a good idea. Carbs he can handle. And don't forget, we want to honor his requests. Make sure Rip van Winkle is a happy camper!"

"Mr. Nielsen, we'll work on the food you wanted," Miles said. "Give us a couple minutes. Meanwhile, let me look you over, all right? Just check a few things, okay?"

Kate was surprised by Dr. Milstein Coleman's suave bedside manner. It seemed honed to perfection, without even a hint of the smartass-Miles side of his personality. Edouard looked on as Miles went through the perfunctory examinations and observations.

"Mr. Nielsen, you are doing very well," Miles said. "I think we can wheel you to your private room now and we'll have some breakfast there for you in no time."

"Thank you, Doctor. I can't seem to remember much right now. You said I was here for surgery?"

"That's right, sir, but you're fine now. We'll build up your muscle tone and you'll be up and about in no time. All right, here we go into the wheelchair." Chrissy, Miles, and Edouard rolled Nielsen to the apartment while Kate scrounged through the kitchen. DePaun, on apartment duty at the moment, was beyond exhilarated as Nielsen approached.

"Mr. Nielsen, it's an honor to finally meet you," DePaun announced as he extended his hand out to shake Nielsen's. No response—Nielsen was still slipping in and out of the fog.

"Look, Mr. Nielsen," DePaun said, "we got *Perry Mason* on the TV for you. It'll be the first show you see now that you're back."

"Oh, I don't really care much for television, young man. Could you turn the volume down, please? I'm sorry," said Nielsen matter-of-factly.

DePaun tried to hide his disappointment. He'd been hoping all the while that he would be the one on duty at the moment when A.C. made his triumphant return. And now this? Mr. Nielsen doesn't 'care much for television'? It couldn't be true.

Mike noticed DePaun's pained expression and placed his arm around him. "It's okay, DePaun. Give him a few days. He doesn't really know who he is yet, understand?"

"Yes, Mr. Burgess. Okay, I get it. I'll be patient."

Meanwhile, Kate had gone to the kitchen and found some freezer-burned microwave waffles. In the cupboard she discovered a tiny bottle of real maple syrup that Deirdre had brought back from a trip to Quebec. She took a guess at which decaf pod might taste like whatever this Chock full o'Nuts coffee was. She could hardly contain her excitement as she prepared Nielsen's welcome back breakfast, placed it all on a tray, and hustled down to the apartment.

"Oh, this is delicious!" Nielsen said, beaming at Kate. "That Mrs. Butterworth's tastes like it's fresh from New Hampshire, doesn't it? It's like the real thing!"

"Yes, Mr. Nielsen, I believe you're right!" Kate grinned. "Sorry, we only had waffles, not pancakes." Truth be told, Kate was in absolute seventh heaven. Here was A.C. Nielsen alive right in front of her, slurping his coffee and gobbling down cardboard-like waffles like a madman.

"Do you think we could turn that TV off?" Nielsen asked. "It's so noisy."

DePaun looked to Mike, not sure what to do. This wasn't how it was supposed to be. He, Bennie, Miles, and a couple other caretakers had been waiting ages for A.C. to return. And now Mr. Nielsen wanted the TV not just turned down but all the way off? Really? Off? Gloria's procession of vintage Magnavox, RCA, and Zenith televisions had been jabbering on for years, and now the person this whole epic production was intended for just wanted to abandon, no, totally destroy the whole conceit? Unthinkable. Impossible. DePaun fought back tears. But he wasn't ready to give up.

"Mr. Nielsen, excuse me, but we've got the TV here to make you feel at home, like all the rest of the nice things here in your room. The comfy Barcalounger chair, the big fancy globe there. The ship in the bottle. Chess set. I'll play you if you want—I'm pretty good. All the famous people with you in the photos on the wall. It's all there for you.

That's what a successful businessman wants, right? A place like that to go to and things that show off all the victories they've had and such?"

"Businessman?" Nielsen said, shaking his head as he squinted hard at DePaun. "No... I'm not a businessman. At least I don't think so. Sorry, I'm still kind of confused, young man."

Mike walked over to the Magnavox TV. He gazed over at DePaun, compassionately mouthed "I'm sorry," and clicked the set off.

CHAPTER THIRTY-SEVEN

Days passed. Nielsen ate more and more, exercised with Bennie's help, became more alert, and regained his sense of humor. He played chess with DePaun and even let him turn the TV on now and then.

"What's this show, DePaun?" Nielsen asked.

"It's called *Maverick*, Mr. Nielsen. Popular show in its day. You knew the star, James Garner. Here, look over this way on the wall. That's you and Garner right there. Not the greatest photo, though. And there's Dick Cavett, Goldie Hawn, and Flip Wilson behind you, see?"

"That's me, DePaun?" Nielsen tapped at the grainy old photo in the $1.99 frame.

"Sure, that's you. A bit heavier than now and you got glasses on there, see? For some reason you don't need glasses anymore, huh?"

"Interesting," Nielsen muttered. "So I was a hotshot businessman, right? You keep telling me that, but I don't remember. I don't recall much of anything other than I like music and a big breakfast."

"You'll start remembering, sir. Just keep looking at the photos. I bet that will jog things loose, sooner or later."

Nielsen strolled around the room. He had looked at the old photos of himself almost every day for two weeks. Nothing had clicked—until just now. "Hey wait, I do know this guy here. Helluva musician, played the piano. Better than most people thought."

"There you go, sir, your first breakthrough!" DePaun patted Nielsen on the back. "That's Steve Allen from *The Tonight Show*."

"That's right. Played the piano. Wrote some songs. Yeah, I knew him! I really did!"

"So look at that, sir. Your memory is coming back. It's a great day!"

* * *

Another week passed. DePaun and Bennie were becoming good friends with Nielsen. Miles would visit the apartment and spend some time with A.C., but he couldn't figure him out. There was something not quite right about him, but Miles couldn't put his finger on what it was. Yet no one else seemed concerned about how odd Nielsen could be now and then.

Nielsen woke on a Wednesday morning about nine thirty, padded into the bathroom, and used the toilet. He turned on the shower. As the streams of hot water pounded away on his shoulders and back, he wondered when the pampering from these folks would end and what he would do when they kicked him out to fend for himself. *Sooner or later they expect me to be a businessman again—not sure how I'm gonna do that,* he mused. He turned the water off, toweled himself dry, then stared at himself in the partly foggy mirror. "Who are you?" he asked himself out loud. "Who are you, really? Answer, come on, answer!"

He brushed his hair, then reached into the medicine cabinet and grabbed the straight razor and the can of Barbasol and lathered up his face. *Now I look like Santy Claus, he thought. Maybe that's who I am!* He started shaving absentmindedly, then suddenly yelled, "Ow! Damn it!" as he sliced his chin badly. He grabbed some toilet paper, moistened it with cold water and stuck it to the cut. The paper turned crimson. He slapped a fresh piece of paper on the cut and finished shaving the rest of his face, still mad at himself for cutting his chin. "Geez, still bleeding—ridiculous," he muttered. He opened the cabinet again. Aspirin, antacids, Q-tips, hand cream. There—bandages. He opened the box, grabbed a bandage, tore open the sleeve, and stuck it over the cut. There, done. *Hey, these are pretty fancy bandages. Like fiber or something. Not the cheapo kind like you mostly see.* He inspected the box, wondering what company was producing such a nice, high-quality product:

HEALTHAID PRODUCTS
FLEXIBLE FABRIC BANDAGES
Long-lasting, Latex free.
Change dressing daily.
Dist. Healthaid Corp.
Sioux Falls, IA
TM & © 2012. All Rights Reserved

Nielsen stared at the last line. He read it over and over and over.

CHAPTER THIRTY-EIGHT

Kate strolled into work in the midafternoon after a nice day of shopping at Plaza del Lago with her mom. Making the rounds of the building, she noticed Miles, Bennie, and DePaun gathered in the hallway outside the Nielsen apartment staring at the floor, not speaking.

"Something wrong, fellas?"

"Yes, Miss Pearson," DePaun said dejectedly. "When I came in this morning Mr. Nielsen yelled at me and kicked me out of his room. Said he hated me. Hated everybody, he said, but especially me and Bennie. Said he thought we were his friends. Then told me to get Mr. Mike Burgess and Franklin Burgess to come see him. The three of them have been in there for hours."

"Franklin's already here from LA?" Kate asked.

"Yeah," Miles said. "Not sure why."

"I do. Mike told me that he and Franklin decided that it was time to tell Nielsen what year it is. He's pretty healthy and getting into shape. Time to do it, Mike said. That's why Franklin was flying in. I didn't know he already got here."

"Listen, Kate," Miles whispered as he pulled Kate aside. "DePaun's really upset. I've been trying to calm him down. He says when he came to visit the apartment Nielsen was bleeding, like his face was bleeding. Do you think he would try to hurt himself?"

"I don't know, but I'll bet he beat Mike and Franklin to the punch somehow and figured out it's the twenty-first century. Why else would he be so mad at DePaun and Bennie? He probably thought his new pals should have told him what's up."

"Guys," Bennie interrupted, "why would he try to kill himself?"

"There's no saying what any of us would do if we were in Nielsen's shoes," Kate said. "I don't even know how I would try to tell him it's 2014. How long did you say they've been in there?"

"Since about ten this morning," DePaun said.

"Wow, that's a long time."

Suddenly the door to the Nielsen apartment swung open. Mike and Franklin emerged, stone-faced. Nielsen remained inside. Kate could hear him locking the door.

"Is Mr. Nielsen okay, Mr. Burgess?" DePaun asked. "Was he trying to hurt himself?"

"No. He cut himself shaving. Just an accident," Franklin said.

"Oh, that's good," Bennie said.

"Not really," Mike insisted. "He was pretty upset. Well, no—extremely upset. Tomorrow Franklin and I were going to help him with his memory issues and ease him into his situation. Help him fathom that it's 2014 and that he's been in cryo for years. We had it all figured out how to break it to him. But you boys fucked it up."

"What do you mean, Mike? What did we do?" DePaun asked.

"Here, DePaun," Mike barked as he tossed the box of bandages at him. "Read the back label. One of you didn't follow the rules."

CHAPTER THIRTY-NINE

July 2014

"A.C. is really doing well, huh, Kate?" Miles remarked as he strolled into her office with a gigantic burrito spilling out of its foil wrapper.

"Hey, stop destroying my office. Here, take a couple napkins. Yes, you're right, he's doing great. I'm glad you were proven wrong that he and everyone else in the world is a Walking Dead prion-zombie in training. You sure got our attention that day."

"Yup. But I do believe that prion contamination is on the upswing. Wait, you'll see," Miles countered, still battling with the black beans and hot sauce trying to spill out and make an escape.

"So, why did you mosey on over here, Miles? Just to spill food all over my office carpet?"

"Kate, have you noticed the simple fact that A.C. Nielsen knows nothing about TV? How the hell does he not remember anything about his ratings business or the TV and movie entertainment field?"

"I wouldn't know so much about the TV thing, Miles, but I've been wondering some stuff, too. I know perhaps not every Danish person is blond and blue-eyed, but he's so dark, and then there's that wavy hair of his. And when he gets upset his voice changes, I've heard him mutter softly in some other language."

"Danish?"

"How would I know? What the heck does Danish sounds like?"

"Dunno. So, what the hell do you think is going on?" Miles asked as he proceeded to stuff the last of his burrito into his mouth, frat boy style.

"I played around with some of his DNA. He is not Scandinavian, his DNA doesn't fit. His genome profile is Mediterranean."

"I see. So the Nielsen name—maybe his Italian or Portuguese or whatever family just took that on somehow at Ellis Island or something?"

"That sounds like a very large stretch, Miles. Anyway, hang on—do you really think that he looks that much like the A.C. Nielsen in all the photos in the apartment?"

"I don't know. Guys looked alike back in those days—the Madmen Don Draper look—Vitalis oiled-up hair, black suit, white shirt, skinny tie, you know what I mean?"

"Yeah, I guess. Well anyway, I have his fingerprints on this glass here. Do you know some way we could run them? Can anyone do that or is it a police thing?"

"Any decent hacker can run them. Hand me the glass. Can I get a date?"

"As soon as you can get it, I guess. How long will it take?"

"No, I mean can I get a date with you if I run the prints?" he asked with a hopeful puppy-dog look on his face.

Kate's jaw dropped, but she caught herself quickly before she'd look foolish. *A date with Miles? Why on earth? He's never seemed to have noticed me before—in that way.*

"Um, what? A date? Well, um, I'm flattered, but I think maybe we need to keep a professional relationship. For now, I guess. So, um, here, then, here's the glass," Kate said nervously, avoiding eye contact as she handed Miles a juice glass wrapped in paper towel.

Miles gingerly unwrapped the glass, looked it over closely, and set it down. He then reached inside a folder he had tucked under his arm, grabbed a couple sheets of paper, and handed them to Kate.

"What's this, Miles?"

"The ID you requested, Miss Pearson."

"Huh?"

"I had a state cop friend run his prints a few days ago. I guess we've both been getting suspicious, huh?"

"That was legal to do?"

"Probably about as legal as you poking your nose into his DNA without his permission."

"Holy cow, Miles," Kate said excitedly "Oh my God, look at this, what the heck? I was right. We were right. He isn't A.C. Nielsen at all. Jesus! This name—totally Spanish or Portuguese, right?"

"Yup. About the same birthdate as Nielsen. Same size and frame. Our guy was arrested a couple times years ago for drunk and disorderly in San Francisco and also in Seattle—that's why we got a print match. Apparently decades-old fingerprints just stay in the files forever. Kate, have you noticed the one subject that makes our friend's eyes light up?"

"Not really. You've spent more time with him than I have. So what do you mean?"

"Mention music and he tends to light up. It's kind of low-key, but noticeable. I think now and then he's still a bit in a fog mentally. Understandable when you've been frozen for twenty-some years."

"Okay, cough it up. I'm getting to know your ways. I can't imagine that you would ID this guy and not dig further, especially with your computer skills. What else do you know? Spill the damn beans. And by the way, thanks for not spilling your burrito beans and hot sauce all over my floor."

"Our thawed-out friend—Mr. Gaetano Raimondo Machado? He was a hotshot jazz musician. And get this—he's Gloria Dunham's ex-husband number one!"

"*What?*" Kate sprang to her feet. She could feel her pulse start to race. "What in the world?"

"It's true. They were married. He played second trumpet with the Jimmy Dorsey band. Second trumpet is the guy who takes all the solos. He went by the name of Ray Machado—pretty famous in his day. Supposedly died in late 1990. Nineteen ninety, Kate! Think what was going on here around then."

"*Oh, my God, Miles. Oh, my God!*" Kate yelled. "I'm texting Mike—he needs to know this."

"Yeah, I agree with you. The whole thing is weird. And if this Machado character is pretending to be A.C. Nielsen, where the hell is the real A.C.? I've been trying to figure this out for three days now and I've got absolutely nothing. I'm glad you wanted to talk about this. And now we can be clueless and confused together. And you owe me a date now, don't forget."

"We'll talk about that later, mister. Okay, I'm contacting Mike now." Kate pulled out her phone and texted Mike, smashing the keys quickly in her excitement.

You busy?

"Kate, I think he went out for lunch. His car isn't here. Does he even text? I've never seen him do it."

"Yeah, he does. We've texted about stuff now and then. He's awful at it. Of course, he's old. Shocking he'll even do it, right?"

"Right."

"Oh, here goes. Miles, he just saw my message. See what I mean? His thumbs are fat, old, and decrepit."

Just doing lnucnh.

        News here.

What?

        AC isn't AC

Wht?

        AC Nielsen isn't AC Nielsen.
        You have an imposter

Seruoilsly?

        Seriously Mike

AC is here w me Kate.
Lunch. Celbrating.

        Can he see our texts?

Yess. Im shpwing him.

        No don't do that Mike NO

Its okay Kate.Everthings
good.Sorry for bad typing.

        Ok. Mike hide the screen ok

OK what

        A guy named Ray Machado is
        pretending to be AC

O Kate. Ray is here too Haha

        What?

There both here

You're drunk right? Machado was
married to Gloria. Where the heck r u?

Fontanas on Devon

OK we're coming over

Keith is hear to We just bought
a trinket or flugglehorm
or something

What?

Here. Keith here too.
sgpuid autospell
Nevr mind Kate come over
Imm buyinh lunch for everyone

You mean security guy Keith?

Yes. We just fixd some stuff

Tell me again who is there Seriously

Me Keith AC Ray haha

What is so funny? We're on our way. Stop
drinking right now

Yes maaam

OK Mike Btw yr shit at texting Miles sez

Hes shit at fashion tell him that

CHAPTER FORTY

Kate and Miles rushed to Fontana's, shooting ideas back and forth about what the heck was going on. Miles braked hard as he narrowly avoided hitting a bike messenger, then slammed on the gas again. Kate's heart was pounding as adrenaline rushed through her body. They finally arrived at the restaurant, squeezed into a parking spot, and raced into the building. Kate spotted Mike and his entourage toward the back of the large room.

"There they are, Miles." Kate grabbed his arm and dragged him with her. "Come on, we have to figure this out. Mike must be clueless about this Machado guy."

"Welcome, Miles. Hi, Kate," Mike said, a bit wobbly as he stood up to greet them. "Join the party. We're celebrating. And A.C. wants to tell you something."

"Hello, Kate, hello, Miles. Please have a seat. Yes, I have something to tell you—something serious. My real name is Raimondo, or simply, Ray Machado. I am most definitely not A.C. Nielsen. I am sorry for the ruse, but it was necessary for a while. We'll explain. Both of you have been wonderful, so I hope that there are no hard feelings. I told Mike and Franklin that you two would probably be on to me before long."

"Hi, guys," Keith, the security guard, said, barely looking up from his jalapeño poppers appetizer.

"So, will someone *please* tell me what's going on?" Kate said, flustered and still half out of breath. "This is crazy. Mike, you've known all along that Machado—I mean this guy Ray here was pretending to be A.C. Nielsen?"

"Totally. Franklin and I were the ones who thought it up over twenty years ago! Oh, here comes the waiter. Order something to drink and eat. We'll tell you the story, but I'm not going to watch you sit there without some grub and a drink. We're celebrating, Kate. We're imbibing."

She and Miles glanced through the menu quickly and ordered. They didn't care what they ate or drink—they just wanted to know what the hell was going on.

"Hey, look at this trumpet I bought for Ray. Beautiful, huh?" Mike opened the plush new case, lined with crimson velvet and satin. The shiny, polished-to-perfection instrument lay there as if it were some kind of royalty.

"It's actually a flugelhorn, Mike—remember?" said Ray Machado. "It's easier to blow through. I'm going to get my lip back in shape for fun. Dr. Radelet gave me the okay to try it."

"That's a beautiful instrument," Miles said. "Chuck Mangione played this kind of horn back in the day, right?"

"Yes. Not that I could ever play like him," Ray answered sarcastically.

"Okay, so please, please, please somebody tell me what's going on," Kate begged. "What are you celebrating, Mike?"

"We've had a security leak at ExitStrategy for a while. But Keith and I figured it out now. I see now it was really no big deal, but for a while it was driving me crazy. I was very worried. And now that we've solved it, every employee can now know that A.C. isn't A.C.—he's actually Ray. You beat everyone else to it by a bit."

"Okay, the suspense here is killing me. What's the story? How did Ray turn into A.C.? And where is the real Mr. Nielsen?" Kate implored.

"Shall I tell it all to them, Mike?"

"Of course, Ray," Mike said, nodding and lifting his glass dramatically in the air. "You have the floor, sir."

"Well, Kate, I saw your text. You've figured out that I was married to Gloria Dunham many years ago. It wasn't a great marriage, we both had our faults. We were trying to patch things up, so we decided that Gloria would go on the road with my jazz group up the West Coast to see if a little travel might respark our marriage. Well it sparked, but not the way I was expecting. One day we got in this big fight and she clocked me—knocked me totally out. This doctor saw me and checked me out and said I better stop playing trumpet or I might blow out my heart. I figured he was nuts. A couple days later we were finishing up a gig at the Black Hawk in San Francisco. The crowd was going nuts over our music and I had just been signed to a recording contract. Other than the situation with Gloria, things were really looking up. So when we got done with our last set, some musicians who were at other clubs came over and we had a jam session. It started at midnight and just kept going. Maybe about three a.m. we were doing some down and dirty blues. I took a few choruses, kind of started easy and then kept building. The crowd started egging me on. They wanted to hear me roar those blues. And so I did, I started really wailing, high notes like way in the sky, all sorts of crazy stuff, and then I blew this ridiculously ultra-high note and I was holding it and the crowd was going nuts, and then I passed right out and fell off the stage. I was told later that it was sheer mayhem there while everyone in the club tried to figure out how to help me. They rushed me to the hospital." Ray paused, took a small sip of his sparkling water, and fiddled with a napkin. Kate's mind was still fully agitated, anxious to hear where the story would go. Finally Ray continued, "Of course, I don't remember any of this, and I was in intensive care for a week or two with serious heart problems. The doctor from a few days before was right, you see. Playing the trumpet was killing me. I had to quit or I would have more problems, maybe blow my heart out and die. In fact, that's what happened to a great trumpet player named Don Ellis in the 1970s. Blew out his heart and died at forty-four."

"Wow, that's awful," Kate said, shaking her head. "You had to quit what you loved, like overnight?"

"Yes. I hated the situation. I turned into an ogre. I didn't know what to do with myself. Teach trumpet but not play? No way, I said. I was too proud to not be up on a stage playing. That was my world."

"So what did you do?" Miles asked.

"I laid around the house feeling sorry for myself. Started drinking heavily and took up smoking like there was no tomorrow. Before that, I had been a decent Boy Scout. Not long after that Gloria and I got divorced. That wasn't any fun, but I have to hand it to her. She did something for me a little later, which she didn't have to do."

"What, Ray? It seems weird calling you that now, I just realized," Kate said.

"I bet—sorry. So Gloria felt sorry for me and got me some work in Hollywood. They were always looking for stunt guys and stand-ins who were reliable. She called around and got me work as a stand-in and I was good at it. I was Paul Newman's double for a while. I could sit still with the best of them while the camera was pointed at Newman's lead actress for whatever film they were shooting. I'd occupy my mind by thinking scales and arpeggios over and over in my head while they filmed over my shoulder. It made it less boring. Like I said, I was a major talent at sitting still, except I did crack Faye Dunaway up once on purpose by drooling and crossing my eyes while she was talking. She couldn't stop laughing and we had to take a half-hour break for her to get back to being serious. But otherwise, I was the perfect double."

"And that's how he met Franklin," Mike explained. "Ray had been doing the double stuff for years and Franklin had come along as a kid. They hit it off immediately. Been friends for years now."

"But why were you pretending to be Nielsen?" Miles asked.

"Well, like I said, ever since I quit playing the trumpet I had been hitting the bottle pretty heavily, smoking a lot, and carousing about town. I was one of about a million guys like that in LA. But it caught up to me eventually." A pained expression passed over Ray's face. It was obvious that this part of the story was hard for him to talk about. He fiddled with the napkin some more, closed his eyes, then opened them and continued. "I became really sick. I was so mad at myself, but it was too late to repent. I was especially pissed off at myself because my sister and I were trying to raise her daughter Grace's children. Grace had two little girls, but one day she and her husband were killed in a car crash. We were raising those two girls, but now I wouldn't be there to see them all the way through childhood. The whole situation stunk and it was all my fault. But what could I do?"

"And that's about when Franklin and I had a situation on our hands," Mike said. "Our business partner—you guessed it—Gloria, had found out that her mentor A.C. Nielsen was dying. She came to us and wanted Franklin and me to be her henchmen. She thought up this crazy plan and wanted us to follow through on it for her."

"What was the plan, Mike?" Kate tried to figure out how this could all possibly piece together.

"She has dough, right? We all know that. She wanted to pay the million-dollar fee for A.C. Nielsen and place him in cryo when his time came. Her gift to her beloved mentor, right? She told him this but he refused. He thought she was nuts. He had absolutely no interest in coming to ExitStrategy. So she wanted us to go in cahoots with the funeral director, commandeer Nielsen's body right after he died and rush it to ExitStrategy for cryo. The family wouldn't know anything. The funeral director the family had lined up was happy to do the deed when Gloria told him the plan. Why? Because she was offering him two hundred grand to pull off her crazy scheme. Greed always trumps ethics, right? Anyway, he would locate a John Doe body to put in the casket and never tell the family. Luckily for Gloria, the family had already requested a closed casket. Come to think of it, the funeral director could have put rocks or peanut shells or porcupines or anything in there if he wanted."

"So you refused, right?" Miles asked. "I mean, I can't picture you and Franklin doing something that insane, and I'm sure, pretty illegal."

"Well, Miles, that's where karma and Franklin's imagination came into play. He had heard through the Hollywood grapevine that Ray was dying. He visited him and proposed a deal. Ray, you want to take back over?"

"Sure, Mike. So Franklin tracked me down. I wasn't in LA anymore, I was back in Mason City, Iowa, where I had grown up. Things had changed over the years. I was no longer the only Hispanic person in town, so I kind of liked being back in the calm Midwest. And as long as I dropped my accent—over the years I had learned how to do that easily from some actor friends—nobody could tell I wasn't an Iowa native. It was actually kind of fun to blend in back in Mason City. I thought Franklin was nuts to come visit me." Ray turned to smile at Mike, took another sip of water, then continued. "When I opened my front door and saw him I was pretty shocked. After some small talk he told me his plan—a con of epic proportions. He, Mike, and Dr. Saltieri would place me in cryo instead of Nielsen. I agreed to keep my mouth shut and let them make the plan work. They would take the million-dollar ExitStrategy fee Gloria thought she was paying for Nielsen's intake and split it up, the whole time keeping her totally in the dark. First, they gave the funeral director a nice one-hundred-grand bribe on top of the two hundred grand Gloria had already paid him. For that side paycheck, we were ensured that the director would tell Gloria that everything had gone according to her plan. Three hundred grand went into my sister's hands to finish raising the girls, another three hundred into trust funds for them for college and such, and finally, the last three hundred grand in a secret fund for me—if and when I came back. At this point my personal three hundred grand has turned into a helluva stack of dough, so I'm told."

"That is incredible! Oh my God!" Kate gasped, then drained her mojito.

"Also, FYI, guys," said Mike, "remember when A.C., meaning Ray here, flipped out over that bandage box with the twenty-first-century trademark on it? Somehow that info shook him up and brought all of Ray's memories back. Until then he was in a pretty total fog. You were all telling him he was A.C. Nielsen. That made no sense to him, of course. But he also hadn't remembered yet who he really was. Franklin and I were about to tell him and figure out a way going forward, but first, obviously, we needed to ease him into the truth. We were too late because of the bandage box and he was flipping out. Remember how long Franklin and I were in there talking to him? We were trying to help him get a handle on who he was, what year it was, all that stuff."

"Yeah, I was totally freaking out. I couldn't believe it was 2014 and I was alive again. And of course, I was me—Ray, not A.C. Nielsen! Thanks, Mike, for calming me down that day."

"Of course, Ray," Mike said.

"I was so mad at DePaun that morning, but he didn't deserve it," Ray admitted. "He just happened to be the first person I came across after I saw the date on the bandage box. I'm going to make sure and have a nice sit-down with him and apologize."

"Amazing. Wow. So wait, tell me if I'm following all this correctly," Kate said. "You're saying that Gloria thinks Mike, Franklin, and this funeral director broke the law, like modern-day grave snatchers or something? She assumes that you—I mean you, Ray, are dead and that A.C. was in cryo at ExitStrategy all this time and now he, A.C., is back? Is that the deal?"

"Yes, Kate. You're a very good listener," Mike said with a big fat grin as he patted her on the shoulder. "And personally I love how ninety percent of her one million went to Ray and his family. Those little girls had a nice childhood and Ray got to survive, and Gloria still doesn't know squat. That one mil is actually nothing to her, but it meant the world to Ray and his family. By the way, she often reminds me that Franklin and I are dastardly criminals and any time she wants to she can call the police and get us arrested. Fat chance!"

Everyone laughed at the funny face he made as he said this. Mike then beckoned the server over to their table and ordered a new round of drinks for everyone. It was a Cold Smokey old-school kind of party he had going. Kate could see that letting her and Miles in on this bizarre secret was lifting an enormous load off of his shoulders.

"What about the funeral director? What's he up to these days?" Miles asked.

"He passed away about five years ago. Scumbag guy, obviously, but to my knowledge he never told a soul," Mike said.

"And when are you going to tell Gloria all this?" Miles asked.

"Hell, we don't know," Mike admitted, taking a big swig and

polishing off his fourth Maker's Mark on the rocks of the day. "Maybe soon, maybe never. It's been pretty fucking delicious to keep it our secret."

"Okay, here's what I want to know next. Where in the world is the real A.C. Nielsen?" Kate asked as she finally attacked her taco salad. She suddenly had realized she was starving.

"Where he wanted to be—at rest in a beautiful cemetery," Mike explained. "He was beloved by his entire family. I'm told that they're wonderful people. They know nothing of all this and I wouldn't think of bothering them with it. It's not their fault or ours that Gloria Dunham is pretty much crazy, and that she was so strangely obsessed with Nielsen. If we ever tell her the truth about A.C. she'll be devastated. Franklin has held off all these years waiting for the right moment."

"And A.C. didn't have cirrhosis—just me," Ray added. "I hear he was a straight arrow. I was the one who had more than cancer since I really screwed up my life. I'm just saying this because a lot of folks believe that people with cirrhosis are bum alcoholics and I wouldn't want anyone to think Mr. Nielsen had that problem. Of course I never met the man—I just played him for a while! And, of course, you were always looking at my medical charts, not his."

"The truly ultimate stand-in role, right? Or lay-in, you might say? This is a wild and wacky story—totally!" Miles shook his head in amazement as everyone chuckled.

"So wait, what was this about a security problem, Mike?" Kate asked.

"Well, Gloria has been calling me a lot lately, pestering me about this, that, and nothing. In talking to her I began to realize that somehow she knows various things going on in our building. Not anything terribly important, but I got the feeling that maybe she had someone spying on us—that an employee was feeding her information. That's why we've been waiting so long to reveal Ray's identity to any of you. We couldn't risk it."

"So what happened? Who's the spy?" Miles asked.

Keith stopped stuffing his face and raised his hand meekly. "That would be me, Miles. She would call and sometimes I would pick up when no one in the office did. She would get me into conversations. I didn't realize she was fishing for inside information."

"Oops," Kate said. "You know she tried to get me to be her spy when we met at The Pump Room—not that she said it directly. So what kind of stuff did you tell her?"

"Well nothing much, 'cause I don't know any of the science stuff. I was probably worthless to her, but I think she believed that sooner or later there might some little tidbit of information that would come out of my mouth that would be of use to her. And of course, I didn't know any of the secret identity stuff. Yesterday I mentioned to Mike that Gloria was calling a lot and asking me a lot of questions and that's when he put two and two together."

"Keith never realized what she was up to," Mike said. "He was just being nice to her over the phone."

"From now on, if the phone rings and rings, I'm letting it go, Mr. Burgess." Keith turned his attention back to his slice of key lime pie.

"You didn't do anything wrong, Keith. But now we're aware why she knew a few things that have gone on in the building. And who gives a flying fuck if she knows what kind of cake James made last week, or whatever," Mike said, laughing.

"So now what?" Kate asked. "A nice lunch, a celebratory musical instrument purchase, what else?"

"Well, we're telling all this to all the employees in a couple days when Franklin flies back in. We trust you all and it's only fair for everyone to know what's going on. And then we'll see what's next. And we'll also see what Ray wants to do next with his life, other than buying flowers for Chrissy like he did yesterday. Right, old buddy?"

"Right, Mike," Ray said as he slapped Mike on the back. "Chrissy's so smart and pretty. Do you think she liked the flowers?"

"I am sure of it, Señor Machado! Her face lit up when they were delivered."

"Well that's cute—an office romance." Kate glanced over at Miles. "You know, Mike, when I signed on for this job I had no idea there would be such a high entertainment value attached to it."

"We constantly aim to please our employees, Miss Pearson. Now pick up your new drink and drain it. You're two or three behind me."

"So, Ray, you basically know nothing about TV or advertising—is that right?" Miles asked, squinting his eyes.

"Yup, you're right. I was doing a pretty bad job of faking it, wasn't I? But I was honest about a couple TV things."

"And what would that be?" Miles asked.

"Remember when I told you that I had the serious hots for Joey

Heatherton and Shirley Jones back in the day? That was the God's honest truth."

CHAPTER FORTY-ONE

"Hi, Miss Pearson. Nice morning, huh?"

"Absolutely. Too bad we have to go inside to work," Kate answered Keith as she grabbed her briefcase and got out of her car.

"Miss Pearson, I've been thinking, why do you always park your car here? The same spot every day? In the winter the snowplow guy likes to mash the snow up right there. And in the summer it's the worst spot, considering all the mulberries that drop, and the birds sitting in the tree eating the mulberries and pooping them. There's also the sap drifting this way from that honey locust tree. So why?"

"That car of Enzo's was right here when I got hired and Mike had you hand me the keys. It's my lucky spot. I'm kind of a superstitious girl."

"Yeah, but you being a scientist and all, that's a little surprising. Oh well, suit yourself. And thank you again for bringing John Cougar back to life."

"Don't mention it, Keith. He's a great kitty. I've been wondering, why don't you take him home with you?"

"I live alone, Miss Pearson. I think he likes it here a lot, what with all the people. Of course, Chrissy is his favorite."

Kate set her briefcase down, realizing that this might be turning into a long conversation. A delightful breeze made this a good thing. "After you, I'm sure. But yeah, Chrissy and animals got a thing going on, don't they? Keith, you look like there's something on your mind besides cats and parking spots. Do you want to talk about it? We can stay out here in the nice breeze for a while if you want."

"Yeah, actually there is something bothering me. You ever make someone a promise and then be sorry later?"

"Sure, I'll bet we all have. Not much fun, huh?"

"No, not at all. I got a problem and I don't know what to do about it. I went and talked to Mike. He said what I should do."

"Well, that's good. I would think Mike gives good advice."

"Yeah, I think so. Miss Pearson, you get frustrated with your work now and then, right? I hear people talk about it. Of course, I'm not supposed to be listening to private conversations. I'm just the security guy, that's all."

"I understand, and yes, I admit, I am often frustrated. It's part of my personality." Kate wondered what this was all about.

Keith kicked at a few stones, then looked up at Kate. "Miss Pearson, ever think that something is right under your nose, but you can't really get it? Like figure it out?"

"Sure."

"Well, there's something here that isn't right underneath your nose exactly—it's under your feet."

"Huh? What? What are you talking about?" Kate eyed Keith closely, squinting into the sun.

"What do you think is below the ground floor, down in the basement here at ExitStrategy?"

"Mike told me—it's the cryo fridge tubes and routing stuff."

"That's true. But there's more down there."

"More than the pipes that run to connect the tower of power to all the pods?"

"Well, yes."

"Wait—seriously? Like hidden chambers? What is this, a Harry Potter story?"

"No."

"Oh, then maybe there are cryo'd creatures in the lower level? Instead of Tom Riddle there's an army of golems, medusas, triffids, and such? Scary evil archetypes just waiting to escape the deep freeze and wreak their terrible havoc on humanity, right?"

"Miss Pearson, you sure have a really good imagination. I don't even know what a triffid is and I didn't mean to get you all worked up about monsters. So here's what I have to get off my chest and Mike said I should go ahead and tell you."

"Yes? What is it? And I'm sorry for being so silly. Triffids are a weird monster in an old movie. I'm not only a *Day of the Triffids* fan, but I'm also kind of sleep-deprived." Now Kate took her turn kicking at the random chunks of gravel by her feet.

"I understand. Anyway, right before he died Mr. Saltieri had me take a bunch of boxes out of his office. He made me promise not to tell anyone about them. We put them in the basement back in a corner behind some pipes, tucked away where no one would notice, except maybe spiders."

"Boxes? What kind of boxes?" Adrenaline began to pump in the pit of Kate's stomach.

"Bankers boxes, I think they're called. Maybe some of the research you've been trying to get a handle on all this time? I don't know. But Mr. Burgess thought it might be important to you, and that's why I'm telling you. He said you deserved to know more details about Dr. Saltieri, and if this helped, it would be okay to not keep my promise to him. Perhaps it doesn't matter anymore since things are going so well now for you. Anyway, it's been really bothering me all this time. See, I made that promise to Dr. Saltieri and I've never broken a promise in my life."

"Dr. Saltieri was sick, Keith. Sometimes he did strange things. He had Alzheimer's, remember? You've done the right thing, I'm sure of that. Can you show me these boxes, like right now?"

"Sure, Miss Pearson. We'll grab a couple flashlights. Like I said, the boxes are way back, tucked in a corner behind some cryo pipes. No one would ever find them, I think. Was he just keeping them safe? Or maybe he was hiding them? Or both? It's pretty confusing to me."

"To me, too, Keith."

PAUL CAREY

270

CHAPTER FORTY-TWO

"Oh my God, Keith, look at this."

"I'm sorry, Miss Pearson, I guess I should have told you ages ago."

"It doesn't matter—we're here now. Do you know if Mike is in the building? Edouard or Miles? Deirdre? Can you run and get them for me?"

"Sure, miss."

There was Kate, in a corner of the ExitStrategy catacombs with eight or ten bankers boxes Keith had stashed there before Saltieri died. Kate opened the first box—old store receipts just crammed in, not in folders, totally disorganized. She pulled one out and read it—a receipt from some drug store. She pulled out another—same thing. Vitamins, pain meds, heating pads, sleeping pills—seemingly random purchases. Kate opened the next box in front of her. She stood there dumbfounded. Handwritten card files. She thumbed through them. Here were the missing cards on many of the C wing patients. Gold stars, the "E.S. signed" notations, and other scribbled notations she and Deirdre had slogged through months earlier with no resultant understanding. "Jesus, this is the mother lode," she mumbled to herself. Just then, she heard voices coming her way from down the corridor.

"Kate, what is it? What did you find?" Deirdre scurried toward Kate, followed by Miles, Edouard, and Keith.

"All the missing records," Kate answered. "Or some of them? I don't know yet. I only looked in a couple. All in all about ten or so boxes' worth. I've already come across some of the missing file cards we talked about ages ago, Deirdre. There's a box stuffed full of random receipts. And look here, a box of old VHS tapes. I think I remember Mike telling me when I first got hired that some of the patients recorded themselves toward the end to document their wishes. That might be what these are. Maybe the death certificates for the C wing patients are in here somewhere, too?"

"Oh my God, Kate," Edouard said as he leafed through the box with all the receipts. "What do you want to do with all this?"

"I don't know. Look through it all, of course. Who wants to help?"

"All of us, I'm sure," Deirdre answered.

"Is Mike in the building?" Kate asked.

"No," Miles said. "He's off visiting old GM friends in Michigan. Franklin, Norm, and Ray went with him, I think."

"How are we going to play these tapes?" Edouard asked. "Anybody still have a VCR hooked up to their TV in the year 2014?"

"Hmm, I know somebody," Kate said. "Anyone up for a trip to my mom's house? She bakes killer cookies. And she absolutely loves mysteries."

CHAPTER FORTY-THREE

"Hi, Mom, can we invade your house?"

"Well, of course, dear," Jeannine Pearson said, smiling at Kate and peering past her at the cars in the driveway. "You've got some friends there? Who are they?"

"Coworkers, Mom. You'll like them. We've got a mystery on our hands. Want to help sleuth it out?"

"You're kidding, right? You know what kind of books I read and TV shows I watch. I've got all of *Murder, She Wrote* and *Diagnosis, Murder* on tape."

"And that means your VCR still works, right?"

"Of course. I haven't gone all modern like you millennials and bought a DVD player."

"That's actually good, Mom. Wow, you know what a millennial is, huh? Okay, guys, it's a go," Kate yelled to Miles, Edouard, and Deirdre. "Bring all the boxes in."

"Hi, everyone. Welcome to my home," Jeannine crooned a bit nervously. Since her husband's death she hardly had anyone over to the house. She had distracted herself from the outside world by diving headfirst into her loves: gardening, baking, and her biggest guilty pleasure—anything written or filmed in the who-done-it genre, all the way from Agatha Christie's Miss Marple series to Gillian Flynn's *Gone Girl*.

"Guys, this is my mom, Jeannine. Mom, this is Dr. Coleman. You can call him Miles. Dr. Edouard Radelet from Haiti, and Deirdre Cunningham; she's a math whiz. We found stuff at my company that had gone missing and we need a VCR to watch some tapes. Here's my company credit card, Mom. Order pizza, okay?"

"Thanks for letting us in, Mrs. Pearson," Deirdre said. "Sorry to trouble you right away, but Kate says you bake killer cookies. I have low blood sugar problems, do you happen to have some?"

"Of course, Deirdre. Do you like snickerdoodles? I made some this morning."

"Oh, I love those. Thank you!"

"All right," Kate said. "Let's see what we're dealing with. Miles, what's in that box you've got there?"

"All those old videotapes. Maybe fifteen or twenty. There are people's names on the label. And look here, another box of them."

"Good. Edouard, what have you got?"

"That receipt box you opened already. Here—same thing in this box. Oodles of receipts. The ink has faded away on some of them."

"Okay, keep those two together."

"Here are some boxes stuffed with manila folders," Miles announced. "Looks like random paperwork. Some old photographs. Lots of different stuff."

"And here are the card files. The ones you said were missing from C wing patients, right, Kate?" Edouard asked.

Jeannine and Deirdre returned from the kitchen a few minutes later with a tray of cookies, cheese, and fruit.

"Okay, Kate, I ordered plenty of pizza and garlic bread. Forty-five minutes, okay?"

"Yes, Mom. Hey, can I give you a job?"

"You bet, Katey!"

"It's going to be annoying, but go through all these old receipts. List the purchases in some kind of organized way. See if there's a pattern or something."

"Got it. It's like that episode of Columbo from way back. He caught the killer because of the mountain of old receipts he didn't destroy. Like a hoarder before they had hoarder shows on reality TV! This should be fun. Are we tracking a killer?"

"Whoa, your mom is a TV freak like me, Kate?" Miles asked. "And you never told me?"

"I was afraid you'd knock on her door and ask her for a date, Miles!"

Jeannine blushed for a moment. She hadn't been on a date yet since her husband had passed away. She tugged at her hair, rearranging it, then dug into the first box of receipts, pen and legal pad at the ready.

"Okay, the rest of us, let's brainstorm these cards," Kate said. "Deirdre and I have already looked through the ones at ExitStrategy. We've got a bit of it figured out, but there are notations we couldn't fathom at all. Let's pull some out and see what we have."

"Okay, Kate," Deirdre said, "here's Julianna Souza, C15. The usual, like you and I have already seen. A 'VT' notation, the usual gold star, the 'E.S. signed' thing. Miles and Edouard, we're stumped on this 'E.S. signed' thing. It's Enzo's initials, but we have yet to find anything with his signature in the files we have back in Kate's office. It's crazy."

"Is it something only in the C wing people?" Edouard asked.

"Yes, starting with C3 or C4 or something like that," Deirdre added.

"Hell, I don't know. Wait, what if he signed something but gave to it someone else, Deirdre?"

"Right. Kate and I thought about that, mostly in regard to the lack of death certificates for the C wing people. Maybe Enzo might have given items to patients' lawyers for safekeeping? We've muddled through this before."

"Kate, honey. Who is this E.S. person you're discussing?" Mrs. Pearson asked. Kate didn't have time for this now. She had hoped the busywork of going through the receipts would keep her mother out of their hair.

"Dr. Enzo Saltieri, Mom, my predecessor. These are all files and stuff that he apparently hid in the company basement."

"Enzo Saltieri, you said, dear?"

"Right. E.S., Mom. His initials."

"Yet wouldn't E.S. also be the initials of your company? Either one, I guess—Energy Source, ExitStrategy?"

Jaws dropped. Could that be? 'E.S. signed' didn't refer to Saltieri's initials? Could it mean 'Exit Strategy signed'?

"Holy cow, Mrs. Pearson," Deirdre exclaimed. "You might have nailed something. We never thought of that. Okay, if it could be 'Exit Strategy signed' and we only see it starting about patient C2 or C3 or whatever, what does that mean?"

"Maybe the Exit Strategy is a document or agreement—something that requires a signature?" Edouard wondered.

"Sounds right," Miles said. "An agreement between a patient and the company? A final decision or choice on how to exit their diseased existence? Why wouldn't Mike tell us any of this?"

"He doesn't tell me anything, that's for sure," Kate vented. "I think he wants me to prove I'm smarter than him. Like it's a condition of continued employment. If I can't prove I'm a genius, I'm out. Plus I think he just likes secrets, period. Franklin loves playing tricks on people, Mike loves keeping secrets, right?"

"I guess," Miles said.

"Okay. Let's assume my mom is right. E.S. is a document of some kind. Now, what about 'VT'? What the heck does that mean?"

"Duh, Vermont. All the patients are from Vermont," Miles quipped.

"Dork. Come on guys, think," Kate said.

The crew took turns riffing on possible meanings for VT:

"Vagrant Titmouse?"

"Variant Treatment?"

"Ventricular Tetracycline?"

"Um, Velociraptor Testing-ground?"

"Shit, I don't know—Veneral Tisease?"

"Ugh, Miles. Wow, we're getting nowhere on this," Kate lamented. "Mom, what have you got so far over there?"

"Well, your doctor seemed to like the Rex-All in Morton Grove. I like the Walgreens better when I'm near there. Anyway, he bought lots of stuff there over the years. Over-the-counter stuff: vitamins, antacids, pain killers. Lots of antacids actually. Maalox, mostly. Oh, there's the doorbell. The pizzas must be here. Here's your credit card back, Katey. I paid for the pizzas."

"Mom, you didn't have to do that. Anyway, guys, ugh. VT has us stumped, right?" Kate moaned. She felt like she'd never get past this wall. *But if I keep banging my fool head against it, sooner or later it has to give,* she thought. *Time to keep trying and be the leader. I'm supposed to be that.* "Wait, Deirdre, VT went back into the B wing, too, didn't it?"

"Yes, about halfway through B wing is where you and I saw the VT thing show up on the cards."

"Okay. Miles, open another box, please," Kate said, sensing a tiny new crack in that damn wall.

"Yup, okay, here we go—photos," Miles announced. "Random people—patients, I'm guessing. No names or labels on them. Poor photography skills. Some of the people don't look so good, so yeah, I'm guessing these are patient photos. Oh wait, here's a weird one. Saltieri with a little old bald lady holding a stuffed animal, and some really sad-looking woman."

"Whoa, hand that here, Miles," Kate said excitedly, yanking the photo away from him. "I think it's that girl with Hutchinson-Gilford syndrome. I've never seen an old lady play with stuffed animals." She waved the photo around for everyone to see. "Guys, this must be Jenny Loves Rainbows and her mother, Jenny's Mom. Norm told me about these two. He said the mother hassled Mike and Franklin or something like that. But he never told me what that meant. They're C3 and C5, right next to each other, right, Deirdre? Guys, look closer at the one holding the stuffed unicorn. See how short she is, the baldness, and the bulging eyes? That's a little girl with the syndrome. She's maybe ten, but she looks like she's sixty or seventy. That's Jenny—I'm sure of it."

"Kate, I'm pretty sure we do have the cards on them back at ExitStrategy, remember?" Deirdre said.

"You're right. I'm trying to jog my memory. C3 and C5 were definitely the cards where we first saw 'E.S. signed,' correct? Enzo must have goofed up and not hidden away all the cards. That's probably the only reason we have a few of them back in my office."

"Right, Kate," Deirdre said. "He just dumped stuff in these boxes and didn't even get them all, apparently. The Alzheimer's."

"Can we find the cards for C1 and C2?" Kate asked. "Dig in there, Miles. I know C1—that's Touchdown Jerry, another person Norm taught me about."

Miles sifted through the cards. Meanwhile, Kate got up to stretch her legs and went over to give her mom a hug.

"Got it!" Miles yelled. "C1—Jerry Hastings, like you said, Kate. He's got the VT but no gold star or 'E.S. signed.' And here's C2. Same thing. So your new notations start at C3 like you thought."

"Okay, so the mom and the girl are next to each other on one wall—C3 and C5. Who is across the way in C4?" Edouard asked.

"C4 is a vacant space, dude," Miles said. "That was A.C. Nielsen's number to begin with, but then they moved his pod down to the apartment when they created it."

"Wow," Edouard said. "I never noticed the C4 station is empty. Shows you how little I stray from the lab."

"Yet you stray on over to the cafeteria for pie and cake just fine, Edouard!" Kate teased.

"Whoa, Kate, do you see that wall in the back of the photo?" Miles tapped at the photo.

"Yeah, I've seen walls before. So?"

"Look—see that big diagonal crack in the drywall? Seem familiar?" Miles asked.

Kate peered closely at the photo, like some fifty-year-old in need of bifocals. "Jesus, that's my office! But there are two cots in there. Looks like a portable clothes hanger-thingy. A big pile of pots and pans and dirty dishes in my mini-kitchen?"

"They were living in your office, maybe, before it was your office?

These two people, and maybe others? Am I right?" Miles said.

"Hey, new friends, grab some pizza before it gets cold," Mrs. Pearson said.

"All right, thanks. Hey, Mom, so far what are the receipts for? You said just miscellaneous?"

"Yes. But it's kind of weird. Lots of antacids. You're talking about sick people at your work, right? I guess they would need that. A whole lot of vitamins, too. Almost like he was putting people on high levels of vitamin therapy. In fact, I found a shopping list your doctor dropped in the box. It said 'A-B-C-D-E.' Then he scribbled 'B complex—All. No K.' Next to it was a giant scribble, 'VT.' Didn't you tell me you were doing that, too, these days, Kate? Giving that patient of yours extra vitamins in a drink or bath or something?"

"Wow, Kate. Your mom just nailed it. VT means vitamin therapy!" Deirdre said excitedly

"And why no vitamin K, my friends?" Miles added, piecing things together now. "Because it promotes clotting. He wouldn't want any annoying blood-clotting if he's soon going to drain their blood and replace it with cryoprotectant."

"Hey, everyone," Edouard said, holding a slice of pizza in one hand and a file card in the other. "I'm looking at that card you pulled before, C15, the Souza woman. I also found an envelope, too. She was diagnosed with late-stage pancreatic cancer on March 2, 1994. The doctor gives her four to eight weeks. Her card says 'VT, March 6.' 'E.S. signed' is dated March 13. Then there's the goofy little gold star, whatever that means. Then she dies and goes into cryo March 14. Somehow she's gone in no time."

"That's less than two weeks. Edouard, is that possible?" Kate asked.

"Maybe. Hard to say how much time people have with these deadly cancers. Pull some more cards, people. Is there a pattern here?"

"Here. C21, Everett Sinclair, the film critic," Miles said. "Brain cancer. *Glioblastoma multiforme*—bad stuff, right, Edouard? Doctor's diagnosis is six months. Then 'E.S. signed' about four days after he's in contact with ExitStrategy. He goes into cryo six days later."

"Six months? Then gone in a matter of days? What the heck?" Kate wondered. She grabbed a slice of pizza and began nibbling on the crust as she started pacing the room.

"Do you remember how you said you couldn't tell me what your company does? Hint, hint, Katey."

"Yes, Mom. But I told you anyway. I'm okay with these people knowing that, if that's why you're saying 'hint, hint.' I've gotten pretty tired of all the secrecy."

"No problem, Kate," Deirdre said. "My fiancé knows, too. Fuck cloak and dagger secrecy. Mike's goofy about that. I don't think it matters that much, right? We're all dedicated and we're professionals at what we do. All along he should have trusted us and told us what's going on, right? And I bet Norm and Chrissy knew some or all of this stuff. He must have told them to clam up and not tell you any of this stuff we're discovering."

"Yes, obviously," said Kate. "But Keith said Mike thought I should get a chance to look at whatever was in the boxes."

"Obviously he finally trusts you now, what with all the success you've had," said Deirdre. "He's probably glad Keith told him about these hidden boxes. It gives Mike a chance to watch from the sidelines while you sleuth it all. Of course with awesome help from the rest of us here, including your mom and her amazing snickerdoodles and magical legal pad." Deirdre grabbed another snickerdoodle from the tray and smiled over at Jeannine.

"Maybe Mike just can't tell you all the secrets face-to-face. Some people are like that," Edouard ventured.

"Okay, so can I go ahead and speak freely now, Kate?" Jeanette asked.

"Yes, Mom, go ahead," Kate said, downing the last of her Diet Cherry Dr Pepper.

"All right, then. I assume you all have heard of Jack Kevorkian, right?"

"Um, sure, Mrs. Pearson. Dr. Death," Miles said.

"I think you've got a Kevorkian situation on your hands," Jeanette pronounced. "Although probably a Kevorkian situation that's quite user-friendly, I might guess. Like smiley-face Kevorkian-ish."

"Mom," Kate said in a hushed tone, "explain, please, although all of sudden I think I know where you are going."

"Kate, first go through the rest of the boxes. Let's see what's there, honey."

Miles and Edouard ripped open the last three boxes. More files. One giant discovery.

"Look. Documents titled 'Exit Strategy,'" Miles said as he dug into the box. "These are the 'E.S. signed' papers, apparently. I'll bet it's

some sort of living will. Look!"
"Read one out loud, Miles," Kate said.

EXIT STRATEGY
Recorded this day June 9, 2003
I, Muriel Gough, being of sound mind but failing body, do hereby declare that I have freely chosen my Exit Strategy. In a few days, I shall pass into cryonic stasis. I do so of my own free will and have not been coerced into this decision. I shall control the instruments which shall cause me to go into the beginning of the cryonic stage. I consider myself to still be alive while in cryonic stasis, and believe that my body, mind, unique memories, and soul shall be revived by doctors of the future. This is my choice. This is my decision. My choice to pass into cryonic stasis is not a form of suicide. Those who have helped me are blameless, they have only assisted me in surviving beyond the disease currently attacking my body. I have chosen to accelerate my passage into stasis before my illness destroys every fiber of my body.
May God bless my family, my friends, and all who read this document.
Signed,
Muriel Gough

"Jesus, Mrs. Pearson, you were right," Deirdre said. "It's just like Kevorkian. No wonder Saltieri hid all this. He was afraid of what would happen if he got caught. Or what could possibly happen, worst case scenario, to Mike and Franklin later on, after he was gone."

"Caught doing what?" Jeannine asked. "I simply mentioned Kevorkian because the situation shares some of the same mechanisms. But that's where the similarity completely ends."

"Mom, these people were killing themselves," Kate protested. "Oh my God, why did I ever take this job? I should have known better. I'm going to be sick."

"Kate, calm down. Please stop acting like a child," Jeannine insisted. "What was their other choice? To endure an agonizing death? For what reason? It sounds like all these people were really ill. No chance to survive. And they actually didn't commit suicide. At least they didn't view it as such. In that sense it is the opposite of the Kevorkian situation. They were fortunate that they found your company. I wish your father could have had that opportunity."

"This has nothing to do with Dad. I'm quitting—tonight. I can't be a part of this," Kate said, her voice shaking.

"Hang on, Kate," Miles interrupted. "I know you're upset. But let's see what else is in here, okay?"

"Why the hell couldn't Mike and Franklin tell me the goddamn truth? They hid this from me for so long. Goddamn bastards," Kate yelled.

"Kate, like I was saying before, they were afraid to tell you," Edouard said. "It's obvious. They didn't know how. And they figured you would quit on them if you knew. And look—they were right."

"Here, take a look at this, guys." Deirdre skimmed through about a half-dozen letters. "Letters from a patient to Mike, Franklin, and Enzo. Some just to Mike and Franklin. Give me a couple minutes to read through them a little."

"What about the tapes, Kate?" Miles asked. "That's why we came to your mom's house. Should we look at them?"

"Hang on for a sec, guys. Here, listen to this," said Deirdre. "It's from Andrea Carlsen. She's the Jenny's Mom patient. She must have been critically important to all of this. Listen:"

Dear Mike and Franklin,

My doctor says that I still have weeks to go. My body is disintegrating. There is so much pain now that sometimes I just want to crawl in a cave, a cave where I can let my mind go blank as if I am not even me anymore and I don't have to acknowledge the pain's existence. And through all this I still have to see my daughter grow worse and worse, too. Without the love of my husband she and I would be lost, utterly lost. I am pleading with both of you once again to listen to common sense. As you may know, Dr. Saltieri agrees with me now. There is no reason to play this out to satisfy other people and society, I cannot play by those rules when my life, but especially my daughter's life is also at stake. If you insist that I die a slow, painful death where my body is racked with this cancer, how shall anyone repair me? Do you really expect a doctor in the future to be able to repair EVERYTHING? Why not give them a fighting chance? Freeze this body and also this disease now before it goes further. It's so logical, Mike and Franklin. I have the courage to go forward today, this very hour if you would stop being afraid. So is Jenny. How can you look at her, see the aging accelerate, and deny her a future? Now is the time to proceed. You know Enzo has a way to make this happen. And Enzo thinks Jenny's condition can be cured, maybe ten or twenty years from now. Please, please, please reconsider your position. She already looks like a

shriveled old woman—my poor little girl. The tears I have cried over her form rivers, oceans. Please let us go, and let us go now.
    God bless you both,
    Andrea

Kate stared at the floor, tears streaming. Deirdre as well. No one spoke. The emotions in the letter sliced through everyone's heart.

After a minute or two of total silence, Miles stood up and walked over to the box of VHS tapes and rummaged through. He brought three tapes over to Kate.

"Here's the Jenny Loves Rainbows tape and the tape for Jenny's Mom. They have gold stars on them, just like the cards. Kate, I think the gold star meant they didn't wait until a natural death. They exited on their own terms. Really more courageous than virtually any of the rest of us could hope to be, I think. They convinced Mike and Franklin to join them in having the courage to not be afraid of societal consequences. Do you want to watch them?"

"No, I can't. My heart will break if I do," Kate murmured.

"I understand. I also have A.C. Nielsen's videotape. A gold star and a red one. I'm guessing the red star is Enzo's little way of notating that something different is going on—meaning it's not really Nielsen. He's the only one with a red star, right? Just a guess, and it probably doesn't matter much. Anyway, how about we watch that one?"

"You know, I have half a mind to call the FBI or the state's attorney right now on Mike and Franklin, just expose all this!" Kate stated defiantly.

"Sorry to say this, Kate, but half a mind is about right," Edouard said. "You'd destroy ExitStrategy. Before even weighing the consequences, and probably totally ignoring the fact that Ray Machado is alive, the government might shut the company down and arrest everyone they can round up. People might go to prison. Some DA under public pressure or swayed by the media would think of some kind of charges that could stick. So why would you drop a dime on Mike? Just to satisfy those precious constipated morals you continue to hold on to all this time? We've been through this before—you and your outdated moral standards."

"Kate, didn't you and Deirdre say there are no death certificates for any of these people?" Miles asked. "You thought people's lawyers might have them? I'm guessing that the company and all these people decided to take a stand and say, 'Hey society, I'm not dead, I'm in stasis. I refuse to have a death certificate made up for me just to play your game.'"

Kate stormed out of the room, disappearing into the bathroom. Everyone could hear her vomit up all the pizza she had eaten. They heard her exit the bathroom, but she didn't rejoin them. She was in the kitchen banging around pots, pans, and dishes.

"Mrs. Pearson, your daughter is a remarkable person, also a sensitive one—maybe too sensitive," Edouard said.

"I know. Just the way she was born. Her father and I were never so insistent on everything being so black or white. It's just how she is."

"I wasn't trying to criticize. We all love her."

"Thank you, Edouard."

Kate stopped her banging. She sank to the floor, deep in thought. The tape Miles found would show A.C. Nielsen—well, actually Ray Machado—committing suicide via some type of Kevorkian-style device rigged so that Ray would initiate the procedure himself. That would make it appear that ExitStrategy could not be guilty of murder. Only an inner circle would know about the procedure—Mike, Franklin, Saltieri, Chrissy, Norm, and a few other carefully handpicked, highly trusted freelance nurses and doctors attending various of the procedures. Of course, they would be extremely well compensated financially considering the career risks involved. Enzo probably employed a drug that would stop the heart without causing tissue damage, then initiate the cryo process immediately, or for that matter, simultaneously. Admittedly, for these patients this would be the most medically optimal way to enter cryo. A few days preparing in the apartment that was now Kate's office, stoking up on vitamins, resting, then do it quickly, avoiding further physical decline. Everything on the patients' terms. Screw society, screw ethics, screw the church—all those worthless, ridiculous taboos.

Kate tread slowly back into the living room. "This is all so fucked up, guys," she said softly. "Sorry for swearing, Mom."

Jeannine came over and hugged her daughter. "That's okay, my Kate. You're a big girl now. You can swear all you want!"

"If we play that tape we're going to see Ray kill himself," Kate said softly. "But he actually didn't kill himself. Because if he did, he couldn't be back with us now, right?"

"Yes, Kate. You're totally right," Miles said. "It's kind of like a time-travel movie with all the usual mind-numbing paradoxes. Except here it's a life and death motif, with a new set of conundrums and contradictions. Totally weird."

"Jesus Christ, I hate Mike Burgess," Kate whispered ferociously.

CHAPTER FORTY-FOUR

"Hello?"

"Hello, Mike. It's Randolph Morgan calling from Los Angeles. Do you have time for a chat?"

"Sure, Randolph, go ahead. I'm making some coffee for myself here."

"How is our mutual friend A.C. Nielsen these days?"

"He's doing quite well. Healthy as a horse. Probably ready to take on the world soon."

"That's good to hear, Mike. Gloria would like to come visit him."

"I don't think he's ready for outside visitors yet, Randolph. So in his best interests I think we'd have to say no for now."

"I understand. I'll tell Gloria. Also, I have some good news and a little bad news for you."

"If this has anything to do with Gloria any slice of good news is welcome." Mike fumbled with the Keurig K-cup, almost dropping his cell phone.

"Right. Understood. You know how she's been dragging her heels on the money issue? Refusing to be part of any new bank loans?"

"Of course. We need more money for more research. Why won't she help us? Franklin and I don't understand. Hang on—I'm going to put you on speaker."

"She's being extra stubborn lately about a lot of things," Morgan said. "I can't fathom it. Anyway, I have convinced her to go another route if it meets your approval, and Franklin's as well, of course."

"What is it?"

"She's willing to give you more money for more shares of the company."

"We could consider that. In fact, Franklin and I have already discussed it. But we're not handing her majority control. You'd have to tell her that."

"She assumes that already. But she says she would be happy to help you."

"Like a python helps a baby bunny, perhaps, Randolph?"

"Well, I can't comment on that. Though I might say something in Latin, like caveat emptor."

"Yes, of course. So was that the good news?"

"Yes. Here's the other part. While Gloria was visiting family, her great-grandnieces showed her some things on TV—shows they tune into when their parents aren't looking. Reality TV shows."

"And what am I supposed to do about that?"

"Oh, it's very simple, Mike. She wants you and Franklin to do her a little favor, give her a little reward for her agreeing to create fresh capital, the liquidity you desire. She thinks it will be of no great difficulty."

"Jesus, Randolph, what does she want from us?" Mike grabbed some cream from his mini-fridge, poured it in his coffee, and took a sip. Miles sauntered slowly by and Mike waved him into the office.

"Calm down, Mike. Here's the deal. She wants you and Franklin to find James Arness, the actor, and along with A.C. Nielsen's expertise, kidnap the star of the TV show Dimi and Khail: U Wish It Wuz U. Ridiculous title. I've never seen it, but according to Gloria it is toxic trash not fit for human consumption. She's absolutely terrified that these little girls are watching it."

"Wait—rewind. Kidnap a TV star?" Miles gave Mike a surprised shrug. Mike shook his head in disbelief at where the conversation was going.

"Yes, and hold her for ransom."

"That would be slightly illegal, correct, barrister?"

"The law is always open to interpretation, sir. Why doesn't anyone understand that? Anyway, perhaps along the vein of interpretation or reinterpretation you can find a creative new way around the criminal code, re: kidnapping."

"You're quite verbose, today, Randolph. You surprise me. Why doesn't Gloria just tattle on the kids and have the parents turn the TV off? I can't believe you and I are having this conversation."

"But we are."

"Yes," Mike sighed, "we are." He put down his coffee mug and slowly rubbed his eyes, wishing he hadn't taken the call. "And who's paying the ransom and how much is it? And besides, why does Gloria need more money?"

"She never wants money, Mike. She's after power. You must know that by now after all of these years."

"Okay, so tell me the rest. Get it over with."

"The ransom is that this overly endowed in the mammary gland category woman named Dimi Konstantos and her male-model husband Khail Santana must give up making their reality TV show— actually, all the shows they appear in or produce. That's what Gloria is after."

"That's all? Just kidnap someone, hold them against their will, and insist that they bankrupt themselves?"

"That's it, Mike. It's doable for the mighty Burgess brothers and that idiot savant doctor you have there, don't you think?"

"Idiot savant doctor, Randolph? I have no idea who you're talking about," Mike lied. "Anyway, tell Gloria to go fuck herself with a rusty pickaxe."

Miles had to fight to suppress a belly laugh. Mike gave him a thumbs-up as he grinned back at him.

"I never speak to my clients like that, though I might think it. Mike, listen to me—this could all turn out very well for you and ExitStrategy. I can feel it. You simply need to stop taking Gloria so literally. Think outside the box. You've done that as an engineer for years, haven't you?"

"Oh my Lord. So if we promise to kidnap this woman, Gloria will sign for more money?"

"Yes. She says she'll sign right away. She knows that you and Franklin need the money and the two of you would never welsh on an agreement. She told me that she is proud of how reasonable she's being right now."

"Yeah, right. Only one more rewind please, Randolph. Did you say something about someone else being part of this? Who did you mention a minute ago?"

"Oh, James Arness. The star of *Gunsmoke*. She calls him Jim. Lifelong friends, the two of them. In fact, she says you can have Peter help, too. That would be Peter Graves, the star of Mission: Impossible, James Arness's real-life brother. Gloria believes she has created an all-star Scandinavian lineup: the Arness brothers plus her mentor A.C. Nielsen. Of course, you would have to start convincing Mr. Nielsen to take part somehow."

"Uh-huh, I see, Randolph. And now I'm afraid to ask this next question, seeing as it's the year 2014, but here goes. Where can I find James Arness and Peter Graves?"

"There's a website your Dr. Miles could look up. I know your geek doctor loves the Internet. This one is called find-the-stars-grave dot com."

CHAPTER FORTY-FIVE

Kate was seated in the garden section of The Dragons Den in Chicago's trendy Bucktown neighborhood, sipping a decent pinot grigio and watching the self-absorbed millennials stroll by. She and Aria were veteran people watchers, and the sidewalk restaurants in Bucktown and Wicker Park were excellent viewing zones for their little vice. They'd never been to this place before so she thought she should scout it out. The weather was gorgeous, about seventy-five with a little breeze that kicked up now and then.

"It's about time you got here," she said as Miles walked up to her table.

"It's my day off—chillax! Parking is a bitch around here, you know." Today he was dressed like the old Miles—Einstein sticking his tongue out T-shirt, twill cargo shorts, and his old orange Crocs.

"Ew, those shoes again, really?" Kate grimaced.

"Yes. Lay off. There's a famous chef who wears 'em."

"And probably a hundred more that don't—duh."

"Well, you look nice today. Even without Crocs," Miles said, remaining cheerful and noncombative.

"You look nice today"? He really does want a date with me. To think that before a few months ago Miles-slash-Milstein never even noticed how I look. Or that I'm even a woman, like with breasts and not boy parts.

"Oh, thanks," she said. "This is actually one of Aria's blouses. We share a bit."

"Well, you definitely look nice in it. Your hair's pretty, too. It's kind of, um… wispy."

Wha—what the heck? Wispy? He's not even hiding the fact that he's hitting on me. Maybe you can play only so many video games before your gonads rebel and insist on seeking out the opposite sex.

The waiter, a young fellow with spiky hair named Chaz, came over and asked Miles what he'd like.

"Do you have any quality IPAs on draft or something good in a bottle?"

"Yes, sir, here's a list for you. Any food for you now, ma'am? Appetizer?"

"No, we're good, maybe later. Another pinot when you have a

chance."

"Very good. Sir, did you find something you'd like?"

"Yeah, I'll take the Sculpin IPA."

"Very good, sir. I'll be right back with that."

"Ugh, I hate being called ma'am. It's like an old lady name," Kate protested. "And—segue—speaking of old ladies, that's why I asked you to meet me here."

"Do we have to talk about her?" Miles said, making a face like he'd been asked to kiss Scary Old Gloria flush on the lips—and add a little tongue.

"Yes, we do. We're the only two people smart enough to plan and pull off a con to fool Gloria. And anyway, I'll bet you have the skills to be a con artist. Think about it, Miles. She's almost blind, thinks the Arness boys are still alive, et cetera, et cetera. She's delusional, right? Really, how hard could it be? Her lawyer told Mike to be creative, think outside the box. All we have to do is fool her for a short time. Get Mike's hands on her money and at least look like we did what she wanted."

"She may be blind, Kate, but she's still an ancient devil. Probably has some kind of a pact with the actual Devil himself. And she's twice as smart as us, I think."

"Look, if we don't figure out something she won't keep funding our research, whether it's via bank loans or giving up shares to her. And she figures that all the money she's made available to Mike and Franklin over the years means they owe her pretty much anything she asks for. If we don't play the game and deliver Dimi, even in appearance, the sugar mommy goes away."

"So what? With what we can do now, Mike and Franklin can make trillions. Cure for cancer, live-forever stuff? Mike is Smaug sitting on a Himalayan-sized mountain of gold!"

"Yes, Miles, but you forget—what can we do now? Making that mountain of money is years away."

"Since when are you so concerned about Mike and Franklin? I thought you hated their guts after we discovered what the gold stars meant? You almost quit that night."

"I still kind of hate them and I haven't really forgiven them, Miles. But I love my work and the people at ExitStrategy. The main thing is what my mom said—those dying people were fortunate to know about ExitStrategy and what we do. Anyway, that's why I didn't quit. And I think I also discovered that, push comes to shove, I'll never be a quitter. I've grown up. Edouard kind of shamed me into it along the way with some of his comments. But that's okay, I adore that man!"

Chaz brought out Miles' bottle of beer and a nice glass.

"What is that? Fish beer?" Kate asked, noticing the bottle's colorful label with an image of some fancy frilled fish. "You're drinking fermented dead fishies? Ick!"

"No, silly! It's a Sculpin, from Ballast Point Brewery in San Diego. They put pics of different fish on the labels. The IPA has a sculpin fish on it. You know San Diego, right? Where I grew up? The ocean, Balboa Park, a nice breeze and sweet weather every day of the year? It's not like here. I mean today is really nice, but we sure don't have this every day here. Anyway, to summarize, I am drinking a very nice craft beer from San Diego. Contents: water, yeast, hops, and malt. No fish in it—just on the label."

"Yeah, right. No, I bet it's fish beer in that bottle. You know—fish tacos, fish beer. Yeah, San Diego, uh-huh." *Oh, my God, am I flirting with him? He does have nice eyes. Oh Jesus, Kate, stop it. It's just Miles. Don't get distracted.* "So let me taste your fish beer, hotshot."

"Of course. Like I said, Sculpin IPA—India Pale Ale from Ballast Point in sunny San Diego." Miles slid the glass over to her.

"Yeah, whatever." Kate took a big sip. "Hmm, not bad," she said, slurping and rolling the beer around in her mouth in a loopy, exaggerated way. Aria's wacky skills at physical comedy had rubbed off on Kate over the years. "Yes, quite nice—tweets of ocean-side citrus, lurking red algae, and a subtle hint of swim bladder."

"Ha, ha, ha!" Miles broke into laughter. "That was good. I'll have to take you with me to beer tastings around town. Knock the bearded beer aesthetes down a peg or two."

"Yeah, whatever. Okay, enough small talk. Let's get to work and make this kidnapping plan, whether it's fake or for real," Kate said.

"I'll make it simple for you. You tell her you want to take her shopping for old lady shawls but instead you drag her to a psychiatrist and get her declared incompetent. Easy-button stuff. You're trying way too hard."

"But she's not incompetent, Miles. She's a consummate actress and she can fool anyone, any time she wants. She'd play cat and mouse with any psychiatrist. She'd be the cat."

"Okay, okay," Miles finally conceded. "What's your plan? And make it good."

"The premise is simple. We do exactly what she told us she wants. Get Jim Arness and his brother Peter Graves to kidnap Dimi. Hold her for the ransom. Dimi and Khail Santana have to agree to abandon their crappy reality TV empire, yadda, yadda, yadda, as Elaine Benes would say on *Seinfeld*."

Miles stared at her for a moment with one eye squinted, took a big sip from his glass, then said sarcastically, "Right, the Arness brothers. And as I believe they're both dead, and not in a Cold Smokey Burgess cryopod, you're thinking that we're gonna go to some Los Angeles cemetery, dig them both up, and defib their rotted corpses back to life? The Arness Zombie Brothers? Jesus Christ, how many damn glasses of wine did you have before I got here?" An overly cute young couple a few tables away stared over at them, wondering what was going on.

Chaz popped back out. "Can I get you two another round?"

"Yes," Kate said firmly, glaring at Miles. "To hell with pinot grigio. Serious work demands a serious drink. Chaz, does your bartender know how to make a vodka gimlet? A real fricking vodka gimlet with actual fricking vodka in it?"

"Yes, ma'am. We have excellent bartenders inside. We don't just pour Budweiser here."

"Good answer, Chaz. And please call me Katherine or Kate. I hate the ma'am stuff. So, anyway, get me a real vodka gimlet. Tito's or Belvedere—not any cheap crap. Crushed ice, not cubes, and a lime wedge—a big honkin' real wedge of fucking fresh lime."

"Wow, look at you all riled up. I've hardly ever heard you swear!" Miles declared.

"Fuck you!" Kate looked away from him. She had tolerated his bullshit long enough.

Chaz didn't react. He knew how to stay out of peoples' personal shit. "Coming right up, Katherine. And another Sculpin, sir?"

"Yes, definitely another Sculpin, another fish beer." Miles grinned. Kate's flash of anger didn't bother him one bit. In fact, her feistiness was amusing. Chaz dutifully went on his way.

"Oh, darn!" Kate yelled.

"What? Hey, calm down. People are staring at you," Miles whispered.

"Aria's here with her new boyfriend Lucas. I told them to meet me here, but she's over an hour early."

"Good. Then we don't have to talk crime sprees!"

"Kate, hi!" Aria yelled from across the way, dragging Lucas by the hand through the mosh pit of umbrella-topped tables and crazily askew chairs.

"Hi, Miles, how are you?" Aria smiled. Miles smiled back, tongue-tied. Aria, the symphony "it-girl"—classy, young, fun, and drop-dead intimidatingly gorgeous. "How the hell could a bassoon player land a woman like that?" Miles mumbled to himself sotto voce as he shook Lucas's hand. They had met once before.

A couple minutes later Chaz reappeared, bestowing another fish beer on Miles and then, with a flourish and gracious smile, presented a classic vodka gimlet to Kate. "I supervised the preparation myself, ma'am—I mean Katherine," he said.

"Thank you, Chaz. You are a dear."

"Hello, ma'am," Chaz said as he turned to greet Aria. "Is that a violin you have in that case there?"

"No, actually it's a damn old crappy viola. I'm actually a real musician and I do play the violin. I was subbing on viola for someone. Not sure it was worth it. Stupid tuning pegs kept slipping."

"What's actually the difference between the violin and the viola?" Chaz asked.

"Well, considering that we are at a drinking establishment," Aria said, "the official difference is that a viola holds more beer."

"Also it burns longer," Lucas added. "After the beer is gone, I guess!"

"Chaz, here's one for you," Aria said. "What's the difference between a viola and a trampoline?"

"Hmm, I don't know."

"You take your shoes off to jump on a trampoline!"

"Ha, that's good. Do you have any more?"

Aria rolled her eyes. "Do I have any more? Seriously? I have buckets more. Chaz, what's the difference between a viola and an onion?"

"Oh, I know that one," Lucas said. "No one cries when you chop up a viola!"

"Very good. Excellent jokes, but I better stay on task with my job." Chaz smiled, happy that there were more people at the table now. "What can I get for you two funny musicians?" Chaz took drink orders from Aria and Lucas and disappeared.

Kate took a good long gulp of her icy green concoction. The frigid shards of ice and the acid of the lime jolted her taste buds and sent Arctic waves up through her sinuses. The subtle pepper tang of the premium vodka built some heat as it flooded the back of her throat. *Damn good drink*, she thought. *Bravo, Mr. Bartender, bravo.*

"So, Miles, what's up? You two look like something's wrong," Aria said. "Did we interrupt something important?"

"Work stuff. Annoying work stuff." Miles shrugged.

"That you won't help me with," Kate complained. "Bullshit—I put up with goddamn fucking bullshit all the time and get no help!" She took another swift gulp of the gimlet, slammed the glass down, stood up and stomped away, disappearing into the dark bowels of The Dragon's Den.

"Well, that was dramatic. Damn, she never swears like that. For her that's ultradramatic!" Aria chimed.

"Yeah. Wow, she's mad—really mad," Lucas said. "What's going on?"

"Nothing." Miles shook his head.

"You know, Miles, I really have no effing idea what you two are up to," Aria said in frustration. "From what I can surmise, everything where you work is fucked up. And you two seem to just accept whatever the hell it is, huh? Honestly, I don't even understand why she works there. It's ridiculous!"

"She works there because she gets paid gobs of money and she's good at what she does. Really good. We're doing cutting-edge scientific work there. Has she told you that?"

"All I know is that my best friend has become a stranger to me because of her stupid job. She's constantly stressed and she never has time to hang out anymore. Do you realize how all that makes me feel? Do you?" Aria glared at Miles, but all he did was sink lower in his chair and stare at a sparrow hopping through the area, picking up crumbs of food. "So, jerkoff, this job of Kate's—is this something she's going to regret being a part of at some point? I won't forgive you if it is."

"What, are you her mom now?" Miles sneered.

"Fuck you, asshole!" Aria barked.

Miles almost lashed out, then kept himself in check. "I'm sorry, Aria," he said, sighing heavily in frustration. "Please, calm down and listen to me, okay? Calm down and listen for a minute. What I can tell you is this—at our company we're about to start saving lives, actually saving lives of people who had no hope. Zero hope. We're creating medical history on an epic level. We're doing this—Kate, Edouard, me, Mike, his brother, other people with us. We really are. But it's all very stressful for each of us. I get that you are protective of her. You and Kate are tight like sisters. I know all the stuff you did to hold Kate together when her father died. I know you talked her into staying in school and not drop out when all that happened."

"Okay, then. Thank you," Aria said quietly, her shoulders slumping. "I'm sorry, Miles, sorry for calling you names." Aria grimaced as she bit her lip. "It's hard for me when I see her so stressed. It's really hard. You know she likes you now a little. At first she thought you were a total moron."

Chaz appeared again. He was a great server. Appear, disappear, appear, disappear. Satisfy needs. Earn a big tip. He brought Aria the malbec she had ordered plus the hefeweizen for Lucas.

"So can you hint what is going on that has her so mad at you today?" Aria said as she checked out her wine. "Tell me some of it at least. Maybe I can help. I've known her for years."

"Talking about little old nutcase me, I assume?" Kate said to no one in particular as she arrived back to the table. She still looked ready to ignite at the tiniest provocation from anyone.

"Sort of," Aria said. "I'm worried about you, Kate. Why don't you tell me at least part of what's going on and let big sister fix it for you."

Kate sat and thought for quite a while, biting her lip as she mulled over her options. Aria waited patiently. Finally Kate spoke. "Hmm, okay. Okay, yeah I will. Look, Miles, I'm telling her. I'm sick of having all these damn secrets. My mom knows what's going on, well so can Aria. I'm telling her and Lucas. If he's with Aria he can hear it, too."

"Sure, go ahead. I don't have a problem with it, not at all. Screw the secrecy stuff we signed. Like Deirdre said at your mom's house, haven't we all been good employees above and beyond the call? Okay, everybody raise your glass. You ain't gonna believe what we're trying to pull off," Miles said, holding his glass high and clinking all around. "Pull up your chairs, children. It's story time!"

CHAPTER FORTY-SIX

"So that's it. That's where we are and why we have to pull off some kind of con game on a totally crazy old lady." Miles grinned. "Epic, huh?"

"Amazing!" Aria said.

"Yeah, incredible!" Lucas added.

Kate hadn't said a word for ages. She had let Miles explain everything. *Well, he didn't explain everything,* she noticed. He had wisely, at least for now, left out direct mention of a certain A.C. Nielsen, or a certain Ray Machado, or anything about ExitStrategy's most delicate secrets. No need to confide in the newbies too much right now. Besides, just grasping the main thrust was enough. The pressing concern was how to con Gloria and make Mike and Franklin happy.

"Are you sure she doesn't have Alzheimer's?" Lucas asked. "I mean, look, she thinks James Arness and Peter Graves are alive? Hell, it sounds like she thinks Marshal Matt Dillon can ride into town and clean up Dodge. Literally!"

"Is she crazy? Don't know." Miles shrugged. "Does she have Alzheimer's? Don't know. Doesn't matter. This is all part of a power game she's been playing against Mike and Franklin for years. I think the three of them like it—too much, actually. But heck, you should see the research and financial plans for the future Mike and Franklin are putting together. Gloria may think she can take over control of the company, but nope, not gonna happen. She's too greedy and that will be her downfall. We need her for one thing right now—to sign over more money so we can afford to do our research, all of it. We're talking five years at least."

"It's interesting, strange and interesting," Lucas said.

"Okay, so hire a couple guys to play the Arness brothers. They fake it. What's the problem?" Aria asked. "And why couldn't you hire *all* actors, film it somewhere and do this without having to mess with Khail and Dimi?"

"Gloria's got bad eyesight, but she'd catch that in an instant," Miles explained. "Don't forget, she's been around sound stages and cameras her whole life. Anyone like her can tell the real world from something being faked. Even just getting two guys to pull off playing the Arness brothers is not going to be easy. We can't tell them anything, especially about ExitStrategy. And what if they're crappy at doing a con? Or crappy at acting? How would we even go about finding the right people? And it's got to be two tall guys with deep voices and a certain amount of brains but maybe not too much. Gloria will want to meet them. They'll have to pull off talking to her. Yeah, she's blind, but not one hundred percent. And what if they screw up and rat to her, or panic and call the police or something? There is no way that Mike and Franklin want any kind of law enforcement poking around at ExitStrategy, especially not right now. Too many sensitive things going on."

"Lots of what-ifs, huh? Yeah, I see. I get it." Lucas nodded.

Kate remained silent, yet thankful that Miles seemed to be dropping his lazy objections to getting rolling on a plan. Besides, Aria and Lucas were smart. Hell, they might have an idea or two that might help, you never know. Chaz brought out another round of drinks—on the house. Snacks on the house, too. Everyone thanked Chaz, especially Kate. He was her new favorite server in the whole city, she told him. His gesture of generosity brightened her earlier foul mood. She tried to turn her frown upside-down like her mother used to tell her to do when she was a kid.

Aria had noticed Kate was trying to smile, so she directed a question to her. "Kate, I'm not an old-timey TV person. Hey, why should I be? I'm only twenty-seven. So I know who Peter Graves was on *Mission: Impossible*. Cool theme music, right? Lalo Schifrin. In five/four time—very groovy. I've seen six or seven episodes. Lots of double-crosses and high-tech equipment for the day. Not a bad show, I think. But those Tom Hanks movie versions I've seen were pretty crappy. Too confusing, for one thing."

"No, not Tom Hanks, that was Tom Cruise," Kate said.

"Oh yeah, right. And who was the other brother?"

Miles rolled his eyes. Aria seemed to know essentially nothing about American television history. "*Gunsmoke*, Aria, the longest running TV show of all time. CBS, Saturday nights mostly. The star was James, or Jim Arness. He was a giant star. The little brother was in his shadow for years until he finally snagged *M.I.*"

"And so these two are brothers, with two different last names?" Lucas asked.

"Right, they actually had the Swedish last name Aurness, spelled A-

U-R-N-E-S-S," Miles explained. "Tall, handsome, manly men. From Minnesota, just like our dear friend Gloria. Peter took a new last name to distinguish himself from the big bro."

"Bro, right. So they were brothers, you're saying?" Aria pressed.

"Yes, we have established that fact, ma'am. They were the Arness *brothers*. They had the same mommy. You know how that works, right, Aria? How mommies and daddies make babies?"

"And you said you need two guys with some brains but not too much, right?"

"Yes, Aria! Yes, yes, yes," Miles said in frustration.

Aria squinted her eyes, blinking over and over while furrowing her brow. Everyone watched the little show playing out on her face. "The Arness Bros!" she spat out finally.

"Sure, Aria, the Arness Bros, if you wish," Miles said, nodding his head, trying to help her out. *Jesus, how dumb is she?* he wondered.

Aria stood up abruptly, raised her chin high, and yelled at the top of her lungs, "THE ARSE BROS!" She quickly grabbed her drink, power-chugged what was left, spun the glass in the air, caught it, and slammed it upside-down hard on the table.

"What? What?" Miles said incredulously.

"The Irish boys I play fiddle for. The Arse Bros—Arness Bros— perfect fit. And you guys didn't even think of it. Obviously I'm a genius," she boasted, a little bit tipsy and pleased with herself to no end.

"Wait. What, so what do you mean?" Miles asked.

"They can pretend to be your Arness brothers. Pull you off a Mission: Impossible. They're both tall, and at least a little rugged. Some brains, but not too much. We can dye their hair, dress them up."

"They've got Irish accents, Aria," Kate chided.

"They put those on for the act. Their family came over from Dublin when they were wee lads. They can speak perfect Joe-Average English. They only do the heavy Irish accent onstage. Or in front of you, Kate, ha-ha!"

"Really?" Kate said, surprised.

"Yeah, and they'll listen to you. Especially Patrick, since he's got a perpetual hard-on for you. Slip on your black vinyl catsuit and crack the whip and he'll do as told, Katey-Kat. They're both very trainable, I'm sure."

"And they'll kidnap Dimi and her famous breasts, too?" Miles asked. "Ransom her back to Khail somehow? Are we talking about doing that for real? People, talking about it over drinks is one thing, doing it sober is another. I mean, come on."

"Maybe we just tell her we tried to pull it off and then tell her it didn't work. Mike's getting his money up front, you know," Kate said. "Aria, do you think the boys would do it if we hatch some kind of plan?"

"Are you kidding?" Aria said. "Offer those two a paycheck and they'll do anything. They're broke 24/7!"

"Chaz, hey, Chaz, another round here!" Miles yelled.

CHAPTER FORTY-SEVEN

"Good morning, everyone! How are you all this fine day?" boomed Cold Smokey Burgess, looking as happy as a clam at high tide. "I have to tell you I woke up feeling great. Best night's sleep in a long time."

"We're pretty damn good," Miles said as he peered around the room at Franklin, Kate, Patrick and Colm Flynn—the Arse Brothers, aka the Arness brothers—Aria Grumman, Lucas Cranach, and last but not least, Ray Machado, aka Mr. A.C. Nielsen.

"Yeah we're good, Mr. Burgess," Patrick said, without even a tiny trace of an Irish accent. "Colm and I have practiced our parts. Franklin's makeup lady is awesome. Check us out!" Colm had the icy white Peter Graves hair color and wore a finely tailored *Mission: Impossible*-era suit. Patrick, standing tall and confident, yet with more girth, took the role of James Arness.

"We've even kind of got their voices down," Patrick said. "Check it out, 'Well howdy, ma'am. You say there's some rustlers out by the old Johnson place? I'll get on over there just as soon as Festus and I get a shot of whiskey and some sweet pussy over at the Long Branch.'"

"Jesus, Patrick, be serious for a bit, will you?" Kate lashed out. "This isn't all just stupid fun and games, like you playing around tossing darts at some crappy pub when you're drunk."

"I disagree, Kate," Franklin said. "If we approach it like a game, it will have the best chance of working. It's basic human psychology and the root, the basis, of all acting. Why do we call a stage production a play? Because it is just that, play framed for an audience. Besides, they're gonna be great. I know a natural actor when I see one. And right now I'm seeing double."

"Aye, seein' double 'e is, an' wit'out a drink in 'im," Colm chuckled in the thickest brogue he could come up with, all the while winking like a fool at Kate.

"I agree with my dear nephew," Mike said, still feeling jovial. "And remember, we're all in this together. Everything will be just fine. Anyway, Miles, what did you find on Gloria's vision issues?"

"Amazing what crappy firewalls people have—absolutely amazing. I accessed her files at a fancy ophthalmologist to the stars in Sherman Oaks. She's not quite legally blind. She can sort of see a bit, way up close, but she's got serious blind spots, floaters, and blurring. You saw how close she got herself to the TV last time we saw her, like six inches away? She's probably still like that or even worse. She's told almost no one, I bet. The hair and makeup on the boys should work like a charm. And speaking of that—just be charming, guys, that's all she desires, that her male admirers be charming and attentive."

"Remember, Marshal Dillon," Franklin said to Patrick, "she guest starred on your show twice, and if she mentions those episodes play along."

"And the lawyer who thinks I'm a child?" Kate asked. "Randolph Morgan? Morgan Randolph? Do we owe him something?"

"It's Randolph Morgan, Kate," Franklin said. "He does whatever Gloria says or he facilitates whatever things she's agreed to. Whether Gloria's playing someone or vice versa, he just does what's needed at the moment, all for a very healthy paycheck out of her vault of moolah. He'll never rock the boat about anything unless it threatens his job in some way. He told Mike that this should go well for us. Not sure I trust that statement or the person making it, but there it is."

"Ray, what do you think of all this?" Mike said.

"It should work. But be on the lookout. You should never underestimate the power of her inner bitch. I'll be sitting back and watching, mostly. But if I'm needed in some way I'll step forward."

* * *

A few minutes later Keith escorted Gloria and Randolph Morgan to the conference room. She was in a wheelchair, wearing giant 1980s-style sunglasses a la Sally Jessie Raphael, and was decked out in designer clothes. *She might be ancient, but she can still dress to impress*, thought Kate.

Franklin and Mike bent down to give her a kiss on the cheek. She swiveled her head around the room, trying to make out faces, but this was difficult for her.

"Mr. Nielsen? Mr. Nielsen, are you here?" she cackled.

"Yes, Gloria, dear." Ray hid his natural voice as he affected a Minnesota accent. "I'm right here, back among the living, thanks to you." Ray reached his hand out to touch hers gently. "It's so good to see you. You're looking wonderful," Ray lied.

"Oh, you flatter me as always, Mr. Nielsen. Such the dapper gentleman. There should be more of you in the world, my dear." Ray grinned—the ironic truth was that, literally, there were more Ray Machados in the world and less A.C. Nielsens.

"And I believe Jim Arness is here—Jim?" Gloria said. "Jim, it's been far too long."

'Jim' stepped toward Gloria and grasped her hand lightly, like a gentleman marshal would do. Gloria slowly moved her right hand up to caress Jim's face. *That's it, boy*, thought Kate. *Let her lead.*

"Please excuse me, Jim. My eyesight is not the best." She felt his chin, his cheekbones, then playfully ruffled his hair. "Handsomest man on television!" she announced to all. She finally let his hand go, after a final squeeze. "And, Peter, you're here, too?" 'Peter' stepped forward and thrust his hand out to Gloria. She shook it matter-of-factly. It was obvious which Arness man she preferred.

"Jim, do you remember the second time I was on your show? When Amanda Blake was late to rehearsal and for a laugh, I stood in for her and messed up her lines on purpose? I cracked you up, remember? The grips and everyone were laughing their fool heads off. Remember the look on Amanda's face when she finally walked in and saw me clowning through her part—her precious part? Oh, I wish I had a picture of that face she made, Jim. I really do."

"Of course I remember, Gloria," 'Jim' said. "You know, Gloria, you were my favorite guest star."

"Oh, you flatter me. I'm sure there were many great ones."

"But you were the best. You were magical both times. After the first time, we knew we wanted to bring you back. It took a while because you had your own series going. We were always on the phone to your agent. He might not have told you." *Yes indeed, Patrick knows how to lay it on thick, thought Kate. Why did I ever doubt his ability to be a conniver and a ham?*

"Jim, I was blessed to be on your show. It's so good to see you and Mr. Nielsen… and Peter," she added.

"May I?" Miles motioned to the assemblage. Everyone looked his way. He pulled a small device out of a Trader Joe's bag, laid it on the meeting-room table, and then slid it over to Colm. "This is for Mr. Phelps." It was a vintage 1970s cassette recorder, appearing as if it were straight out of the *Mission: Impossible* prop room. "I customized it.

You'll see."

'Peter' picked it up, looked it over, then pushed the play button:

Good afternoon, Mr. Phelps,

Your mission, should you decide to accept it, is to kidnap the dreaded leader of The New Turd Order, Miss Demetria Konstantos. Miss Konstantos and her husband Khail Santana have left a trail of odiferous floaters across the vista of modern television entertainment. Once you have captured her and her enormous breasts, you will ransom Demetria, code name Dim Dum, back to her husband and his wranglers, only on condition they promise to cease and desist their methane gas-based pollution of the airwaves.

As always, should you or any of your IM force be caught or killed, the Secretary will disavow any knowledge of your actions. Good luck, Jim. This tape will self-destruct in five seconds.

Everyone giggled—all except Gloria. She remained stone-cold serious. Morgan was stone-faced, too. If you wanted a smile out of him you'd have to cut him a check.

"Very clever, Miles." Mike grinned. "Quite the tinkerer you are."

"Wait, there's more," Miles said.

"More?" Mike said. "What do you—" Suddenly tiny flames and a whoosh of gray smoke rose up from the machine.

"Wow, holy cow! Just like in the show," Kate said.

"Hm, be glad you didn't set off my sprinklers, young man," Mike said. The room erupted into laughter. There was a pause while Miles cleared away his most excellent prop. Finally, things settled back down and the meeting continued.

"Well, Mr. Coleman, that was an interesting touch," Gloria said, "but I prefer that we handle this more in a Marshal Dillon–type of way. I don't think we need spy games or the like."

"Gloria, we're not even sure we can pull off what you want—kidnap Dimi and hold her for ransom. What if we get caught? And we still need people to help Jim and Peter pull this off," Mike said.

"You will do it because I have decided so, Mike," Gloria said, the gloves coming off.

"Mr. Nielsen has offered to help, by the way, Gloria," Franklin said.

"Yes, Gloria, I'm as disgusted with reality TV as you are," A.C./Ray said. "I've decided to go back and run the A.C. Nielsen Company again. If the kidnapping doesn't work I can always, ahem, rig some ratings. I'd never do that in the past. Never. But this is different, by God. Dimi and Khail are an abomination. We have to take them down some way, somehow." Ray surprised himself. He hadn't planned any of this speech, but it came out sounding impassioned and convincing.

"Gloria, I understand your feeling of urgency about the TV thing, but let's not lose sight of something far more important—that is, the work we're doing here," Franklin said. "We really need more funding for our research and long-term planning. Our bank lines of credit are running low. As you know, Mr. Morgan and I have drawn up some papers, which you've indicated you'll sign. He's explained it to you, correct?"

"Yes, he has. You want more of my millions, as usual," Gloria snapped.

"Yes, but it's for another ten percent stake in ExitStrategy."

"I understand. I'll sign the papers. I'll gladly dilute your shares and take more control of the company whenever you and Mike desire to offer it, Franklin."

Lord, she sounds like Mr. Potter in It's A Wonderful Life, thought Kate. *I had no idea she was this much of a mean old miser. What can she possibly do with all those hundreds of millions at her age, anyway?*

Morgan reached into his briefcase, and with a grand flourish, produced the document and a very expensive new pen. With a few strokes from the ancient lady, fifty million US dollars would flow directly into ExitStrategy's bank account. This was fresh capital that Kate needed for research—real research, not just for piddling around. Gloria took the pen and Morgan guided her hand here and there to sign or initial. As she finished her last pen stroke she leaned in close to Morgan and whispered, "You know what to do now."

"Yes, ma'am," he responded quietly. "I'll take care of everything."

CHAPTER FORTY-EIGHT

Gloria's bank transfer to ExitStrategy went through without a hitch. The company was again flush with cash. Mike, Franklin, and a few topnotch financial advisers discussed how to proceed with real research, probably at least five years' worth. Hiring someone younger to oversee everything needed to happen, too. After all, Mike and Franklin both admitted they weren't spring chickens anymore. They also decided not to take on any new cryo clients other than the ones already contracted. There was too much at stake on so many levels to confuse things by adding clients. It was time for research, time to crunch numbers, time to slow down and accumulate data—no more hit-or-miss guessing at things like they had fallen into doing in the short term. Where were the prion brain cell problems coming from? And were the prions accelerating during some part of the cryo process? If so, when? At the onset, during the long freeze, or during the revivification? Or all three? So many questions. How would Kate's info from the Iceland institute affect the research and what they were doing? And how was cryo seemingly curing cancer—Kate's realignment theory? Or something else? You could guess at the answers to any or all of these questions, but it sure would be nice to use the good old scientific method. Create a hypothesis or two—or twenty. Fifty million dollars sounded like a lot of money, but it could disappear quickly if they didn't use it wisely.

Meanwhile Mike, Franklin, Kate, and Miles held a few meetings on the Gloria issue. They knew they still had to rig up a dog-and-pony show for her. Aria's idea was adopted. Kate felt it was actually quite elegant and had to explain to Franklin why the concept of elegance was something scientists were into. They would make a videotape of Patrick and Colm as the Arness brothers attempting to kidnap Dimi, something to show Gloria that they had at least tried to save the world from the godlessness of reality TV and its top stars, Dimi and Khail. Mike, Franklin, Kate, Miles, Patrick, Colm, Aria, Lucas, and Ray gathered in the company lunchroom for the last planning session.

"Okay, people, so here's the final plan," Miles said. "So Dimi, Khail, and a small entourage will be flying into O'Hare next Tuesday morning. They usually travel with three or four bodyguards. These guys are unarmed, but they are very big dudes with very big biceps. You don't want to run into these guys' fists, trust me. They glare at you and your head might explode. Anyway, when we do this, things will probably be a bit crazy. The paparazzi will have found out which flight they're on and the fans may know, too, since it's public knowledge that Dimi is flying here to appear live on *The De'Vanna Show* that day. The idea is to do this fast and get the hell out. All we need is some footage."

"Right," Franklin said. "Everybody stick to the script. It's damned simple. You all get out fast and don't get punched."

"Exactly," Miles agreed. "Our four actors will be there ahead of time. Aria and Lucas will be in disguise. As Dimi approaches, Aria will bump into one of the women in the entourage and create a diversion for a moment. Lucas will help keep her safe once this starts. The bodyguards will be distracted and the Arness Bros will swoop in and then pretend to kidnap Dimi, but they'll keep it vanilla. The bodyguards will come in fast at the boys once they see a bigger threat than Aria, and Patrick and Colm will break the whole thing off and disappear, as will Aria and Lucas. Arse Bros, I'm reminding you two to steer clear of Khail. He's a total hothead in airports and knows how to land a punch. I'm sure you've seen clips on entertainment TV of this doofus going ballistic and pounding people. This will all look great on camera. Franklin and the video camera men have worked with the boys on it. Speaking of cameras, our guys will be pretending to be normal paparazzi. They'll be catching video of all this from two different angles. Who knows if we really need all our video, since the usual paparazzi will be on hand, plus it's possible that Khail's reality show camera crew may be there, too. But one way or another all this will get caught on film for our dear Gloria."

"Besides, her money's in our account," Mike said. "We're just giving her a show and, in true Hollywood manner, sort of keeping our end of a bogus Hollywood deal. Sort of," he repeated.

"Sort of," Kate said.

"Yes, sort of. That's all we need, my friends," Mike said, smiling over at Patrick and Colm.

"Hey, I've got a new idea for a reality show. *The Real Paparazzi of LAX*. Could be pretty cool, right?" Lucas said. "'Follow the exploits of underappreciated, underdog cameraman Joe Schmoe as he valiantly keeps the American public satiated with the awesomeness of Hollywood royalty.'"

"I've got a better idea. How about the *Lucas Keeps Aria Safe Show?*" Kate said.

"All right, all right. Be nice to each other, people. You're all a team, remember?" Ray cautioned.

"What if one of the bodyguards really does land a mean left hook on Patrick or Colm?" Aria asked.

"Hell, we're Irish. We can take a punch and send it right back at 'em, we can," Patrick declared, doing a bit of airboxing.

"No, you'll get out. Damn it, Patrick, no fighting. Period. Jesus, we talked about this already, guys," Miles said, looking quite frustrated. "Anyway, folks, the boys will have their wigs and makeup like you saw at the meeting with Gloria. To her they're the Arness brothers. You all saw that we fooled her at the meeting. Who knows what's going on in that teeny skull of hers, right? But it really doesn't matter, because this will all happen in twenty seconds or so, and then all four of you will disappear into the crowd like that." He snapped his fingers. "Hell, it's O'Hare, it's friggin' enormous."

"We're not worried about Chicago PD or airport security or anything?" Lucas asked.

"Ha! That's funny. Next question!" Franklin laughed.

"Sounds great, folks. Very doable. A real live fake *Mission: Impossible* micro episode!" Mike proclaimed. "We show this to Gloria and we're off the hook with her for anything and everything. Thank you all for creating this. It's truly excellent."

"Hey, Franklin, were you ever on *Mission: Impossible?*" Miles asked.

"How old do you think I am, Miles? I'd have to be like ten or twelve at the time to manage that! But I did some TV stuff with Martin Landau, if that impresses you at all. Barbara Bain showed up to the set now and then. They were married, you know. Classy lady."

"Okay, Mike, why the hell does Gloria have to come to Chicago for this?" Kate said. "I hear she's coming in. I wish she would just stay put in California."

"I think it makes her feel more important. Actually, it means we can show her the tape quicker. So get over it. She'll be sitting in her hotel twiddling her thumbs or something. She'll be at her usual room, 525 at the Winston House Hotel."

"She should stay in 666," Colm said in an eerie voice.

"No, it's always 525. Something good must have happened there back in the day." Mike laughed.

"I could tell you, but then I'd have to kill you," Ray said grimly. Everyone had forgotten he was in the room, he'd been so quiet. They all went silent, wondering what secrets he might know.

"Gotcha!" Ray yelled. Everyone laughed.

CHAPTER FORTY-NINE

"What do you think of my hair, Kate?"

"Weird. Blue? No way, Aria—you're supposed to be able to blend into the crowd. It's not little girl dress-up day in the attic. I hope you only spent your leftover pennies for that thing at the dollar store, because you're not wearing it today."

"Grump. So no blue hair? Can I dress up as a hippie chick? Beads and bell-bottoms? Leather fringe vest?"

"No, wear something drab. Drab little you bumps into the entourage, gets everyone confused, and then gets the hell out. We've been through this a thousand times."

"Wow, you really are a grouch today. Okay, I get it. So how about *this* wig?" Aria pulled out a dull, brown cheapo purchase from her WigWag DiscountTag Hair Supplies bag.

"There, that's more like it. You were just messing with me with the blue thing, weren't you? I should have known," Kate said. "Someday maybe you'll grow up, but in the meantime I guess I'll have to just enjoy your early years. Put it on, let's see."

"Okay."

"Wow, babycakes, you actually look like crap in that. Amazing!"

"Thank you very much for that assessment," Aria groaned.

"Listen, stick to the plan. I am scared to death your Arse Bros are going to do something stupid today."

"They'll be fine. Any further concerns or lectures, oh Anal Retentive One?"

"Remember, I'll be circling with my car and Miles in his. Get out to the curbside and when you spot either one of us, you and Lucas get in and we're outta there."

"You know, Kate, this really is just like *Mission: Impossible*. I watched some more of it on YouTube. I think overall we need some gadgets."

"Right. I'm gonna be happy when I can put my lab coat back on and be done with this kind of nonsense. Damn Gloria and her A.C. Nielsen daddy fixation, her stupid crush on Marshal Dillon, all that. God, she's an idiot."

"I know you'll be happy when we're done. Everything will go just right. Colm and Patrick aren't as stupid as they act. You do know that, right?"

"Aria, based on the empirical evidence so far I know nothing of the sort. So what are you going to do with the twenty grand Mike's paying you for today? That's a damn fine paycheck for a ringer, huh?"

"What any violin playah would do, buy a wicked bow or two!"

"Wow, that truly is total nerd territory," Kate remarked. "A stick with horsey hair on it? Should be like two hundred dollars tops. Unless it's fluffy rainbow unicorn hair instead. Now that might be worth something."

"*Oy*, you don't know from music, my little *meshuggeneh*. You can't play a great violin with a crappy bow. It doesn't work that way."

"Okay, dear. I'm just picking on you because if it's about music, you're an easy target. So, if you're done futzing with the malnourished dead polecat wig and that ill-fitting jacket we can go, right?"

"Right, sir. Peppermint Patty reporting for duty, fearless leader, sir." Aria saluted Kate over and over as she stood up.

* * *

Kate and Aria picked up Lucas and headed toward O'Hare. Meanwhile, Miles picked up Patrick and Colm and were on their way, too. Mike, Franklin, and Ray were back at ExitStrategy with nothing to do other than wait for updates via texts. They wound up swapping stories about the old days—Ray's jazz club stories, Mike's three-drink lunch glory days at Frigidaire, Franklin's days as a TV character actor. Manly stuff the young kids wouldn't understand, that was for sure. It was enjoyable not to have some damn smartass kid like Miles or that boyfriend of Aria's, whatever the hell his name was, trying to hang out with them. Young guys who had never smoked a nonfiltered cigarette, or who didn't know who Ursula Andress was, or who hadn't a hint of what the free love 1960s were like. When a car had eight cylinders and there wasn't a catalytic convertor in sight, when Burma Shave signs were along the road, and Dean Martin was on the television. When people actually worked nine to five and didn't dick around on their cell phone or the Internet at work. Goddammit, back in the day people put in an honest day's work for an honest day's pay.

Kate dropped Aria and Lucas at ORD Terminal One arrivals. Perfect timing. They had thirty easy minutes to get into a good position to ambush Dimi, Khail, and their entourage.

"Remember, Lucas," Aria said. "Khail likes to slug people. Steer clear of him if you want to keep your front teeth."

"Yeah, okay. But if he does slug me I could have a nice, juicy lawsuit against him, right?"

"Just play it by the book, honey," Aria purred with a grin.

"Where do you think the camera guys are?"

"Back that way, obviously. Don't worry about them. They're professionals. Worry about the Arse Bros if you want. You and I got our act together and I guarantee you those camera guys will be smooth."

"So you're not nervous, Aria?"

"Nope. Dude, we're professional musicians. This is just another performance. When's the last time you were actually nervous playing a concert?"

"Yeah, okay, I get it. It'll be easy-peasy, then. Cool," Lucas said, looking much more relaxed.

Miles arrived about five minutes later and dropped the Arse Bros off. The boys looked great in their nicely tailored suits and carried new expensive leather briefcases. They entered the terminal, walked for a while, and then spotted Aria and Lucas ahead of them, blending in and waiting. The boys positioned themselves about thirty yards downstream from Aria and Lucas. Patrick and Colm went into blend-in mode as well, pretending to read newspapers at the newsstand. Everything was good to go. Meanwhile, Kate and Miles slowly circled back to the cell phone waiting area to waste time. They could sit there and monitor the flight in from LAX and eventually start circling the pickup area.

A few more minutes passed. *Just kill time*, Aria thought, *just kill time. Wait, what the hell is this?* "Lucas, look at the boys. What is Patrick doing?"

"He's opening his briefcase and taking something out," Lucas said. "I thought those were empty, just for looks. What is he doing, anyway?"

"I don't know. Oh Jesus, look, he's got clothes in there or something. He's pulling something out and now he's taking off his suit coat. Colm is helping him. They're messing with the plan."

"Call Kate or Miles," Lucas said.

"Hell, no. What can they do? We're in position. Dimi and Khail will probably be coming through soon. Look at the board. They just switched it from inflight to arrived. They'll be coming off first class in a jiffy."

"Hell, he's putting on a vest, like a cowboy vest," Lucas said. "Is he trying to look like Marshal Dillon? Oh no, a fucking cowboy hat, too!"

Aria let out a series of loud coughs—loud enough that people stared over at her. Also, loud enough that Patrick and Colm looked her way, too.

"Look at those bastards," Lucas said. "The big doofuses are standing there with shit-eating grins on their faces."

"If we were in Dallas Patrick would blend right in." Aria said. "But not here. Why do I feel like I'm in an idiot cowboy version of *American Hustle?*"

"Unbelievable."

"Yup, unfuckingbelievable," Aria echoed harshly. "Oh, look over there. It's Khail. They're already off the plane, look!"

"Geez, that's a lot of people coming our way."

Sure enough, paparazzi were scrambling to take pics as Khail led out front, trying to run interference, followed by Dimi, her sister Konstantina, two female friends, Chris Bronsteyn, and then the three beefy bodyguards—Antoine, J.T., and Theo. Dimi and her girls all carried Marchesa Valentino crocodile skin handbags, and they were already yakking away on their bling-bling cell phones, pretending they couldn't care less about the vapid fans gawking at them.

"I assumed the bodyguards would be in front. I thought we could flank them and maybe they wouldn't all see us right away," Lucas said.

"Well, we know Khail likes to be the hero. That's why he's out front—the Alpha male, you know," Aria exclaimed.

"Yeah, I get it. Geez, he's such an idiot."

"Doesn't matter. Ready?" Aria glanced back at the Arse Bros, fuming again for a second as she saw 'Marshal Dillon' and his cohort lurking. "I hope they know what they're doing. Shit, it was my idea to use them. Damn, damn, damn."

"It's okay. All right, now, on an angle. Let's go!" The two turned toward the approaching entourage, aiming to flank just past crazy Khail and bump into one of the girlfriends near Dimi. Just as they were about there, two paparazzi tripped over each other, bumping into Aria, which gave her a perfect excuse to shove the smaller man right into Dimi's sister Konstantina and one of the glitzy girlfriends.

"Hey, what are you doing, *asshole*?" Konstantina yelled, but Aria didn't respond. She made sure to get tangled up with them, which wasn't too difficult since the strap from the nearest paparazzo's camera wound up wrapping around both Konstantina and Dimi, causing things to go further amok. Lucas bumped smack into Dimi, causing her cell phone to go flying out of her hand. Khail grabbed the closest photographer he could find and shook him silly. The bodyguards rushed forward and sprang into full motion.

"Mr. Santana, we got this!" yelled Antoine, the head bodyguard. "We got it, sir, take it easy. You all right, Miss Konstantos?" Dimi was still trying to untangle herself from Aria and find her precious cell phone in its Swarovski full crystal case. Aria was just about loose, so she glanced over her shoulder and saw that Colm and Patrick—he in his preposterous cowboy getup—were about to walk right into the mayhem. They would be right on top of the skirmish in about two or three seconds. Time for her and Lucas to walk away briskly from the brouhaha. The plan was working. Time to get away, get out of the airport, and step into one of the trawling cars.

"She's got a gun! She's got a gun! There! There!" Konstantina screamed.

"I don't have a gun, idiot. What the hell are you talking about?" Aria mumbled. She and Lucas were side by side now, past the craziness and making a clean getaway. But then they both looked back. Some crazy woman, a total stranger, had come out of nowhere and was pointing a .44 Magnum straight at Dimi. *How the hell could this be happening?* Aria wondered as adrenaline pumped furiously throughout her body. "Oh my God, run, Lucas, run. We have to get out of here!" They took off as fast as they could down the long walkway toward the transportation pickup zone. At the very same moment, Patrick and Colm, without ever breaking their stride, walked right through the potential line of fire.

"Colm, grab her, grab Dimi—come on quick! We have to get her out of here," Patrick said, thinking quickly.

"Get out of my way. She's got to die. Get out of my way, I'm gonna shoot her!" the gunwoman shrieked. While everyone else froze, the boys kept moving, gathering up Dimi, one on each side of her and quickly pushing her forward.

"Come on, Miss Dimi, run! We have to run, come on. Go, go, go!" Colm urged. Dimi, in a panic, hardly moved at all. The boys literally had to lift her off her feet and trot her away from the crazy woman, risking getting shot in the back. As the boys disappeared with Dimi, one of the bodyguards tried to talk the gunwoman down. People in the immediate area were screaming, not knowing whether to flee or stay still. The madwoman was still snarling at everyone, "Bring her back here. Bring her back *now!*" she screamed. "She destroyed my marriage. Now she has to *die!*"

No police came. It was now a standoff between the gunwoman and Khail's crew. As the crazy woman kept waving the gun wildly and babbling on about her ruined marriage, Konstantina gradually circled behind her without being noticed. Antoine saw this and tried to engage the woman, coaxing her into a dialog, working to keep the woman's focus on himself. Gradually, Konstantina snuck up from behind and then took a gigantic swing with her crocodile bag, knocking her toward Antoine, who grabbed the poor soul, turned her upside-down and backward, shook her so she dropped the gun, and then executed a classic pro-wrestling pile driver move, landing on his ass as he propelled her head into the concrete floor. The woman squirmed for a moment, then went motionless, down for the count. She would wake up later in the hospital under police watch with three cracked cervical vertebrae. The growing crowd cheered for Antoine. Danger averted, but now what?

"Where's Dimi? Where's my Dimi?" Khail yelled.

"I dunno," Antoine yelled. "Those two cops saved her. They came outta nowhere and saved her. We'll find her soon. She's safe, I'm pretty sure. We got to keep moving. Look at this crowd now, it's getting bigger and bigger. We got to go, got to go, Khail. We'll call the police once we're out of here." Antoine motioned to Theo and J.T. "You two keep watching the nutcase until security shows up, if they ever do goddamn show up!" Khail, Antoine, Konstantina, and the girlfriends speed-walked away from the mayhem, not realizing that ordinary folks had wrestled each other for a valuable celebrity souvenir—Dimi's cell phone.

* * *

"Keep your head down, miss," Patrick said. "Just try to walk fast. We can't carry you all the way without getting noticed. Walk fast, and don't yell or anything. We'll get you out of here. There's a car outside." Patrick and Colm were lifesavers, but they weren't out of danger yet. They had, in a sense, quite accidentally kidnapped Demetria Konstantos. Somehow Gloria's ridiculous goal had willed itself into reality!

"Okay, okay." Dimi trembled. "Oh my God, she wanted to kill me. Were there shots? Did she shoot? I'm shaking so much, I can't remember what happened."

"No, ma'am, no shots," Colm said. "I'm sure your husband has karate-chopped her weak little ass by now. But keep moving, we'll get you out of the airport. Cover your face so people don't recognize you, okay? We're almost there."

"Are you police? FBI?" Dimi asked.

"No, ma'am, we're marshals. See my hat?" Patrick quipped.

"I think I might be sick. Can I sit on this bench for a minute? Just a minute and then we can keep going to your headquarters. Is it close?"

"Yes, ma'am. Sit for a minute, put your head down a bit, and stay incognito," Colm said. While Dimi was trying to catch her breath and calm herself, the boys could whisper back and forth.

"No police all this time. Wonder why? Maybe looking in bathrooms?" Patrick said.

"Or eating donuts somewhere? Heck, did dumbass Khail not even call the police yet?" Colm wondered. "Maybe they thought we were Men in Black. Saviors of the universe, you know? Well, at least I look like an MiB dude, right? You look like some stupid guy who just flew in from Oklahoma. And you even forgot your goddamn spurs."

"Hey fuck you, Colm. I wanted to do the part right, okay?" Patrick hissed.

"Yeah, whatever. Okay, let's get the hell out of here. And what are we doing with her, anyway?"

"I don't know. Let Kate and Miles figure it out. They're the ones with all the college degrees."

"Okay, Miss Dimi, let's go now. There should be a car outside," Colm said, slipping back into his confident MiB persona. Dimi took a big gulp from a bottle of liquid antacid she had stashed in her purse, then they started out the door.

Kate had been sitting there at pickup aisle seven for only a minute or two. No cop had shooed her away yet. She saw the boys come out and squinted their way as they crossed over the taxi and shuttle lanes on their way to her. "What the heck! What is this nonsense?" she yelled out loud even before they got to her car. The Arse Bros opened the back door of the car, wedging Dimi between the two of them.

"What did you guys do? You morons! What is she doing here?" Kate hissed.

"I suggest you drive away from here, ma'am," Patrick said, trying to act cool and calm.

"And what is with the getup? Oh my God, I knew you were going to do something stupid. So help me!" Kate continued to rant. She slammed on the accelerator and almost ran into a hotel shuttle bus. "Do you not have any brains in your mucked-up heads? Oh my God, I'm gonna have a heart attack!" *Why in the world did they kidnap her? How stupid could they possibly be? We're all going to jail.*

"Ma'am, just drive. Get away from O'Hare. We'll explain later," Colm said.

Dimi sobbed uncontrollably. She looked a mess, her hair ratted all across her face, her mascara dripping down her cheeks.

"It's okay now, Miss Dimi. We'll keep you safe." Colm stroked her nasty hair.

Kate looked back at the three of them via her rear-view mirror. This was crazy. *We'll keep you safe?* What the hell? They had kidnapped her. How was that keeping her safe? Kate tried to breathe more deeply and get her heart to stop pounding. It didn't help that traffic leaving O'Hare was a bear. Time to hurry back to ExitStrategy and figure out what happened, what went wrong, and what the hell they would do with reality TV's biggest star now that they had, in some ridiculous manner, caught her. Kate glanced back again. *There she is. Dimi the precious ass, looking like crap, crying like a five-year-old, surrounded by the two stupidest goons on the planet. Jesus H. Christ! Oh, wait—where are Aria and Lucas? I've forgotten about them.* Kate took a couple deep breaths and tried to calm herself. There was already one sobbing basket case in the car, no need to make it two.

"So," Kate said as matter-of-factly as she could manage for the moment, "our other *friends*, are they okay?"

"They're fine, I'm sure," Colm said. "They walked on past."

Kate let out a big sigh. That meant Miles would have picked Aria and Lucas up and they too would be headed back to the lab.

Suddenly Dimi went crazy. "Let me out of here, let me out of here," she screamed. She tried to spring free from the squeeze the boys had on her, pulled herself up and above them, then grabbed Kate's hair as hard as she could. Kate screamed out in pain and the car swerved wildly, almost hitting a taxi as she tried to get herself free.

"Stop it!" Kate yelled.

"Let me out, let me out. She's got a gun. She's gonna shoot me!" Dimi yelled, then pummeled the boys.

"She's in shock, Colm, do something," Patrick said.

"Miss Dimi, calm down. Everything is okay. You're safe now," Colm said.

"No, no, no, she's still got the gun. She's still got it." Dimi went to pull Kate's hair again. She grabbed ahold and pulled even harder this time. Kate had to work like crazy to keep the car in its lane. *The woman's whacked out, and what was that about a gun? A gun? Makes no sense. If a cop sees me swerving like this I'm gonna get pulled over. There is no way that can happen—no darn way!*

"Do something with her, Patrick. Do something now!"

"All right!" he yelled back. He made a fist, reared it back and slammed a left hook into Dimi's pretty little Hollywood face—*pow!* Score the knockout for the newly crowned Light Heavyweight World Champion of the Backseat, Mr. Patrick Seamus Flynn.

CHAPTER FIFTY

Back at ExitStrategy, Franklin was on a roll regaling Ray and Mike with stories of wild antics he had been part of during his TV career. Franklin's material was killer. Mike and Ray alternated between laughing their fool heads off and sipping their Johnny Walker Black Label on the rocks. The three of them had been doing a number on the brand new bottle Mike had cracked open barely half an hour earlier.

Suddenly, the lab door swung open. Keith, the security guard, motioned to Mike.

"She insisted on coming in, Mr. Burgess. She barged in and wouldn't give me time to call you. Is this okay, sir?"

"Yes, Keith, I guess." Mike stood and tried to walk a straight line after all the hard liquor he'd put away so quickly. "Gloria, what are you doing here?"

"It's barely noon and you're already drinking? You should be ashamed of yourself!" Gloria squawked, as Randolph Morgan wheeled her into the room. "Oh my heavens, is that you as well, Mr. Nielsen? Drinking at this hour? Randolph, roll me closer. Dear Mr. Nielsen, you shouldn't let these rough men be a bad influence."

"No, ma'am, I shouldn't," A.C./Ray agreed, then burst into laughter. He'd called Gloria lots of names before, but a down-home respectful "ma'am" certainly had never been one of them. Mike and Franklin laughed, too. In their inebriated state, the sight of Gloria still totally clueless that her ex-husband was playing the part of her precious Mr. A.C. Nielsen was too much to handle.

"Randolph and I have been watching the local news. It's quite apparent that you three haven't been," Gloria said, imperiously.

"No, ma'am, I swore off TV weeks ago," A.C./Ray said, still with a case of the giggles. Gloria sent him a harsh, disapproving look.

"Mr. Burgess," Morgan said dryly, "you might want to turn the local news on. It will be of interest to you, I am sure."

"Okay, whatever," Mike said. What's this all about, he wondered. *Paparazzi shots of our con are already on the news? That's great. Hey, old lady, we can watch it together right now. I'll pour myself another drink to enjoy while we pull the wool over your eyes!*

"Come on over this way. There's a big flat-screen TV in the

cafeteria," Mike said as he stumbled out of the lab, the rest following. Ray made sure that Johnny Walker came with.

Franklin grabbed the remote and turned on the set, clicking to the channel 5 noon newscast: *"...officials have no idea how long these wildfires in Southern California will continue to ravage the—"*

Click to channel 7. *"...seek medical help if you experience an erection lasting longer than—"*

Click to channel 9. *"...thanks, Miriam, we'll be looking forward to the next segment of your fascinating series, 'Scabies and Rabies: Part Three of Exploring Diseases that Rhyme,' but now this just in—reports are coming in from O'Hare International Airport that reality TV megastar Dimi Konstantos was attacked this morning by a woman wielding a large caliber gun. Miss Konstantos, arriving from Los Angeles, was on her way here to appear on* The De'Vanna Show. *Eyewitnesses report that a bewildered-looking middle-aged woman with a drawn gun approached Miss Konstantos near the baggage claim area in Terminal One, but that Miss Konstantos was whisked away to safety by government agents, possibly Texas Rangers, as one of the agents was dressed in a cowboy hat. Miss Konstantos's current whereabouts is unknown. Meanwhile, the gunwoman was apprehended by Miss Konstantos's personal security detail. We'll have more on this breaking story, so please stay tuned. And next we turn to Micah Oliphant's 'Lunch-Counter Creations for Millennials.' This week's recipe is for a sous vide prepared coyote meat with quinoa and avocado pita sandwich you'll just howl for. Micah?"*

"Holy shit, why would Aria pull a gun on Dimi? Where the hell did she get a gun?" Mike wondered.

Suddenly they heard the main lab door bang open loudly and then the sound of shuffling footsteps. They all moved toward the doorway to see who was entering.

"Kate, you're back. What's going on? Oh my God, what's she doing here?" Mike yelled and pointed at Dimi, still unconscious and propped up by Patrick and Colm. "You weren't supposed to actually kidnap her. Damn! Wait, she's alive, isn't she?"

"What's going on?" Gloria said, fidgeting in her wheelchair. "Did they get her? Oh, I hope so. What's going on? I can't see."

"Yes, ma'am," Morgan said. "They've kidnapped Dimi Konstantos. It's the Arness boys, as some of you like to call them. She's either dead or she's passed out. They're holding her up right now."

"Oh, goody!" Gloria cackled, giddily clapping her hands together like a schoolgirl exacting revenge on a rival third-grader. "You did it,

THAWING A. C. NIELSEN

Jim! You really did it. I'm so proud of you, Jim. And you, too, Peter!"

"Shut up, Gloria," Mike barked. "Kate, why the hell did Aria have a gun? We heard it on the TV news. What was she thinking?"

"You tell him, Patrick. I'm too stressed." Kate sank into a chair, disgusted by the chain of events.

"Wait, first put Dimi down on the sofa. You don't need to keep holding her up like that," Ray suggested.

"Aria wasn't the one with a gun, Mr. Burgess," Patrick said. "Just as Franklin and Miles' plan was working, some crazy woman came out of nowhere with a giant handgun, yelling at Miss Konstantos and threatening to shoot her. Colm and I grabbed Dimi as fast as we could and got her out of there. Kate called Aria a little while ago. She and Lucas are safe and Miles and they'll be here any minute."

"You caught her, Jim!" Gloria screeched. "I knew you could do it, I knew you could. Now we can destroy her TV shows. What's next? How do we ransom her?"

"Someone get her to shut up before I lock her in the closet," Mike exclaimed.

"Miss Gloria, please calm down," Morgan said, annoyed at virtually everyone present. More footfalls echoed in the hallway. Everyone looked up to see Aria, Lucas, and Miles tumble breathlessly in.

"You guys okay?" Aria asked. "What's wrong with Dimi? And who the hell was that woman with the gun? Geez, that was fucking surreal."

"We don't know—some crazy woman. She never did fire a shot. Dimi froze so we just grabbed her and kept moving," Colm said.

"You saved her life. You guys are heroes," Franklin said. "But I gotta ask, what's with the cowboy clothes, Patrick? I mean—really!"

"Sorry, I shouldn't have, it seemed like I should really be Marshal Dillon for the gig, not just James Arness in a business suit."

"Who's Patrick?" Gloria asked. "That's Jim's voice. Mr. Morgan, why are they calling Jim 'Patrick'?"

"I'll explain later, miss," Morgan said, rolling his eyes.

"And what happened to Dimi's face?" Ray wondered.

"My bad," said Kate, raising her hand meekly. "I told Patrick to make her shut up. She wouldn't stop yelling and grabbing my hair while I was trying to drive. So he clocked her!"

"Nice!" Aria said. "She ain't so pretty right now, is she?!"

"Oh, look—she's coming to," Mike said. "Somebody get her an icepack and give her some space." Dimi looked terrible. She had a bright reddish-purple welt across her right cheekbone and temple. Her hair was a disaster from being tangled in the camera strap, and her dress was torn. Her makeup was a mess, too. Her eyes opened and she looked around, startled. Suddenly, her hand shot up and felt here and there around her face—the pain from the punch had just registered.

"Ow, ow, oh that hurts!" Dimi whimpered. She spotted Patrick and Colm. "I thought you were rescuing me? You—you punched me!" she said, pointing an accusing finger at Patrick. "What in the hell is going on?"

"Sorry, ma'am. Yes, I punched you," Patrick said. "You were in shock. You were pulling our friend's hair and making the car swerve dangerously." Lucas handed Dimi an icepack. She put it to her face, wincing.

"Ugh, you're all awful, whoever you are. Oh dammit, I think I'm gonna be sick." Dimi grabbed for her purse. At first it looked like she meant to use it as a barf-bag, but then she reached in and pulled out her antacid, opened it, and chugged down about a quarter of the bottle. "Damn, where's my phone? You stole my *phone?*" she yelled, glaring at Patrick.

"I don't have it."

"I thought you were FBI or undercover police. But you don't look like that now. You look like scum. Do you realize who you are messing with? I'm Demetria Konstantos. I'm the biggest celebrity in Hollywood. Where's my Khail and why are you holding me here?"

"Young lady," Gloria said, in the most commanding voice she could muster, "you are here because Mr. A.C. Nielsen and I can no longer tolerate the damage you are doing to the television industry and our great American values."

"Who the hell is the freaking old lady?" Dimi demanded, still wincing now and then, as she pressed the icepack to her raw face. "People, I said who the hell is the dried up old bitch?" Dimi grabbed her antacid and chugged away.

Suddenly Kate had a lightbulb moment. *There it was right in front of her. Why hadn't Miles or I figured it out,* she wondered. *Oh my God!* "Miles, look at her, look at her drinking that antacid. Do you see it?" Kate whispered.

"See what? Who cares, we have a crisis on our hands—hello?"

"Miles, I've solved it. I know the answer. Why A.C. is alive—I mean why Ray is alive. Dimi Dimwit solved it for me!" Kate said with a huge smile on her face.

"Shut up. It will have to wait," Miles said.

"I said I got it!"

"Shut up. Not now!"

After a few commercials the TV news anchor came back on-screen, with the graphic "Breaking News From O'Hare" perched in space above his left shoulder.

"Quiet, everyone. Look." Lucas pointed to the screen.

"And now we have a live report from O'Hare, where our correspondent Stacy David has further info about this morning's melee there. Stacy?"

"Thank you, Peter. In a bizarre bit of news here in the arrivals area of Terminal One, reality megastar Dimi Konstantos was the apparent target of a woman brandishing a large caliber handgun, screaming at an astonished Dimi, her husband Khail Santana, and her entourage. We have a few seconds of amateur cell phone video taken of two daring mystery men whisking Dimi away to safety. You can see the video right now on the screen, Peter, but the images are a bit shaky. As you see, the unknown man on Dimi's left is dressed in a black suit while the man on her right was dressed in some sort of cowboy attire. There was speculation that these men were FBI, US Marshals, or Rangers of some sort but now authorities state that these two men are not from any known law enforcement agency. Right after they stepped in the line of fire, blocking the assailant's view of Dimi and moving her out of danger, Konstantos's entourage was able to subdue the suspected assailant. We believe that no shots were fired. The suspect has been identified as Meryl Donahue, a recently divorced woman whose ex-husband had taken out an order of protection yesterday against her. We're currently trying to get a statement from Dimi Konstantos's spokesperson. The current whereabouts of Dimi Konstantos, Khail Santana, and the two mystery rescuers remain unknown. Peter, we'll have more on this story as it continues to unfold."

"Well, you got back on TV again, Jim and Peter," Mike said, trying to cover up for Franklin calling Patrick by his real name. "How's it feel?"

"Oh, it's great," Jim Arness/Patrick said. "Like the old days, rescuing womenfolk from bad guys—or bad women, I reckon."

"I reckon"? Oh that was good, Patrick. Keep up the cowboy talk, thought a suddenly amused Kate.

"You're all dead," Dimi hissed. "When Khail gets a hold of you, you're all dead meat." Again there were loud noises in the hallway. People yelling, was it the police? How was Mike going to explain any of this? This time, uninvited guests spilled into the lab—Khail,

Christopher Bronsteyn, and the three bodyguards, Antoine, J.T., and Theo.

"What's going on here?" Khail yelled. "Who the hell are you people? Get away from my Dimi. Are you okay, sweetheart?"

"Mr. Santana, we're from the US Marshal's office. Stand your men down and we'll settle this," Franklin bluffed, cool as the proverbial cucumber.

"Khail, I lost my cell phone. Did you find it?" Dimi asked.

"No, Dimi."

"How did you find me here? Did you follow these stupid-ass people here?"

"No, Miss Dimi," Antoine said.

"So if you didn't have my phone to track, how did you find me here, honey?"

"We just did," Khail ventured, looking apprehensively at Antoine.

"Go on," said Dimi.

"Well, we found you another way."

"What do you mean?" Dimi said, noticing the nervous look on Khail's face. All the ExitStrategy folks had been forgotten about for the moment. For some reason all Dimi wanted to know was how Khail had found her.

"Well, Miss Dimi," Antoine said hesitatingly, "you know your husband loves you very much. In fact, he loves you so much and worries about you and wants to keep you safe. Look at what happened today. That's what it is, miss."

"Yes, Antoine, I know Khail loves me. I also know he can be a total ass. I think you're hiding something. In fact, all that double-talk and the look on your face right now gives it away. I'm not as stupid as everyone thinks."

"Oh no, Miss Konstantos, you're not stupid. We don't think that."

"Quit stalling, Antoine, and tell me how you found me here."

Antoine exchanged glances with Khail, hesitated, and then explained. "Well, ahem, Khail loves you so much, um, like I said, that he had me put GPS microtags in your, um, your clothes. We tracked you from the GPS signal, um, you know... in your clothes."

"You did *what?*" Dimi screeched, then winced as the pain in her face greeted her again. "My clothes? What clothes? Which clothes, *Antoine?*"

"Well, miss, I'm sorry, but the GPS microtags were sewn into all of your bras, usually under the strap adjustment or near a snap. That's where we put 'em. We knew you'd wear a bra every day for support of your—you know, endowments. Khail said sometimes you don't wear panties. So that's why we did bras."

"We track you to keep you safe, honey," Khail pleaded. "Even the life insurance company liked the idea."

"What the hell?" Dimi howled. "Our insurance company knows you're tracking my titties and I don't? And now, Antoine, you've announced to the whole room here that I like to go commando? Goddamn you, Khail, goddamn you, Antoine, goddamn you all." Dimi stood up, fussed with her hands under her dress, unhooked her bra, yanked it out, looked it over in disgust, and threw it with all her might at Khail's head. "Here, *honey*, it's yours now. You can wear it and track your own stupid self. Wrap it around your limp dick and Antoine can track that little worm of yours."

Mike and Franklin exchanged grins. This was fucking great theater. "Too bad the reality show didn't have cameras rolling for this," Franklin whispered. "Jesus, Khail hasn't even ask what happened to Dimi's face. Weird!"

"Well, look at the poor reality star. Strange men are playing in her undies drawer. Why am I not surprised?" Gloria cackled.

"Okay, goddamn it, what *really* is going on here?" Khail yelled. "Who the hell are all y'all?"

"Khail, calm down," Chris said. "You're forgetting that these people saved Dimi's life. I don't know what they're up to either, but we should listen to them and find out what's going on."

"Mr. Santana, Miss Konstantos, please bear with me," Mike said. "I would really like you to hear what the most senior person in the room has to say to you. Let's slow it down and let her tell you why, somewhat surprisingly, you're here today. Gloria, go ahead. I told you to shut up before, but now it's only fair for you to get to speak." Mike knelt down next to Gloria and whispered, "Whatever you do, speak your mind without going on some kind of ridiculous tirade."

Gloria nodded. She smiled at Mike, then sat taller in her wheelchair, closed her eyes and took a deep breath. When she exhaled and opened her eyes it was obvious that a transformation had taken place. She had become the Gloria Dunham of yesteryear—the Hollywood actress, not just a strange, decrepit old lady.

"Miss Konstantos, my name is Gloria Dunham. I was once a very famous actress. You probably don't know who I am at all. I understand that times change and I accept that. Those golden days of entertainment are gone—the world keeps spinning. In addition to myself, there is another famous person here. That man is someone I have admired and respected for decades—Mr. A.C. Nielsen of the A.C. Nielsen Company. Mr. Nielsen, can you nod to them, please?" A.C./Ray nodded to the group and smiled. "As you all can see," Gloria continued, "I am well into my latter years. I have recently been confined to this wheelchair and my eyesight is very poor. I can hardly make any of you out, but I can recognize voices with the best of them, and as a trained actress I can hear your words and understand the emotions embedded within them."

The room grew ever more still as Gloria commanded everyone's attention. Dimi was the only one not listening intently. She played with her icepack and kept chugging her antacid like she were draining a forty-four-ounce Coke at the movie theater. Kate again eyed her closely. *Yep, there's my answer*, she thought.

"Miss Konstantos," Gloria continued, "the two men who saved you, or perhaps we should be honest and say that they captured you, are not from the US Marshal's office or the FBI, or any such thing. Franklin, why ever did you say such a thing?" Franklin gave a sheepish shrug. "The two tall, handsome men are Peter Arness, generally known as Peter Graves, and the great star of *Gunsmoke*, James Arness. They are brothers and they are very good friends of mine. All of us—Mr. Nielsen, myself, and the Arness brothers—are proud Scandinavians from Minnesota. And as ethically responsible Minnesotans and Americans, we shall not abide the destruction you and people like you have caused to the world of television and the havoc you wreak on traditional American values. That's why I asked the Arness brothers to help us. We wanted to kidnap you and hold you for ransom. The ransom would be the solemn promise that you would stop making all your terrible shows."

"I was right. They kidnapped me, then they slugged me. See, Khail, they're all criminals!"

"Shush, Dimi, let her talk," Chris said. "Khail, you want to just get Dimi and leave, or call the police, or stay and listen? It's your call."

"Let's listen. Somethin's going on here."

"I think I can help explain," A.C./Ray said. "In the old days, back in radio and TV, we had writers—great writers with high aspirations.

Some of them had written great short stories, even great novels. Some of them were already famous for that and yet somehow we convinced many of them to come and write for radio, but especially for the new medium, television. They wrote scripts about the human condition: love, hate, fear, loss, joy, all the many emotions that define us. There were also great comedy shows that helped people relax and forget their cares. But these comedies weren't simpleminded shows poking fun at little people, or 600-pound folks or anyone else that might have appeared in circus sideshows decades ago. And there weren't any TV shows about boobs or buttholes, or snake-handling preachers or toddler beauty pageants."

"Oh, go to hell! You're criticizing me, right? People like our shows, so you can go to hell!" Dimi said.

"Excuse me, I still have the floor, Miss Konstantos. In my time, when I ran the A.C. Nielsen Company, a famous marketing adviser to large advertisers, gods strode across the American stage and screen reciting the words of those great writers. Great actors like Henry Fonda, Jimmy Stewart, Cagney, Hepburn, Olivia deHavilland, Bette Davis, Cary Grant, Peter O'Toole, the list goes on and on. In television as well, there were great actors whom the American public loved and admired."

"What you people have created is a travesty, an embarrassment," Gloria continued. "Taking real people and putting a camera on them and encouraging them to make fools of themselves. Paying them, I understand, but then throwing them away when their frailties finally bore you and your fickle audiences. Miss Konstantos, I wouldn't have even known of your so-called reality TV productions if my young great-grandnieces hadn't made me aware of your shenanigans—the show where you try to cram your enormous breasts into bras five sizes too small, where you go out in public and demean any store clerk or valet who doesn't bend down and kiss your feet. Do you think I want these young girls to believe that your behavior on that show should be emulated? And then I asked them more about this reality TV. So they showed me other programs you people produce—some ridiculous show about swamp people that believe there are aliens trying to mate with their daughters, another show where deaf mute people worship monkeys and cicadas as gods. I couldn't believe my eyes and ears when I saw all this." Chris shot an "I told you so" look at Khail. The two shows Gloria happened to mention were the horrifically tasteless co-winners of the reality show contest Dima and Khail had run months earlier. Chris had tried, without success, to convince Khail and Jak Hammer to keep them out of production.

"Yeah, it's a lot of crap. How you get away with it I can never figure out," Miles said.

"We know it's crap, I guess," Khail said, "but people watch it. Listen, I got to tell you all, Chris and me, we been thinkin' up new shows. Good shows to balance things out. It's true, tell 'em, Chris."

"It is actually true. I've been working on Khail lately to get him to see some of what you're saying here."

"And nobody tells me?" Dimi said. "You don't tell me what's up with the new shows, you have your boys in my bras, insurance companies know my personal business. You're a sick man, Khail Santana."

"Give it a rest, Dimi. You got some things to learn," shot Khail. "So wait—you're not FBI or US Marshals—you're TV actors? Washed-up old actors? James Arness, the *Gunsmoke* guy? C'mon, man, I think you're probably dead, right? And you're the *Mission: Impossible* guy? I think I saw your obit a while back. I do read *Variety*, ya know."

"Khail," Chris leaned over and whispered, "knock it off. I think the old lady believes these guys are the real deal. It's obvious they're made up to look like those actors. Get it?"

"Oh, yeah, so anyway—you boys saved Dim's life," Khail said. "I got to give you props for how you got her away from that crazy woman. But I don't think you get to hold on to her. That old lady talking ransom shit? That's just crazy. But like Chris said, we're starting to devise some better shows. Maybe real actors with a script and no more monkeys and cicadas. You should see the animal wrangler bills for that show—way too much money goin' down the drain there, right Chris X-X? Course we won't drop the shows that are running and makin' us real cash. Too much money there, baby." Khail walked over and knelt by Dimi, taking her hand. "Dimi, look me in the eyes. Those people there, those two tall guys, they saved your life today. That woman had a big gun. That was the gun Clint Eastwood had in *Dirty Harry*. Big-ass gun and it was loaded. You're still alive 'cause they grabbed you and ran you outta there."

"They also punched me, Khail," Dimi tacked on with a pout. Yet her anger seemed to melt away—a little bit.

"Maybe they had reason to punch you, sweetie. Sometimes other people might want to punch you, too, when you get crazy. Dim, listen close—you owe those two men a sincere thank-you."

Dimi turned slowly toward Patrick and Colm. "Thank you," she said softly. She rested her head on Khail's shoulder and sobbed. Everyone waited until she had calmed down.

"So I'm still curious—why would we stop making all our shows?" said Khail. "This whole ransom thing makes no sense. We could make any old promise but once we had Dimi back we'd just make them anyway. Plus I got bodyguards happy to beat all y'all senseless. I thought you people were smart, but all that's just stupid."

"Yes, it was. But all of it was a show we were putting on for Gloria—Miss Dunham," said Kate. "We had to convince her that we cared about it as much as she did. We had our reasons, but things got out of control. We weren't planning on really kidnapping Dimi at all, just cause a scene in the airport as if we were doing it. Of course we weren't planning on some crazy person pulling out a gun. I guess we learned a little about reality today—all of us. Sorry, Gloria. I have to tell the truth."

Gloria stared intently at Kate, trying to fathom what she had just said.

"Is this true, Randolph?" Gloria asked, cocking her head.

"Yes, I'm afraid it is. I encouraged Mike to be creative—make up a show for you. Gloria, you have to admit you've been out of control lately. In a sense, you were actually holding the lab hostage to get your way. You weren't being fair to anyone here. Mike and Franklin did the best they could to keep the lab going, ramp up all the expensive research that Miss Pearson needs done, and still try to make you feel like they supported your feelings about the reality TV world. I think everyone here is sorry how this all turned out." Just then two new people wandered quietly into the room.

"Who are those guys?" Antoine asked.

"Oh, they're the cameramen I hired for this morning," said Miles. "We wanted to be able to show Gloria that we were trying to kidnap Dimi even if she does have to sit with her eyes six inches from the screen."

"What the fuck?" yelled Khail, jumping to his feet. "You shot footage of this morning? Seriously?"

"Oh, we can destroy it, Mr. Santana," said Mike, pleading. "Please don't call the police. Things just got out of control, right? Miles, have your guys destroy the footage."

"Destroy it?" said Khail. "Hell no, you crazy? Damn, white people be so stupid, huh, Antoine?" Antoine, J.T., and Theo grinned back at Khail. "You got live footage? Is that an effing Steadicam?"

"Well no, it's two effing Steadicams, see?" Miles said, pointing to the second camera set down a few feet farther away.

"*Damn*," said Khail, shaking his head at the bodyguards. "You guys staring at Dimi's and Konstantina's asses so much back there you don't even see hotshot professionals with Steadicams?"

"Sorry, boss," said Antoine.

"Never mind." Khail shrugged. "Okay, hurry up, hook it up to the TV. Come on, I wanna see this."

The two cameramen futzed around in their equipment bag, looking for the right cables to hook up to the television monitor. In a minute or two they had it ready to go. Everyone's attention focused on the screen. Dimi chugged the last of her liquid antacid. She'd downed an entire large bottle in the space of a couple hours.

"Look, there we are walking through," said Khail. The paparazzo fellow stumbles and then Aria and Lucas are on-screen. "That's you two," he shouted, pointing at Aria and Lucas. Apparently he had decided to do play-by-play for everyone.

"Guilty as charged," said Aria, sheepishly raising her hand halfway. Then from the left of the screen, the gunwoman enters, weapon drawn, and begins shouting. The lunchroom is filled with gasps.

"Damn, that gun's huge," said Khail. They watched as the Arse/Arness Bros boldly enter, swarm over Dimi, and just keep on trucking. "*Damn smooth*—yeah, oh yeah!" Khail exclaimed, pumping his arm and letting out a whistle.

"We just did what we had to do," Colm said.

The camera then zooms in to catch Konstantina and Antoine taking down the woman with the gun. Everyone grimaced when Antoine's pile driver sends the women's skull straight into the floor. Then the footage goes crooked and haywire, then black.

"That's where you knocked into my equipment, Mr. Santana," said Jake, one of the cameramen.

"Oh yeah, I remember you now. I tried to leap over you, I didn't see you had that camera. I was trying to grab the gun off the floor before it spun away into the crowd," said Khail. "Damn, that is some crazy fucking great stuff. The other video?"

"Same thing from the other side. Wanna see it?" said Jesus, the other camera operator.

"Nah," said Khail. "Dimi, so now you seen it all. They really did save your life. So, fellas, if you're not Marshal Dillon or the *Mission: Impossible* guy, and you're not law enforcement dudes, what the hell are you guys, really?"

"We're musicians, Mr. Santana. We're Irish folk musicians!" Patrick said proudly.

"Damn if that don't beat all!" Khail laughed. "Folk musicians—now I heard everything! Irish guys—you try your best to kick those English butts in soccer, right?"

"Aye, sir, that we do! We're always strivin' ta beat the English, arse an' bullocks bot'," said Patrick in his thickest brogue, causing the whole room to erupt in laughter.

"Listen, folks," Khail said, suddenly turning more serious, "we got ourselves a situation. This many people in a room with issues goin' on, gotta make a compromise. My momma taught me that. Wise woman, but I don't call it a compromise, I call it a business deal. Miss Gloria, I'm truly sorry we hurt your feelings. I want to make that up to you. Mr. Nielsen—yeah I know who you are. Like I said, I read books and magazines. I study history. I know that Nielsen Family box on the TV, the ratings—it's cool. I heard those names—Jimmy Stewart, Cagney and Lacey, Bette Davis. So let's see if we can make a deal here, people. First, who owns these videos?" Mike raised his hand. "Sir, I'll pay you a hundred grand for them, right now. This is hot, I want to be able to sell stills of it now for cash to the entertainment outlets, and I wanna run the whole thing on our show in two weeks. We'll build the whole episode around what happened in the airport. We'll shelve the thing we already got for that week. It's pretty lame anyway. Dimi and her friends shopping for more leopard print thongs or somethin'. We won't ID anyone here—it will all still be a mystery. It'll drive people crazy trying to figure out who those two hero boys are. Ratings will be through the roof. Chris can authorize a check right now on the spot."

"The footage isn't for sale," Mike said. All the ExitStrategy staff stared at him like he was crazy.

"Come on, man," Theo said. "TNZ would only give you fifty grand for that, I bet. Khail's making you a good offer."

"All right, two hundred fifty grand *and* you're not filing charges against anyone here, and my company name is never mentioned. I mean never," Mike said firmly.

"File charges?" Khail said quizzically. "Hell no, I hate cops. We're making a business deal here, man. Maybe two or three of 'em. Okay, I'll give you two hunnert for the footage."

"All right, done!" Mike reached out to shake Khail's hand.

"What's your name, man?" Khail said.

"Cold Smokey Burgess!"

"Damn great name. You sure cold, making a deal like that. Chris, get to work on that check. Listen, Cold Smokey, I give you two hunnert large you better make sure you tip your cameramen. Pay the help well like my man Chris does."

"I always do, Mr. Santana." Mike nodded a thank-you to Jake and Jesus.

"Now, Miss Gloria," Khail said, kneeling down in front of Gloria and reaching out to hold her hands in his, "I want to bring you on to help teach Dimi some charm and some real acting skills. You know, bring some legitimate old-school class to the show. You'll be on-screen plenty. We'll do like a montage of your career. Make sure ole Marshal Dillon is in there, too. Like clips of the real Marshal Dillon, I mean, not these Irish dudes. We'll get a few senior citizen issues going, too, but they can't be lame. Still gotta get people tuning in. You can sort of be like a wise Gram-Mamma to J.T. and Theo. We'll script it to be warm and fuzzy. So, maybe six episodes with options? What do you think?"

"But I still don't like what you are doing, young man. It's all in such bad taste. Isn't that right, Mr. Nielsen?"

"Gloria dear, remember that old saying 'Every journey begins with the first step'?" Ray said in his kindly, wise A.C. persona. "Khail and Christopher have expressed an interest in exploring a new path. If you won't take a few steps with them to get them started, how can you stand back and continue to judge them? What gives you the right to criticize if you won't be there to help? This is your chance to lead the way. See, Gloria? Show them what things were like back in the glory days. You can do it if you try."

Gloria sat deep in thought for a moment, then said, "Mr. Nielsen, you're right as always. God bless you, sir! Mr. Santana, I'll do it. But we have to keep it clean, understand? Make it something my great-grandnieces can watch."

"We'll try, Miss Gloria. We'll really try." Khail smiled at Chris and

Dimi. Always the handsome charmer, he gallantly kissed Gloria on the cheek.

Kate smiled as well, happy that things were turning out fine. She was amazed that Ray, so far, had kept his A.C. persona intact. He had been kind to Gloria when he could have revealed his identity at any time and rubbed her face in it. Mr. Ray Machado was truly just as classy as her supposed hero A.C. Nielsen had ever been. Kate leaned over toward Miles. "Psst, get me all those old drugstore receipts Enzo Saltieri kept and all our patient bloodwork files, especially Ray's. And grab John Cougar's file."

"The cat?" Miles asked incredulously.

"Yes, dammit, the cat. And don't ever, ever, ever tell me to shut up again!"

PAUL CAREY

CHAPTER FIFTY-ONE

Miles stood up and walked toward Enzo Saltieri's old office, then halted suddenly when he heard a shrill voice ring out, "Just where do you think you're going, Mr. Coleman?"

"We're done here, right? Kate wants me to get some files to look at."

"I'll let you know when to go do something, as well as if you will be fortunate to even have continued employment here, and that applies as well to the rest of you." Devil Gloria had made her stage entrance with a vengeance.

"What in the hell has gotten over you, Gloria? I thought everybody was finally happy here," Mike said. "And you're not running this company, I am."

"Really, Mike?" Gloria's voice quivered with excitement. "Don't you recall you sold me another ten percent stake in ExitStrategy? I told you I'd be happy to keep reeling in more shares from you while you diddle away your money. Randolph, didn't I say that?"

"Yes, ma'am," Randolph answered.

"You see, Mike?" Gloria said with a sneer.

"So what? Right now Franklin and I each control fifteen percent, plus I inherited Enzo's shares. That's another fifteen. That makes forty-five. All you've been able to do over the years is grab forty-four, Gloria. Why do you think we made sure it was only forty-four? We're not stupid. And the other eleven percent are spread out between various friends and family of mine."

"Oh, they are?" Gloria challenged, smiling wickedly. "Friends, you say? Family? And you say you're not stupid, dear Mike? Do you still have that drug problem? Is that where all the money goes? Does cocaine cost millions now?"

"Damn, this beeyotch is cold," Khail muttered, shaking his head.

"Randolph," Gloria said, "what did I say to you at the end of that last meeting? You know, while I was signing the papers and handing Mike millions of dollars."

"I can tell you exactly what you said," Randolph answered, standing up to address the room. "You whispered 'You know what to do now,' and then I said, 'Yes, ma'am, I'll take care of everything.'"

"You see, Mike? You see, Franklin? Mr. Morgan has taken care of everything. While you weren't looking he's snapped up all the shares your so-called friends and relatives were holding. Entertain us with how you did it, Randolph."

Randolph Morgan cleared his throat, peered around the room, then began his narrative. His calm, courtroom-trained delivery commanded everyone's attention. "Well, first was Mr. Breedlove, the famous romance author. He didn't want to sell his two percent stake until I told him that there was a young woman running the lab now. He's been divorced now six times—finally sworn off women, he told me. In fact, he's stopped writing romances, too, says he's going to take up men, or stamp collecting, or something. He figures this woman, Kate Pearson here, won't know what she's doing, so he sold out. One shareholder down, four to go."

"Very good, Randolph. Continue," Gloria commanded. The wicked smile remained plastered across her face for all to see.

"Then there was flaky Mr. Friedman, the condom company heir. I told him that the new lab research showed that men revived out of cryo wouldn't be able to get it up, as they say, even with Viagra. Even though this so-called information would really make zero impact on his company's bottom line, he nonetheless panicked and sold his two percent worth of shares there on the spot. I think I was at his estate for all of ten minutes. A very strange man. Two down, two to go."

"This is outrageous, Mike. He's lying!" Chrissy insisted, pounding on the table. "They can't do this to you."

"It's okay. Stay calm. We'll check this out," Mike said, patting Chrissy's shoulder.

"Shall I continue, Mr. Burgess?" Randolph asked condescendingly, completely ignoring Chrissy. "Next on my list was Miss Tatum, the famous retired Olympic athlete. She has many investments, including a thirty percent stake in the country's largest balloon manufacturer. I told her that the world was running out of helium, which is true by the way, and that Mike and the medical team wouldn't be able to do the helium perfusion on patients anymore. Oh yes, she also became aghast about how this helium shortage would affect her balloon company and all the darling little children and their precious little birthday parties. She endured a severe panic attack in my presence, recovered after a bit, and then fired her investment broker via text message while I sat there and wrapped up her one percent share, lazily sipping iced tea by her pool the whole while."

"Mike, Franklin, none of these people called you guys to check on the accuracy of this damn crapola Morgan was telling them?" Miles asked. "None of them?"

"No dammit, they're all elderly or a little *woo-woo*, or both. I guess we should have been more aware of those loose shares," Franklin said dejectedly.

"May I remind you that not everyone involved is old, Franklin," Mike said, letting out a chuckle. "Max, my godchild, is the one he hasn't mentioned yet. He's got the deciding shares. Without Max you've got nothing, Randolph, you fool. Sorry, Gloria, your henchman came up short!"

"Oh yes, dear goth-child Max," Morgan said, shaking his head for dramatic effect. "Community college dropout Max and his delicious six percent stake in the company. This took some expert sleuthing. Mike, you made a big show of giving him stock certificates as a reward for him getting his act together and graduating high school a while ago, correct?"

"Yes, I was trying to get him on track, influence him to make something out of himself. And leave his appearance out of this, he's just a kid, you bastard." Mike glared at Morgan.

"Your darling little tyke didn't realize or perhaps didn't really care what those private stock certificates were really worth," Morgan said. "A few months ago he took those fancy pieces of paper of yours and bartered with the concert management of the rap artist—I use the term artist loosely, let it be known—Master DJ BigBaby, to secure free BigBaby concert tickets and backstage passes for fifty-seven of her besties, as they say. I am sure this horde of slacker friends were most impressed by Max's generosity. *Or not.* Discovering all of this, I donned my gold chains and flat-bill Oakland Raiders cap and paid a visit to Master BigBaby's crib. After a few niceties we got down to business. I told him that Kanye West says George W. Bush hates black people and so does Mike Burgess and I urged him to divest himself from this racist's company. Despite this information, he refused to sell. Having progressed this far in my quest I decided I must succeed. I refused to let this renegade evade me. I visited Master BigBaby again and complimented him on his investing acumen, for while this gentleman and members of his posse never graduated high school, they, unlike the others, had the intelligence to follow due diligence on all that I had said. They unflinchingly stood faithful to their original position since they had decided emphatically that George W. Bush was no longer the enemy, that Kanye was a *boogee mofo cocksucker Kardashian butt-licker*, in their words, that they had no ill will toward either Mr. Burgess and therefore still refused to sell, even when I doubled my offer. I then pulled out all the stops, as they say. I quadrupled my original offering price and finally walked out the door five minutes later with the deal done."

Mike stared at the floor, speechless. Devastated.

"Thank you, Randolph," Gloria chirped. "That was quite an adventure in language there at the end, wasn't it?"

"Damn you, Gloria. What is wrong with you? How could you do this to us?" Kate protested.

"Oh, don't be such a baby, Miss Pearson. I know your kind. You've been far too sheltered in your pretty little upscale suburban world. You like rules far too much. You need to get knocked down a few times, then get back up and show some fight if you want anyone to respect you in the real world."

"You can go to hell, Gloria, that's all I have to say. Just go fucking rot in hell," Miles yelled. Franklin gave him a supportive, yet pained smile.

Kate looked over at Ray. *Why won't he do something, goddamn it? He's just sitting there expressionless. Tell her who you are, mess with her mind, Ray— come on, come on, come on!*

"So, here's the math," Gloria continued. "I had forty-four percent of the shares, add these eleven percent of purchases in and the figure stands at fifty-five. I am easily now the majority shareholder of ExitStrategy. From now on, whatever I say, goes. First order of business—Miss Pearson, you're fired."

"I'm sorry, Gloria, your computation is inaccurate," Randolph interrupted, calmly raising an index finger in the air.

"What do you mean? Forty-four plus eleven is fifty-five, is it not?"

"Yes, but you are forgetting one thing, dear Miss Dunham," Randolph said coolly.

"And what is that?" said Gloria, looking confused.

"When you received the shares recently from Mike and Franklin, thus diluting their ownership, you whispered to me as you signed the papers 'you know what to do,' and I responded 'I'll take care of everything.' Correct?"

"Yes, of course, we already told the people here about that," Gloria said. "So?"

"I took your words literally, ma'am. *I knew what to do and I took care of everything.* I, Randolph Morgan, Esquire, took care of everything. I bought out those shares with my own money, Gloria. I now own eleven percent of ExitStrategy. You are still stuck at forty-four percent. You don't control the corporation, Miss Dunham, and *you never will.*" Morgan grinned ever so slightly at Mike.

"Boo-yah!" Khail yelled, reaching out to Miles for an epic knuckle bump.

Kate let out a whoop while Chris Bronsteyn sat shaking his head in amazement.

"Mr. Burgess *and* Mr. Burgess," Randolph said, turning to Mike and Franklin, "I believe in what you are doing here. My holdings will support you in any way needed. I would also like to offer my services as an attorney should you be in need of counsel now or in the future."

"How could you do this to me, Randolph?" Gloria sputtered. "I'll sue you. I'll destroy you. You're my attorney, my financial representative. This is a conflict of interest. You'll be disbarred!"

"Oh, I don't think so, Miss Dunham. And there's another issue or two. You knowingly haven't paid my retainer fee for the last nine months. When I asked your accountant, James Fahey, about this issue he said you told him to stop paying what you called 'frivolous expenses.' He said that my name was scribbled on a piece of paper, which listed the areas in which you decided to cut corners. My representation for you for the last nine months has been solely at my discretion, as an unpaid free agent, I suppose you could say. I spoke to Mr. Fahey two days ago—oh, did you know we golf together quite often? Anyway, he is ready to vouch for the fact that you have chosen to avail yourself of my expertise for nothing, which could be considered theft of services. Also, Jim and I have also discussed what to do about some creative bookkeeping you devised against our professional advice. Do you recall your generous gift to the Children's Hospital in Temecula? A large, heartfelt donation, no doubt, but a problem for us when you ridiculously insisted on tacking on an extra zero to the sum on your tax return. You may recall that Jim refused to sign that return. Yours is the only signature."

"This is preposterous. Mike put you up to this, I'm sure. Randolph, take me back to the hotel and we'll sort this all out. I'm sure we can get to the bottom of these misunderstandings," Gloria said, trying to save face in front of the grinning audience.

"Gloria, when we left Los Angeles your ticket was round-trip, of course, but mine was one-way," Randolph said. "I've finally tired of you and California as well, frankly. I'm thinking of trying out Chicago for a while—see if I like it here. I'm sure that Miss Konstantos and Mr. Santana will be happy to drive you back to the hotel and will also be fine company when you get back to La-La Land. Best wishes to you on your new career in reality television."

CHAPTER FIFTY-TWO

"Okay, ExitStrategy people, come with me. My office, hurry!" Kate yelled. The whole crew trotted off, leaving Khail and company to sort out what to do with pathetic old Gloria.

"Mind if I come with you?" Randolph asked.

"No problem. Man, you saved our asses. And you really had us going for a while there. Wow!" Miles exclaimed.

"Listen, everybody," Kate said, almost breathless with excitement. "I think Dimi solved the prion issue for me. Now I know why Ray is alive and John Cougar, too. Did you all notice Dimi chugging on that bottle of antacid?"

"Yeah, I guess. So what?" Edouard said.

"Remember the old drug store receipts Enzo stashed?" Kate said. "Vitamins plus also tons of Maalox? Ray, was Enzo giving you all that?"

"Yes, he was. But he didn't really say why."

"Okay," Kate said, digging quickly through files on her desk. "Here—I've got it! This is a thing I printed out from the Internet right after I started. Cryo procedure FAQs for the general public from back in the early 1990s from another cryo firm. Listen to this. 'In the last few days or hours of life, the cryonics team must combat a number of issues which can be problematic. One of these is the acidity of the stomach. Accidental release of these acids into other parts of the body could cause extensive cellular damage. The simple solution to this problem is to place the patient nearing death on a regimen of antacid products, plus induce antacid products into the stomach just before lowering body temperature in the cryonics procedure.' I guess maybe Enzo was doing this, too. Once he started trying the vitamin therapy he was doing the antacid thing as well. So, there you have it."

"Have what, Kate?" Mike said with a look of frustration. "Ray, you were taking a lot of vitamins and antacids right before you went into cryo?"

"Yes, Mike. Enzo would literally force all that down my throat. I just figured he knew best. At least it wasn't castor oil like my parents made me take when I was a kid! And for whatever reason, he never told anyone else, not even Chrissy, his main RN. He constantly changed up his procedures—he told me that himself. He said nobody could possibly keep up with his tweaks, so what was the point of telling them his plans?"

"I'm sorry about all that. But that's how Enzo operated," Chrissy admitted, a somewhat ashamed look on her face. "The rest of us didn't even really know what he was up to in your old office, Kate, once a patient was in there for their preparation for exit. Only when it was time for the actual exit procedure in the operating room would he let us back in the loop."

"Wow, interesting. I guess it makes sense in a way, considering his personality," Kate said. "Say, Miles, on that desk over there. Grab that report from the institute in Iceland. Go to page five, I think."

"Okay, I see. Hmm, it's a list of elements, chemicals, and so on, right? Ones that accelerate prion production and others that inhibit it? Is this what you wanted?"

"Yes. Hand it here. Listen to all the bad boys on the acceleration list. Lead, bismuth, manganese, mercury—basically all the scary metals."

"You just disproved you case. Manganese is in antacids, Kate!" Edouard argued.

"No, you're wrong—it's *magnesium that's in antacids, not manganese.* They're not the same. You need to brush up on your periodic table, Edouard. And look, magnesium is on the good list. It was the magnesium hydroxide in the antacids that Enzo was giving the patients that just happened to thwart prion development. But I doubt Enzo was going to bother spiking the guinea pigs' water bottles with Maalox. So that's why they got prion disease."

"But what about the cat?" Mike asked. "Enzo didn't really like animals that I noticed. I doubt he would have treated the cat with as much care as the people."

"Right, Mike," Edouard, the devil's advocate, said. "So, then, Kate, how do you explain John Cougar not having prion disease? I think you've painted yourself into a corner."

"Somebody please go get Keith—it's his cat," Mike said.

"And right here are the vet's files on the cat. Let's look again," Miles said as he began leafing through the old paperwork. "I only see meds for the leukemia. Nothing else in here. But hey, I also see there's no notation of death."

"Of course not, that's the other piece of the puzzle," Kate said. "We all know that post–Andrea Carlsen people, including Ray, were cryoing themselves straight on in, not waiting for their disease to destroy them day by day and Death himself deciding when to come knocking on the door. Thank you very much for not telling us newbies that little tidbit, Mike. And thank you for telling Norm, Chrissy, and a few others to keep me in the dark about that, damn it. Sorry—had to throw that dig in there. I can't forgive you and Franklin for that."

Mike looked mutely down at the floor, he hadn't figured out a way yet to tell Kate how sorry he was.

"Anyway," Kate continued, "John Cougar was also post-Andrea. I'm guessing Enzo stopped John Cougar's heart and put him straight into cryo. There were two things necessary for us to have success reviving patients: magnesium to fight the prions, no matter when they happened to show up in the process, plus a quick entry into cryo—not waiting for extensive destruction by disease and clinical death."

"So we may know fairly clearly now who here in the building has a chance to be brought back, right?" Chrissy asked excitedly.

"Yes," Kate said. "Sorry to say, but probably no one before the middle of B wing will make it. They had no accidental magnesium therapy and will most likely have prion damage. Anyone starting from the Carlsens on has an even better chance because they went into cryo well before their disease could cause extensive destruction. Plus the transition from normal metabolism to cryonic stasis was very quick and thoroughly controlled."

"You still haven't addressed my question, Kate. You haven't proven the cat had the magnesium advantage," Edouard insisted. "Have you forgotten that?"

Just then Keith entered the room with Norm. "What's up, Miss Pearson? Norm says you had a question for me about John Cougar."

"Yes, Keith. Do you know what meds your vet had John Cougar on?"

"Some drugs for the leukemia. I don't know what they were, except they were very expensive."

"Wait, Keith, I just remembered, didn't John Cougar have hairball problems?" Chrissy asked. "You told me that, I think."

"Oh yes, he did. He'd choke so bad on them. He was getting miserable. I asked the vet what we could do about it."

"And?" Mike asked.

"He told me there were veterinary drugs he could give him, but it would be just as good and way less expensive for me to give him something over the counter to settle his stomach, so it wasn't churning so much. It really seemed to help and it was pretty cheap."

"And what was that over-the-counter drug?" Kate asked, zeroing in for the checkmate.

"He told me to hide about a tablespoon of liquid antacid in John Cougar's food once a day. As long as I mixed it into a plate of tuna, I had him fooled."

"Bingo!" Miles yelled with glee. "Kate, you nailed it! Bravo!"

"Excuse me, who's in charge here?" boomed a loud voice at the door.

Everyone turned to look. There were two police officers in the doorway and someone else peeking in from behind them—Gloria. Kate sighed. *Wasn't Khail supposed to have taken her off our hands?*

"I'm in charge here, officer," Mike said wearily. "What can I do for you?"

"Well, the lady here called 9-1-1 and says there are some criminals here on your premises. She wants me to arrest two fellows named Burgess for grave-robbing. That's right isn't it, ma'am?" The officer looked over his shoulder at Gloria.

"That's right. That's them, right there," she screeched, pointing her gnarly forefinger at Mike and Franklin Burgess. "They stole a body out of a funeral home. You can put them in jail now, I'll testify against them."

"All right, ma'am, let us sift this out, please. So you're Mr. Mike Burgess, then, sir?"

Mike nodded. "Officer, I think you might want to just take the lady back to her hotel downtown. She gets confused about reality quite a bit at her age."

"I most certainly do not!" Gloria insisted.

"All right, ma'am, so where is this body you're talking about?" the officer asked. "Let's see if we can find it. What address might it be at? Or is it here, ma'am?"

"I don't know where it is, but they stole it. They had a cohort."

"And who is that, ma'am?"

"Well, he passed away a while back, officer."

"Wait, you're saying the cohort died already? When are you saying this alleged body-snatching occurred, ma'am?"

"Well, twenty-some years ago, I would venture. But you can still arrest them. They switched bodies and then the one was alive again. He's right here somewhere. A.C., where are you?"

Ray Machado didn't say a word—instead he just stood up from his chair and slowly walked out of the room, shaking his head in disgust as he sauntered off. Kate wondered why he was leaving. Was he finally so fed up with Gloria that he had to get away? The two officers stepped aside for a short conference, occasionally peering over at Mike, Franklin, and Gloria. One of the officers went out in the hall and could be heard talking to his station sergeant. After a few minutes he reappeared, rubbing his chin. "Ma'am. We've checked this out. First of all, we aren't arresting anyone here today. We'll take info down and check it out, but here's the thing—the statute of limitations for an alleged crime of this sort is ten years. My sergeant made a quick call to the assistant DA to ask that question. I'm sorry, ma'am, we can't help you right now. And what was that about one of the bodies being alive again? Are you sure you've been taking all of your medications, ma'am?"

"Goddammit all," Gloria shrieked once the two police officers exited. "When will justice be served?"

"*Callate, puta, callate*," Ray whispered ferociously, reappearing with a framed photo in one hand and his shiny new flugelhorn in the other.

"What? Who said that?"

"Me, myself, and I!"

"Who is that? Is that you, Mr. Nielsen? Your voice sounds a bit different all of a sudden. Do you speak Spanish now?" Gloria squinted in the direction of Ray's voice.

Kate was thrilled, Ray was finally going to let her have it. *Oh man, this is going to be good,* she thought.

"Mr. Nielsen doesn't speak Spanish or English, Gloria. It's hard to speak at all when you are dead and lying peacefully in your grave. But I speak both languages," Ray said, letting loose the rich, full Spanish accent of his youth, before living in LA and Iowa had flattened it out. "My name is Gaetano Raimondo Machado. Remember me?"

"What is going on here? I don't understand. Ray died years ago!" Gloria snarled.

"Understand this, *diabla*," Ray continued as he fingered the valves of the flugelhorn a bit, then put his lips to the horn. He slowly played sweet little phrases of the tune "What a Wonderful World." All the

ExitStrategy team smiled and nodded to each other. It was Ray, the real Ray, the famous musician. Gloria sat speechless, she absolutely could not comprehend what was going on. When he was done playing, Ray walked over to Gloria. "It is me—Ray. Do you understand now? And did you ever hear that tune before? And do you recognize this photograph here in my hand?"

Gloria squinted at the photo. "Of course. It's me, A.C. Nielsen, and the president in front of the Winston House Hotel. I put it into A.C.'s apartment here. So what?"

"That was taken in 1961, the night I found out, quite by accident, that you were cheating on me. You weren't in LA, and I didn't have a gig right then, so I flew in to Chicago to see Louie Armstrong at The Plugged Nickel. Louie had phoned and asked me to come. We'd been friends for years. I thought sure, why not. So I was sitting way in the back in the dark and it was closing time. The audience left and then all of a sudden these guys in dark suits swarmed the joint, looking here and there, serious as hell. Louie had come in back to chat with me, so I asked him what was going on. He said the president was in town and this was a Secret Service detail. The president wanted to hear him play. They were securing the club so it would be a safe place for a special tune or two for the president."

"Oh dear, oh dear," Gloria muttered, cradling her head in her hands.

"That's right, Gloria, except it wasn't an audience of one, it was two—the president and you. Meanwhile, the Secret Service thought I was an employee and left me alone. Louis sang 'What a Wonderful World' for you and then played 'Basin Street Blues' on his trumpet. Then you and the president disappeared into the night. I asked around the next day. Plenty of people were happy to squeal on you. Apparently you had a standing little love nest at the Winston House, room 525—isn't that right? Marilyn Monroe wasn't the only blonde he had his eyes on, huh? Of course, he didn't have to deal with your shit. A few months later was when lucky me had to contend with you and your craziness on that trip up the California coast. I was about to confront you with your cheating when you went goofy that one night and almost killed me."

"Oh, dear. Oh, I can't believe this," Gloria said, looking very ill.

"Remember what I told you all once—Kate, Mike, the rest of you? If I told you why Gloria loved hotel room 525 so much I'd have to kill you? My own little Secret Service joke, I guess. And listen, Gloria, Mike and Franklin Burgess weren't criminals, but you were. They never pulled off your disgusting little plan. They went ahead and buried Mr. Nielsen as per his wishes all along and put me into cryo instead. They saved my life, and here I am."

Gloria coughed and began gasping and wheezing. She turned blue, then purple. She tried to speak but couldn't. Fear was written across her face as she gasped for air.

"Miles, Edouard, do something," Kate yelled.

"Do what?" Miles said, holding Edouard back. "Why should I help a monster?"

"Because you have to. She's having a heart attack, I think," Franklin yelled.

"Not possible."

"Why not, Miles?" asked Mike.

"Because that would presuppose she actually has a heart. She'll be fine. People like her are always fine."

Gloria sputtered, her eyes rolled up in her head, and she passed out. Or had she just died? Kate didn't get it. *Miles is refusing to lift a finger to save her?*

"Miles, do something! This is not right!" Kate yelled.

"Yeah come on, Miles—enough," Chrissy said nervously. "Come on, do the right thing!"

Miles whispered something in Ray's ear, then whispered to Edouard as well. Everyone else looked at the two doctors like they were crazy.

"Miles, help her, damn it!" Norm yelled.

Just then Gloria stirred, sat back up straight, coughed some more, and regained her normal color. She finally composed herself, again grinning like a devil.

"Nice acting, Miss Dunham," Miles said facetiously. "You had most of the people here going, but not me. You see, I'm just a lowly geek who, fortunately or unfortunately, has seen almost all of your movies. That little choking, spluttering, about to die, feel-sorry-for-me act you just displayed? No one else here recognized it, but I sure did. It was straight out of *Her Desperate Times*, a really crappy movie you made in 1947 with Robert Young. You wanted to fire me earlier? Well, I'm going to fire you now for bad acting. Even on your best day you couldn't carry Joan Crawford's jockstrap. So basically fuck off, get the hell out of ExitStrategy, and go back to Los Angeles!"

CHAPTER FIFTY-THREE

October 2014

"All right, people, now that you've been partying for ninety minutes and have become successfully lubed with plenty of free alcohol, Franklin and I have some announcements for you," Mike Burgess declared. "Without a doubt, this is a party in honor of absolutely each and every one of you—the people who have worked so hard to make our company the success it is and to honor what you have done to pave the way for our future."

"That's right. Is everyone having a good time?" Franklin yelled.

"Yes!" they all cheered.

"And it's great to see old friends, of course. Everybody give a cheer for Amman and Ritika. They came in from Boston just to see all of you!" The crowd applauded.

"All right, then," Mike said. "I am announcing right now that we are starting a new profit-sharing program for all employees. Franklin and I expect the company to be worth hundreds of millions, billions, or trillions once the truth is known to the world. Also, we have hired a publicity firm to handle all aspects of our future as it relates to the media and the public. The publicity firm will be introducing our dear Ray Machado here to the world next month. Expect things to be totally crazy here for a while when that happens. We'll have media arriving here from around the world when this announcement is made. We'll have to hire extra security, no doubt. And on that note, I'm announcing to you that Keith will be retiring in a few weeks. He'd like to keep his life on the quiet side and we all know things will be crazy here for a while. So three cheers for Keith!"

"Hip, hip, hooray!" everyone yelled. Keith waved and smiled. John Cougar Mellencamp was sitting in his lap purring as Keith stroked his ears.

"You can also expect that we will be up for Nobel prizes in medicine, and who knows what else. Sure, there will be many doubters, but all of you know that Ray here is the real deal. And if we really do get a Nobel Prize, we're all going to the ceremony. How about three cheers for Ray!"

"Hip, hip, hooray!"

"Nobel in medicine, you say, Mike?" Miles asked. "What about physics?"

"Physics? We didn't do any physics here, Miles. Just some awesome medicine and engineering mixed with a heapin' helpin' of luck," Kate said with a wink.

"Well, hey, folks, not sure if you noticed who came to the party with me—remember Theo Gaddis here?" Miles asked, putting his arm around his guest. "Theo, one of Khail's bodyguards, remember? Theo has quit his job and is hoping to find a way to go to college full-time. He's done some junior college already. He was even teaching Khail some vocabulary, math, and so on. Right, Theo?"

"That's right," Theo said. "I got tired of that job. It was truly beyond crazy. Anyway, it's great to be here with all y'all."

Clink-drink went everyone in the room.

"What was that?" Theo asked, a bit disoriented.

"Oh, Norm made up a drinking game," Ray said. "Every time Chrissy says *y'all* we clink and drink. She's from North Carolina and the more she drinks the more *y'alls* she says."

"Oh, damn," Theo said. "I'm from Kannapolis down near Charlotte. I best watch myself, then, huh?"

"Wait, Miles," Norm said, "what was that about a Nobel for physics?"

"Well, Theo and I have been hanging out lately. He's got some ideas you might want to hear. Y'all want your mind blown?"

Clink-drink.

"Sure, why not?" Deirdre said. "What's it all about?"

"You tell 'em, Miles," Theo said.

"No, don't be shy, man," Miles countered "It's your concept. Go ahead."

"Okay, but can I have a beer to wet my lips?"

"Of course," Edouard replied. "Here you go."

"Thanks, man," Theo said. "Okay, this is what I got to say, y'all."

Clink-drink.

"Oh, damn, I wasn't trying to get them going again. Man, these people are wasted, Miles."

"It's okay, Theo. They're nerds. Their brains still function even when inebriated. Go ahead and tell them your ideas."

"Okay, people. So your Mr. Machado here. How old does he look to you? Like maybe fifty, sixty tops, right? Mr. Machado, how old are you by the calendar?"

"I'm eighty-eight, my friend, and feeling great," Ray announced, winking at Chrissy. Their little romance was still developing quite nicely.

"There, you see?" Theo asked. "He's like way younger. How do you account for that?"

"It's the cellular realignment the cryo caused," Kate said. "We've figured that out. And I suppose that's physics, sort of. And I just want to toss in that today happens to be the one-year anniversary of us reviving Mr. T!"

"To Mr. T, all y'all!" yelled Chrissy.

Clink-drink.

"Okay, have y'a—oops," Theo said, "have *you people* ever heard the story of the twins? One stays on earth while the other goes into space. When the space fellow comes back, he's way younger than his twin, right? We're talking quantum physics now, get it? I mean all sorts of quantum physics. Did you know brand new ideas in quantum physics say that cause and effect might be able to go both directions? Sounds crazy, but they're getting that going."

"So, Theo, what's that got to do with cryo and Ray?" Chrissy asked.

"Well, I'm building up to that. See now, you froze Ray way down low and slow, I guess you could say, like what they say about our Carolina barbecue. Right, Miss Chrissy? Anyway, his atoms and electrons were going slower and slower. Of course you couldn't see them—you put Ray in a box or a tube, right?"

"We call it a pod, Theo," Mike said, edging closer to hear Theo's theories.

"Okay, sir. Anyway, this is typical quantum physics stuff. Ray was unobservable. You couldn't know what was going on inside that pod, right? So, what I'm saying is that you gave his matter a choice. Like free will. There wasn't any daily what they call human circadian rhythm anymore, everything was slowed way down, and I'm saying that at some point his body decided to change directions and travel the other way. You gave it a choice, free will, and it said, 'Hell, I'm gonna hit the switch and have me some fun—go the other way, back in time.' Not that it had to say that, necessarily, because time probably goes both directions anyway. We really don't understand it too well with our human minds."

"Whoa—hold on a sec," Mike said. "You're saying the cryopods are time machines?"

"And they're not even hot tubs!" Miles exclaimed, as silly as ever.

"That is beyond bizarre, but I like it!" Mike said. "Hey, all y'all, I really like Theo's idea!"

Clink-drink.

"So anyway, Mr. Burgess," Theo continued, "if time inside the pods was going the other direction, it accounts for why diseases disappeared. Bodies were gradually sliding back in time to when they didn't show symptoms and then even further back to when they didn't even have the disease at all. Plus all their cells were getting younger and heathier. Get it?"

"Whoa, you may have something there, Theo," Kate said. "All along I wasn't so sure why we could never see any evidence of the diseases the animals or Ray had. There was like zero evidence. Not a trace."

"Amazing, Miss Pearson. And you got a cryopod cat here, too, right?" Theo inquired. "He's sort of like Schrödinger's Cat. You know that mind game?"

No one responded. Miles shook his head in disappointment. "People, Schrödinger's Cat. It's been referenced three times on *Big Bang Theory!*"

"Anyway," Theo continued, "right before you put the cat in the pod you could observe him. Maybe alive and about to be frozen, or dead and about to be frozen, right? But at least you could observe him right then and decide which of those you personally believed. But once you put him inside that crazy deep-freeze pod and you couldn't see him anymore, he was either alive, or dead, or—get this—*both at the same time.* Quantum physics says there can be multiple realities for stuff like this. Finally, when Ray and the cat came back out they were pretty different than before, right? So one reality was chosen, or at least we see one reality in front of us. We got a live cat, a live Ray, and since time decided it was fun in that deep-freeze to run the other direction, you got a dude who sure doesn't look eighty-whatever who's holding hands with a beautiful woman. She looks at him and sees a much younger man, right? And I hear your cat is frisky, too. More like a kitten than a cat?"

"Holy shit, ya'll. He might be right!" said Chrissy, grinning from ear to ear.

Clink-drink.

"Theo, how did you figure all of this out?" said Mike, who had just been whispering something to Franklin.

"I read books all the time, Mr. Burgess. Lots of books. When I was a bodyguard I had a lot of free time. I wanted to learn stuff. Try to be different than Khail, and especially be different than Dimi. My family is pretty poor. Community college is even tough for us to afford. Khail didn't pay me anywhere near what you might think."

"Well, here's what Franklin and I are gonna do, Theo," said Mike. "Would you like to work here part-time? Security? But real security—not that silly stuff you had to do for Khail and Miss Konstantos. And we'll pay your way through four-year college. You can start part-time for a while at that. What do you say?"

Theo looked at Mike for a moment, as if he couldn't trust his ears. "Yes, sir. I would very much love to do that. I didn't come here looking for a job or a handout. Miles said I should just come share my ideas."

"Welcome aboard, then, Theo!" said Mike. "Hey, all y'all, welcome Theo aboard!"

Clink-drink, then shouting.

Everyone was laughing, smiling, proud of each other for everything they had done and all they had been through. But after a few minutes, things grew quieter.

"You know, folks, we're all pretty tipsy right now, kind of getting mellow and oh so happy, right?" Kate asked. "And I have to say, if Theo might be right about the backward time thing, that our cryopods are time machines—wow, that blows my mind—there is an enormous amount of joy in my heart right now. Does anyone understand why I might be saying that?"

"I do," Norm responded, giving a little bow of the head to Kate while tapping his chest gently with his hand.

"I do, too," Mike said. "Everyone, Kate's thinking of Jenny Loves Rainbows. If she is going backward in time, she can survive. She can thrive. She can beat that disease. She can come back and have a childhood. She won't look sixty or seventy. She'll look half that age or even better. Jenny has a chance now. I guess we won't know for a while yet, but hope is a beautiful thing, right?" They all clinked their glasses, softly this time. Hope. All cryo had said it ever was. Hope—'The thing with feathers—that perches within the soul,' according to Emily Dickinson.

Miles left Theo's side, angled over by Kate and squeezed her hand. "I'm sorry if this quantum physics and time-travel stuff took the air out of your own theories, Kate. Hell, I have no idea if Theo could be correct about any of that. He may have four or five threads of quantum physics all jumbled together and it doesn't really make any sense. But I wanted to encourage him to use his mind and share his ideas with great people like we have here."

"That's a very, very good thing, Miles. I'm so proud of you," Kate said, tearing up.

"Yeah, but this party was supposed to be about you, Kate. You're the one who made all this happen."

"It's not about one person, Miles. It's never been that."

"But you're the one that holds us all together."

"Yes, I know that. I know that now. All of you are crazy and I'm just here holding on—holding on for dear life. And I wouldn't ever change a thing," Kate said, gently planting a kiss on Miles' cheek.

Hi!
If you liked the
book, please
write a quick
review on Amazon
Thanks

ABOUT THE AUTHOR

"Thawing A.C. Nielsen" is Paul Carey's literary debut. He is hard at work on his next book, a bizarre alien-invasion sci-fi tale for lower-upper middle-grade readers, "The Grandma Apocalypse". Following that will be another Kate Pearson book, tentatively titled "The Mozart Murders", in which a fairly foul, and Voldemort-like Wolfgang Amadeus Mozart is unleashed upon the twenty-first century. It's up to Kate, Aria, and Miles to bring him to heel!

In addition to writing, Paul continues his prolific career as a choral composer, which has led to thousands of performances of his award-winning music by choirs across six continents. He wishes that he lived on a tropical island somewhere, but in reality he resides in Oak Park, Illinois (birthplace of Ernest Hemingway and the Hostess Twinkie).

Twitter: @gotspellcheck
Blog: paulcareyauthor.blogspot.com
Facebook: Paul Carey, Author
Amazon Author Page: www.amazon.com/author/paul_carey